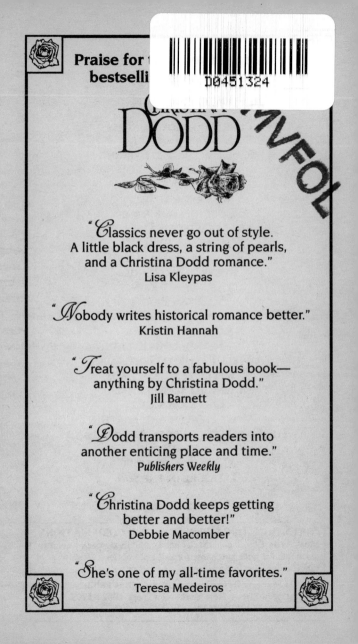

CHRISTINA DODD

My Fair Temptress

AVON BOOKS

An Imprint of HarperCollinsPublishers

This is a work of fiction. Names, characters, places, and incidents are products of the author's imagination or are used fictitiously and are not to be construed as real. Any resemblance to actual events, locales, organizations, or persons, living or dead, is entirely coincidental.

AVON BOOKS
An Imprint of HarperCollins*Publishers*
10 East 53rd Street
New York, New York 10022-5299

First Avon Books paperback printing: October 2005

Avon Trademark Reg. U.S. Pat. Off. and in Other Countries, Marca Registrada, Hecho en U.S.A.
HarperCollins® is a registered trademark of HarperCollins Publishers Inc.

Printed in the U.S.A.

10 9 8 7 6 5 4 3

Adorna, Lady Bucknell, sole proprietress of
the Distinguished Academy of Governesses,
as part of the continuing series called
The Governess Brides
Presents

RULES OF SURRENDER
RULES OF ENGAGEMENT
RULES OF ATTRACTION
IN MY WILDEST DREAMS
LOST IN YOUR ARMS
MY FAVORITE BRIDE

And now

MY FAIR TEMPTRESS,
the story of Miss Caroline Ritter,
accomplished flirt and disgraced debutante,
who, destitute and desperate,
takes a position teaching Jude Durant,
the earl of Huntington,
how to catch a wife, and discovers that
sometimes the teacher becomes the pupil
in a most improbable seduction . . .

My Fair Temptress

Chapter 1

The Distinguished Academy of Governesses
London, 1849

$\mathcal{M}$iss Caroline Ritter squeezed a handful of her damp, shabby skirt. "I need to procure some method of providing sustenance for myself."

Adorna, Lady Bucknell, the proprietress of the Distinguished Academy of Governesses, folded her hands on her desk and gazed at the young lady seated before her. Outside, the March rains lashed at the windows, the occasional splatter of sleet a reminder that winter hadn't yet loosened its hold on London.

Rather more forcefully, Miss Ritter said, "In other words, I need a job."

Pinning her with a direct gaze, Adorna asked, "What are your accomplishments?"

Miss Ritter hesitated a telling moment.

Adorna tried to make it easier for her. "What do you do best?"

"Flirt," she said promptly.

Adorna believed her. She had seen many a young lady come through her study at the Distinguished Academy of Governesses, all of them in need of assistance, but she had never felt such a kinship as she felt now for Miss Caroline Ritter.

This young lady was beautiful. Her smooth, tan complexion reminded Adorna of the tale repeated about the Ritters—that four hundred years ago Mr. Ritter brought home a bride from some exotic locale, and since then the women of the family had been temptresses who led all men astray. Miss Ritter certainly fit the role.

She was tall, almost gangly, with long arms and slender fingers, yet she moved with a grace that pleasured the eye. Her high bosom and narrow waist would naturally rivet any man's attention, and her voice, low and warm, gave the impression of interest and kindness. She had gathered her straight brown hair into a severe chignon at the base of her neck, yet fine strands had escaped their confinement, and the auburn highlights encased her striking face like a summer sunset. Her wide chin gave the inference of defiance, and the dark lashes and brows that decorated her slumberous aquamarine eyes strengthened the impression of unusual and delicate beauty.

Never had Adorna seen so exquisite a visage since the day, thirty years ago, when she had gazed into a mirror and realized that she herself was a diamond of the first water.

Yet time had wrought changes on her own face, so that now Miss Caroline Ritter could accurately be described as the loveliest woman in England.

Leaning back in her chair, Adorna said aloud what she had been thinking. "I remember you. Three years ago you were all the rage."

"And I've heard of you." Caroline met Adorna's gaze directly. "You were the most famous debutante of your time."

At the tribute, Adorna allowed a small smile to cross her lips. "I was."

"Some say you were the most famous debutante of all time."

"So my husband says, but I tell him that is simply flattery. It works, of course. He is very good at getting his way." Adorna allowed her mind to drift back thirty years to her debut. "Do you know, I had fourteen offers of marriage in my first Season?"

"That is extraordinary." Miss Ritter modestly lowered her eyes. "I had fifteen."

Ah. A rivalry. How delicious. "Four abduction attempts, two by the same man."

"Only three abduction attempts, but all by different men."

"And fifty-three stolen kisses." This game amused Adorna. "I kept a tally."

"I kept a tally, too, and I assure you, you're far ahead of me in that contest." Miss Ritter's mouth drooped in disappointment. "My chaperone was far too watchful until . . . until she wasn't."

"Mine was having her own scandalous evening." Adorna chuckled warmly. "She is my aunt, Jane Higgenbothem, now Lady Blackburn. Perhaps you know of her?"

"The famous sculptress? Indeed, I do! Her work is magnificent. My father . . . my father invested in some of her works . . ." Miss Ritter eyed the crackling fire with some longing. "I imagine her dedication to her sculpting distracted from her duty to keep you untouched."

"Something like that." Lifting the bell at her elbow, Adorna rang, and when the maid appeared, she requested a generous tea be served. Returning to the matter at hand, Adorna said, "Unfortunately, Miss Ritter, there is very little call for such a talent as flirting."

The girl half rose from her chair and leaned across the desk to seize Adorna's hands. She fixed her with her amazingly bright aquamarine gaze. "Please. Lady Bucknell, I truly have need of employment. You have a reputation of finding a position to fit every young woman. You must have *something* I can do."

"Your circumstances are difficult." Adorna's sympathy was unfeigned. "I understand you were compromised during your debut Season?"

Miss Ritter kept her chin up and a brave smile on her lips. "Not just compromised. Ruined."

Adorna hated to press her, but if she was responsible for placing the young lady into a household, she had to know the circumstances. "By a married man."

"By Lord Freshfield."

"He is very handsome." The viscount had followed his family tradition and ruthlessly used his face and figure to marry an older woman—a woman with money.

"Very handsome, indeed. He could turn a girl's head." Miss Ritter's eyes froze to the color of the winter sea. "But not to that extent, my dear Lady Bucknell. I was a foolish girl, but not a wanton."

That was the damning part of the tale Adorna had heard. That Miss Ritter had been infatuated with Lord Freshfield. That she had encouraged him to behave badly. But Adorna well knew how gossip twisted the truth. "I've met Lord Freshfield, and he's not an admirable character, scarcely fit for society, much less the company of a young lady." Shrewdly, she added, "I hope he hasn't bothered you since."

"We no longer move in the same circles." Miss Ritter sank back down into the chair. "We never shall again."

Miss Ritter hadn't really answered the question, Adorna noted. So Lord Freshfield had not only destroyed her life, but now sought to destroy her innocence. That man was nothing but blond hair and smiling teeth held together by his own imagined allure.

"He hurt my reputation, he hurt it badly," Miss Ritter said, in a voice she kept under rigid control, "but my father is the one who ruined me."

"Your father believed you had done wrong."

"My father's dearest wish is for a title. He said my stupidity, as he called it, ruined those chances." Miss Ritter's mouth was the kind of mouth men convinced themselves signaled the soul of a seductress. Yet if those same men saw its intelligent, humorous quirk right now, they might be cautious, even frightened, for she appeared both savagely amused and furious.

"You are without resources," Adorna said delicately.

Miss Ritter gazed into Adorna's eyes. Adorna gazed back, trusting that Miss Ritter would recognize the common bond between them.

And it seemed she did, for with a dip of the head, she said, "My mother . . . my mother was from the Aquitaine in the south of France. Her family has written repeatedly asking that I come to them. But I can't. My younger sister . . . she needs me. We visit every chance we get, when my father goes out, the servants let me in and she . . . he doesn't see in Genevieve the potential he saw in me, so he doesn't have time for her. She's lonely. She's a child, only fourteen years old. If I could make enough money to support us both, I would take her to the Aquitaine . . ."

Adorna gestured in the maid who carried the tea tray, and listened.

"Which is silly. I can't make enough to support myself. But I must stay here in London, for although she has enough to eat and shelter over her head, doesn't a girl need kindness and encouragement and, most important, love, to develop?" Miss Ritter seemed to be repeating a conversation she had often had with herself. "Yes, I know this is true. Mama died when I was that age, and I miss her dreadfully. How much more terrible for Genevieve that she lost her mama, then five years later, she lost me. I can't leave, no matter how much sense it makes or how rapidly I might return for her."

Adorna stood and she led the way to the chairs by the fire. "You're right, of course." She glimpsed the warm gratitude in Miss Ritter's gaze as she followed, and resolved to fix this situation. "Do you have a place to stay?"

"Yes, thank you, my lady."

Adorna waved her to the settee close to the fire, then seated herself opposite. She examined the platter of foodstuffs and, satisfied with the selection, dismissed the maid. Taking one of the plates, she asked, "Lemon cakes, Miss Ritter?"

Miss Ritter's eyes glowed. "Yes, thank you, I *love* lemon cakes."

Adorna placed a lemon cake on a plate. "Cinnamon biscuits?"

Stripping off her gloves, Miss Ritter said, "Yes, thank you, I *love* cinnamon biscuits."

"Clotted cream?"

"Yes, thank you, I *love*—"

Removing a few items off the heaped platter for herself, Adorna placed the platter close to Miss Ritter. It was easier that way.

She poured tea, added milk and sugar, and extended the cup.

Accepting it, Miss Ritter took a sip, her eyes closing as if tasting the finest ambrosia.

She might have somewhere to stay, but she had gone hungry more than one night. Smoothly, Adorn asked, "What have you done to support yourself?"

Miss Ritter put down the cup. "I have sewn." Leaning down, she rummaged in the large valise she carried with her and produced a sealed paper. "Here's an affidavit from Madam Marnham, the noted seamstress, confirming the dates of my employment. I have worked in the kitchens of Lord Barnett." She produced another letter. "Here's an affidavit from the chef also confirming the dates of my employment. I have taught singing and pianoforte, and for that I have a very sweet recommendation"—she handed it across—"from Mrs. Charlton Cabot explaining why she had to let me go. Poor woman. She felt so guilty, but I quite understood."

Adorna waved Miss Ritter to silence and broke the seals. As she examined the letters, a pattern became clear. Miss Ritter had tried to find employment on her own, but she was nothing less than dreadful at sewing and cooking and teaching. Yet her employers had loved her, had hated to let her go, and gave lengthy explanations about their reasons for releasing her from their employ. Miss Ritter's efforts had endeared her to her employers, and they wished her only the best, but in truth, she was only good for one thing—flirting.

Now she sat and stared at Adorna. Her bonnet was frayed, her hem was frayed, her composure was frayed.

The finger of one glove had a hole, badly mended, her lips were chapped from the cold, and her dress had been turned too many times. She had hit bottom, and something had to be done.

"Very well." Standing, Adorna went to her desk. Digging down to the bottom of the employer requests stacked on her desk, she found the one she wanted and pulled it out. She reread it, and nodded. "Miss Ritter, I have the perfect position for you."

Chapter 2

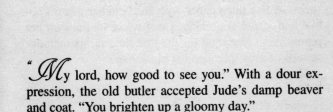

"My lord, how good to see you." With a dour expression, the old butler accepted Jude's damp beaver and coat. "You brighten up a gloomy day."

Jude Durant, the earl of Huntington, fought a revealing grin. He knew very well he brightened the day. With his orange neck scarf and his yellow waistcoat, some might even say he rivaled the sun in all its glory—not that anyone had seen the sun in London these past months. "Thank you, Phillips. My father sent for me?"

"He did. I'll announce you at once." Phillips started across the magnificent entry that the duke of Nevett had ordered in his new town house in Mayfair.

Jude followed and laid a restraining hand on Phillips's hunched shoulder. "First—where is Mum?"

"In the library, but my lord, the wishes of the duke of Nevett reign supreme in this household, and he asked that you be shown into his drawing room before—"

"Thank you, Phillips." Uninterested in his father's autocracy or Phillips's opinion, Jude strode to his stepmother's study. She had had a difficult eight months—they all had, but her especially—and these days, he visited only too seldom. Duty called, and revenge, and a great many other emotions, like guilt and impotent fury. Mum had a way of seeing too much, so he stayed away until he had finished his self-appointed task.

Now he paused in the doorway.

She sat at her desk, dressed in the lavender of half-mourning, a lacy cap perched on her hair. Before her spread an array of stiff, cream-colored invitations and sheets of fine linen paper—yet she held her pen immobile and stared at nothing. Grief wrote its lines on her plump, kind face, and for the first time in his memory strands of gray threaded her black hair.

He said softly, "Mum?"

She looked up, and her gray eyes lit with instant pleasure. "Dear boy, you came to see me!" Rising, she hurried toward him. His stepmother had captured his father's interest eighteen years ago when she had been the debutante of the year. As Father told his two young sons, Lady Nicolette Vipond possessed good breeding, pretty manners, and an obedient nature, so the forty-year-old widower had wed the nineteen-year-old girl . . . and ever since, she had been the center of the household. Soft, sweet, and affectionate, she had tamed the rebellious boys, loving Jude and his elder brother Michael as if they were her own—which made Michael's death in the distant country of Moricadia all the more wrenching for her.

Embracing her, Jude kissed her cheek, and said bracingly, "You're looking well."

She pulled a long face. "Pale and boring, as always."

Holding his hands, she looked him over, and with a dimple of a smile, she asked, "My, isn't that a fetching costume? Is that the style in France?"

"In the better parts of France."

Laughing, she led him to the couch. "Someday, you'll have to tell me what parts of France those might be, because I don't remember seeing anything like this." She touched the large silver anchor-shaped pin that decorated his scarf.

"Father escorted you fifteen years ago. Things have changed." Deftly, Jude changed the subject. "And speaking of that trip, how is Adrian? How's his school this year?"

Mum blushed. She had come back from France increasing, and nine months later produced another son to carry on the proud name of Durant. As Michael had privately told Jude, it was good to know the old man still had it in him to make a woman happy.

"Adrian is fine. He's studying hard and looks forward to coming home for the holidays. I look forward to having him here. Since you and . . ." She faltered, then rallied. "Since you and Michael went off to tour the Continent, it has been very quiet in this house."

Very quiet? Yes, indeed. No carriages dropped gaily dressed guests on the stone steps. No music played in the majestic ballroom. The closed curtains allowed no light to escape the tall windows.

Jude's mouth tightened. This is what he had done. Thrown his family into mourning for their eldest son, their endearing son, the son who had been the light of his father's eyes and the joy of his stepmother's life.

Now Jude prepared to make amends. In a rallying tone, he said, "Adrian's not much of a hellion. If it's noise you want, I shall have to come and rile him up."

"You're not much of a hellion, either." This time she didn't falter. "That was Michael."

"He always chased adventure until it turned around and chased him." *Until it killed him.* But Mum didn't need to know that. In a jolly tone, Jude asked, "Do you remember the time when he was thirteen and decided to put the fear of God into Cook's husband so the ruffian would stop beating her?"

"And Michael dressed up like a ghost and convinced you to do it, too!"

"—And it wasn't until we slipped into Cook's bedroom that we discovered they were *both* terrified of spirits." Remembering the scene and his own panic, Jude chortled.

"Cook pulled her knife, and that man chased you all the way down from the attic while he screamed the place was haunted." Mum clasped her hands at her chest. "I thought the house was on fire, but your father said it was probably Michael getting into trouble. And he was right." She was laughing . . . while tears dribbled down her cheeks.

"Oh, Mum." Heart aching, Jude hugged her shoulders.

She dug a handkerchief out of her sleeve. "No, I like to talk about him. It hurts your father to mention Michael's name, but it keeps him alive for me, and I shall conquer this ridiculous tendency to turn into a watering can every time he's mentioned. I swear I will." She mopped up, then asked with forced cheer, "Now, tell me why you're really here. Did your father send for you?"

"I could have come to see you," Jude protested.

"But you didn't. You're having much too much fun cutting a swathe through society. Don't you think I hear about it? Every fascinating thing you say, every wonderful thing you wear, every single young lady to whom you speak?"

"Of course. All the old biddies in London keep you apprised." That could cause trouble if he weren't careful.

With a hint of a dimple, she protested, "I'm one of those biddies."

"No. Not even when you wear that silly matron's cap." Insistently, she tugged at his sleeve, and Jude surrendered. "But you're right. I'm here on Father's summons. What have I done to cause him enough displeasure that he should summon me?" *There was no way the old man could know the truth . . . was there? The duke of Nevett had his sources, but lately he hadn't gone into society.*

"I don't know." Her lips trembled. "He's been fuming ever since the word came about . . . ever since you returned."

"Without Michael."

"Yes, without Michael." She wasn't being cruel. Jude had wanted to rush home from Moricadia, to be the one who gave his parents the evil news. Alas, he had been wounded, almost killed, in the berserker fury that had possessed him after Michael's murder, and had spent two months near death hidden in the cellar of a tavern. By the time he made his slow, secret journey back to England, it had been too late. The Home Office had already visited the duke and duchess, and Jude returned to a house draped in black crepe and filled with sorrow.

Jude touched the signet ring that, for time eternal, had decorated the hand of Nevett's heir. Michael had worn it with pride from the day of his eighteenth birthday. Now the worn inscription had been melted by intense fire, and if not for the glorious ruby at its heart, it would be unrecognizable. "Is Father angry at me?" Jude asked.

"No! No, dear, not at all. He loved Michael, but he knew his propensity to rush into danger. Nevett doesn't blame you for what happened." She tapped his cheek. "You must believe me."

"I do." Yet Jude knew the facts, and he blamed himself.

"It seems that lately, your father's been aware of the passage of time, and his own mortality. He had spoken again and again how he failed in his duty to Michael."

"*He* failed. How so?"

"Instead of allowing Michael to cut a swathe through the ladies of London society, he should have arranged a marriage for him."

"I would have liked to see him try." Michael and Father had always butted heads, and on this matter Michael would have had plenty to say.

"Your father can be autocratic when he chooses," she warned. "He comprehends the frailty of life now, and while he has always shown the utmost of care for all of us, he now worries about Adrian, and you, and me."

"Then I shall assure him I live a clean life."

She eyed him doubtfully. "Not too clean, I've heard. Something about actresses . . . ?"

"Good heavens, what is it the old biddies discuss when they get together with you?" he asked, appalled.

Her smile blossomed into real amusement. "Not much. Only everything men would like to think we don't know."

In the doorway, Phillips cleared his throat. "My lord, His Grace grows impatient."

"You'd better go, dear." Mum returned to her desk. "Will you stay for dinner?"

"I wish I could, but I have an appointment."

"Ah." She nodded wisely.

Jude wanted to tell her this had nothing to do with an

actress, but really, her suspicions were better roused that direction. With a bow, he left her and strode ahead of Phillips toward his meeting with his father.

"Your Grace, the earl of Huntington has arrived," Phillips announced with a pompousness honed by years of practice.

Paxton Durant, the duke of Nevett, sat ensconced in his favorite chair in his favorite drawing room, and kept his gaze fixed to his newspaper. "Send my son in, Phillips."

The old butler tottered off to do his duty by roasting another inexperienced footman over the coals of propriety until the fellow was servile enough to serve in His Grace's household. Because, as Jude knew very well, everything that surrounded His Grace must be perfect, as it had been for fourteen generations before them and no doubt would be for fourteen generations to come.

Jude walked toward the older man, his high-heeled boots ringing on the hardwood floors. It was obvious by Nevett's flinching that the sound aggravated him, and that was enjoyable. Then the Aubusson rug muffled Jude's steps, and Nevett's color subsided.

Jude didn't know why Nevett allowed anything to irritate him. He was wealthy, he was powerful, he was, at sixty, as healthy as a stallion, and he had all the comforts those three enviable traits allowed. The drawing chamber had been designed to Nevett's own specifications, built to convey a sense of hushed importance and decorated in shades of maroon and gold. A branch of candles lit the gloom of the rainy day. A coal stove in one corner radiated heat, and a crackling fire lent the room atmosphere. His leather armchair was the largest, the deepest, and the most comfortable. Placed at the center of a grouping of seats, it clearly displayed Nevett's importance for any visitor who might be in doubt. A carved teak Oriental screen hid the alcove that housed his father's desk—a new addition, and one that surprised Jude since his father had forcefully expressed his scorn for the fad for Asian furniture.

Stopping a short distance away from his father, Jude bowed. "You sent for me, sir?"

His father visibly braced himself for the first, horrific vision of his oldest son. Lifting his gaze, he considered Jude for only a moment before closing his eyes in pain.

Jude couldn't lie; he enjoyed sticking needles into the old man, so in an affected tone, he said, "Don't you *adore* it? It's the newest color from France. It's called sunrise, and I'm the first to use it on a waistcoat. You can imagine the attention I attracted on my way over here!"

"I can indeed." With a weary rustle, Nevett lowered his paper into his lap. "It is very yellow."

"With a mere tinge of orange." Jude kissed his fingertips and tossed the kiss into the air. "So stylish I know I shall single-handedly lead London society away from this dull obsession with black and white."

Nevett looked down at his own staid black-and-white garments. "I wouldn't count on that." He indicated the seat opposite. "Sit. I want to talk to you."

Jude minced to the burgundy velvet straight-backed chair and drifted down until the base of his spine struck the seat. He crossed his legs, placed both hands on the knob of his walking stick, swung one foot.

The room smelled of cigars, leather, and wool, exactly as it had during the twenty-nine years of Jude's life. The scent itself recalled stern lectures, given to Michael and Jude, on how a Durant should at all times behave. With proper civility had been the correct reply, and indeed Jude had never seen his father behave in any other manner.

Of course, neither had he indulged in obvious displays of affection for anyone, although since Michael's death and Jude's return from Europe, Jude had begun to suspect his father hid feelings deep within his portentous breast. But that was not a suspicion he could express to his father, and in return, his father been restrained in expressing his thoughts about Jude's lifestyle or his manner of dressing . . . although the provocation had been extreme.

Jude hid a grin as Nevett said abruptly, "It was a mistake to send you on the Grand Tour. I acknowledge that now."

Jude bowed his head.

"Not because of Michael. Not because of that. That . . . happened. It was regrettable." Nevett turned his face toward the miniature of Michael, painted when he was sixteen, which sat on the table by his elbow. The portrait-maker hadn't captured the twinkle in Michael's eyes or the laugh with which he greeted life, but the paints represented his fiery red hair and green eyes all too realistically for those still mourning his memory. "I'm concerned with you now. Only with you."

"Then why the regrets, sir?" Jude had left three years ago, at the age of twenty-six, and returned three months ago, a new man. Before, he had been studious, industrious, the second son who took his responsibilities seriously. Now he was a bon vivant—and a man with a purpose. "Italy, the Alps, Russia, the Rhone, France, the Pyrenees—they broadened my horizons, which was your expressed reason for our going."

"And you're living proof that there is such a thing as

horizons that are too broad and, er, colorful." Nevett cut off Jude's protest with a slash of his broad hand. "You were the perfect son when you left. Restrained. Strong. Silent. And now you are . . . are . . ." Words failed Nevett, but he gestured feebly at Jude's slouched figure.

"More perfect?" Jude suggested.

"Not quite that." Nevett's mouth settled into a grim line. "You are Frenchified."

Jude sat up straight. "Do you really think so? That is the finest compliment you've ever given me, sir! When I visited France, it was as if I found my cultural home. The food! The art! The fashion! So superior! So grand! On the grounds of Versailles, I swore I would live the civilization as it was meant to be lived." Drawing his fan from inside his coat, Jude snapped it open and fanned his face in simulated excitement, hiding a smile.

The duke of Nevett was a man who had been taught from his cradle the traditional English contempt for the French. The English and French were now allies, of course, united in their struggle to keep Russia from taking the lucrative continent of Asia under its control, but Nevett remembered Napoleon and the trouble he caused across Europe. Nevett eschewed the rage for French chefs and served good English beef at every occasion. Only English tailors dressed Nevett. Now his son, his adult son, raved like a madman about French culture and its superiority, and only Nevett's vaunted English reserve kept him from shouting his hostile opinion.

Jude wondered if this would prove the breaking point, if His Grace would give his honest opinion at last.

He did not. He ground his white teeth like a frustrated bear and fixed Jude with a hostile gaze. Folding his newspaper, he dropped it beside his chair. "You know why I called you here."

"No, sir," Jude said in all truthfulness.

"I want a grandson."

Jude blinked. "Sir, I'm unwed."

"That is painfully clear. And how you'll manage to attract a bride in your current condition is beyond me."

"In my current condition?" Standing, Jude strolled languidly across to the mirror and considered his own reflection. Dark brown hair, swept into a careless, dashing style. Black tailcoat. Plaid trousers. White ankle boots, polished to a blinding shine. The yellow waistcoat, so bright even he blinked. And in his blue eyes, an amusement that he quickly veiled.

After all, his father was not stupid.

As Jude adjusted the orange silk scarf tied about his neck and draped over the expanse of his chest, he said, "Any woman would be proud to call herself the countess of Huntington."

"Of course she would!" the duke said with unfeigned impatience. "After I die, your wife will be a duchess, and that's not a position to be taken with a pinch of snuff and a hearty sneeze."

His father did not, Jude noted, consider Jude himself a good catch, only the title.

His Grace rumbled on, "But until you apply yourself to the process of obtaining a wife, I fear you shall remain single and I grandchildless. So I have taken steps to remedy the situation."

Little surprised Jude, but he was surprised now. Swinging around on his father, he surveyed the man whom he resembled so greatly. With an unconscious return to his own crisp intonation, he said, "You don't imagine I'll marry a girl of your choosing."

Nevett raised his eyebrows. "I hadn't imagined that, no. A man should choose his own wife from among the panoply of young ladies presented to him. But you've proved woefully inadequate in your ability to woo these young ladies."

Jude had been busy in quite another manner, but he did not admit that to his father. He already knew what Nevett would say about a Durant lowering himself to deception for the sake of God and country—and it wouldn't be flattering. It wouldn't be flattering at all. "Find me a young lady worth wooing, and I will do so at once."

"There are at least ten maidens of unexceptional birth and fortune on the market right now."

"I said find me one worth wooing. One with conversation and intelligence and—" He caught himself. "Not a pockmarked, unfashionable lady, but one whose sense of style matches my own."

"Lady Amelia Carradine dresses well."

"Too short. Clothes do not drape well on her."

"Miss Richardson is tall."

"Her complexion! She should refrain from sweets until the blemishes have diminished."

"Lady Anne Whitfield is young and trainable."

"Too young."

"Lady Claudia Leonard."

"Too old."

"Miss Naomi Landau-Berry."

"Please! Can you imagine being married to a woman named Naomi?"

"Then you wouldn't want to wed Lady Winnomena Bigglesworth."

"Actually, Winnomena falls upon the ear like a tune well played." Jude frowned. "It is her deplorable habit of eating shellfish when it is presented to her that must be the deciding factor."

Nevett sputtered, "Eating . . . shellfish? Why shouldn't she eat shellfish?"

"I saw her eat scallops. Scallops are *round*."

"Round? Well, of course they're round. Square scallops would be ridiculous." Nevett realized he was being ridiculous, too, and he hissed in fury. "Who in hell would you wed?"

"A lady of France would be most acceptable."

"You're taxing my patience."

And Nevett was taxing Jude's. Reining in his own annoyance, he seated himself once again and said in a softly apologetic voice, "Sir, I would never wish to do that."

Nevett dragged in a deep breath and choked, "Of course not. Not *you*." He was freezingly polite, when actually he loved nothing more than a good fight, especially with his sharp-witted son.

But His Grace wasn't helpless. He had his ways of calling Jude to heel. "I've hired you a tutor."

"A tutor." *What was the old man talking about?*

"To teach you how to woo a woman."

"How to woo a woman."

Nevett struck the arm of his chair. "You sound like a prating parrot."

Jude *felt* like a fool. "You've hired me a tutor to teach me how to woo a woman?" For the first time since he'd started carrying his fan, he actually needed it. With a flip of the wrist, he fanned his hot face. "What will he use? Diagrams on a slate?"

"*She* will demonstrate by example."

"You've hired me a whore?" Not even in his untried youth had his father hired him a whore.

A rustle sounded from behind the screen. Jude registered it. Saw his father glance toward it, and realized he

was not surprised. Realized Nevett had planted someone there, and that that someone had heard every word
spoken.

His father looked outraged and thunderously angry.
"Son, for a dandy, you've a nasty mind. I hired a tutor
from the Distinguished Academy of Governesses. The
young lady is recommended by Lady Bucknell herself."

Who was behind the screen? What possible reason
had his father for concealing someone there? Jude
glanced sharply at his father. Nevett was relaxed, so . . .
ah, it must be the female his father had hired.

Yet Jude wondered if she could be more than Nevett
realized? Was there suspicion about Jude? Could she be
someone sent to spy on him? On Nevett?

For the rest of his life, would Jude see danger in any
situation? It was a grim consideration—and a real one,
yet a quick review of the conversation eased his worries. If she had been sent to report his activities, she had
heard nothing that would incriminate him.

"I don't understand, sir," Jude said with an airy
laugh. "Why would you hire a governess? Women
adore me."

"Not enough to wed you."

"A man has to have standards!"

"You have to be wed!"

"Who is this person?"

"What difference does that make to you, boy? She is
the person I hired."

Catching at his fraying temper, Jude managed the
correct question. "What does she look like?"

"She looks well enough for this task," his father said
dismissively. "She'll flirt with you. You'll flirt with her.
She will show you how to win a wife. Then you will go
out into society and put your lessons to good use!"

"Tell me one good reason why I should submit to such a humiliation."

"For my peace of mind."

"That's not nearly good enough."

His father rose from his chair, a slow, majestic rise that brought him to his full height of six-foot-two and displayed not only the broad-boned frame which Jude had inherited, but also the imposing authority he could exhibit as he wished.

Jude rose, also, but at that moment, he knew he had met his match. Jude might be younger and stronger, but he respected his father too much to go head to head with him. So it was with a rare sense of defeat that he heard his sentence.

"Very well," Nevett said with freezing courtesy, "if you don't care about my peace of mind, you'll care about this. If you don't accept this tutor, if you don't give this tutor your full cooperation, I'm going to find you a maiden, arrange a contract of marriage, and let's see you get out of that one, my lad!" Nevett lifted his fist. "Let's see how you'll manage to avoid an energetic mama when I've promised her you'll make her daughter the next duchess!"

Jude recognized defeat when it stared him in the face. And this was defeat, a complication unlike any other he could imagine. Lowering his head, he gazed at his very shiny boots. "Very well, sir, you win. When will the lessons commence?"

"Tomorrow. She'll meet you in Hyde Park. You'll know her by the red rose she wears in her lapel."

"Good God, sir, how trite!" Jude said, irritated beyond measure.

"Trite or not, willing or not, you'll do as she instructs, or b'God I'll sic the entire Fairchild family of females on you, and you'll be lucky to escape with your sanity, much less your freedom."

Knowing the Fairchilds as he did, Jude took that threat seriously. "I'll do it." Feebly, he flapped his lace handkerchief as if whisking away an evil smell. "But I won't like it."

Chapter 3

In high dudgeon, Lord Huntington removed himself from Nevett's study, and Caroline walked around the decorative screen. She met Nevett's gaze directly. "His lordship seems displeased."

"It's to be expected. He is . . . or rather, he *was* strong-willed." Sinking into his chair, the duke groped for his glass of brandy. "I don't threaten him often, but when I do, I mean what I say. He'll do as he's told."

"He didn't sound as much of a dilettante as you painted him." Indeed, for a good portion of the interview, Huntington had *sounded* like a vigorous man of action. More than that, he had sounded . . . magnificent. His deep, melodic voice had resonated in her soul like a declaration of strength and security.

"Did you *see* him?" His Grace demanded.

She had. After listening to his voice, she had peeked through the holes in the screen and laid eyes upon the most striking man she'd ever had the good luck to view.

The impact of his form, his visage, remained with her still.

Huntington was tall, taller than she by at least six inches, and he sported a pair of shoulders that gave a woman a sense of shelter. His body was strong-boned and sturdy, not willow-thin like so many stylish aristocrats. His hair was a luscious, dark brown, with kisses of gold, and he wore it long and tied at the base of his neck, like some aristocrat of old. His face was sculpted from the finest clay God ever created, with jutting cheekbones, an authoritative nose, and a jaw too pronounced to be called anything but obdurate. The sun had toasted Lord Huntington a lovely brown, providing a striking setting for a pair of eyes so blue they shocked with the impact of his gaze.

And he hadn't truly looked at her. He had seen only the screen behind which she was hidden. Yet she had drawn back in alarm.

He didn't fit in the modern age. If he were stripped of that silly costume, he could easily stride from the mists of myth, a warrior who conquered by the strength of his body and the skill of his arms. He would have looked at home in a glittering suit of armor, with a sword clutched in his broad hands, or in a kilt, holding a claymore . . . or as a druid, clothed in secrets and magic. He sported a fierce male beauty, and she feared he would see all the way down to her silly, shallow core.

"He's very handsome." With the words came the memory of the time, only a few days ago at the Distinguished Academy of Governesses, when she had said much the same thing about Lord Freshfield.

Lord Freshfield, who had set out to ruin her and succeeded beyond all hope of redemption.

Lord Freshfield, who despite Caroline's assurances

to Adorna, stalked her still. Caroline had to make this job work. She had to, for with each failure Lord Fresh-field pursued her more closely, his soft white hands outstretched to touch her . . .

With a snap that made her jump, His Grace asked, "What did you think of my son's clothing?"

"Ah, his clothing." She had a vision of that yellow waistcoat, that orange silk scarf, the plaid trousers that mingled the two colors.

"Those boots." His Grace's voice vibrated with contempt.

"Yes, the boots." She fought the desire to laugh as she recalled the incongruity of those huge feet in those shining white boots.

"You have to admit, he looked absurd."

"*Absurd* is too strong a word." She gave a faint gurgle of amusement. "A better word would be *silly*."

"And that fan! And his handkerchief!" Nevett clutched the arms of his chair. "And his manner. Be truthful and tell me what you think of it."

Truthful? She stared at His Grace. He looked like his son—or rather, his son looked like him. Nevett had been a duke most of his life, and he sat in his thronelike chair in stolid dignity, a big, strong man who demanded the truth as if it were his right. As if anything he desired was his right—and probably it was.

"He's frivolous, but that should not preclude a wealthy, handsome man from marriage." Heaven knew she'd met enough frivolous men during her Season. Her best friend had married the biggest fool in society, but money had soothed Edith's distress and Caroline had to admit the fool had a kind heart, for he'd uttered not a word of reproach when Edith had assisted Caroline in the darkest days after the scandal.

But His Grace had a single goal, the marriage of his son, and he drove toward that event relentlessly. "Huntington's title and wealth attracts the ladies. His manners and his interests drive them away."

"Not completely. I can't believe they are completely repulsed."

"No. Regardless of his idiocy, they try valiantly to win his regard. But he doesn't seem to notice, or care. The ladies might as well be . . . be . . . invisible!"

If that were the case, the problem might not be so easily resolved.

But Nevett noted her silent, questioning glance, and said with a snort of impatience, "I'm not a man given to dreams for my son to which he is unequal. From his tenth birthday, he displayed an eager interest in the fair sex. The lad visits actresses on a regular basis. Never the same one twice, mind you, but he's still got the needs of a, er . . ." His Grace seemed to remember he spoke to a lady, albeit a lady he had hired. "Never mind."

"You've had him followed."

Lord Nevett viewed her forbiddingly, and she understood him. He was a duke. He would do as he wished, and a chit like her should not question him.

With a scornful twist to his mouth, he said, "Lady Bucknell recommended you as the best flirt to be had, but now that I've met you, I have my doubts. You seem light-minded and inexperienced. Do you think you can do it?"

"Teach your son how to flirt?" Could Caroline teach Huntington how to flirt? Of course she could!

For the first time since she had been compromised, she allowed herself to submerge into the sweet and downy personality of Miss Caroline Ritter. Her eyelashes sank down to rest on her cheeks, then up to gaze adoringly at Lord Nevett. A small, secretive smile lifted her full lips. Her posture changed; she leaned against the desk, and her shoulders developed a seductive slope. She took a deep breath, bringing her breasts to his attention, then in a low, husky voice, she said, "I have no doubt I can teach Lord Huntington how to flirt."

"By George." The duke's gaze fastened to her in masculine appreciation. "If I were twenty years younger and unmarried, I'd hire you to teach *me* how to flirt."

She answered automatically, as he—as any man—would have wished. "You, my lord, need no instruction. Not now. Nor, I wager, not twenty years ago."

He chuckled deeply, and she realized with a shock she probably had spoken the truth. He was a very attractive man.

"You're very good," he said. "Very good indeed."

She *was* good. She knew it in her heart, for although she had been careful, these past four years, to appear plain and capable, she had been playing a part. As she once more plunged herself in the role of a flirt, she returned to her true persona. As her father had repeatedly told her, she was born to be a coquette, nothing more, nothing less—and that was a lowering reflection, indeed.

His Grace bobbed up from the depths of his appreciation. "As impressive as was that exhibition, I would have to point out that that is feminine flirting. How will you teach Jude to act like a man?"

"He will not act, he will react. In my experience, when a man is confronted with a lady who calls forth his sentient male predatory instincts, he responds appropriately. My task, as I see it, is to hone that instinct in Lord Huntington so that every time he sees a skirt, he automatically flirts."

Nevett's remarkable brows rose to his hairline. "You've thought this through."

"I have, indeed. If I am to be a success in this position, it will take more than a simple tap of my magic wand. I'm gathering all my forces, all my intellect . . . such as it is . . . all my experience." With every intent of impressing him, she removed the green leather-bound journal from her bag. She showed him her graceful penmanship marching its way down the pristine white page. "I've planned every lesson with care."

With a frown, Nevett took the book from her. "Planned . . . you said you were going to cultivate his instincts."

"Absolutely, but flirting is a fine art." She waxed enthusiastic on this, her area of expertise. "He must know how to flirt in every situation, how to flirt with an unknown yet desirable lady in the lending library . . . how to judge a lady's station in life and therefore her suitability as a prospective mate. This is no small project, Your Grace. It took me eighteen years to learn the subtleties of flirting, all of which I must teach your son by the end of the Season."

Nevett donned his glasses and read her first entry aloud. *"Week 1: Test Lord Huntington to see if his command of basic social skills are tolerable. Improve if necessary."* With a frown, he looked up. "He knows some of it, or at least he used to, before he went to"— loathing filled his tone—"France."

"With all due respect, Your Grace, that he could lose his skill in France seems unlikely." A light smile played around her lips. "The French I have met seemed not only experts at the art of light romance, but at the same time extraordinarily pragmatic about marriage and fittingness."

Nevett handed back her journal. "They have corrupted him."

In her experience, corruption involved more dire cruelty and carelessness than Huntington had shown. But she kept that information to herself.

In a whiplash tone, Nevett asked, "How are you going to make sure he doesn't fall in love with *you*?"

"With . . . me?" She laughed. It had been a very long time since she had been under the misapprehension any man loved her. "Your Grace, I can't imagine anything more daunting to a man than discovering that every languishing glance, every coy compliment has been paid for by his father."

"You're right."

Caroline suspected few people had ever heard those words from the duke of Nevett.

He surveyed her critically. "That gown is last year's fashion. To play the part, you'll need to wear different garments."

She looked down at the plain blue skirt. "Sir, this is the best I have." The best by far, provided by Lady Bucknell.

"Very well, I'll provide what's needed. My butler will arrange for you to visit a couturiere for day wear. We'll add more as necessary." With his gaze, Nevett dispassionately weighed and measured her. Then his eyelids drooped, and he tapped his fingertips together. "We'll do as they do in the nursery. We shall teach Jude by arranging situations such as he will encounter in society. Tomorrow the park. The next day, an encounter in the lending library."

She knew she had to take her role as a teacher seriously, so she made her protest respectfully yet with great seriousness. "I will assess Lord Huntington tomorrow in the park. The next day, I'll start his training according to my schedule."

At this contradiction of his plans, Nevett's eyes bulged, and his voice rose. "What?"

Hastily, she backed off. "If that's all right with you, Your Grace, that's what I'll do."

He picked up Adorna's letter and studied it. Then he nodded, and in a grudging tone, said, "Yes. Well. Yes. Of course. You're in charge."

"Yes, I am," she said faintly. Although she didn't quite believe it herself.

"How long do you think it will take you to get him whipped into shape?"

"I don't know, sir."

He gestured impatiently, his hand rolling as he urged a reply.

She guessed, "If we work together every day, perhaps a fortnight for afternoon affairs, more for evening events."

"The duchess will host a small party with a few of his cronies and a few select young ladies."

"Who won't object to my presence among them, I trust?"

Nevett's lip curled haughtily. "The young ladies will do as they're told."

Caroline hated to break it to him, but he needed to know. "I . . . I can't go into society with his lordship. I don't know if Lady Bucknell made my circumstances clear, but it is impossible."

"Lady Bucknell did make your circumstances clear."

He pshawed as if the scandal was of no matter. "If I say you shall go into society, then into society you shall go. Let anyone who disagrees carry their complaints to the duke of Nevett."

She stared in fascination at the aristocrat so sure of himself he feared neither society's censure nor judgment. "Sir, with all due respect for your influence, I've found that society will gossip about a single woman who is unprotected by her family regardless of who is her patron, and in fact the higher the prestige of the patron, the greater the delight in the gossip." She could imagine how Lady Reederman would harrumph, how Mrs. Gibben would hide behind her fan and smile as she spread the most vile rumors conceivable.

After all, they had done it before.

With finality, Nevett said, "I need you to accompany my son into society. Every facet of society. How else will you supervise and correct him?"

The situation was fast escaping Caroline's control. If she weren't careful, she lose this position before she even started. "I'll create situations like the ones he's going to face at the theater, at balls—"

"No." Nevett struck the arm of his chair. "You'll go *with* him to the balls and the theater. I depend on you to introduce him to the right young women. The ones who'll engage his interest. And at the same time you'll guide him in the correct behavior for a gentleman seeking the delights of matrimony."

The very thought of going to a ball made Caroline shudder with horror. To face those outraged matrons with their freezing contempt, those smirking men with their lascivious eyes—she couldn't do it. *Wouldn't* do it. Not even for Lady Bucknell. Not even for this job. "I can't," she said faintly. "It won't work."

"I admit it," he said. "You're right."

She breathed a sigh of relief.

Like a charging bull, Nevett continued, "You need parental approval bestowed upon you. So I'll make your father approve of you at once."

Had Nevett run mad? "Your Grace, my father and I haven't spoken since he threw me from his home in a theatrical production worthy of Shakespeare."

She might as well have not spoken, for all the notice Nevett took. "We'll arrange a meeting between the two of you. He'll speak to you courteously. You'll answer him with daughterly respect. It will be done."

"But . . . he won't do it."

"Don't be ridiculous. He'll do as he's told."

It seemed Nevett had used that phrase already. She tried to think back . . . ah, yes, he had said that same thing when talking about his son and heir. And, as a matter of fact, about the young ladies who would attend his soirees.

She pictured her father's corpulent face, his ingratiating smile. She remembered his fervent desire to lift himself in the ranks of society, in his worship of the aristocratic state.

His Grace was right. Manfred Ritter would do as he was told.

"We should easily have this thing wrapped up before the end of the Season." Now Nevett's gaze rose to rake her face, and she realized he hadn't been deep in thought. He had been biding his time. "Miss Ritter, you heard what I said to Huntington. I've arranged it so the lad will do his best to learn from you. Now hear what I say to you—I know your circumstances. All of your circumstances."

Mortified, she asked, "Your Grace, what does that mean?"

So he told her.

Caroline went to the servants' entrance. She rapped softly, and when the door opened, she slipped down the stairs and into the dim, cavernous kitchen below her father's town house.

"Miss Caroline, ye're taking a terrible chance. 'E's at 'ome." Cook wrung her hands. "If 'e catches ye, ye know 'ow mean 'e'll be to ye."

"And to you, so I'll be especially careful." Caroline pushed her hood back from her face.

Cook shrugged as if she didn't care. "There's a lot o' positions fer a good cook."

"Yes, but I need a cook who cares for my sister as you do." Caroline pressed the worn hands. "Where is she?"

"She's reading in the classroom. Stay 'ere. I'll go get 'er." Cook moved softly for a woman of her girth. She had to. Mr. Ritter was a strict taskmaster who demanded his servants provide faultless cleanliness, perfectly cooked meals, and absolute silence. He did not accept mistakes of any kind. Many a serving maid had been dismissed without a reference for dropping her duster, and the result of such strictness was a house as still as a tomb. And dark, and grim.

Stepping back into the shadows, Caroline pulled her thin coat close around her shoulders. She hated to come back here. Hated more that Genevieve had to live here. But she had the solution. She had the solution at last.

She heard the swift patter of Genevieve's footsteps on the stairway and irresistibly, her smile blossomed. As Genevieve entered the kitchen, Cook on her heels, Caroline stepped into the light.

The single lamp showed a tall girl of fourteen. She moved awkwardly, as if her own hands and feet were alien to her. Her features looked too large for her face. She had spots, and she slumped to compensate for her height. In fact, she was the image of Caroline at that age.

"You're beautiful." Caroline spoke softly and embraced her.

"Huh." Genevieve hugged her back, but her scowl seemed to have put permanent lines between her eyebrows. "Nobody agrees with you."

"They will." Caroline stepped back and took her hands. "I have the most wonderful news. I have a position with the duke of Nevett."

"That's good," Genevieve said cautiously. "Doing what?"

"Teaching his son to flirt."

"That's dumb," Genevieve said, with uncensored adolescent scorn.

"Maybe so, but it's something I know how to do, and you know what he said?" Caroline squeezed Genevieve's hands in excitement. "He said that if, by the end of the Season, his son is betrothed to a girl of good family, he's going to give me a bonus of *one thousand pounds.*"

"Miss Caroline!" Cook dropped into a chair as if she'd been shot.

"One thousand pounds?" Genevieve stared as if she didn't quite understand. "Are you sure?"

"Yes! A thousand pounds if I deliver his son to the altar." Caroline lifted her skirt and curtsied to Genevieve. "Do you know what that means?"

"We can go to France and live with Mama's family?" Genevieve guessed.

"Yes!" Caroline did a few dance steps.

Genevieve's eyes, the exact color of Caroline's, widened. "Can you do it?"

"I most definitely can." Caroline vowed, "Lord Huntington's bachelor days are numbered."

Chapter 4

$\mathcal{J}$ude straightened his cuffs as he entered the party that night at Blythe Hall. The Throckmorton home in Suffolk lay a short train ride away from London, and the place hummed with celebration and laughter, with dancing, good cheer—and with intrigue.

Garrick Throckmorton worked with the Home Office, as did his lovely wife, Celeste. Throckmorton's mother, Lady Philberta, his brother, Ellery and Ellery's wife, Hyacinth, were off visiting Italy, and Jude would wager they, too, performed some duty to the crown. The Throckmortons were a dynasty of spies, yet Garrick Throckmorton was also a financier of some repute, the man to whom many applied when they wanted investment tips. To top it off, the Throckmorton family reigned as scions of society, and an invitation to one of their parties was a coup d'etat for any member of the ton. So Jude wasn't conspicuous as he greeted his many acquaintances—not conspicuous, unless one considered his silver velvet evening jacket trimmed in beads.

Throckmorton separated himself from a laughing group and came forward to greet Jude. "How unexpected! I had not hoped to see you tonight."

It didn't sound like a question, but it was, and Jude answered heartily, "Heard you were having a do. Had to come out to show off my latest acquisition"—he slid a finger along his lapel, and in a lower tone, added— "and I have an inquiry about an unforeseen companion I've acquired. I hoped to speak with you alone."

"A companion. Of the female variety?"

"Most undoubtedly female."

"How intriguing." At the approach of his charming wife, Throckmorton took her hand, tucked it into his arm, and led them both toward his study. "Darling, Huntington has acquired an unexpected female companion."

With a smile that lit the dim, private corridor, Celeste said, "He needs one. He is isolated."

Jude suspected that she meant it, which both made him want to deny it and wonder what deep-seated loneliness she saw in him. "Actually, my companion isn't my choice, and I'm afraid she causes me a bit of a conundrum."

Throckmorton frowned in concern. "Who is she?"

Now that the moment had come, Jude didn't want to tell him. It sounded so absurd. "It's a trifling matter, really."

In the study, Celeste went from lamp to lamp, turning up the low-burning wicks until warm light reached into every corner of the room. "Trifling matters frequently become larger matters."

"You cared enough to bring this to our attention," Throckmorton reminded him.

"It's probably of no moment."

"For heaven's sake, man, what is it?" Throckmorton demanded.

"My father has hired a female to teach me how to flirt."

Silenced, Throckmorton and Celeste stared at him. Then Throckmorton's solemnity gave way, and he chortled.

Celeste rested her hand on Throckmorton's arm. "We should not laugh. This is obviously"—her voice quivered with amusement—"a serious problem for Lord Huntington." Her gaze wandered up and down his colorful garb. "And a much-needed improvement."

Throckmorton and Celeste both burst out laughing. The couple was incongruous, she so light and cheerful, he so dark and somber, and they complemented each other as did the moon and the night.

Jude crossed his arms and waited until their merriment had subsided a little. "I wondered if someone might suspect me of—"

"Bad taste?" Throckmorton suggested.

Jude had to wait again, and this time he glared forbiddingly. His annoyance was tempered by the knowledge that if Signora Eloisa Vittori could hear about his predicament, she would chuckle, too. It was Jude's ability to flirt that had convinced the famed Italian opera singer to allow him in her bed, and his skill as a lover that kept him there during his three-month sojourn in Florence. But of course, in Florence he had dressed with taste and behaved with the savoir-faire of an urbane English gentleman.

"Sorry, sorry." Throckmorton seated Celeste on the sofa, gestured Jude toward the comfortable chair opposite, and seated himself beside his wife. "Suspect you of working for me? Yes, anything's possible. What's this young lady's name?"

"He wouldn't say."

Throckmorton raised astonished eyebrows. "You don't even know who she is?"

"No. He didn't tell me, which makes me all the more suspicious." Jude sank into the chair. "I didn't anticipate my father's action, but on reflection, I should have. Nevett is not one to wait on events. He wants me married, and I can't tell him what I'm doing."

"No. Heaven forfend. From where did this lady—I assume she is a lady?" At Jude's nod, Throckmorton continued, "From where did this lady arrive?"

"Someplace called the Distinguished Academy of Governesses." Jude waited for their reaction.

"Oh!" Celeste dimpled. "No, you need have no worry about your companion. If she is recommended by Lady Bucknell, the proprietress, then the young lady is trustworthy."

"It's through the Distinguished Academy of Governesses that Celeste came to work for me." Throckmorton ran his finger up her arm and when she turned to him, they smiled at each other as if remembering a great romance. "And Lady Bucknell has on occasion done work for me."

"Oh." Jude hated to surrender, but he saw no way out. "Then I suppose I shall have a governess."

"It'll do you good to put some frivolity in your life," Throckmorton said.

"Yes. Spying is serious business, but that doesn't mean we can never enjoy ourselves," Celeste added.

For them, perhaps, but for Jude, the decision to become a spy had been forged in fire and pain. "I came into this business by a different route, and until I've trodden the whole path, I can't truly enjoy anything. Although I do owe it to Michael to live as he did, I'm still learning. Still learning." Jude closed his eyes and, as always happened, he saw again the scene that had etched itself into his mind. Once more, he saw the fire, felt the heat, experienced the agony of knowing he'd failed his parents, the dynasty, and Michael.

Jude held the summons from his brother. Come at once to the old square. I need you! P.S. Pay the girl. It was scrawled on a torn piece of paper, delivered to his rooms by a waif. He stared at the message with the sense of helpless rage Michael frequently engendered in him. Michael, who was always falling in and out of adventures and wanting Jude to come to his rescue. Jude always had, but after the last caper, which resulted in a broken arm and two blackened eyes, and all for the love of a barmaid, he had sworn to Michael he would aid him no more.

And he wouldn't.

He paid the messenger, who bit the coin, then disappeared into the night. He seated himself on the chair, crossed his arms, and stared into the darkness. He had known Michael was heading for trouble.

Jude lived down near the bottom of the hill. He visited the museums, attended classes at the university, drank at taverns with the impoverished students, and listened while they fomented revolution.

Michael lived at the top of the hill at the spa with the wealthiest, most dissolute people in Europe. He drank champagne, he danced all night, he gambled and gossiped and philandered, and for the first time in their years as brothers, Jude despised him. Michael had never been so callous before, so determined to frolic while, not far away, people suffered and starved. Jude had tried to tell him, but Michael laughed, and said, "Don't worry so much, little brother. We've all got to die sometime."

Maybe Michael's time was now.

Jude leaped up. Michael was his brother. No matter what, he would always go to the rescue. Loading a pistol, he stuck it in his belt. He strapped a leather holster to his arm and into that he slid the long, sharp, thin-bladed knife that was the weapon of choice in this small country. He donned a dark coat and dark hat and started for the square in the depths of the old town. Above him, at the top of the hill, he could hear music, see light, but as he got closer to the valley floor, poverty closed in around him. By the time he approached his destination, hardship pressed so close it seemed the buildings were ready to topple from the weight.

It was just past ten o'clock. Pubs lined the narrow, littered street. But no light spilled from the doorways. Shutters covered the windows. Nothing moved. Not a drunk, not a cat, not the breeze.

Where was everyone?

Disquiet crawled up his spine. He stayed close to the buildings, his hand on the grip of his pistol, and he smelled a whiff of smoke carried on the evening breeze. And saw something. Light from the square. Not a lot, but a flicker. Something was burning. Something that shouldn't be. A building. A bonfire. Another trace of smoke wafted past.

Then a blast of smell, the stench of burning wood and metal, and mixed in with that, an odor that lifted the hair on his neck. He found himself running, slipping on the stones beneath his feet, running right to the edge of the square. Then he stopped abruptly. He would do Michael no good if he rushed in to be killed. He peered around the building into the empty square.

A fire had been set right beside the fountain. A big fire. A fire fueled by sturdy chunks of tree and, if the smell was to be trusted, fed more than a few bottles of brandy. The occasional flame still licked at the twisted branches, but most of the wood had burned down to coals. And laid out like a lesson on the hearth of embers . . .

Caution forgotten, Jude walked slowly toward the center of the square.

A body smoked, blackened and crisp.

Jude stared down at it. Flinched, horrified . . . disgusted.

No. No. Not Michael.

But in the light of the dying flames, gold glinted in the cavern of the ribs. Jude didn't have a moment of doubt. He knew what it was.

With a stick, he speared the family's signet ring, the one Michael had donned on his eighteenth birthday, the one the Durant heir always wore. Jude dropped it into his palm. The gold, so shiny, so bright . . . so hot it sank through Jude's skin and into his flesh. He didn't care. He welcomed the pain, the searing heat. It was real. He deserved it, and it gave him a moment's relief from the taste of his own guilt.

This was his brother, and he was dead.

Michael was dead. Michael was dead, and Jude had failed him.

Not just failed him. Refused to aid him. Agony clutched at Jude. He bent, holding his belly in silent agony.

When out of the corner of his eyes, he saw a dark shape creeping toward him. Whirling, Jude pulled his dagger.

A boy stopped, stood there, hands up.

For all that the lad was skinny and a child of perhaps eight, Jude recognized the menace of his motions. A pickpocket and a sneak thief. Jude slipped the ring into his pocket, kept the blade pointed steadily at the lad. "Tell me what happened now."

"Can't you see? They killed him, Mister," the lad said. "They claimed he interfered. They said if we knew what was smart, we'd all stay down here where we belong and not make trouble, or we'd end up just like him."

"Who did this?" Jude contained his anguish in a whisper.

The lad backed up a step as if he expected Jude to explode. "Men from up there." He indicated the mansion near the top of the mountain where gamblers came to take their chances, where aristocrats danced, and the de Guignard family tossed their gossamer net and pulled up gold with every cast. "They killed this chap, burned the body. They threw gold pieces on the floor of my father's tavern. They took a cask of ale and my sister and rode down the road toward the border of Serephinia."

Jude heard a different anguish in the lad's voice, the torment of a boy who had lost his sibling. Slipping his dagger into its shield, he said, "Get me a horse."

"Why should I do anything for you? You're a foreigner. You're a gentleman." The boy spat at Jude's feet and cast his worst insult. "You're like them."

Jude didn't waste his time denying or explaining. Picking up the lad by his ragged jacket, Jude tightened his fist and shook him. "Get me a horse."

The lad hung there.

"And I'll get you your sister back." Jude dropped him back to his feet.

"How're you going to do that? There're four of them."

Jude pointed to the blackened body. Sorrow clawed at him, seeking escape. "That was my brother. He taught me to fight by landing me in all sorts of desperate situations. He taught me to be cautious the same way." Grief and guilt won its way over his control. "And now—he has taught me how to go mad." He dropped to his knees. Lifting his face toward the black sky, he howled his fury and his anguish. Like a wolf. Like a beast. Like a man who had nothing to live for except vengeance.

When he finished, the boy was back with a horse. "Bring back the gelding." He dropped the reins into Jude's hands. "Bring back my sister." With glorious relish, he added, "Never mind the bodies. When you kill 'em—let 'em rot."

He had fought them, four against one. He had saved the lad's sister, and killed the men. Two had died easily, but one had sliced Jude's arm open with a broken bottle. Another had shot Jude in the shoulder and in the gut. That blackguard suffered special treatment. Jude had questioned him before he dispatched him, and pulled two names from the villain's lips—Comte de Guignard and Monsieur Bouchard. They had hired these men to kill Michael, but why, the blackguard didn't know.

Looking down at the circle that branded his palm, Jude brought himself back to this with the Throckmortons. "When I dream, I dream that I made a mistake, that he's still alive and off on another grand adventure. But I always wake up, and he's dead." He looked up to see Throckmorton examining him with a sharp eye, and he knew the speculation that ran through Throckmorton's mind. "I found Michael's coat nearby, and the blackguards had his boots. His boots, Throckmorton, no one else's, for no one except me wears such a large size."

Throckmorton nodded. "As you say. I simply hoped that—"

"Believe me," Jude said, "I tried in every manner to convince myself that body was not my brother's, and the more I tried, the more I convinced myself it was."

Celeste's eyes swam with sympathetic tears. "You have done so much with no thought for yourself!"

"I think too often of myself." Jude rubbed the hardened round scar in the palm of his hand. "That's why my brother was killed."

"You accept blame when it is not due. He was killed because someone wanted him dead." Celeste had lived in France for several years, and occasionally Jude could hear the echo of French pragmatism in her tone and accent.

"Because that's true, I'll be able to forgive myself—when I have my vengeance."

"Good. Self-loathing makes a good man bad. Vengeance is a great cleanser of the soul." She nodded in satisfaction. "I have help for you. I found two gifts that were given to Garrick and me on the occasion of our marriage. You can present them to the Moricadian gentlemen as a bribe to get their attention."

Throckmorton cleared his throat. "Would the gifts be the snuffboxes that Uncle Julian gave us?"

"Yes, as a matter of fact." Celeste's voice was crisp and clear.

"Because they are expensive—"

"And in dreadful taste, and suitable only for a man, and just the sort of thing you would expect from someone who disapproves of your marriage to the gardener's daughter." Celeste tapped her slipper-clad foot in annoyance. "What difference does it make, anyway? When the time is right, Maltin's going to break into the Moricadians' apartment, steal everything back, and do another search for clues as to their purpose."

"I know." Throckmorton put his hand on her shoulder. "I know, darling."

She took a steadying breath, then closed her eyes as if she were groping for her temper. She must not have found it, for she snipped, "You cannot help it if some of your family are jackasses."

Throckmorton met Jude's gaze and made a gesture over his belly, then sliced a glance at Celeste.

Ah. She was increasing. That explained her sensitivity about a matter she would have normally shrugged away. In a chatty tone, Jude said, "Comte de Guignard and Bouchard believe that Englishmen are worthless, good-for-nothing fribbles, and I've worked hard to confirm their prejudice." He had tagged along after them, contrived to meet them wherever they went, and played the part of a simpleton and a sycophant so in love with Continental culture as to be oblivious to insult or innuendo. "I've succeeded. They believe me to be the country's biggest fool."

"Have they realized you're Michael's brother?" Throckmorton asked.

"Yes, but they don't know I was in Moricadia at the same time as Michael." Bitterness etched Jude's smile. "That's part of the reason they despise me so much. They ordered the death of my brother, and I appear to be so stupid that I want their approval."

"Do you yet have any inkling why they've come to London?" Throckmorton asked.

"No, but they've begun to lower their guards. It's Bouchard we need to watch," Jude leaned forward. "The key lies with him."

"We don't know that for sure." Throckmorton leaned forward, too, caught up in the recitation of the facts and seeking the answers that must be there.

"I do. I lived in Moricadia for months waiting for Michael to stop gambling . . . although now I know he was doing more than gambling." He had been playing the hero. Damn him. "It was Bouchard who advised Comte de Guignard and Prince Sandre to bring in the spas and the gambling, and their success is beyond anyone's imagining. Along with the money, Bouchard brought in the criminals to run the country. He's a thug in fancy dress clothes. The people in Moricadia are downtrodden and angry, and they hate him as they do no one else. They *fear* him as they do no one else."

"When I lived in Paris, even then there was talk that France should absorb Moricadia, take over the spas and the gambling, and put the money into their own treasury." Celeste sounded almost normal.

"De Guignard and Bouchard don't want that—but why not go to France to argue against union?" Throckmorton demanded. "Why come to England?"

"To make trouble between the two countries," Celeste said.

That was easy enough to do. The state of affairs with the Russians had grown dire. They wished to take over the continent of Asia, and Britain and France had too much money and power at stake to allow that to happen. So the two unlikely allies were putting aside centuries of distrust to join together and fight the Russians.

At least, that was the plan. In truth, the French diplomats despised the English, the English diplomats de-

spised the French, and certain men were willing to go
to any lengths to destroy the alliance. "If de Guignard
and Bouchard make enough trouble, they'll distract
France from Moricadia."

Celeste dabbed at her eyes. "Like a house of cards,
the peace between France and England would be easy
to knock down, and that would mean war."

A faint tap sounded on the door, and in his low voice,
Throckmorton's secretary said, "Sir, she's here."

With a flounce and a smirk, Celeste said, "How fortunate you've come tonight, Lord Huntington, for our
visitor concerns you."

Throckmorton's mouth grew tight, and to his secretary, he replied, "Send her in."

The most extraordinary young woman walked
through the door. She was young, perhaps twenty, beautiful and plump in a toothsome way, petite in height
with a presence that commanded the eyes. Her sumptu-
ous bosom quivered as it spilled over the top of her
low-cut gown, which was sewn to perfection, yet the
scarlet color easily outshone Jude's most outlandish
costume. Her abundance of blond hair was caught at
her neck, and her slumberous green eyes surveyed the
room, then settled on Jude.

She moved toward him, her skirts swishing with
each step she took. He found himself on his feet,
watching her. As she drew near, an earthy scent swam
in his head, and when she placed her hand on his arm,
he discovered a heretofore overlooked affinity for petite, curvaceous, green-eyed blondes. "What a glorious
gentleman you are." She drew each word into a caress
that made him wonder what her order of business might
be—and he knew that if she wished to make him her
order of business, he would submit to her demands.

But Celeste interrupted her, and pointed at Garrick. "This gentleman is Mr. Throckmorton."

"Oh." The woman glanced at Throckmorton's somber, distinguished outfit and sighed. "Of course he is. I beg your pardon, Mr. Throckmorton."

"He doesn't mind," Celeste said blithely. To Jude, she explained, "Miss Gloriana Dollydear is an opera singer, and our newest weapon in this war. Sit down, Miss Dollydear, while I explain the situation to Lord Huntington."

Chapter 5

"*A* lovely afternoon after so many days of rain, Lord Huntington." Lady Rutherford's affected voice brought Jude to a halt.

"Indeed, Lady Rutherford. So good to see you and your lovely daughter, Miss Jordan!" Jude bowed so extravagantly he might have been in the courts of Versailles rather than a gravel path in Hyde Park. "A most splendid day, and a chance to try out the newest spring styles."

Poor Miss Jordan. She was only seventeen, new to London, and was torn between acknowledging him as the heir to a dukedom, a man wealthy in his own right, one of the prime catches of any Season . . . or as one of the most laughable men in London.

When, with deliberate insouciance, he tossed his emerald-and-tan paisley scarf over one shoulder, Miss Jordan lost the battle. Covering her mouth with one gloved hand, she dissolved into muffled laughter.

Her mother jabbed her bony elbow hard into the girl's ribs.

Straightening at once, Miss Jordan choked, "How lovely to see you, my lord. Your costume is most magnificent."

"But of course!" His brow knit with sham concern. "Yet you sound as if you're not well, Miss Jordan. I fear from your glassy eyes you're coming down with an indisposition." He drew back as if from the plague. "Please! I'm too important a gentleman, and too much in demand at parties, to be exposed to such a threat."

This time, she couldn't contain a snort, and he stepped back to the far end of the path. "Really, Lady Rutherford, she should be in bed and away from the rest of polite society. Away from *me*."

Lady Rutherford nodded, grabbed Miss Jordan's arm, and jerked her down the path.

He strolled on, doffing his tall hat—his *very* tall hat—to every lady he passed. The wise mamas and their title-hungry daughters curtsied gravely to him, but there were always the young ladies like Miss Jordan who couldn't contain their amusement, and to them he gave a special smile. His oblivion caused further gales of merriment as he minced along.

As he had hoped, the first spring sunshine drew enough people to Hyde Park to make his outing unremarkable. Unremarkable, that is, except for the vibrant lime green greatcoat he matched with a brown-checked suit and brown, high-heeled ankle boots, making him the most outrageously dressed man on parade—and a nincompoop of the highest order. Such was the title he had cultivated with painstaking care.

Sometimes he wondered if, after this escapade, he would ever return to his former self, careful of manners, of propriety, of all matters that were unimportant, and contemplative to the point of indecision.

He thought not. He hoped not. None of the ton who strolled the paths imagined that he noted each of them: how they walked, the tones of their voices, the attention they paid to their surroundings, and, of course, what they wore. It was possible to tell a lot about a man or a woman by their attire, and Jude watched and weighed everyone who crossed his path as, all the while, he avoided the puddles left by the rain and kept a lookout for the two Moricadians who were his prey.

He also watched for his tutor.

His tutor. The dour female his father had hired to teach him how to flirt. The one his father said, "looked well enough"—a euphemism if Jude had ever heard one.

And there she was, a horse-faced female carrying a nosegay of red roses held under her chin. Her complexion was absolutely white, either painted on with powder or caused by a lamentable lack of sun. Her nose was squashed flat, as if she'd walked headlong into a door. Her shoulders were rounded, her bosom unremarkable, and she wore fine clothing so badly she would have done as well to have donned a sackcloth.

What in the devil had his father been thinking?

The tutor batted her brown eyes at him in vapid adoration.

Lifting his hat, he bowed, and resolved to return to Nevett's town house as soon as the lesson had ended and ask.

She skittered forward, then stopped a few feet away as if uncertain.

Fiend seize her, she was playing coy. Hat still held high, he bowed again, and indicated the place before him.

With a triumphant glance around at the aristocracy strolling past, she minced toward him and curtsied.

Settling his hat back on his head, he said in a low voice, "I don't suppose I could convince you to tell His Grace I've reformed."

She narrowed her eyes as if in confusion—or as if she needed glasses. "My lord?"

"Silly of me to ask." How was he to flirt with this . . . this creature? The gossip would no longer be about his clothes, but his taste in women. His friends would think he'd run mad, and if he tried to explain that his father had blackmailed him, they would laugh themselves into bedlam just as Throckmorton and Celeste had done. "His Grace will have made this whole travail worth your while somehow. So we shall do this thing, heh?"

She visibly swallowed. "What thing, Lord Huntington?"

"The politeness, the flirting, the courtship." Looking on the bright side, Jude knew his interest in this female would, without a doubt, cement his reputation as a cretin with Comte de Guignard and Monsieur Bouchard. "Must make it look good, and the sooner we succeed, the sooner we are done. Very well." He indicated the path. "Shall we walk?"

In a voice with all the appeal of chalk on a slateboard, she said, "Why . . . yes, my lord. Thank you, my lord. I would be delighted—"

"My lord," he finished for her.

She blinked at him. "My lord?"

"Nothing. I realize the circumstances are unusual, and we have not been formally introduced, but you know me, and I would be delighted to make your acquaintance." She didn't seem to know what he meant, so he prompted, "Won't you tell me your name?"

"Yes! Of course! I'm . . ." She paused and gasped, her pale lips opening like a fish out of water. If he didn't know better, he would say she had forgotten her name. At last she managed, "I'm Lady Pheodora Osgood of the Rochdale Osgoods."

"Indeed?" She surprised him. There really were Osgoods in Rochdale, a respectable family although singularly plain. "Now that you mention it, I see the resemblance. I hadn't realized—" He paused, on the verge of being indelicate.

"You hadn't realized what, my lord?"

He hadn't realized they suffered from the loss of fortune that required them to send one of their young ladies away to earn her living—but he *had* been out of the country. "I hadn't realized the Osgoods had brought a young lady of such exceptional beauty here to town."

She squinted up at him. "My lord, are you completely well?"

"I'm fine, I thank you." He bent his most charming smile on her.

"Are you sure? Because no one has ever called me . . . that is, I have never before heard . . ." She squinted at him yet more.

Irritated beyond belief by her stammering and her uncertainty, he snapped, "Do you wear spectacles?"

Deliberately, as if she'd been instructed to do so many times, she widened her eyes. "Spectacles? What do you mean, spectacles?"

"Eye apparel which would make you see more precisely. Here." Taking her reticule off her arm, he rummaged inside. "There they are." Taking the plain gold frames, he perched them on her nose.

She stared at him, and this time her eyes were sincerely wide—and a rather pretty brown.

"That's better. Now we can get along swimmingly. And after all, it's not as if you have to truly impress me with your beauty." Remembering his father's injunction to flirt, Jude added in a low, seductive tone, "I'm already overwhelmed."

She stopped in the middle of the walk, and said to herself, "I did hear that while abroad you had run mad."

"Is that one of the rumors?" He laughed with wholehearted amusement. "I suppose that is to be expected. No, I'm not mad—but then, madmen never realize their insanity, do they?"

"No." She backed up a step. "No. It was good to meet you, my lord."

"Is the lesson done for the day?" Her retreat rather surprised him. "I suppose you want to go at it slowly."

"Yes, my lord. The lesson is done, and you should go at it slowly." She took another step back. "Perhaps it might be wise to return to your rooms and rest. Take it all slowly." She stepped back, and back.

At that moment, he spotted his quarry. As he had hoped, the sunshine had brought Comte de Guignard and Monsieur Bouchard out for a stroll.

"There they are!" At once Jude sunk back into his role as a dilettante and a coxcomb, examining his cravat as best he could, twisting his fingers in his hair to create an extravagance of curls on his forehead.

"Yes. There they are. Of course. Excuse me." Turning, Lady Pheodora fled back up the path.

Staring after her, he said, "What an odd girl. She'll never have a career that way," and without another thought for her, he hurried to catch de Guignard and Bouchard. His tall walking cane touched the ground with every step, and in an affected voice, he called, "Wait! Comte! Monsieur! Oh, wait, I don't want to splash my clothes with these nasty puddles!"

As the men glanced at him, he saw the contempt they didn't bother to conceal. They didn't feel they had to. They thought him oblivious to any insult, and that meant he played his role well. But they didn't stop.

So he called, "I was hoping to meet you most excellent gentlemen. I've brought you each a gift. It's only a trifle, a snuffbox, but I think you'll find the gold work is quite admirable, and the jewels are of wonderful clarity and cut."

The bribe stopped them in their tracks. Extending their hands, they accepted the boxes he offered, the boxes Celeste had given him. Bouchard, a short, stout man with an amazingly large black mustache and an equally amazing shiny bald head, pocketed his immediately and returned to puffing on the fat cigar he smoked at any possible occasion. But de Guignard opened his box and examined it. Jude thought if he'd had a jeweler's glass, he would have popped it in his eye and assessed the stone right there.

The comte was a man of perhaps forty-five, thin, tall, and handsome, with a gray, well-trimmed beard along his jaw. He spoke fondly of the days of Napoleon and France's position at the heights of power—and Moricadia's rise on its coattails. He also treasured an overweening grudge against the English, who had stripped their glory away, and at the same time, a tight-lipped resentment for the French, who looked down on the Moricadians. He wasn't an easy man to understand; yet he liked gold and he liked women, and on those traits Jude pinned his hopes.

Satisfied by the quality of the gift, de Guignard

nodded brusquely. "Thank you. It was good to have seen you."

Jude grasped their arms before they could turn away. "You can't go off yet! I wanted to ask how you liked the opera last night. I thought the soprano sang off-key, but perhaps that's because she's Mr. Throckmorton's mistress. That's enough to throw any woman off her stride!"

The two men caught their breaths. They looked at each other. Moving in unison, they separated enough to allow him to walk between them.

"*C'est vrai?* She is Monsieur Throckmorton's mistress?" Bouchard's English was strongly accented.

Jude fell in beside them without any indication of the triumph he experienced. The thing he did well, the thing which had led him to create this silly and vapid personality, was his ability to dissimilate. "But of course she is! It's a quiet affair. Mr. Throckmorton has a reputation to maintain, because his very pretty wife"—Jude lowered his voice and the Moricadians leaned closer—"is a shrew."

Interest brightened their faces.

Jude placed his hand on his chest and told the tale Celeste had conjured up. "Mrs. Throckmorton would make his life a misery if she knew."

"Fascinating. I hate to see a fellow gentleman suffer." Bouchard contemptuously blew a cloud of noxious smoke toward Jude. "What is her name, this mistress of Mr. Throckmorton?"

With a roguish wink, Jude said, "Miss Gloriana Dollydear, a lovely young lady with sizable . . . lungs that increase her capacity to sing loudly."

"We shall have to visit with her after her next performance." Bouchard stroked his mustache, a telling gesture he always used when he had received a plum of information.

The two Moricadians walked on, smiling at the oncoming walkers.

Miss Gloriana Dollydear, Jude had discovered, was lovely and shrewd, willing to play her role as Throckmorton's mistress—and as the wide-eyed informant to the Moricadians. She would tell de Guignard and Bouchard what Throckmorton wished them to hear. She would listen to their replies and report them, and in her youth, she cared nothing for the danger.

"I can't remember, do you speak French, Lord Huntington?" Bouchard asked with well-feigned confusion.

"*Oui!* Very well. All Englishmen of my class speak French." What Jude didn't say was that some spoke better than others. In French with an execrable accent, he said, "France filled me with awe." But the word he used for awe meant *timid*.

"France is Moricadia's mother." Comte de Guignard puffed out his chest.

"Oh, how you must wish to reunite with that great country!" Jude clasped his hands before his chest.

"I find myself speechless with desire," de Guignard said sarcastically. "*Mon cher* Lord Huntington, do you speak any other languages?"

"I have a way with languages," Jude said. "Spanish. *Muy bien!* Italian. *Benissimo!* Latin. *Optime!* German. *Sehr gut!*"

"So you speak Moricadian, too? But no, how could you? You've never been to Moricadia." In a masterful stroke, Comte de Guignard conveyed pity.

"I was there! I went through on my tour." Might as well give them that tidbit, so if they ever heard the truth, Jude wasn't caught out in a lie. "I do speak it! I find the grammar to be confusing." Hastily he added, "Although not above my command."

"Of course not." Bouchard stroked his mustache and watched Jude closely. "It is no shame to have trouble with Moricadian. It is an old language, the language of peasants, unfit for a nobleman's tongue."

Jude brightened. "That's true."

"Yet it is obvious *your* command of languages is superior," Comte de Guignard added, "and we find ourselves missing our country. So you do not mind if we speak in Moricadian?"

"No . . . not if you want to." Jude managed to sound both wistful and manly.

"But my dear Huntington, we would not want to exclude you," Bouchard said.

"You don't! You're not! You can't!" Jude assured them. "I'm very fluent. Go ahead." And the truth was, he *was* fluent, as fluent as he claimed.

Enunciating slowly and carefully in Moricadian, Comte de Guignard said, "He is like a child who runs after his betters in hope their authority will rub off."

The words sounded softly slurred, as if each consonant slipped from the tongue. When first Jude had heard it, he had found it difficult to follow, but the year spent in Moricadia had changed that. He would never be mistaken for a native speaker, as Michael had been, but these men misstepped by underestimating Jude.

"His taste in clothing is abominable." Bouchard kept his gaze fixed on Jude and chewed on the damp end of his cigar.

"How true, how true," Jude said in Moricadian, and he mangled the pronunciation.

Bouchard gave a bark of laughter, then abused his taste, his figure, his parents, and his country.

At every pause in the conversation, Jude smiled and nodded vacantly until the two men were convinced of his fatuity.

"Comte, with the singer's help our quarry will be delivered to us," Bouchard said in rapid Moricadian. "All will be as we planned."

What have you planned? Jude wanted to grab them until they answered his question. Instead, he kept quiet and grinned.

"Yes, but will this do as you promised?" De Guignard grew more agitated. "I would not have our friends attempt to console our hosts for their loss."

Their hosts? Who? The British? Yes, the British. Their loss. What loss? "Oui," Jude said as he tipped his hat to Lady Sugden and her daughter.

"Non, mon comte, everything shall be as we wish," Bouchard said, with more eagerness and less care. "You see, when we—" He stopped. He turned his head. In English, he asked, "What is that?"

"Oh, help!" A female's faint call came from a stand of blooming rhododendrons off the side of the path. "I've fallen!"

Jude ignored her, fiercely willing Bouchard to say exactly what they wished.

"Help, help!" The call was stronger now, sweeter, more feminine.

De Guignard and Bouchard turned like bird dogs on point and headed for the bushes.

Jude stood in the middle of the path, his hands flexing into fists. Whoever this girl was, he wished her to perdition. He'd made a fool of himself to discover the information the Moricadians were about to impart, and she had ruined everything. He stalked after the men. She had better be badly hurt, or she would . . . she would . . . He grimaced. What paltry punishment could the ridiculous, elegant Lord Huntington inflict?

She would suffer his sarcasm!

Comte de Guignard lifted the dark green branches, heavy with pink blossoms, to reveal a young lady of unusual beauty, dressed in a riding habit of misty gray, laid out on the ground in an attitude of distress.

False distress, Jude noted. She hadn't hurt herself. This had happened before; her trick was nothing more than a ploy to gain his attention. To gain the attention of that most eligible bachelor, the earl of Huntington.

"Oh." She rested her sleeve on her forehead. "Thank heavens you discovered me. Gentlemen, my horse threw me, my ankle is twisted, and I've been in a faint ever since." Her darkened eyelashes fluttered at each of the Moricadians.

Bouchard turned red from his collar to the top of his bald head and hastily discarded his smoldering cigar in the bushes.

"*Mademoiselle*, we are honored to come to your rescue!" As eager as a boy, de Guignard bowed, then bowed again.

Finally, she turned her dark-lashed, aquamarine eyes on Jude.

He felt the impact of her gaze like a bullet tearing into his chest. He recognized the feeling. He'd experienced that surprise and the agony in the mountains of Moricadia. He'd barely survived his wounds and the fever that followed them.

Now he faced a similar event, and he feared this experience would be as excruciating, as life-altering, and leave as big a scar. A wise man would turn and run from the exotic appeal of the beauty stretched out at his feet. Her smooth, tan cheek invited the touch of a finger. Her mouth, too wide for her face, begged to be kissed. With a single glance, she made him want to forget his duty, to gather the lovely miss into his arms and carry her to safety—which showed how incredibly talented this little performer must be.

"We cannot leave you here." De Guignard dropped to his knee beside her, ignoring the soft squish of the mud beneath his blue trousers.

"You're French." In a graceful gesture, she brushed tendrils of hair back from her face. "How lovely."

"Actually, we're Moricadian," de Guignard said, "although a great many people don't make the distinction."

"I don't understand," she said.

With an enthusiasm that cared nothing for the unlikely surroundings or the mud beneath his knee, de Guignard explained, "You see, two hundred years ago during the reign of our good King Louis XIV, after he conquered Moricadia, he gave my noble family the highest title and asked that we rule the country as a French principality. It was only after the wretched French Revolution of the last century that we realized we had to seize control of our own country and mold its destiny with our own hands without interference from any upstart French government or its peasant leaders. So we are French, but more . . ." At her confused frown, his voice trailed off, and he affirmed, "Yes, we're French."

"It was a French horse that threw me." Her smile trembled as she gazed on the comte. "You understand why I can't allow you to help me, don't you?"

Patent nonsense—and both de Guignard and Bouchard nodded as if they understood.

"Is *he* English?" She fixed her large eyes on Jude in melting appeal.

"Him?" De Guignard cast him a loathing glance. "*Oui*. He is English. He can, I suppose, help you." With obvious reluctance, he made way for Jude.

Jude was hard-pressed not to groan.

When he didn't move forward at once, Bouchard said "My lord! *La jeune fille* awaits you."

"All right," Jude conceded none too graciously. "I'll get her up."

Like a statuesque nymph, the lady lifted her arms in a fluid arc.

Briskly, Jude caught her elbow and brought her to her feet. She was tall. My God, so tall. He could hold her in his arms, and her mouth would be within easy reach when he kissed her. She had a lush, firm bosom and a waist that invited a man to try and span it with his hands. She was a lovely package, firm where a lady should be firm, soft where a lady should be soft, with a glossy finish on her skin one might see on a pearl, and, as he'd expected, she favored the leg, leaning against him for support.

He called himself to attention. He had no time for dalliance. He had a mission to complete—and until she had interfered, the end had been in sight. He steadied her, removed his support, then clapped his hands together. "That's it, then. You're standing, so we'll be on our way."

Shocked, Comte de Guignard staggered back, his hand over his heart.

"But Lord Huntington, see how bravely she smiles while she holds her foot above the ground. She is hurt!" A note of cynicism entered Bouchard's voice. "Surely your English chivalry will not allow you to leave Miss . . . Miss . . . ?" He looked inquiringly at the girl.

"Miss Caroline Ritter." She dropped her name as if

expecting a reaction, although Jude couldn't imagine what that would be.

"Surely you won't leave Miss Ritter here alone!" Bouchard said.

"I'll hail a cab for her," Jude said, from between his teeth.

Now she smiled both bravely *and* reproachfully, her lips trembling, her white teeth flashing in a glorious, smooth complexion that showed the effects of healthy exercise and time in the sun. Copper tipped her brown hair like riches found, and those eyes . . . a man could get lost in those eyes.

But he'd been lost in a woman's eyes before, and somehow he'd always found his way out—and he *had* to hear what the Moridovians had been about to say.

In a voice that signaled heartbreak, she said, "Don't worry about me. I know I'm not important, as are you gentlemen. I'll make my way to my humble place of residence . . . alone. There I will try to heal my ankle from this dreadful fall."

The melodrama was so thick, Jude could scarcely breathe. "Don't you think you ought to find your horse first? Horses are usually valuable."

A single tear slid over one of her high cheekbones. "The horse was a rented hack. Just let me limp on my way . . ." She struggled out of the bushes.

With an extravagant exclamation of Gallic disgust, Comte de Guignard caught her arm. "Please, I am an unworthy foreigner, but I cannot bear to see you in such anguish. Let me help you"—he cast a glance of loathing at Jude—"where your countryman will not."

She sniffed, although her little nose was clear and unblotched. "I accept your offer with gratitude."

Bouchard caught her other arm. "Allow me to assist you, too."

"Yes, thank you, you are both so good." As she walked away, taking both of Jude's Moridovians, and all their goodwill, with her, she glanced back at Jude with twinkling eyes. "Some Englishmen need lessons in how to flirt. Perhaps, if they pay attention, they will get what they deserve—a bride."

At the moment, Jude realized . . . she wore a red rose in her lapel.

He looked up the path where Lady Pheodora had escaped.

He stared the other way at the sinuous figure of Miss Caroline Ritter.

He had wooed the wrong girl.

Chapter 6

$\mathscr{M}$iss Ritter rode off in a cab.

Comte de Guignard and Monsieur Bouchard walked in a wide circle around Jude and indicated their opinion with a haughty sniff in his direction.

How had that happened? In one fell swoop Jude had lost his influence with the Moricadians, and all so he could learn to flirt . . . with a woman who tied his guts to her garters. She was magnificent, a Helen of Troy who could launch a thousand ships, a woman of beauty and mystery.

He should discover where the cabriolet had taken Miss Ritter, follow her, and show her how very well he could flirt.

He should accost Comte de Guignard and Monsieur Bouchard, follow them, ingratiate himself with them.

He was torn between his brains and his balls, being the dashing cavalier he had sworn on Michael's grave to become and the man driven by the need for vengeance for his brother's death.

Before he could make a decision, he heard a voice he'd not heard for many a long year. "Huntington? Huntington, is that you?"

He turned to see Rodney Turgoose, the silliest man in London—and Jude's best friend—bearing down on him.

"I heard you were back, but I didn't believe"— Turgoose looked him over—"the report."

Jude might as well allow de Guignard and Bouchard time to get over their pique and to follow up on the lead regarding Gloriana Dollydear. In addition, he saw no real sense in chasing after Miss Ritter. He'd see her often enough to suffer all the frustration a man could bear.

So, sighing, he fell into the role of fop and fool as easily as he might tumble into one of the shiny puddles left over from the rain. "Turgoose! As you see, I returned to England a new man!"

"Yes, I . . . see." Turgoose stood a full foot shorter than Jude, but the elevated soles of his shoes brought his nose level with Jude's shoulder. A soft fall of reddish blond hair hung artfully over Turgoose's forehead. His lips were full, his smile fatuous, but he was warmhearted and generous to a fault.

Jude flung out his arms in exuberant exhibitionism. "Am I not the finest Beau Brummel you've ever had the good fortune to view?"

Turgoose's eyes widened in alarm. "I heard you looked ridiculous."

"I have my jealous detractors." Jude chuckled humorously.

"No. You really do look ridiculous," Turgoose insisted.

Jude fought the desire to laugh in real amusement.

The two men had attended school together, and as one of the deans said, it was a good thing Turgoose was pretty, for he wasn't smart. But he was honest, incurably honest, and Jude found himself enjoying the novelty. "Come, come, my dear Turgoose, you don't mean that. I'm magnificent!"

"If you like vulgarity. You look as if you fell into a vat of paints from that crude Vermeer fellow." Catching the glint in Jude's eyes, Turgoose pounced. "Let me guess. You're not serious. You're playing a part. You're driving your old man batty so you can take over the family fortune."

Wrapping his arm around Turgoose's neck, Jude pulled Turgoose's head to his chest and knuckled him hard, messing up the careful arrangement of hair.

Turgoose sputtered and groused, and when Jude let him stand on his own two feet, dedicated a full two minutes to rectify the damage done to his coiffure. In an aggrieved tone, he said, "If you don't want to tell me, you could just say so. It's not as if I'm nosy."

Jude stood, hands on hips, and grinned at Turgoose.

"All right, maybe I am." Turgoose grinned back. "But I came by my nosiness legitimately. My grandmum spends so much time looking out her curtains, she caught her rings in the trim and was tangled there for an hour. Grandmum said she would have called for the footman to help her get free, but she caught her neighbor sneaking out in a lavender silk ball gown trimmed with handmade lace."

Jude bowed to a group of four ladies. "So?"

"He was too tall for the style."

Jude laughed again, and realized Turgoose's friendship was worth cultivating for more than just diversion. He also knew London society and its secrets. "Let's walk," Jude said, "and you can tell me what I missed in my absence."

As they started down the walk, Turgoose said, "It didn't take you long to find Miss Ritter, and she herself is no small scandal."

Grabbing Turgoose's arm, Jude yanked him into a fenced garden off the beaten path. "Scandal? What scandal?"

"She's a woman with a past," Turgoose said significantly.

"She's experienced?" Jude didn't believe his father would hire a woman of easy morals. More important, Jude didn't believe it. Didn't want to believe it. Didn't want her to be one of the demimonde, a woman of easy virtue. It didn't make sense, but he wanted her to be exactly as she appeared to be—a lady of perhaps desperate means, a lady who would trap a man with her beauty, but a lady nonetheless. "I don't believe it."

"I know. That angelic face, the perfect figure, the grace, the charm . . . a fellow doesn't want to consider it. But she got tangled up with that scoundrel Freshie and poof!"—Turgoose snapped his fingers—"went her reputation."

"Freshfield," Jude said slowly. "We were up at Eton with him. Brilliant fellow. Cunning and totally without ethics."

"But from a good family," Turgoose said.

Jude stared at him questioningly.

"That's what my mother says when I point out that other stuff. Nothing else matters to her. She says Miss Ritter is totally beyond the pale. Not acceptable. I only wish—"

Sharp and still, Jude asked, "What do you wish?"

"I liked the girl. I liked her a lot. I just wish I had the

bottom to take up the cudgels on her behalf. But my mother would break me like a crust of toast."

"She certainly would." Turgoose's mother, Lady Reederman, was a stickler for propriety, a guiding light of society, and she inspired fear in every one of her seven children as well as in her husband, all her servants, and every debutante who had made her bow for the last twenty-five years. Funny that Jude even cared whether Turgoose, of all people, was eliminated from the competition for Miss Ritter. With an intensity that he felt down to his toes—no, to his groin—Jude said, "Tell me the details."

"Debut year, Miss Ritter was as glorious a creature as any I've seen, and she was constantly in trouble. Men were always trying to kidnap her, or declaring their undying love on their knees in the middle of a quadrille, or threatening to commit suicide for her."

Jude should have been acting languorous, but the thought of her and all those men, all those suitors, kissing her hand, whispering about her charms, trying to sneak a kiss made him furious. They made him jealous, and of a girl he had met once, in the bushes, in the mud. A woman who'd ruined the plans he'd so carefully set in motion and made him lust when he should be focused on vengeance. Yet he managed to sound amused, to look casual, when he asked, "Bodies strewn in her path, eh?"

Seriously, Turgoose said, "Not really. They always stopped short of shooting themselves. But you get the idea."

"The Season was a circus that revolved around Miss Ritter."

"Precisely!" Turgoose clapped Jude on the shoulder.

"You may look like a damned fool, but your understanding is still superior."

"Sh," Jude said softly. "Don't spread that around."

"No, of course not! No man wants to be known as intelligent! I wouldn't like that at all."

"I think you're safe."

"Exact . . ." Turgoose paused as if suspecting sarcasm.

Jude kept his face blank, and prompted, "You were telling me the tale of Miss Ritter."

"Oh. Yes! Mr. Manfred Ritter was mightily pleased with Miss Ritter's success." Turgoose sneered. "He saw the chance to advance his family name at last. He's not only a cold fish, but he clutches the coin so tight his shillings scream in agony."

Jude swung his monocle back and forth on its ribbon. "I don't understand."

"He's cheap! The damned fool didn't obtain a responsible chaperon, and when Lord Freshie started romancing Miss Ritter, that viper of a chaperon took a bribe to convince Miss Ritter of Freshie's good intentions and persuade the gel that he could be trusted."

Jude felt his face settle into grim lines. "But he's married."

"Precisely. She should have known better, and that is what her enemies point to as conclusive condemnation." Turgoose drew out his handkerchief and blotted the perspiration on his forehead. "Walk slower, will you?"

Jude hadn't realized how his gait had speeded up beyond the appearance of a stylish man loitering down the path on a spring day. So he did slow, but with his cane he poked at Turgoose. "So Miss Ritter was a fool." And Jude, who remembered Freshie and his reputation for perversions, thought he might take the time, when he'd finished his mission, to take Freshie apart joint by joint.

"I hesitate to put such a label on that darling gel, but Freshie *can* be charming and she *was* infatuated with him. Certainly she trusted him beyond all propriety, and at a party given at his house, he carried her away to his study. Alone. And locked her in with him." Turgoose ran his finger under his collar. "I was the one who realized what he had done. I broke into the room."

"Really?" Jude examined his friend with renewed interest. "I didn't know you had it in you."

"I was rather more than infatuated," Turgoose mumbled.

"You were in *love*," Jude teased, but he wasn't laughing. He was furious. This was his friend, and he didn't even appreciate Turgoose's efforts on Miss Ritter's behalf—because Jude wanted to be her rescuer.

"Buckle your beak." Turgoose put his hands on his waist and glared. "We're talking about Miss Ritter, and my dedication is undiminished."

He was simply, Jude diagnosed, too afraid of his mother to do anything about his passion, and that was fine. Turgoose's fear almost made him likeable again. "My apologies. Go on with the tale."

"Trouble was, that whoreson Freshie had more than seduction on his mind. He wanted to use Miss Ritter to obtain a separation from his wife. Figured Miss Ritter was safe because her commoner father couldn't call him out. So when I tried to get her out of the room, Freshie made a fuss to attract attention." Now Turgoose blotted his upper lip, and his perspiration wasn't from exertion, but from remembered horror. "It was a nightmare. A nightmare, I tell you. When his wife broke in, she shrieked like an Irish banshee and blamed it all on Miss Ritter. Freshie came off innocent as a rosebud."

Jude scarcely moved his lips as he asked, "With as many suitors as you said Miss Ritter had and Freshie's reputation, why wasn't she able to find someone who would marry her?"

"Because her father threw her from his town house in a dramatic scene. You can imagine the calumny for her." Turgoose's color fluctuated. "Eighteen-year-old girl. No resources. No dowry. Reviled by her family. Frightened . . ."

If Jude had been there . . . what would he have done? Until the day he had stared down at his brother's body, he had been shallow, conceited because he wasn't a worthless bon vivant like Michael, superior for no more reason than the ability to hold his liquor and a talent for logical thinking. He probably would have shrugged and agreed that no *beautiful* young woman should have to suffer such an inequitable fate . . . yet, remembering his reaction to her face, perhaps he would have been as indignant as Turgoose. "Why, my good man, what did you do?"

"Nothing. I did nothing untoward!"

Lifting his monocle, Jude fixed his gaze on his friend.

"I didn't," Turgoose insisted. "Her younger sister gave her her allowance. The servants sneaked her food. But she was truly destitute, so I recommended her for a position teaching singing and pianoforte." He scuffled his feet. "She lost the position. But Mrs. Cabot loved Miss Ritter, as does everyone who meets her, and she gave her a glowing reference that found her another position."

Seeing the developing pattern, Jude suggested, "Which she lost?"

"If only the dear gel could discover something she did well for which she could be paid."

A plan slid easily to the surface of Jude's mind. For the first time he blessed his father's interfering ways. "She may have already have done so."

"Really? As what?"

"I imagine if someone attempted to resuscitate her reputation, it would cause an immeasurable fuss."

"But what kind of fool would attempt that?" Turgoose's gaze slid up Jude's frighteningly green jacket, and he backed up a step. "I mean, it would be absurd to think anyone could bring her back into the fold."

"You insinuated she had been used for nefarious circumstances by a known libertine and yet remained innocent."

"Yes, of a certainty." Turgoose rubbed his shining forehead. "But no maiden can survive such a blow to her reputation."

"What if a duke's heir attended her at the opera?" Which, considering her face and figure, would be a labor most enjoyable.

Turgoose chuckled weakly. "You are jesting. Why would you do that?"

Because the Moricadians liked her. Because the resultant scandal would both draw attention to Jude and allow him to do his work under the cover of gossip and resentment. And because—this was no small matter—it would make his autocratic father think twice before he again attempted to control his second son.

Turgoose pleaded, "Jude? You are jesting, aren't you? *Aren't* you?"

"No." Jude smiled a sharp, predatory smile. "I don't believe I am."

Chapter 7

Caroline picked her way through the refuse in the narrow alley toward her flat. The westering sun shone at an angle across the high rooftops three stories above, but here below, the shadows were deep and the stench obnoxious. The scene was, she reflected, much like her own life. Somewhere, she saw evidence that light and happiness existed, but no matter what she said, no matter how hard she worked, no matter how much she climbed and clawed, she couldn't reach the light.

A croaking voice came from a recessed doorway. "Ahoy, Miss Ritter!"

Caroline peered into the shadows at the pile of rags that shifted as she stared, becoming a man—or what was left of a man when a cannonball ripped off both his legs more than thirty years ago at Trafalgar. "Greetings, Harry. My day has been fruitful, and I trust yours has been the same."

"A difficult day, Oi'm afraid. Very difficult." She

couldn't see his eyes beneath his hood, but his pale, pointed nose quivered like a rabbit's scenting fresh feed. "Oi lifted six pocketbooks off the gennamen goin' in the Bank o' England, and no' one carried more than shillings."

"Rather thoughtless of them. Perhaps they've heard you were working the area?"

He nodded dolefully. "Aye, a beggar's life is 'ard, and just when ye get a territory set up, along comes a bunch o' coves who ruin a man's 'onest labor."

"Not honest and not—" She stopped herself. She had previously tried to point out the error in Harry's ways, but he saw nothing wrong with begging, and certainly nothing wrong with picking the pockets of any gull who stopped to throw money into his hat. He said the gentlemen owed it to him—after all, hadn't he sacrificed everything to preserve their country? And no thanks except a sawbones to cut off the shattered remnants of his legs.

His voice changed from the whine of a professional beggar to the deeper, surer sound of a man defending his territory. "I thought ye ought t' know. Ye've got a visitor."

"A visitor? Here?" No one of import came here, where shattered hopes met implacable poverty. "What kind of visitor?" A creditor, waving a bill and demanding satisfaction? Or . . . *him*, Lord Freshfield? She drew a painful breath. Had he found her here?

"'Tis a man, young, tall, 'andsome. Rich-looking sort o' fellow all dressed up fancy."

Her fear subsided a little. "Fancy? Really, really fancy? Colorful fancy?"

"I'd call 'im positively eye-popping."

Huntington. Her savior. She was surprised he had found her so quickly. She gave Harry a lopsided smile.

"Then I know who it is." The handsome Lord Huntington. In the bright sunshine in the park, his clothing had looked even more absurd than in Nevett's study, and his selfish disinterest in assisting a beautiful, helpless young woman provided a challenge to her skills as a flirt—and as a matchmaker. If all he cared about was himself and his clothing, she'd have to find some other leverage than desire to make him want to marry. She needed to make another notation in her planning book, design another strategy to make him want what his father and she wanted for Huntington—to wed.

She *had* to get Huntington married to some poor debutante, and with the money Nevett would provide her, she could take Genevieve and go to France. Their mother's people weren't rich. She didn't expect to live off their generosity forever. But somehow, she would find something that she could do to earn a living. Something that would give Genevieve a chance at a life unmarred by their father's indifference. As it was, in the dark of night, Caroline feared she was fit only for life as a mistress—or a prostitute.

She *had* to teach Huntington to flirt. She *had* to find him a wife. For when she remembered the slow crawl of Lord Freshfield's fingers over her leg, she wanted to vomit.

"Don't look like that, Miss," Harry said. "Ye're not one t' end in such a manner."

How did he know what she was thinking?

"I've seen it time and again," he answered as if she had spoken. "Poverty eats ye alive, but ye've got an aura. It surrounds ye like sunshine. Ye're one o' the lucky ones. Ye'll see."

Although her lips trembled, she smiled. "Harry, you're a philosopher and a seer."

"Don't ye recognize me, Miss? I'm a fallen angel, I am, a curate's assistant who went t' war and came back 'alf a man." He pulled back into his rags, as if he were sorry that he had revealed so much. "As long as ye're sure this gennaman is not a threat t' ye, I'll not worry further."

"Thank you for the warning," she said softly. "It would be unpleasant to come on him unexpectedly." She turned away, and heard the rhythmic squeak of Harry's wheels as he pushed his low-slung cart toward his pitiful home. She didn't look back; the man deserved his dignity.

Sunlight still slipped into the dark corridor of her building, and for the first time since she had rented this third-floor flat, she climbed the stairs with a kind of lively interest. She wondered what Huntington would demand: that she leave him to his own devices, probably . . . or perhaps he would welcome her as a sycophant. Who knew? He was an odd sort of fellow, apparently more interested in the Moricadians than in her. Yet she'd recognized that glint in his eyes when he'd first looked upon her; he was very much a man, with a man's strong appreciation of a handsome woman.

For a moment, when he looked at her that way, she had experienced a thrill, a kind of heady anticipation and girlish alarm. Foolishness. She knew her place.

When he noticed her red rose, she had enjoyed his start of surprise more than she should, and now she unfastened it from her bodice and twirled it, and the pin, in her fingers.

She would take pleasure in this interview.

Opening the door into her flat, she found a candle already lit. Of course. The son of a duke would never think of the price of a candle. She saw the bulk of him sitting there in the one chair beside the bed, and as she stepped inside, she said in an amused tone, "I've been expecting you."

The man rose. She saw the flash of his golden hair, and in that split second, she realized—this wasn't Huntington.

It was Lord Freshfield.

She took a hard, frightened breath.

In that suave, knowing voice she despised, he said, "I would have come sooner if I'd known."

She stood frozen, paralyzed with revulsion. She wanted to run, but if she did, he would know how much he frightened her. She wanted to shriek, but he would like that, too. She wanted . . . she wanted him out of there. "How did you get in?"

"Your landlord saw no reason to keep me out." In other words, Freshfield had bribed him.

Her heart thudded against her breastbone. He was so handsome, a glorious creature of sunshine and shadow, and only the discerning could see the corruption that tarnished the gold.

She hadn't been discerning. She had been a trusting fool. That night . . . that night, Lord Freshfield had offered her a drink in private, and she, imprudent, infatuated, and enjoying the intrigue, had agreed. He had slipped away from the party. She had slipped away from her chaperon—although, looking back, she realized that had been all too easy.

He toasted her. "To my beautiful release."

She didn't understand what he meant. She didn't wonder, either. She just drank of the deep, rich wine . . . and after that, memory came in bursts. Disoriented, she giggled. When she staggered, he led her to his study.

Then what started as an adventure became a nightmare. He shoved her down on the sofa. She protested.

He tore her bodice. She pushed at his hands. He touched her breast. She cried out. He slid his hand up her skirt. She kicked at him with her soft slippers.

But she didn't gouge his eyes with her nails. She didn't scratch his face, or punch him, or bite him. God help her, she had been trained to be a lady, never to hurt anyone, and she couldn't bring herself—didn't even think of—seriously defending herself.

People burst in. Men, three men, she thought. Mortified, she cried harder. They stared, then averted their eyes as if she were soiled. Dear Goose—Rodney Turgoose—tried to remove her from the chamber, but her knees collapsed beneath her. More people arrived, women this time. Lady Freshfield shrieked. She slapped Caroline, a blow to the face that sent her staggering.

And from the murky depths of remembrance, Caroline could hear someone in the crowd murmur, "She's drunk. She's ruined."

Everything that had followed was humiliation, and horror, and disgrace.

She would never be so weak again. She would never be so stupid again. She had learned. Through the last painful years of poverty and struggle, she had learned. No man would ever use her as abominably as Freshfield. Looking at him, she knew—she'd kill herself first.

And a voice that sounded like doom echoed in her head—*and Genevieve would be alone.*

There was no escape for Caroline. She had to make this employment work.

Determined not to be trapped in the room, she stayed in the open doorway. "I'd like you to leave."

"Darling, you don't mean that." He swept his arm around her pitiful hovel of a room. "Let me take you away from this. I can provide a house for you, and luxury such as you've never imagined."

"I can't afford the price." Her gaze fixed on his cravat. It was a bright orange color, like the one Lord Huntington had worn the day before. No wonder Harry had thought Freshfield was positively eye-popping. The marquess was imitating the earl.

"Of course you can. Every woman can afford that price. Women are made to let men pay for their every little whim."

"I thought it was your wife who paid for your whims."

He lunged toward her.

She jumped back into the corridor. Her hand tightened on the rose stem. It snapped. "I'll run screaming."

With a sneer that distorted his handsome face, he asked, "Who would hear you in this neighborhood?"

"Men who would attack you and steal everything you own right down to your boots." This she understood, and in a contemptuous voice, she said, "I'm surprised you made it this far."

"I can protect myself." He showed her the sword hidden in his cane.

She almost laughed. Was he bragging or trying to intimidate her? At one time, she would have been impressed. Now she knew the kind of men who lurked in dark alleys, who would club Lord Freshfield unconscious before he had time to draw steel. "It's almost dark. Go out and try your luck."

He gazed at her, at the way she stood, at the amusement on her face, and his gaze dropped. She wasn't the unwary fool she had been before, and he didn't know how to bully her. "How can you, a female raised as a lady, bear to live in this slum?"

She tucked the long, sharp pin that had held the rose between her knuckles, facing out. Harry had taught her that, his low, hoarse voice morose with intensity as he suggested weapons like hatpins, keys, and writing pens. At the time she had thought it was kind of him to worry about her so. Now she was thankful. Profoundly thankful. In a cold, clear voice, she said, "It makes you wonder, doesn't it, why would I prefer to live here than in a house with you?"

"I'll make you sorry you said that." He lunged toward her again, a long-legged leap that threatened violence.

She lifted her fist. She was no longer the girl she had once been. She *would* defend herself now.

But from the landing below her, she heard the rattle of footsteps, and an airy, male voice call, "Miss Ritter, are you up there?"

Lord Huntingon.

To Freshfield, she said, "But you won't make me sorry today."

"Who is it?" Lord Freshfield demanded. "A lover?"

"You have a mind like a sewer." She called down the stairs, "Yes, my lord, I'm here."

Freshfield stood, arms straight at his side, hands clenching. She knew what he was thinking. She could see it in his face. He wanted to confront the gentleman whose boots tromped up her stairs, but he didn't dare. He was a coward. He liked to frighten those weaker than himself; he didn't want to confront a man who might handle him with the flat of his fist.

As Freshfield brushed by her, he grabbed her arm hard enough to bruise. "This is not over."

She knew that. Unless she got away from London and hid herself so well that he could never find her, it would never be over.

He ran down the stairs, his boots creating an angry clatter on the aging boards.

She listened to see if Huntington stopped him, but heard not even the murmur of a greeting. In the darkness of the stairway, perhaps they hadn't recognized each other. She hoped not, for if Huntington thought she entertained Freshfield in her rooms, he would be justified in demanding her dismissal.

Huntington loomed in the doorway so recently vacated by Freshfield.

She drew back into the darkness of her room. Perhaps Freshfield had heightened her fears, but to her, Huntington presented the appearance of a dangerous man, one given to manipulation, one with a plan and a purpose.

Then he moved forward, exclaiming, "It's dark. How do you bear the darkness? It's frightening in here. Aren't you afraid?"

And she relaxed. The ominousness he had projected was nothing but a figment of her overactive imagination. "There's a candle burning." She gestured toward it.

"A single candle," he scoffed. "It's dim. I can scarcely see where I'm stepping—or what I'm stepping on." He looked down at the rough, bare boards beneath his boots, then around at the shabby surroundings.

She winced in mortification. She hadn't minded that Freshfield had viewed her surroundings. She very much cared that Huntington did. It wasn't pride, she told herself, but rather a matter of gaining and holding his respect. He was obviously a man who set much store by appearances.

He bowed to her, a lovely, flourishing bow, and said, "Introductions are not necessary, for I know who you are, Miss Ritter"—he waggled his finger at her—"and how naughty of you to play such a trick on me at the park!"

So he did know who she was. Had his ignorance at the park been an attempt to shake her from her task, or had one of the onlookers informed him of her identity? Probably the latter.

He continued, "But the formalities should be observed." He bowed again. "Jude Durant, the earl of Huntington, at your service."

She curtsied. "Miss Caroline Ritter, at your service, my lord." His insistence on the proprieties made her feel as if she were on solid ground, as if she could do the task set before her, for she'd been raised in the world of society and proper behavior. With complete solemnity, she extended her hand. "I'm your new governess." Had he come to refuse her services? For she wouldn't allow him to intimidate her.

Taking her fingers between his two gloved hands, he held it firmly, and in a tone new to her, a tone of deep appreciation, he said, "Hm. Yes. When I was a lad, I dreamed of having a governess like you." His intense gaze swept her from head to toe, stripping away her clothes—or was it her pretenses?

Once again she thought he was bigger than she had realized, a strapping man with broad shoulders that looked out of place in that absurd jacket. In the wavering light of the candle, his face no longer looked smooth and young. A line bracketed either side of his mouth, as if bitterness had placed it there, and his eyes were sharp and far too observant.

He didn't look like a dandy. He looked like a man who had met the world and found it harsh and unforgiving.

With a jolt, she realized—she might be in as much danger from Huntington as she was from Freshfield.

They were alone. She was an unprotected female. And with a single glance, Huntington had proved he was obviously, shockingly, completely male. Furthermore, she had seen his expression at Hyde Park, and she had not a doubt that she had irritated him. Irritated him, and intrigued him, and made him look like a fool.

Then he let go of her hand. Petulantly, he demanded, "Why should I learn to flirt? I've always planned to coast through life on my looks. Look at me." He posed with his profile to her, his lips pursed. "Like chiseled marble."

She almost laughed. Almost. She had to stop imagining a threat where none existed. This man might appreciate the female form, but he was absorbed in a lifelong love affair—with himself. "There's more to finding the right woman than wearing the right clothes and posing to show off your perfect chin."

"Do you think it's perfect?" She would have sworn his eyes were twinkling. "Because I've thought so, too. Strong, manly, yet sensitive, with a rather dashing cleft in the chin."

He did have a rather dashing cleft in his chin, one that made her want to press her finger in it and see if it sprang back like well-risen bread. But such sentiment was foolish; he would be a duke, and she . . . before long, if she were lucky, she would be taking a ship to France. In a firm tone, she said, "Nevertheless, your father has contracted my services for whatever reason, and I intend to fulfill that contract to the best of my ability."

"As if I need to learn to flirt!" He waved his handkerchief with petulant fanfare. "Why, I have ladies fawning on me at every party."

With a brutality brought on by desperation, she answered, "For no other reason than you're the heir to a dukedom."

Radiating indignation, he drew himself up. "That's not true! The ladies also enjoy conversing with a gentleman who understands fashion."

Words failed her. Fashion? What he wore wasn't fashion, but an abomination against good taste. But if she said so, she would violate more rules of courtesy than she had already. "I imagine the ladies do enjoy speaking with a lord who comprehends the intricacies of material and color."

"Exactly." Her trepidation fell away as he continued, "I must tell you, that color you're wearing is an outrage with your skin. What made you select gray? It makes you look sallow and does nothing for your hair."

In shock, she looked down at her new riding costume. "I think it's quite attractive."

"Ha, ha!" He laughed in a manner so affected she gritted her teeth. "Quite amusing. So. You will teach me to flirt—as if I really need such lessons!—and I will teach you to dress."

"I have gowns being sewn right now, gowns ordered by your father."

"I will inspect them all. I shan't be embarrassed by the companion on my arm."

"I won't be the companion on your arm." Painstakingly, she explained, "I'm the female who'll help you find a companion for your arm."

"If you must." He touched the wall. He grimaced as his white gloves came away soiled, and with elaborate disdain, he pulled out his handkerchief and wiped at his fingers. In his old, light, society voice, he said, "This will never do! Not at all. I can't learn to flirt here."

She spoke in a tone pitched to reach his ears and not

pierce the thin walls where others listened. "You're not required to learn here. I intend to visit His Grace's home, and it is there you will learn the art and the subtleties of flirting."

"Exactly." He looked around fretfully. "Are you packed?"

"What?" What was he talking about? Was he always so arbitrary in his conversation? "Packed? For what?"

"Weren't you listening? My father sent me here to bring you to his home."

"You didn't say that," she pointed out, head spinning.

"A woman of superior understanding would have comprehended and been packed by now." Huntington moved into the room, found the stack of clothing she had placed on the table beside her bed, lifted them, and looked around. "Is there a bag anywhere to be had?"

He confused her with his rapid change of subject and his arrogant insults. "I didn't think His Grace would care where I lived, and if the only reason the ladies enjoy speaking to you is your appreciation of fashion, your ability to find a suitable mate is impaired by contradictory interests."

He waved her clothes at her, and she leaped forward when the frayed leg of her drawers dangled downward. "Let me pack for myself, please." She had, she realized, given in to his imperious command without knowing whether he spoke the truth. And even if he did, she could scarcely believe the arrogant duke of Nevett would send his heir to arrange what a servant could do better. Yet what other reason besides his father's command would Huntington have for taking her in his custody and transporting her to Nevett's town house?

She looked around the tiny, grimy room and wondered—why did she care? She had the chance, an honorable chance, to escape the poverty of London's East End and the terror of Lord Freshfield's pursuit, and she would seize that chance with both hands.

Pulling her bag from beneath the bed, she packed her clothes.

From the cover of darkness, Freshfield watched as Huntington removed Caroline from her room and herded her down the street. Freshfield had plotted to have her for three years, and now Nevett's heir had swooped in and taken her from underneath Freshfield's nose. He wouldn't have it. He had put up with Brenda's shrieking and nagging ever since his aborted seduction undertaking. He had successfully sabotaged two of Caroline's attempts at employment. He had stalked her throughout London, and damned if that ridiculous fool Huntington would have her first.

Perhaps after Lord Freshfield had tired of her, but not yet.

Not yet.

Chapter 8

$\mathcal{A}$s Jude paid the driver of the cabriolet, he heard Miss Ritter take a long breath. "I really don't think this is the proper thing to do," she said.

She was a shadow on the stairs of the elegant town house. The light spilled from the windows and over her shoulders and outlined her glorious curves. Her face was in shadow, she stood completely still; nevertheless, she attracted him like some nymph with mystical powers. And she didn't seem to realize it. Because of the way he dressed? God, he hoped so. It was better than thinking she felt indifference where he suffered lust, or that she was so used to fascinating her companion that she found his interest commonplace.

"You have met my father, I believe. Do you intend to tell him he desires an improper act?" Jude didn't wait for the reply, of which there could be none, but took her firmly under the arm and ushered her to the door. Lifting the huge iron knocker, he let it drop and listened with satisfaction to the thud.

Beside him, Miss Ritter flinched.

Was kidnapping her the proper thing to do? No, certainly not. To use her to distract the Moricadians was the act of a scoundrel, and Jude knew he trod a fine line, for a man tempted by a woman always ran the chance of revealing his true self.

The butler opened the door and stood astonished as Jude escorted Miss Ritter inside. "Here you go." Jude handed Phillips her bag. "Please take this to the silver bedchamber for Miss Ritter."

Phillips looked down at the bag in his hand. "But my lord, the silver bedchamber is not made up."

Miss Ritter made a small squeak of distress.

Jude tsked in disgust. "Did His Grace not warn my stepmother of Miss Ritter's arrival? How like him. Better prepare the room." Turning to Miss Ritter, he said, "If you'd take a seat in the lesser drawing room, I'll locate my stepmother and inform her of the circumstances."

Miss Ritter had seemed bold in the park, setting her plan to capture him in motion with timing and flare. In that pathetic little flat, she had been determined, straightforward, and brisk. Yet when faced with a time spent in the luxury of Nevett's town house, she viewed Jude with suspicion. She held her shabby parasol uneasily clasped in her hands.

Jude hoped she would prove brave and stalwart, for she was a useful addition to his plans.

"Thank you, Lord Huntington." She entered the small drawing room he indicated. "I think."

He couldn't completely ignore her trepidation. Not now that he had her in the house. Taking her gloved hand, he bowed over it, and to build her confidence, he put all of his charm into his smile. "I assure you, you'll be pleased with your quarters, and my stepmother is a dear. The two of you will get along felicitously."

When her eyes widened, he realized he had lied to himself. He hadn't smiled at her to build her confidence. He'd been testing to see if he could capture her interest. He had. Her lashes fluttered. Color stained her cheeks. Gently, she withdrew her hand, and she looked shy and confused and as if she wanted to smile back but didn't dare.

Of course not. Last time she had trusted a man, she had been betrayed and destroyed, and if Jude tampered with this girl, if he took advantage of her vulnerability, he would be no better than Freshie. Freshie hadn't wanted to be noticed—although with that bright cravat, there was no way to miss him—and when Freshie wanted something kept quiet, it was because what he intended was slimy and cruel and would reflect badly on himself.

Miss Ritter had definitely not wished to discuss the matter with Jude. He understood her wish for privacy, but he also knew he would have to put a stop to Freshie's pursuit of Jude's governess. Jude had plans for her.

He straightened. "Please sit down. I'll send my stepmother to you."

He found Mum alone, reading in her study, and her bright, welcoming smile told him only too clearly how dreary she must be.

Kissing her cheek, he said, "As my father commanded, I've brought the lady."

She tucked her finger into her book to keep her place. "What lady are you talking about, dear?"

"The lady Father hired to teach me to flirt." Obviously, his stepmother knew nothing about Miss Ritter, and Jude rather enjoyed the progression of expressions that crossed her face.

Disbelief, anger, and amused resignation. She laughed as if she couldn't help herself. "To flirt! That old devil. I told you he was up to something."

"You were right." Jude seated himself across from her, discarded his gloves, and adjusted the crease in his trousers. "He hired a governess from the Distinguished Academy of Governesses to help me snare a wife." Smoothly, Jude moved to his falsehood. "Father requested she be housed beneath his roof, I suppose so he might more easily retain control of the proceedings." And to provide protection as well as a refuge for her. Jude could feel easy that Miss Ritter would never be in danger from his clandestine activities.

This was the kind of maneuver at which he excelled—lightning assessment of the situation and the ability to arrange matters to his best advantage.

Yet at the most important moment of his life, long-range planning had availed him nothing. He had hesitated, and so he had lost his elder brother. The heaviness of remorse weighed on him, and nothing could wipe the stain on his soul clean. He would go to hell for his misdeed—but not until he had first sent de Guignard and Bouchard to the flames.

Mum laughed again, her tired eyes alight with a glee directed at him. "Who is your governess?"

"You might know her. A Miss Caroline Ritter."

Mum's mirth died. "Yes, I know her. The poor child. Is she reduced to this?"

"I would say she has not been reduced to this, but elevated. I found her in a hovel." He valued Mum's opinion, so he asked, "You like her, do you?"

Mum placed her book on the table and folded her hands in her lap. "It is—or rather was, for I haven't seen her since her disgrace—impossible not to like her."

Remembering Turgoose's report, Jude said, "That's not what I heard. I heard a great number of people disliked her."

"She was the belle of the season, a diamond of the first water, and from a less-than-aristocratic background. She generated a great deal of jealousy, which contributed to her downfall." Mum smiled slightly. "But for herself, she was charming."

"Yet she lost all."

"She's a silly girl." Mum rested her plump cheek on her hand. "But I was a silly girl once, too. One does not deserve to have one's whole life ruined for a single mistake."

"It happens more than we can imagine."

"Yes." She looked at him thoughtfully. "It seems it does."

Her insight startled him. Had he been so transparent in his guilt and anguish that she knew he was to blame for Michael's death? Remembering the charred body of his brother, he rubbed the warped signet ring on his forefinger.

"Everything conspired to make her *faux pas* fatal to her reputation. Lord Freshfield's secret plan, which ended by being no secret at all, Lady Freshfield's persecution, and, of course, Mr. Ritter's refutation."

All Jude could remember of Lady Freshfield was a voice that grated the flesh with its high notes. "Isn't Freshie's wealthy wife from a merchant background?"

"Yes, and unattractive, and married for her money. That made her all the more venomous in her vendetta against the pretty, common, popular Miss Ritter." As only she could, Mum made a moue that expressed disdain. "Five hundred years ago, Lady Freshfield would have lit the torches, tracked Miss Ritter with dogs, and burned her at the stake."

"Lovely woman." And another bump in the road of restoring Miss Ritter's respectability. It looked like an exciting Season, filled with social intrigue and personal vengeance. When Jude was finished, he would have helped a wronged young woman regain some measure of respectability—and he would have vengeance on his brother's killers.

He rose. "At any rate, Miss Ritter has brought her belongings and is ready to occupy one of the bedchambers. Would you make her comfortable? I wish to go to the opera." *To see if my tip has sent the Moricadians chasing after Miss Gloriana Dollydear.*

"Of course." Invigorated, Mum rose as if on springs. "I'll take care of her."

"By the way, Father ordered clothes for her. You might want to check and see what he deems as appropriate wear for a young lady."

"Heavens," Mum said faintly. "He has appalling taste."

"Exactly. If she's to go out in public with me—"

"Is she?"

"So Father says, and I won't be escorted by a fashion disaster." He sniffed. "It would be fatal for my reputation."

Mum examined him as if not quite sure if he was jesting. "As you say. When do the lessons start?"

"Officially, tomorrow morning." He gathered his

gloves. "I instructed Phillips to make up the silver bed-chamber for her."

"Absolutely!" Mum bustled out of the room, then back in. "Where is she?"

"In the lesser drawing room." As she left once more, Jude reflected with satisfaction that his father would never notice Miss Ritter was staying under his roof in one of the numerous bedchambers, and his stepmother would have someone to coddle and promote. Unlike Jude, Mum did things out of pure kindness.

Jude had turned his father's plan to his own advantage, and his stepmother's, and Miss Ritter's. All in all, a most profitable situation.

Caroline sat with her knees together, her feet placed directly below her knees, her hands in her lap, and her heart in her throat. Occasionally, when she wasn't completely intimidated, she sneaked glances at the gilded frames around the portraits, the lush carpet threaded with inky black, sky-blue and soft peach, and the velvet curtains hung on gold rods. Then she remembered this was the *lesser* drawing room and was properly intimidated again. Ducking her head, she watched her hands as they flexed on the rod of her parasol and considered the difference between this chamber and the one in her father's house. This chamber reeked of wealth, as did her father's, but while her father's house had been designed for show, the chair on which she perched was gloriously cushioned and so comfortable she fought the temptation to put her head back and nap.

If only her room had been ready! Not that she disbelieved Huntington when he said his father wanted her here, for what reason had he to lie? Yet in his carriage, something about the way he watched her gave her the sense he was playing his own game, and she had already been a pawn in one game, with disastrous results. She didn't ever want to revisit that humiliation.

She heard footsteps and the murmur of voices out in the foyer. The outer door opened and closed.

The duchess of Nevett herself entered, hands outstretched. "My dear, how good to see you again. I suppose you don't remember me, but we met during your Season."

"Your Grace, of course I remember you." As if she would forget a duchess! Caroline scrambled to her feet.

"Please, don't call me that! Save the exalted title for my husband. My name is Nicolette."

Beside the petite and gracious lady, Caroline felt tall, skinny and gawky. "Your Grace . . . Ma'am . . . I couldn't . . ."

"Of course you could, at least in the confines of my own home." Taking Caroline's hand, the duchess squeezed her fingers companionably. "You want me to be easy, don't you?"

Caroline swallowed. "Yes . . . Nicolette."

"There. That wasn't so difficult. And I shall call you Caroline."

"Yes, please. Only my sister calls me by name now, and I miss hearing it." That was the truth.

"Jude tells me he brought you to stay with me. I'm so glad, for you may have heard we had a tragedy recently, and I've been dull and lonely."

"A tragedy?" Then Caroline wished she knew the gossip, for Nicolette's smile faltered.

"I'd forgotten you have been out of society."

A tactful way of expressing Caroline's exile.

"Our son Michael was killed while abroad, but our

deep mourning is over, and having a beautiful, vivacious young lady in the house will provide just the tonic we need." The duchess tucked Caroline's hand in her arm and led her toward the foyer and the stairs. "It's very clever of you to find a way to use your talent. I always envied your skill at flirting, and Lady Bucknell recommends the best governesses!"

"You're too kind." She was. Caroline was dazed by the welcome.

The stairs rose from the foyer in a graceful arc, and Nicolette continued to escort Caroline upward. "Jude says you're to start teaching him tomorrow."

"I taught him a little lesson today." Caroline's mouth curved as she remembered.

"You look like the spirit of mischief. Tell me!"

Caroline found herself confiding the whole incident to the duchess, who laughed with seeming glee and approved Caroline's tactics.

As they approached a closed door in the corridor, a footman sprang to attention and opened it.

"Here we are," Nicolette said. "Jude suggested the silver bedchamber for you, and I know why he did. It's the perfect setting for you."

Caroline knew she shouldn't allow her jaw to drop. It was unfeminine and unattractive. But whatever she expected of her bedchamber, it wasn't this. Not this spacious, graceful room decorated in cool blues and warm browns. The fireplace was laid with wood and waited only a flame. A dressing screen stood in one corner. Gleaming silver vases stood on either side of the curtained bed, and the chambermaid was filling them with flowers.

She dropped at curtsy. "Just a few final touches, Yer Grace, and it'll be ready fer yer guest."

"Thank you, Daisy. You'll act as Miss Ritter's maid while she is staying with us."

"Very good, Your Grace." Daisy bobbed a curtsy at Caroline, and her gaze examined her up and down. "'Twill be a pleasure. May I have yer hat and gloves?"

Caroline peeled off her gloves, but she didn't have to untie the ribbons under her chin. Daisy stepped close and did it as if Caroline shouldn't weary herself with such labor. Carefully, Daisy removed the bonnet and took the gloves and parasol. "Are the rest of yer bags coming later, Miss Ritter?"

Caroline cleared her throat. "I believe there'll be deliveries with more clothes, yes."

"Then I'll freshen these up fer tomorrow." Daisy took them away to the bedchamber.

Caroline had begun to feel as if she had fallen into an odd sort of dream, where she lived in a beautiful house, was attended by a maid, visited with a duchess, had her garments bought by a duke and approved by an earl . . . It was hard to remember who she was. Not the debutante, but not the same desperate young woman poised on the brink of starvation, either.

"Miss Ritter will have a tray in her room," the duchess instructed, when Daisy returned.

Daisy curtsied and went to the door.

To Caroline, Nicolette said, "Nevett and I had an early supper, and I know you must be exhausted after your fall from that fractious French horse." She laughed again.

"It was very fatiguing." Caroline laughed with her. "What a beautiful chamber this is!"

"Yes, it is nice, isn't it?" Nicolette gazed about her in satisfaction. "Come and visit while we wait for Daisy to finish." She seated herself on one of the comfortable

chairs placed beside the fireplace, and when Caroline
had joined her, she confided, "When Jude returned
from abroad, he was much changed from his previous
self, and I find myself longing for the old Jude."

"Changed . . . how?" Caroline's curiosity was more
than just politeness. Huntington had aroused her interest. While in society, she'd met a number of fops, and
Huntington was singular. Caroline couldn't put her finger on it, but he showed flashes of a powerful masculinity. He observed everything around him intensely, and
she, who took pride in understanding men and catering
to their inflated sense of self-worth, didn't quite know
how to handle him. She needed to handle him, for she
had to complete this task Nevett had assigned her.

She had to. This was her last chance. She would not
fail.

"Most obviously, he didn't used to dress like a
French coxcomb." The duchess rolled her eyes. "It's
driving his father mad. But also, Jude always got his
own way. He would manage me and everyone in the
family."

"Oh!" Caroline remembered how he had swept her
out of her poor room before she had time to truly consider the situation.

"I see you have experience with his autocratic ways."
At Caroline's nod, Nicolette continued, "The only one
Jude could never manage was his father. They're too
much alike—or rather, they used to be. Jude used to be
cautious and thoughtful. He dressed with dignity. He
pondered literature and logic. When he was a lad, he
was complex, not easy to understand. Rather . . . stuffy,
and solemn beyond his years. Now"—Nicolette shook
her head in bewilderment—"he blurts out what's on his
mind, and it's seldom of import. He's frivolous. He

flings himself at every event as if it is his last." In a lower voice, the duchess said, "I suppose that's the legacy of Michael's death. We've all been changed."

Caroline thought about the dark green journal she had in her bag. She had filled its blank sheets with her plans for flirting lessons, and even now she wondered if her simple strategy would work with Jude. "But to have changed so much seems improbable."

"I think that sometimes, too, but what game could he be playing?" Nicolette smiled. "Of course, you didn't know him, he had left before you had your Season, so how can you answer?"

Caroline winced, and reluctantly approached the matter she knew must be on the duchess's mind. "I'm so grateful for your kind offer to house me while I teach Jude, and I promise there'll be no embarrassing incident while I'm under your roof." When the duchess looked startled, Caroline decided she liked this lady more than she had ever liked anyone before.

"I would say not," Nicolette said. "The people who should be embarrassed by that incident four years ago are Lord Freshfield and his harridan of a wife! You must be so very angry about what happened to you."

Astonished, Caroline blinked at Nicolette. "Angry? No. No, how could I be angry?"

"How could you not be? You weren't guilty." The duchess's eyes shot gray sparks. "Everyone knows you were a victim of Lord Freshfield's desire to obtain a divorce. He ruined your reputation, yet he is still accepted. Your father tossed you out without challenging Lord Freshfield or his dastardly deeds. Your friends couldn't help you. Of course you're angry."

Such thoughts had never occurred to Caroline. "But

it was my fault. I flirted with Lord Freshfield even though I knew he was married."

"You were young. You were inexperienced. He had bribed your chaperon. What happened was not your fault—but you and you alone have suffered."

"I deserved everything that's happened to me. What's more, I ruined my father's expectations—"

Nicolette raised her eyebrows.

"All right," Caroline admitted. "I don't really care about Father. But I do care about my sister, and she's so alone without me."

The duchess reached across, put her hands over Caroline's, and said, "If it were me, I would be angry."

"No. I'm not." Caroline truly didn't understand what the duchess was saying. She did not. "I'm *not* angry."

From the duke of Nevett's box in the rapidly emptying opera house, Jude watched Monsieur Bouchard walk to the stage. He handed Miss Gloriana Dollydear a bouquet of flowers and a folded piece of paper. She accepted both with a coy smile and broke the seal on the note. She took the money within, tucked it into her copious bosom, then read the note. Nodding at Monsieur Bouchard, she indicated her acceptance and watched him walk away. Her gaze swept the theater, never seeking Jude in the shadows, but she slid her hand over the back of her neck as if she were exhausted.

It was a signal arranged between them. She had directed them to meet in the alley behind the opera house.

Throwing his concealing black cloak over his beaded jacket, Jude slipped into the darkened corridor. The opera house smelled of dust and greasepaint, and the gilt decorations glinted in the dim light. Only a few people lingered; now that the performance had concluded, the ton made their way to parties or dinners. He walked backstage where the hands shouted and joked as they put away the props and the costumes. The chorus threw cloaks over their stage clothes and left in a steady stream. The stage door opened and closed, letting in puffs of fog and chilly air. People called out good-byes, and no one paid attention to Jude. Male visitors backstage were common; several of the girls cast inviting smiles his way. He kept moving right out the door. The pale fog shimmered in ribbons on the night breeze. He hung back, straining to see the light of Gloriana's lantern or hear her voice.

And then there she was, smiling into de Guignard's face while Bouchard held the veiled lantern.

"Mr. Throckmorton is a lovely gentleman, quite the craftsman with everything he does." Her husky tones carried clearly to his ears. "But he's got an air about him that's dangerous, if you understand me, and I'm not likely to cross him."

"I do understand you, but I assure you, I can protect you from him." De Guignard smiled so charmingly Jude wanted to vomit. "I'm quite a rich and powerful man myself, and noble, too."

She tilted her head and studied him. "What is it you want to know?"

"I understand Throckmorton is an important man in this Home Office, where the English make their decisions about foreign policy."

"I'm a simple opera singer, dearie." Placing her hand on her hip, she fluttered her eyelashes. "It's not commerce he talks with me."

"You could find out, couldn't you?" Bouchard asked impatiently.

Gloriana transferred her smile to Bouchard. "I could—for the right incentive."

De Guignard nodded at Bouchard. More folded bills exchanged hands.

"What do you want to know?" she asked in a businesslike tone.

Celeste Throckmorton was a genius.

This was going to work.

Chapter 9

Caroline's early training had covered many things. It covered how to dance with a man while appearing both modest and appealing, what a man liked to talk about (himself), how to walk in a manner guaranteed to catch a man's eye.

Yet her early training had never covered how to enter the breakfast room of the duke of Nevett while in his employ. She didn't even know that she should be there at all, but the previous day, as Her Grace had hospitably welcomed her to the home, she had informed Caroline of the time and location of breakfast.

So there Caroline stood, hovering in the doorway while His Grace remained ensconced behind his paper and the duchess read a book. The utter quiet in the cozy room intimidated Caroline; not even the footmen made a sound as they trod back and forth with fresh rashers of bacon and steaming plates of scones.

At last, the smell of food and rich, hot coffee drew

Caroline into the room. Lately, as she made her money stretch farther than she had ever imagined possible, she had only allowed herself two meals a day. She wanted to laugh as she remembered how, in the days when she had stood poised on the edge of social success, she had imagined she would escape the coldness of her father's house and spring into the warmth of an adoring man's arms. What a fool she had been.

Now she made her way toward the duke's intimate table, her planning journal held in her hands, making an effort to be as silent as the gliding servants.

And her stomach growled.

"Damn it!" Nevett smashed his newspaper onto the table. "Do you have to be so god-awful noisy?"

Caroline froze.

The duchess was on her feet before he had finished speaking. "Come and sit down, dear Miss Ritter, we have your place set." Taking Caroline's arm, Nicolette ushered her toward the table while Nevett glared with unmitigated wrath. "We don't make a sound around Nevett until he's had at least two cups of coffee," the duchess confided in a low voice. "We find they substantially improve his disposition."

"I heard that! I'm not yet deaf," Nevett trumpeted.

"No, dear." Tranquilly, the duchess signaled to the footman, who began offering platters of food to Caroline.

"I do not require coffee at this or any other time." Picking up his cup and saucer, Nevett held it as if he disdained the brew within. "I am always even-tempered—except when people are excessively loud and unable to maintain their composure." He took a sip, then set it down.

At once, a footman filled it with fresh, hot coffee.

Distressed, Caroline put her planning journal beside

the place setting. She ignored the plates of kippers, eggs, and fruit, and stared at the still-glaring duke. He must be angry that she hadn't yet thanked him for allowing her to stay there. He must consider her ungracious to the extreme. Faltering, she said, "Your Grace, I'd like to express my gratitude for your hospitality—"

The duchess touched Caroline's arm and shook her head.

But it was too late.

"Are you going to be joining us every morning?" Nevett demanded. Before she could answer, he spoke over the top of her. "Because if you are, you're going to have to learn not to chatter every damned moment of the day."

Tears sprang to Caroline's eyes.

"And crying won't get you sympathy." Picking up his newspaper again, he flapped it in front of his face. To the newsprint, he asked, "Don't people have a palace they can go to anymore?"

Nicolette pushed his coffee cup toward him.

His hand came out, groped for the handle, and pulled the steaming brew beneath the page.

Then the duchess patted Caroline's hand, but Caroline could see the twinkle in her eyes. Her husband amused her. Rich, powerful, he held her life in his hands, yet his wife laughed at his foibles. Perhaps he was not as fearsome as Caroline feared. Perhaps he was not cold and exacting like her father.

Once again silence reigned, broken only by the click of porcelain against porcelain as Nevett drank his coffee.

Without making a sound, Nicolette filled Caroline's plate and, with a smile, encouraged her to eat.

Caroline found her distress wasn't the equal of her hunger. She reasoned if she didn't eat, her stomach would growl again, and Nevett would be furious. She took her first bite of an egg poached in chicken broth and laid on a slice of ham, and she could scarcely stifle her exclamation of delight. She hadn't put such an exquisite flavor in her mouth for far too long.

Nevett put down his paper, and, as if that were a signal, the footmen moved more briskly, their shoes made noise on the floor, the dishes clattered in their hands.

From the entry, a door slammed and voices murmured.

"Dear," Nicolette said, "Jude says you hired Miss Ritter to teach him how to flirt."

"That's right," Nevett said in a tone so reasonable he might never have snapped in his life.

"I wish you had consulted with me first. The plan is fraught with peril."

"Don't be ridiculous." He dismissed her trepidation as easily as any husband ever dismissed his wife's concerns. "I've thought it through."

"Have you thought that when Jude goes to the opera with Miss Ritter, the ton will gossip?"

He smiled at his duchess with such charm, Caroline was startled. "Not if you go with them, Nicolette."

The duchess's eyes grew round, and her complexion heated. "I hate the opera!"

"You're a female," he said. "All females like opera."

"I don't," she retorted. "A flock of squawking men and wailing women carrying on and on until they collapse on stage and die."

Caroline listened and ate. She liked the opera—the costumes, the music, the stories about honor and infidelity moved her to tears. And it seemed that she was to have the chance to go once more, and sit in the ducal box.

Nevett pulled a coin out of his pocket. "We'll toss for

it. I'll take heads." Before Nicolette could object, he tossed the coin. "Heads," he said with satisfaction. "You have to go. It's better that way. Your presence will be unremarkable at the opera."

The duchess blew a stray strand of hair off her face. "The gossips will natter more, believing that we're giving sanction to a match between Miss Ritter and Jude."

"I'll tell them it's not true" he said, complacently. "I'll explain that Miss Ritter is a friend of the family."

"I believe that will only fuel the rumors."

"Don't be ridiculous. I'm the duke of Nevitt. They will gossip as I command." Finishing his breakfast, he touched his lips with his napkin, folded it neatly, and placed it on the table. As if noticing Caroline for the first time, he said, "Good of you to arrive early, Miss Ritter. Good job. As soon as my son gets here, you can go to work." Dropping a kiss on the top of his wife's head, he left the room.

He was so calm, almost pleasant, that Caroline stared after him in amazement.

"It will last until three, when he takes tea, or until someone irritates him. He is the quintessential duke, who wants nothing more than to live his life exactly as he wishes." Lady Nevett turned toward the other door as Jude strolled in. "Dear, your father and I tossed a coin to see which of us had to escort you to the opera, and he won. He always wins. Is he using a two-headed coin?"

Jude looked amused, and bowed to his stepmother and to Caroline. "Are you calling my father a cheater?"

Jude looked different in the morning light. The hint of aristocratic dominance had disappeared beneath his overly stylish green-and-white-striped trousers, green waistcoat, and cravat embroidered with fleur-de-lis. A purple splash of a scarf rested across one shoulder and a large brooch shaped like a lavender flower pinned it in place. His smile could only be described as amiable, and his eyes were wide and indolent.

Nicolette turned to Caroline. "That means he's not going to tell me. It's difficult being the only female in a household of males."

Seating himself beside his stepmother, Jude lifted her fingers and kissed them. "It guarantees you're always our favorite lady."

"Such a compliment!" She touched Caroline's arm, and for a moment, Jude and Caroline were joined by the hands of the duchess. "I'm glad to have Caroline share the privilege of being the favorite and having the gentlemen tease."

He watched Caroline eat so intently she became self-conscious and put down her silverware.

"How good to see you here," he said. "You look as lovely as a flower this morning." He examined the new day gown she wore. "A very badly dressed flower."

Smoothing the skirt, Caroline said, "I rather like it."

"Yes, on a petite debutante. But you should never wear vertical stripes; it creates the illusion you're as tall as a giant. You should never wear a plain style; it, too, contributes to the impression of overwhelming height. And never should you wear pink"—he sighed and flapped a hand—"because you shouldn't."

Now Caroline felt as if she were an awesome Goliath.

The duchess studied Caroline. "You're right, Jude, this is an unfortunate choice. I shall take over the ordering at once."

"I shan't need many more," Caroline objected.

Nicolette pulled a long face. "Sh. You'll take my fun away from me. I always wanted a daughter to dress.

Now I have you." She studied Caroline. "What do you suggest, Jude?"

"Some lace, a few furbelows that would take down her height so she doesn't intimidate lesser men." His gaze mocked Caroline, and she knew very well he wasn't intimidated, nor did he consider himself one of the lesser men. "I want to approve the choices before they're made up."

"And create more rumors, and those of a less-respectable nature?" Nicolette answered crisply. "I think not."

Jude looked offended. "But I have impeccable taste!"

Tired of being discussed as if she didn't exist, Caroline said, "No, you don't."

His eyebrows shot up. His fingers went to his brooch. "Whatever do you mean?"

"I mean you can have the right to approve my clothing," Caroline said crisply, "when I have the right to approve yours."

"But you like that pink gown!" His eyes grew round and horrified. "You obviously have no taste."

"Then we're at an impasse, are we not?" Caroline retorted.

Nicolette laughed, a brief chuckle, and when both sets of eyes turned to her, she rubbed her hands together. "So, Caroline, what do you have planned first for Jude?"

"Breakfast?" Jude suggested.

"If you'd arrived earlier, you could eat. As it is, you'll have to wait until your governess takes pity on you," Nicolette said decisively.

"And I'm pitiless." A silly statement, of course. Caroline was no such thing, but she liked saying it, as if the words would make it come true.

She flipped open her planning journal as Jude sneaked a scone off her plate and consumed it. Although she knew exactly what lesson came first, she made a show of reading what she had written while Jude picked up several pieces of bacon and wrapped them in a slice of toast, and ate those, too, and swallowed a steaming cup of coffee as quickly as he could. Jude wolfed his food like the kind of man who relished horseflesh, boxing, and fast women, and nothing at all for fashion, and she wondered at the dichotomy between appearance and reality. Or perhaps all men, no matter how fussy, were the type to drink straight from the brandy decanter when given a chance. "I thought first I would see what he knows and what I can build on." She asked the duchess, "Do you have a piano and a place we can dance?"

"The ballroom! It hasn't been opened since last season. How lovely to have a chance to air it." Nicolette rose to her feet and hurried out of the room.

Caroline lingered behind and observed as an elderly footman slipped Jude a sausage and another scone. "You could have eaten before you came," she said.

With a toothy smile, Jude said, "I did."

As Caroline hurried after the duchess into the ballroom, she considered that he had none of the puffiness of a glutton. Jude was, in fact, lean and muscled, with the kind of healthy appearance a sportsman might exhibit. He truly was a mystery, flippant and serious, kind and mocking, intelligent . . . and the worst sort of fool.

He followed on Caroline's heels, so when she stopped short at the door of the ballroom, he trod on her skirt. She didn't care. She could only gape as the footmen threw the draperies wide. The sunshine lit the giant chamber, sparkled through the crystal chandeliers that hung from the ceiling and the crystal candelabras that sat on the tables. Rainbows danced on the gleaming golden oak floor and up the warm, cream-colored walls, and the gilt-trimmed cove moldings that decorated the ceilings. The windows looked out over the small garden, where spring roses climbed the wall, and the first yellow buds opened to the sun.

"This is magnificent," she breathed, then realized how much like a waif she must sound. She supposed she'd seen rooms as lovely as this in other homes during her Season, but the years between had been filled with paltry, dingy flats overlooking open sewers and rotting refuse. She'd forgotten what it was like to stand in the middle of the floor and smell the clean odor of beeswax, and see nothing but glossy wood and unmarked walls, or how her heart lifted at the sound of dance chords on a grand piano.

"It is beautiful," Jude agreed. "Mum decorated all the rooms in the town house, and she is universally acknowledged as a leader of style in London."

The duchess sat at the piano, running through the keys, limbering her fingers. "I doubt if Lady Reederman would agree."

"Of course not. Everyone knows she's deathly jealous of you," Jude answered.

"There *is* an advantage of being the only female in the house, Caroline." A smile quivered on Nicolette's lips. "The men flatter you at every turn. Are you two ready to dance?"

"I'd hoped to play for you," Caroline said. "I need to observe Lord Huntington and his skills."

"You're young." Nicolette waved an impatient hand. "You should dance. Are you ready?"

Ready? Caroline supposed she was. For four years

she hadn't skipped in happiness, hadn't heard music even when it played, and didn't know if she remembered the steps. She should have worn gloves, but the only decent pair she owned were for riding. Jude had already expressed his dismay for her gown.

So was she ready? She had to be. She was the governess.

She placed her journal on the piano. She nodded to Nicolette, and to Huntington. "I beg Your Grace, let us proceed."

She thought Jude would be like most men, impatient with the necessity of learning what he thought he already knew and anxious to get it over with. Instead he bowed as elegantly as a beau to his love, and begged, "Miss Ritter, may I have the pleasure of this dance?"

Caroline curtsied. "My lord, I would be delighted."

"We're the best amusement Mum has had for months," he added, *sotto voce*.

That explained his curious tolerance with their pretense, and she liked him for his open affection for his stepmother. "I trust we shan't amuse Her Grace too much, or I'll find myself covered with chagrin." She put her hand in his.

He slid his arm around her waist.

And the duchess played the first chords of a lively waltz.

As Jude and Caroline swung onto the floor, she was pleasantly surprised to find that Jude danced very well indeed. He led firmly, but without bullying, he kept time with the rhythm, and he displayed his partner at an advantage. Every eligible young man should be so adept.

Which made her task so much easier. She had set aside several days to teach him to dance, if necessary, but his skill put her far ahead in her schedule. If she were lucky enough that he could converse at the same time, she'd be that much closer to having him ready to become the most sought after beau of the Season. After that it was an easy leap to his betrothal, his marriage, and her independence from poverty and despair. She'd be able to take her sister—

"I have never before danced with a woman who was not truly there," he observed.

"What?" She glanced up from her calculations to see him smiling at her quizzically. "My lord, what do you mean?"

"We've circled the room twice, and you've frowned and concentrated on some private agenda the whole time. I can't imagine where you got the reputation as being a flirt. You've ignored me every step of the way."

She snapped to attention. They were circling the ballroom in great, sweeping spirals. The walls, the tables, the piano all blurred on the wings of the music. Her petticoats rustled, and her skirts flew. She hadn't danced for so long, and the practicalities of her situation had stripped away her enjoyment. She hadn't allowed herself a moment to revel in the movement—and if she didn't pay mind, he wouldn't learn his lessons, and she wouldn't get her reward.

"Sir, forgive me." With deliberate charm, she smiled back at him. "I have a checklist in my mind of things to teach you, and your excellent dancing has moved our schedule forward by days and days."

"Ah, praise! But pray, don't tell me we're done with the dancing! Because with such an excellent partner, I hate to ever stop."

At his words, a small thrill climbed up her spine.

"No, we are not done. Dancing is merely the framework for flirting—but I think you know that."

"What do you mean?"

"Your flattery was duly noted."

"It isn't flattery when it's true," he said, in a deep, warm voice.

Another thrill shook her, and for the first time since the dance started, she noted other details about Huntington: the arm around her waist was strong and fit, he smelled of clean linens and spice, he moved with the lithe grace of a cat, only he was bigger. Much, much bigger. Better . . . or worse, depending on how she looked at it, he watched her as if she were the most interesting, exciting woman in the world.

For she was not immune. She, who had spent the last years fending off unwelcome male attentions, now basked in the heat of one gentleman's admiration. It was a heady feeling, one she had almost forgotten. Yet she wasn't there to enjoy herself. No one knew that more than she. So with a merry smile, she tempted him with the chance to make an exhibition of himself. "Think how wonderful it will be to attend the grandest ball of the Season. Think how London will gossip when they see how handsome you are, dressed in your wonderful clothing and clasping a classic beauty in your arms!"

His arm tightened, and he swung her in a series of turns that made her head whirl. "I already know the pleasure of dancing with a classic beauty."

"Thank you, my lord." *Why* was she teaching him to flirt? He seemed only too skilled—and she was only too susceptible. "However, no one but Her Grace can see us. When you're with the right lady, you'll cause a sensation. Your name will be on every pair of lips!"

"In the dance, the man is not important. His only desire should be to display the woman like a flower for all to admire. As long as I hold you in my arms, I am invisible." He leaned close to her ear. "And in all of England, I could never find a woman more beautiful than you."

She surrendered. Only for the moment, but she did surrender. She gave herself up to the sensation of flying across the floor, to the one perfect moment of happiness that recalled youth and foolishness and passion, to the idea that this man thought her flawless and beautiful. It was as if they were making love to music.

Until the door to the ballroom slammed against the wall.

Chapter 10

*N*icolette's fingers smashed the chords to bits.

Huntington and Caroline whirled to a stop and broke apart.

In the doorway, a scarlet-faced Nevett shouted, "What are you blasted fools doing?"

"Father." Huntington used his scarf to fan his face and became, before Caroline's eyes, a fop once more. "We're dancing."

Nevett's gaze drilled into Caroline. "Why?"

Going to the piano, she picked up her journal, turned to the first page, and offered it to Nevett. "It's part of my plan."

He ignored the proffered book. "Why would he need help with dancing? I spent thousands on dancing tutors for him!"

"Thousands?" Huntington murmured.

Nevett scowled at him. "Hundreds!"

"Yes, Lord Huntington is fabulously proficient." She

had enjoyed the dance. She hadn't planned to, but Huntington made Caroline feel like a flower, like a beauty, and if she could coax him to do the same with the debutantes in the ton, he would be the most-sought-after gentleman in London.

Like the autocrat he was, Nevett made his pronouncement. "Then you're wasting time."

"No, I have to see where Lord Huntington is proficient and where he's inept before we can move on." At Nicolette's gasp, Caroline realized she had contradicted the duke, and obviously that never happened. Hastily, she added, "Flirting is like playing the piano or learning a foreign language. The more one practices, the better one is. The trick, Your Grace, is to practice flirting so often and so continuously that one can walk and flirt, dance and flirt, eat and flirt, listen to opera and flirt. The last is not as easy as one might suppose, since the object of one's affection could be in another box."

Nevett huffed. "Yes, well, but . . ."

"The first time we met, I did show you my planning journal," Caroline reminded him.

He clamped his lips shut.

His wife moved quickly to keep him subdued. "Nevett, what did you envision Miss Ritter would do to teach Jude how to flirt? Have him sit in a classroom and write a paper?"

Huntington drew a handkerchief from his sleeve and flapped it in wild enthusiasm. "I'm good at writing papers!"

Nevett stared at his son, with his foppish clothes and his affected mannerisms, and with a grim expression, he yielded. "Very well, Miss Ritter, continue." He backed out of the room.

Caroline swore she saw triumph glinting in Huntington's eyes. Then it vanished, and he sighed in exaggerated weariness. "Miss Ritter, did I pass the test on dancing?"

With flying colors. She had taken far too much pleasure in the music, the dancing . . . and his embrace. "I'd like to observe as you dance with Her Grace, if you please," Caroline said, in the repressive tone she'd heard so often from her own governess.

He smiled at her, smiled as if he knew what she thought.

"And if Her Grace doesn't mind," Caroline added.

"She loves to dance." Huntington took Nicolette's hand. "Don't you, Mum?"

"I do, but it's been months . . ." Her voice trailed off. Months since they'd received word of Michael's death, she meant.

Caroline admired the determination with which Huntington handled his stepmother's reluctance.

"Then of a certainty you must dance." He gestured Caroline toward the piano. "Miss Ritter, if you please?"

"Do you know what I saw today when I went out?" Nicolette sounded amused and looked amazed as she poured tea in the great drawing room late that afternoon. She handed the first cup to Caroline, who handed it to the duke.

Nevett grunted as he accepted the fragile white porcelain.

"At the corner, we have a beggar who has taken up residence," Nicolette informed him.

"That will never do," Nevett blew on the hot brew. "I'll send a footman to chase him off."

"Lady Reederman already tried that." A smile

curved Nicolette's lips, and she glanced at Caroline as if she expected her to share her wicked glee.

And in truth, it did Caroline's heart good to know *something* could defeat the formidable Lady Reederman.

"He won't go," Nicolette said.

"He'll go with a good swift kick in the arse," Nevett retorted.

"You don't want to do that." Nicolette sobered. "He lost both his legs at Trafalgar."

Caroline froze, her gaze fixed on the tableau before her—the duchess, her expression fraught with sympathy, and the duke, scowling at the story, yet watching his wife with concern.

"How do you know that?" he asked.

"I stopped and talked to him," Nicolette answered.

Harry. Somehow, Harry had followed Caroline.

"Nicolette, I have told you. You must have a care," Nevett scolded. "Beggars are scoundrels."

Caroline couldn't agree more.

"He's as likely to slit your throat as to answer your charitable queries." Nevett placed his cup on the table.

Not that, but Harry was far too adept at liberating a reticule from its owner, and if he took Nicolette's, the theft would be in part Caroline's responsibility.

Nicolette put her cup down, also. "He would have to coax me down to his level, then. He *has* no legs."

Caroline wanted to faint.

"Your soft heart will be the death of me." Nevett sounded as if he had never meant anything more.

"My maid accompanied me." Nicolette smiled at her husband. "Listen, dear. Harry is a charming fellow."

Standing, Caroline wandered to the window and peered out, looking for the familiar figure on his cart.

"He could be spinning you a Banbury tale," Nevett said.

"He could be," Nicolette answered, "but the fact remains, he has no legs."

"I heard you the first two times," Nevett said dryly. "How much did you give him?"

Caroline waited in dread to hear what Harry had done.

"I emptied my reticule into his hat, a sum of perhaps two pounds." Nicolette burbled with laughter. "He said I was such a generous lady, he wouldn't cut my purse this time."

Putting her hand to her chest, Caroline sighed with relief.

Going to Nevett's side, Nicolette perched her hip on the arm of his chair and slid her arm over his shoulders. "You'll have to admit, any beggar who refuses to do Lady Reederman's bidding is a man worth knowing."

Remembering Lady Reederman, Caroline had to agree.

Apparently, so did Nevett. "Has he actually faced off against the old witch herself?"

"And sent her scuttling back to her house." Nicolette burbled with laughter. "How I wish I had seen it!"

"Man deserves a medal for bravery under fire. Wonder if he has one?" Nevett mused.

Without thinking, Caroline said, "No. He was only a common sailor." Both sets of eyes turned to her. "I assume," she added, "or someone would be caring for him, and everyone knows the sailors were shamefully abandoned after they wrestled control of the seas from the French." Harry's words, although without the street accent. "If Your Graces would excuse me, I had thought I would take advantage of the sunshine and go for a walk."

"Good idea." Nevett examined her. "Put some roses in your cheeks. You're too blasted skinny for a gel your height."

"Yes, Your Grace." Caroline skittered from the room.

She requested her outer garments in a low, intense tone that sent the footman scurrying after them and raised Phillips's eyebrows. "In a hurry to go out, Miss?" he asked in sonorous tones.

"Yes." She snatched her mantle, hat, and gloves from the footman. "Thank you."

Her regal disdain brought Phillips's eyebrows winging upward. She knew she acted more like an imperious duchess than a disgraced debutante. Let Phillips make what he wanted of her manner. She didn't care.

She sailed out the door and down the street, hoping Harry remained on his corner, and desperate to discover why he had followed her—for she didn't for a minute imagine his appearance was an accident.

Was he checking on her?

Did he plan to blackmail her?

Briskly, she walked toward the corner, her mantle flapping in the cool spring breeze. She had had so many men use her, abuse her, she could scarcely imagine a man who would not take advantage of her bettered circumstances to improve his own.

As she rounded the corner, a voice at her feet said, "Hit's a sad day when a lady o' yer caliber steps on a poor legless veteran o' the great sea battle o' Trafalgar."

"Harry, I didn't step on you." She looked around to make sure they were unnoticed, then back at him. His cart was nothing more than a board nailed onto four lopsided wheels. His shoulders were broad, his arms muscled from the effort of pushing himself along the street. He wore wool gloves with the fingers worn-out from his ceaseless efforts, a short, ragged brown cape with a deep hood, and the face that peered out at her was pallid from lack of sun and lined with old pain and constant disappointment. Yet his pale eyes watched her with lively respect and the area around them with suspicion, and she never doubted she was safe here with him.

He continued his loud lament. "Poor wounded ol' soldier sitting 'ere minding 'is own business and the beautiful young lady 'as no respect or care." He rattled his cup. "But a bit o' coin will help assuage yer guilt, m'lady." In a lower tone, he added, "And no one will be any the wiser if we talk a bit."

No one was peeking out any windows that she could see. Only a few carriages traveled along the main road. Hopefully no one would notice at all, but at least if they did, she would appear charitable and he grateful. Slowly, she opened her reticule. "What are you doing here?"

"Someone's got t' watch out fer ye. Did ye think ye could wander off in the company o' an unknown gennaman and not come back without me worrying?" He sounded sincerely concerned.

But she watched him with wary eyes, wondering what game he was playing.

He must have read her trepidation, for he snorted. "What, do ye think Oi'm like yer father, out t' use ye fer me own purposes?"

She had never told him about her father.

"Hit's a sad day when a young lady can't tell 'er enemies from 'er friends." Harry sighed with gusty dismay and pulled such a long face, she couldn't help herself.

She chuckled. "You're right. You've been a wonderful friend to me." She looked down at the meager amount of coins in her wallet. "But really—why are you here?"

"Oi 'eard ye took yer bag and went off with a gennamen, and Oi wanted t' see that ye wanted to. Some gennamen have a habit o' taking young ladies where they don't want to go."

"Not Lord Huntington. He escorted me to his parents' house, where I have taken a position as governess." Wisely, she decided not to fill him in on the details, and tossed a coin into the cup.

"'Ere now. A pretty lady like ye can afford more!" Harry said loudly. Then more quietly: "Good fer ye! Oi told ye ye'd come out right."

"So far."

"What about the other gennaman? The first one? Oi heard 'e wasn't such a welcome visitor as ye thought."

Goose bumps rose at the thought of Lord Freshfield. "Harry, how do you know these things?"

"Oi 'ear things. The 'ores and beggars gossip, and the gennamen and ladies think Oi'm deaf as well as lame."

Taking another coin from her meager store, she tossed it in the cup. "The other gentleman is not a gentleman."

"Well, then. Oi'll keep an eye out fer 'im and warn ye when 'e comes about."

"Are you going to stay here?" she asked, aghast.

"Hit's a good corner. People come and go, and there's one lady 'oo really wants me t' leave, so Oi 'ave t' stay, ye see." He smiled and showed the gaps in his teeth. "Why's that, 'Arry, ye say."

"Why's that?" she repeated obediently.

"Oi can't let the uncharitable ol' besom wallow in 'er sins. If she don't see the error o' 'er ways, she'll go t' 'ell." He patted the ground beside his chair as if the flames were burning his hand. "So ye see, by staying 'ere, Oi'm saving 'er soul."

"You're not doing yourself any harm, either," Caroline said shrewdly.

"'Ey, there, cynicism isn't nice in a pretty girl."

She wondered when that had happened. Four years ago, she hadn't known what a cynic was. Now it appeared she was one. "At one time I was nice. I don't think I am anymore."

"Ye're practical. That's better." Harry's voice grew softer again. "Ahoy, there. Ye've got a surprise sailing up on yer port side. Best look lively!"

Caroline glanced to her left. A man walked toward her, right toward her, and although Nevett had warned her this moment would come, she was ill prepared for the sight of her father's florid face, and even less prepared for the fulsome smile he directed toward her.

That smile made her skin prickle and the hair on the back of her neck lift.

Mr. Ritter never smiled like that except when he was foreclosing on widows and fawning on aristocrats. The duke must have truly put the fear of God in him that he bent it now on his erring daughter.

He stopped before her, every inch the prosperous merchant: stout, with a snub nose, two chins, and lengthy gray whiskers that crawled down the side of his face. He wore good, solid, conservative clothing, carried a gold-headed cane, and took pains to preserve the shine on his black boots.

"Daughter Caroline, how good to see you." He glanced down at Harry. "Is the beggar bothering you? I can kick him away."

"No!" She took a breath, not wanting her father to see her revulsion. It would never do to let her father know she had a friend such as Harry. Mr. Ritter used every bit of knowledge to his advantage, and the less he knew about her and her circumstances, the better. "No, thank you, sir, I was simply putting a few coins into his cup."

"He'll spend them on drink." Mr. Ritter took incredible care to present the appearance of nobility, yet didn't comprehend that servants spread the word about his stinginess throughout London. He took equal care to present the appearance of philanthropy without actually performing charitable deeds, and failed to understand the difference.

At their feet, Harry rattled his cup, and whined, "Alms fer a poor veteran, m'lord?"

"No. Get away from us!" Mr. Ritter lifted his cane threateningly.

Caroline realized she might have to intercede, and she didn't want to.

But without a word, and that was uncharacteristic, Harry pushed his cart around the corner and out of sight.

Caroline knew he remained within hearing distance, and that was fine. Some people might say Harry was a frightening man with his disability and his chosen career. For Caroline, those people were fools. It was Mr. Ritter who was frightening. He had never laid a disciplinary hand on Caroline, yet he terrorized her beyond even Lord Freshfield's abilities, for Mr. Ritter had a way of cutting her that was both personal and devastating. She never felt as insignificant as when she was with her father.

"Daughter Caroline, how have you been?" Mr. Ritter asked.

"Fine, sir, and you?" And when had he decided he

should remind her of their relationship every time he spoke her name?

"Fine."

"Is my sister well?"

"Very well, although she's given to weeping at inconvenient times."

Caroline wanted to ask him when it would be convenient for his daughter to cry; but sarcasm would avail her nothing, and she didn't have a doubt that, if it pleased him, he would take out his discontent on Genevieve. Besides, she could imagine Nevett's displeasure if she foiled his plan to bestow upon her respectability, and she had to admit respectability would make her life easier. So she smiled and nodded, and searched her mind for more useless, indifferent conversation. She should have known she needn't have bothered.

"Do you have a position doing something?" Mr. Ritter clasped the head of his cane and leaned hard on it.

"I'm working for the duke of Nevett"—*as you very well know*—"and will keep this position until the end of the Season."

"The duke of Nevett, heh?" Mr. Ritter's small blue eyes narrowed. "I imagine he's a tyrant."

"A bit of one, yes, but nothing untoward."

"You wouldn't want to offend him."

"That's the last thing I wish to do."

"So at the end of the Season, you'll be pleased to come home."

"What?" She felt as if she had swallowed a stone. Whatever she expected him to say, it wasn't that. "What? You're inviting me home?"

"Yes." His gaze drilled into her. "I imagine you're grateful."

"To live?" she clarified.

"Of course to live. What do you think?" He managed to sound insulted, which was an insult in itself.

What was the reason? The duke of Nevett was kind in the way that most aristocrats were kind; if it availed him something, then he would do it. But he gained nothing by pressuring Mr. Ritter to allow her to return to their house in Cheapside, so that couldn't be it.

Had her father finally comprehended that the act of tossing his erring daughter from his home in a rage had labeled him as an irredeemable vulgarian? That the ton considered it better form to quietly retreat to the country than to create a scene in the street? That seemed unlikely, too. He understood the value of money in all its guises, but not the value of gentility or the appearance of loyalty and graciousness.

When she didn't at once curtsy and show her appreciation, he glared and blustered, "I'm your father. When I say you shall return, you shall return."

During the lowest moments of her life—a week ago—she would have leaped at the chance to return home. Of course she would be miserable, but at least she'd be warm and fed, clothed and dry.

Now she could see the possibility for escape—from poverty, from her father, from Lord Freshfield, and from England, and she wasn't giving up so easily. "Sir, really, whatever impression His Grace made on you, I assure you, he doesn't expect this kind of sacrifice on your part."

"What do you mean? You're my daughter. You should live in my house. I don't want you to anger the duke of Nevett, naturally, but when this is over you shall come home." Mr. Ritter rapped the tip of his cane hard against the ground. "Until that time, good day." Tipping his hat, he stalked off, an offended bowl of blancmange in a suit.

Harry wheeled himself back around the corner, and joined her in staring after her father. "Well. What do ye expect that was about?"

"The duke of Nevett ordered my father to have a public reconciliation with me." Now that the meeting was over, she felt nauseated. She hadn't seen the man for almost four years, and he had neither spoken a kind word nor offered an embrace. She had expected nothing else, but the whole event left her cold and far too aware of her own vulnerability. One wrong move, and she would be on the streets . . . like Harry. "I suppose His Grace was too emphatic and my father too eager to please, and he made an unnecessary offer."

"Why did yer father have 'is reconciliation 'ere?" Harry waved a hand around at the desultory traffic. "This is 'ardly public enough t' generate gossip."

"I don't know." With a glance down at her friend, she said, "I don't know how often I'll be able to come down and see you. That *would* generate gossip."

He waved an arm. "Ye know where t' find me if ye need me. Go on, now, before the ol' hen yonder starts 'er cackling."

He meant Lady Reederman, and as Caroline hurried past her house, she saw her peeking through her curtains. Now Lady Reederman had another reason to dislike Caroline—Caroline cavorted with married men *and* with beggars. What a diversity of sins.

Returning to the house, Caroline divested herself of her outerwear, and this time she smiled as she thanked Phillips and the footman.

Phillips sniffed when the footman smiled back. Phillips, who liked to supervise every servant in the household, had no right to supervise her, and obviously he didn't like that—or her.

She couldn't help it. She wouldn't submit to his management. She wouldn't have a stuffy old butler telling her how to give Huntington instructions.

"Miss Ritter, are you back?" Nevett called. "Come in here, please."

Warily she entered the great drawing room.

"How was your walk, Caroline?" Nicolette asked.

"A little colder than I expected." Standing directly in front of the duke, Caroline asked, "What do you desire, Your Grace?"

"How long are you going to be here?" Nevett asked.

Again he wanted an accounting of the lessons. And again she would give it, because he was the duke, and she the governess, and she would do well to remember that. "Lord Huntington is most graceful at dancing and most skilled at the art of fetching a lady food and drink. His conversation is entertaining."

Nevett looked diverted. "Then why in Hades hasn't a female captured him?"

"I suppose he hasn't chosen to be captured. I don't believe any lady would care so much about his clothing that she would discourage his advances."

"It must have been chilly outside," Nicolette observed. "Your cheeks are quite rosy."

Caroline put her palms to her face. She felt warm, not cold, but she nodded in agreement. "Your Grace, you said you would arrange a party here. If I could be in the background and see how Lord Huntington disports himself, it would show me which areas of his deportment need adjustment. In the meantime, I'll continue to work with Lord Huntington. I'm sure I can refine his skills."

"The invitations for our tea are going out tomorrow." Nicolette clasped her hands in delight. Then, with a worried frown: "Do you think it's too soon, Nevett?"

"Don't be ridiculous. If it was, I wouldn't have started this." Nevett considered Caroline. "Before I forget, I'll send a message to your father, arrange to have him run into you in a public place and speak to you. That should take care of the problem of paternal approval."

Staggered by this turn of events, Caroline said, "But Your Grace, he did speak to me, just now, while I was on my walk."

"Really?" He spoke as slowly. "I wonder why."

"Perhaps he was moved to charity toward the plight of his daughter," Nicolette said.

Both Nevett and Caroline gave identical, disbelieving laughs.

"Not *my* father," Caroline said.

"No." Nevett was in complete agreement. "Not Mr. Ritter."

Chapter 11

"Miss Ritter, yesterday proved to you I can dance." Huntington waved his handkerchief in a mad display of impatience. "What shall we do today?"

Although Caroline knew, she made a pretense of opening her journal and consulting it. "I had hoped to create a party situation and judge how you deal with the details of being introduced to a lady and caring for her needs." To the duchess, Caroline said, "If we could have glasses, plates, napkins—"

"Of course, a party." Nicolette clasped her hands. "You'll need food and wine, although perhaps it's early for wine. Water in crystal glasses, Jude, just like when you were young." She confided to Caroline, "Actually, he's very good at this."

"I'm sure he is." Caroline was sure of no such thing.

"I'll have it set up in the library. There's always a fire laid there. Give me ten minutes." The duchess bustled out of the breakfast room, where Jude had once more put in a late appearance.

Jude stared after her and smiled.

"I suspect, my lord, you avoid your father's early-morning mood by arriving late for your lessons," Caroline said.

Jude turned that smile on Caroline.

Goodness. His excellent teeth more than made up for his execrable taste in clothes.

Then Caroline scolded herself for being shallow. It was that kind of thinking that had gotten her into this fix in the first place. She had looked on Lord Freshfield and believed that beauty equaled character. It wasn't true, not with Lord Freshfield, and certainly not with a man who wanted to consult on her wardrobe so that in public, she wouldn't disgrace him or in private, distress him.

When she turned her gaze on Huntington again, she wondered for a brief moment if he knew what she was thinking. *Ridiculous*.

Yet Lord Huntington had a way of dominating the room at the oddest moments. Sometimes, like now, when they were alone, she was very aware of his height, his breadth, the odd, deep blue eyes that slashed at her composure when she should have felt a lady's contempt for a dandy.

"I don't recall—is my father irritable in the morning?" Seeing Caroline's disgust, he chuckled deeply. "Actually, I must rise early every morning. It takes time to achieve the perfection of my toilette."

"Of course. I should have thought of that." It must take an immense amount of time to put colors together so badly, to torture his hair into a pile of curls over his forehead . . . to scrape his face clean of whiskers and show off that resolute jut of a chin. He could be so handsome—was so handsome—if only he stopped wearing those absurd clothes!

"Yesterday and again today, my stepmother is happy. I haven't seen her so entertained since I returned from Europe." Taking Caroline's hand, he kissed the backs of her fingers. "I thank you."

The touch of his lips against her bare skin sent a thrill up her arm. She started, and he felt her shock.

Looking up into her eyes, he smiled again, observing her every motion and reading her every emotion.

Absurd! No man cared enough to bother with a woman's emotions, at least not unless he could get something from her, and Caroline had nothing this man could desire.

Then, turning her hand, he kissed the tender skin of her wrist. His lips rested there long enough to feel the suddenly hastened beat of her heart.

Ah. Bitterness curled up in her. She'd forgotten. She *did* have something this man desired. The same thing Lord Freshfield desired, the same thing every man wanted. She pulled her hand free. When he rose from his bow and quizzically lifted his brows, she said, "My lord, it's obvious my reputation has preceded me, but let me make something perfectly clear—I'm not now nor have I ever been willing to lower myself to becoming a man's leman. If I had, I wouldn't now be your governess, but a woman of means. Please remember that—and keep your lips and your hands to yourself."

Jude hadn't expected Miss Ritter to so fiercely throw down the gauntlet, but then, he hadn't expected to kiss her as intimately as he had. The kiss on her fingers had been prompted by gratitude, but her skin was bare against his lips and the impulse to taste her caught him by surprise. He'd given in to the whim, kissed her wrist, and caught a much-wronged lady on the raw. Yet while he knew she had every reason to be tender of her reputation, and that he should humbly apologize, still his temper rose.

She thought he was cut from the same mold as Freshie.

He stepped closer, not away, and looked down at her fierce expression. "You don't know me, Miss Ritter, but I don't take advantage of young women felled by misfortune. That is the act of a cad. I, madam, have no need to act the cad. I have enough women in my life, and they've deliberately charted their way in life. I have no interest in victims."

"Good. Because I'm not a victim." As she realized what she had said, the invitation she seemed to have given, a bright blush lit her cheeks.

Jude relaxed. This flirting business was more fun than he'd expected.

"I mean—I'm not afraid of you." She tucked the journal under her arm.

When Nevett had first told Jude about this project, Jude had expected these lessons to be time to unwind from the pressure of tracking the Moricadians, time to think of strategy . . . he had expected to be bored. Instead, Miss Ritter proved delightful and interesting and much cleverer than he'd been led to believe—and perhaps, because she was gorgeous, he had imagined she would be dim-witted. Not even she understood how bright she was, and he was only beginning to see that she could be dangerous to him. With a sweep of his hand, he called attention to his outlandish garb. "Of course not. I'm a civilized man. I eschew those dreadful fistfights and those muddy horse-races and all those ridiculous activities other men do to prove their masculinity. So how could you be afraid of me?"

"Yes. You're right." She walked toward the door, moving with languorous grace; her long strides made her seem to flow from one place to another, and made a man wonder how it would be to have her under him, or on top of him, pouring her smooth sensuality over his naked body. She stopped. She looked back at him, and even now he could see wariness in her gaze, as if she no longer noticed his garments and instead saw the man beneath. "How could I be afraid of you?"

It was all very well to desire that this woman see him as he was rather than as he pretended to be, but it would not do. He had to maintain his disguise, or he would fail to avenge Michael's death.

With a few long strides, Jude caught up with Miss Ritter. "With your help, I shall find a bride as all men long to do and settle into a blissful state of matrimony."

Her sharp glance examined him thoroughly. "Every young lady in the land would be proud to accept your suit. I'm sure you can find one who will make you blissful."

"Did I not just say so?" He paced beside her along the corridor, his hands behind his back, and distracted her with a subject guaranteed to catch her interest. "May I ask a question?"

She braced herself as if expecting an inquiry into her personal life. "You may ask."

She was very good at this game, promising nothing, holding the mystery of herself close so that a man wanted nothing so much as to decipher it. "You're teaching me to flirt, yet so frequently I don't know what a lady wants to hear. It's a mystery with which every man struggles."

She turned those oddly bright, aquamarine eyes on him. "Yet I think you know the answer."

Taken aback, he replied, "If I do, I don't know that I know."

"You very skillfully give me that which flatters and entices."

"I have no idea what you're talking about." He'd never meant anything so sincerely.

"Even when you criticize my clothing, I'm more pleased with you than I am with most men, for you give me the one thing I've never had—you give me your whole attention."

"Attention." One side of his mouth quirked up. "Fascinating."

"Yes. Your attention, without any trace of superior masculine assurance that you're more intelligent than I am because I'm pretty and none of that irritating indulgence as if I were a treasured pet you could scratch under the chin, then forget." She watched him with the kind of smugness she said she detested in men. "Attention—that's what all men want, too."

"Men want attention?" More and more he realized that Miss Ritter was an astute observer of human nature. How to distract her lest she penetrate his masquerade? Perhaps he should flirt with her in earnest and make her fall in love with him . . . and perhaps that wasn't his mind making suggestions. Perhaps the organ making suggestions was lower and less inclined to intelligent decisions. Miss Ritter caused him a turbulence and an arousal that could only produce embarrassment.

She stopped outside the door of the lesser drawing room. "Think about the most fascinating woman you know."

"All right." That would be Miss Ritter.

But he shouldn't think of Miss Ritter.

Yet he could think only of her. For God's sake! This was his father's house, his stepmother was nearby, Miss Ritter had been much wronged, and he intended to use her for his purposes. He had to subdue his undue and obvious interest in the young lady . . .

. . . Who seemed unaware of his fascination. "What does she talk about?" she asked.

"Who?"

"Pay heed!" she said. "The most fascinating woman you know."

He tried to pay heed. Tried to remember.

"She doesn't talk," Caroline informed him. "She listens. She listens with every appearance of interest as you babble about your horses and your gambling and your"—Caroline's gaze swept his garments—"style. She hangs on your every word while you bore the entire dinner party senseless going on and on about politics."

Was she accusing him of being interested in politics? After he had worked so hard to create the persona of a man enamored of nothing but fashion? Pointing to his chest, he said, "Politics? Not me."

"Of course not. You care nothing for manly pursuits." She threw out the phrase almost as a challenge, as a test.

"Manly pursuits are fatiguing and frequently splash mud on one's garments," Jude said indolently,

As if she were disappointed in the answer, she snapped, "Exactly," and strode ahead of him into the drawing room.

He watched the irritated sway of her petticoats and smiled. No wonder she had been the belle of her Season. She could reduce a man to obsession.

Today she spoke without the usual maidenly restraint, without the annoying fluttering of the eyelashes and the pretended bashfulness which so many debutantes affected. Of course, the reason she spoke to him so freely was because she neither expected nor could accept his courtship. Unlike most single ladies, her goal was not her marriage to him, but rather his marriage to anyone else but her. Fascinating, indeed.

He followed her into the room.

There the footmen bustled in and out, placing a small repast on the cupboard against the wall, and as the duchess promised, there were crystal glasses and fine china, and on platters a series of simple appetizers and pastries laid out on the buffet, which stood against one wall.

Breezing into the drawing room, Mum placed her hand on Jude's arm. "This isn't as difficult as you feared, is it, dear?"

"How hard is it to take two beautiful women in my arms and dance with them one day, then feast with them another?"

Rather tartly, Caroline said, "Let's see if you still thank me when the Season is over."

"I'm sure I will," he said meekly.

Wisps of chestnut hair had fallen from Caroline's chignon and teased under her chin and around her amazing eyes. Now those wisps caressed the pale, velvety nape of her neck in the same way he would if given the chance—softly, lightly.

Catching sight of herself in the mirror, she sighed. "Would you excuse me? I'm untidy." She placed her journal on the table. All unconscious, she lifted her arms and displayed the long, clean line of her torso, her perfect bosom, her strong arms. In the space of a few seconds, she rearranged some pins and tucked most of the errant stands back into the severe style.

As Jude stared, his mouth grew dry.

This beautiful woman failed to realize that her efficient motions could carry a man's imagination into the boudoir, that her simple task drew him into a reverie where she wore nothing but a robe, where she let down her hair rather than put it up as she prepared to join him in bed.

Turning back to the room, she didn't seem to notice that Jude had been struck dumb. "Shall we proceed?"

He shook away the fantasy and indicated the sofa, inviting her to seat herself. "Mum, will you join us?"

"If it's part of Caroline's plan, then I would like that," Mum answered.

Miss Ritter's smile blossomed. "I would like that, too."

Seating herself beside Caroline, Mum suggested mischievously, "Shall we ask for a jumble of things to eat so he has to strain to remember?"

"My memory is excellent," he warned, and when he brought them their food, he had remembered everything. He presented them each with a well-filled plate, a napkin, and placed their goblets of water on the table nearby so they could sip at any time they wished. He filled his own plate, balanced it on his knee, and proceeded to please Miss Ritter by being the perfect suitor. "Miss Ritter, tell me—if a woman is in love with a man, does she find his discourse interesting?"

"What an excellent question." She knit her brow as she thought. "I do believe that's possible. Once I observed a very lively conversation during which the host was quite left out, and the hostess quite ruthlessly steered it back to him. But the truly amazing thing was—in the drawing room after dinner, he did the same thing for her! I was quite astonished."

"So they have a true love match," Nicolette said.

Caroline blinked as if she'd never considered the matter in that light. "I don't know."

"Do you know anyone who has a true love match?" Jude asked.

"None that I've ever seen," she answered.

"You *are* a cynic," Jude snapped.

"A realist." She didn't seem offended, nor did she wish to argue with him. Rather, she seemed rapt when she asked, "Have *you* ever seen a true love match?"

"Indeed I have." He turned a smile on Nicolette. "My father adores my stepmother, and she loves him. You wouldn't believe how much she's softened him through the years."

Nicolette blushed, and inclined her head, and shook it, acknowledging the compliment and declining it at the same time.

"He's softer than he used to be?" Caroline asked.

"Most definitely." Jude tugged at his collar in mock dismay. "He used to be a despot. Now he's more of a . . ."

"Tyrant?" Caroline asked tartly

Jude gave a shout of laughter, an amusement so pure it should have been illegal. He might look like a fop, but he laughed like a pirate.

Then the nightmare repeated itself. The door slammed against the wall. Nevett stood in the doorway, bristling with indignation. "What are you doing? Having a tea party? Miss Ritter, are you the best Lady Bucknell can provide?"

Caroline found herself on her feet, staring into Nevett's furious eyes.

The duchess stood beside her.

Phillips, that self-satisfied old beast of a butler, stood behind Nevett.

And Huntington lolled in his seat, his gaze mocking, leaving Caroline to manage on her own.

"I do not believe you know anything about teaching flirtation, Miss Ritter." The duke attacked the very foundation of her knowledge. "You're simply repeating what your betters have taught before you."

Caroline's temper rose—and she was surprised. A lady's equanimity never flagged. A lady never grew angry. Although the duchess had said Caroline should be livid at the way she'd been treated in the past, Caroline took responsibility for her actions, for she had been told, time and again, that turbulent emotion was unfeminine.

But right now, she faced an indignant Nevett and a smirking Phillips, and knew they had no right to treat her with disdain. None at all.

Although she might not currently have the circumstances of a lady, she certainly had the upbringing, so she controlled her irritation and modulated her voice. "Your Grace, as I've said, I have to observe Lord Huntington interacting with society before I can judge where he needs assistance. I *am* an expert, Lady Bucknell *did* recommend me, and you *did* hire me to teach him. If you would please allow me to do so without interference, my task would be a great deal easier."

She must not have hidden her exasperation as well as she'd thought, for Nevett's eyes bulged with affront. "I say . . ." he sputtered.

"Your Grace, if you would like, I'll see about hiring a more suitable governess." Phillips gloated in premature enjoyment. Caroline recognized his type, a petty tyrant who imagined he could manage her as he did the rest of his staff.

But before Caroline could speak, the duchess said, "I find Miss Ritter quite suitable." And she looked at Phillips. Just looked at him.

Somewhere in the past, when the duchess was first wed, Phillips must have tried his tricks on her and failed, for now he bowed, and he bowed, and he faded back into the foyer so rapidly Caroline blinked at the place that he had inhabited.

"Come, dear." Going to Nevett, Nicolette placed her hand on his arm. "Let's leave Miss Ritter to work her magic."

"I wouldn't allow a footman to use that tone with me," Nevett huffed, "much less a young woman."

"Nor would you allow a footman to teach your son to flirt." Nicolette guided him out of the room, then returned, and to Huntington she mouthed, "Lock the door behind us."

The footman shut them in.

Huntington turned the key.

Caroline stared at the door. The last time she'd been locked in a room with a man, her whole life had been destroyed. Now she wondered—had she lost what was left of her pitiful reputation or won the war to keep her position?

Chapter 12

"Don't look so worried." Huntington took her arm and sat her back on the sofa. "Father's bark is worse than his bite, and he rather likes people who stand up to him."

"Are you sure?" It wasn't safe to exasperate her employer, especially not when he was a duke. A duke who had promised to pay her a lot of money.

"I'm positive. He likes a challenge."

"I did stand up to him, didn't I?" Irrationally, her heart lifted.

"I'm impressed. I was under the misapprehension that you were too soft and feminine to speak so brusquely. But that's nonsense, isn't it? You've survived in London for four years without family or money. It's a rare young lady who can do so. I greatly admire you for that." Huntington's voice sounded so sincere, as warm and as personal as a lover's.

Taking a startled breath, she stared at him wide-eyed. This wasn't flirtation. This was seduction.

Then she looked at him again.

He stood flipping his handkerchief back and forth, back and forth, and he watched it as if fascinated by the motion.

She shook herself. No, this wasn't seduction. By pure accident he had managed to say the thing she wished to hear, but clearly, he had no idea what he'd done or how to follow up on his success. And if he really wanted to seduce her, he would have interceded with his father.

"I should practice my manners." Picking up her goblet, she crooked her little finger and smiled politely at Huntington. "I've been out of society for so long, I say too much."

Huntington sat beside her at a perfectly respectable distance, yet too close for her comfort. "You say what you think. That's an admirable quality."

"No. It is not. Honesty shakes the foundation of civilization." She inched back an infinitesimal amount.

He didn't follow, didn't seem to notice or care. "At least that."

Irony? From such a man? Was it possible?

"You are my governess. You're my instructor." He faced her, his arm braced against the back of the sofa. He looked soulfully into her eyes. "You're the woman who will guide me into the holy state of matrimony."

Oh, yes. Irony. It was definitely possible. He was more subtle than she had hoped, which meant he was more intelligent. "My lord, tell me true. Are you determined not to marry?"

As if her accusation pained him, his dark lashes

closed over his remarkable blue eyes, then opened, and again he stared at her like a languishing beau. "It's my penultimate objective in life."

If, as she suspected, he masked his reluctance with florid speech and suggestive glances, that made her task all the more difficult. She could leave nothing to chance. She would have to search out the woman of his dreams, thrust them together, and somehow create an atmosphere of irresistible yearning. It would be difficult, but possible. She faced him, as determined to seek out his wife as he was to evade his fate. "Tell me, my lord. When you're at a ball, and you see the whole line of debutantes sitting, talking, smiling—who is it you choose to grace with your attention?"

"Ah. That's easy." He leaned back against the arm of the sofa and surveyed her. "I like a tall woman, a slender woman, one who moves with notable grace. I like a woman with a healthy color—no pallid beauty for me. I like dark hair, and unique, aquamarine eyes that bewitch me and draw me closer."

With a shock, she realized—he was speaking of her.

Earlier in their lesson, he had been trying to impress her with his flirting abilities—and succeeding admirably—but she had detected nothing personal about his attention. He had produced the kind of engaging conversation every man employed to ease a social confrontation. This . . . this was different. This was blatant flattery. He was testing her mettle.

So she mocked him with a smile. "It's a well-known fact that tall, graceful women prefer men who wear somber colors and have unaffected mannerisms."

He flipped his handkerchief as if shooing away a pesky fly. "What else do tall, graceful women want?"

The spark of challenge in his eyes drove her on. "They like men who like to dance."

"I like to dance."

"More than that, tall, graceful women like men who, when they dance with another woman, come back with a glass of chilled champagne, present it with all admiration, and converse as if that other dance was so unimportant it didn't rate a mention."

He nodded slowly. Going to a side cabinet, he poured her another glass, brought it, and with a bow presented it.

She took it, took a sip, and although it tasted like water, she wondered at the contents. It must be an intoxicating beverage, for she was behaving recklessly. "After the dance, tall, graceful women want a man who worries if they're cold, who would take off his coat and drape it on them as they wait for the carriage."

He moved closer. "Are you cold, sweet Caro?"

"There. You see? You show a natural talent for flirtation." A big-boned, polished, alluring talent for flirtation. But she was his instructor. She maintained control of this lesson. "If you pick up conversational clues as quickly when speaking with an appropriate young lady as you do with me, you shall be mobbed with ladies who recognize your allure." Hastily, she added, "As well as your style."

He smiled at her. Just smiled, and her breath caught. He was truly handsome, with thick brown hair as luxurious as mink. The strands begged a woman to sweep it off his forehead. His warm eyes conveyed appreciation without ever looking below her neck, and that was rare in a man. His chin was smooth-shaven, yet a few hours' growth of his stubble gave it a texture she imagined would feel like velvet. He still flipped that ridiculous handkerchief, and the motion called attention to his hands.

She liked his hands. They were big, almost absurdly big, with long fingers, broad knuckles, and weighty palms. They looked capable, as if they could crush the duchess's goblets, and gentle, as if they could cradle a baby's head.

"So what else can you tell me about women that will help me in my pursuit of the perfect wife—what, besides attention, do women want?" he asked, as idly as a man who didn't even realize he was flirting.

"A clean house, happy servants, healthy, well-behaved children, enough money to pay their bills, and a husband who doesn't stray." She smiled. "In short, the impossible."

"Miss Ritter, you are a cynic."

Harry had said so. Now Huntington, too. "I fear that's the truth."

"Yet you know the secret, and you must tell me." He leaned close to her. "You're my governess, and I can't succeed without you. What is it that *all* women want?"

A vague irritation preyed on her nerves. "Why do men think that women all want one thing, as if we were one big female blob with but a single mind and all the same desires?"

He cocked his head and seemed to consider the question in all gravity. "Because, I suppose, it would be easier that way."

She subdued her irritation, for if he understood what women wanted, he would be better prepared to find a wife. "I can't speak for the whole gender," she warned him.

"Then speak for yourself," he commanded.

"A woman wants a man who has his own pet name for her."

His eyebrows rose. "Like Oogy-Sweetie?"

"No! Like . . . well, for instance, if we were talking about me, it would be a name like . . . like sweet Caro."

"I'm flattered that you like my name for you."

"Yes. Well." She fluttered her lashes at him. "If you were mine, I would love that you gave me a nickname and used it at appropriate times."

"Sweet Caro," he experimented.

She straightened, her spine snapping upright. She shouldn't be responding to him. What was she thinking? They were student and governess. Her future depended on making a success of this post. In a businesslike tone, she said, "When a woman's distraught, she wants a man to take her part."

"I think a woman could depend on me for that." He didn't seem to notice the change in her demeanor. He seemed as intent on her as before.

"About anything. Even when things look the worst. Even if her guilt is authenticated by a hundred witnesses." Grimly, she reminded him of her past.

Just as coldly, he answered, "A man should be willing to challenge those who sully the reputation of his woman. He should kill them on a dueling field."

"Well." He shocked her with his stern gaze and his formal tone. He looked . . . he looked like a man who could kill. Who had killed. Who feared nothing, not even death. That didn't equate with the Huntington she thought she knew—but she liked to think he would be her champion. Such an idea was a gratifying seduction unlike any she'd ever allowed herself. "That's admirable. But in my experience, usually those who pass judgment are women." She gave up pretending she was talking about someone else. "I can't stick a sword through them—no matter how much I want to."

"No. But there are other ways to vanquish the beasts. You'll see. I promise." With a hearty, "Ha ha!" and a fashionable slouch, he transformed back into the giddy leader of fashion. "But my dear Miss Ritter, you're being coy. Tell me, what do *you* want?"

Was he truly interested in *her?*

No. Not at all. He was simply talking, acting, seducing, when he should be learning. He was being a man, and Caroline knew she should be glad, for that meant she could find him a likely mate. After all, that was all there was to love. Timing and compatibility. Shaking her head, she smiled.

He coaxed, "Surely there must be something that you want. Really want. Want more than anything in the world."

"I want to take my sister to France to live with my mother's family in peace and happiness," she said with brutal honesty. "That's what I want—and I will have it, because I'm going to get it for myself."

He placed his fingers on his lips as if he were surprised.

Unfortunately, that caused her to notice his mouth, to wonder how he kept his lips so rich and soft-looking, the kind of lips a woman would like to kiss. Yet despite his garb, he projected an aura of intense masculinity. She'd noticed it before, but she hadn't been affected. Not really. Not like now, when they were locked alone in a room and she could hear nothing but the sound of her own breathing. And his.

He broke the silence. "I have complete faith in your ability to get anything you decide to have."

"You do?" She sounded too surprised. "I mean, you

do." Well, why not? It had taken him to point it out, but she was strong. She'd survived on her own for four years in London. Survived when most women would have starved or been killed. She had won a confrontation with the duke of Nevett and his abominable butler, and she would wager not many could say that.

"Yes, you're an amazing woman." Again Huntington moved closer. "And I have complete faith in your ability to find me the right wife. Tell me more about the things women want."

"All right." She took a long breath. Some ladies might not want to tell him the secrets of their gender, but if he were to succeed—if *she* were to succeed—he needed to know things, things other men only vaguely understood. Grasping Huntington's collar in her hands, she looked into his eyes. "All right. Listen to me. A woman wants presents for no reason. Not because it's a birthday or Christmas. Just because it's Thursday, or because you saw a muff that would be pretty with her eyes. A woman wants a man to save her the best cut of the roast and the best ripe strawberries. A woman wants a man who lifts her feet into his lap after a long night of dancing and rubs them."

"You have charming feet."

"Don't be ridiculous," she said with disdain. "I have very large feet."

"So do I. Thus I find your feet charming."

"There you go." She bestowed her praise honestly. "A woman wants a man who turns a skilled compliment tailored only for her."

"I'll remember that," he said meekly.

He was truly good at this. Amazingly good. With this information, and the proper woman, Caroline could motivate him. She could get him married! With rising excitement, she told him, "When a woman wants to go somewhere, she wants a man who makes sure she gets there safely."

"Naturally."

"If a woman is crying for no reason, she doesn't need a man to point out that it's for no reason, as if that will make everything better." Caroline put her face close to his and emphasized each syllable of that most important rule. "Every woman likes a man who bathes frequently."

Huntington's mouth crooked on the edge of merriment. "A great number of women must be disappointed."

"A great number, indeed." But not her. Not now. He smelled like fine soap and powerful masculinity. "A woman likes to be kissed. A lot."

"Tell me more." His lips puckered as he formed the word.

"A woman likes a man who *enjoys* talking to her, and kissing her. You're only a man, so I don't know how best to explain it, but try to understand—a woman likes a man who understands romance."

"Or at least a man who pretends to," he said wryly.

Her mirth caught her by surprise, and she giggled like a girl.

He reached toward her face as if trying to catch a note of her laughter, and his eyes comprehended far too much. "You've been kissed before."

Trust the man to pick that out of her list of instructions. "Wait! I didn't say *I* like to be kissed."

His hand fell away.

"But women talk, and I listen. Women—other women, most women—delight in kissing. They wish that men would linger over the exchange rather than sprint toward some desperately important goal." Her smile lingered. "I know about the rush, for when I was kissed, it was usually by a young man who charged at my lips as if he were the cavalry, and I was a hill to conquer."

Huntington chuckled. "Who else kissed you?"

"Once Lord Duchesman kissed me in his garden, and that was interesting, a kiss from an older man who showed patience and skill and—" She stopped. And who had, after the scandal, been kind.

"Any more?"

"One quite disgusting kiss." That Lord Freshfield forced on her.

"Let me see if I can do better than that." Huntington leaned forward until his lips barely touched her cheek, and his breath whispered along her skin. "Let me know where I fall on the list."

The other kisses had been things done *to* her. This was so different. Nothing about this kiss frightened or amused her. He pressed his lips to hers, but softly, as if seeking a response as tart and interesting as their dialogue. She answered him in the same spirit, skating her lips along his because . . . because she wanted to answer his challenge.

For this kiss was a challenge between two worthy opponents, a salute after one battle and before another. She kept her hands folded comfortably in her lap, and kept her attention on maintaining perfect relaxation in every muscle of her body, as if that proved that she could kiss, yet remain apart. Only their lips meshed; no other part of their bodies touched, and she experienced a kind of triumph when he slid his arm behind her shoulders, because that meant she had remained aloof while he surrendered to her allure.

Or did it? His lips seemed no more desperate or insistent than before, and she realized his move simply upped the stakes. He challenged her to keep her composure while he touched her.

Very well. She drew back, smiled into his eyes, and slid her hands up his arms to his shoulders.

At her tactic, his eyes narrowed.

Still smiling, she leaned in and kissed him again. With a slight thrill of enthusiasm, she identified that which made him such a worthy opponent. Beneath the clean scent of soap and fresh linens, a subtle scent clung to him. Not perfume, but rather it seemed his skin and hair were imbued with the fragrance of him. He had wonderful lips, plush as velvet, well shaped, yet skilled at imparting wordless compliments that brought a warmth to her skin. And, most important, with her eyes closed, she didn't have to look upon his garments.

When the last consideration popped into her head, she smiled against his lips, an openmouthed smile, and some imp of mischief led her to touch her tongue to his lower lip. Just a touch. Just a tease.

And his surprise brought a puff of his breath into her mouth. It was heady, like good wine, and intimate, like . . . she didn't know like what. Nothing she had ever done compared to this. There was nothing in her lesson journal about this. She had to improvise . . . but she was the best. She would improvise.

She found herself kneading his shoulders, her fingertips sinking into the muscle beneath his jacket.

She didn't remember the last time she had been so close to another human being. So close that she could inhale his warmth, revel in his closeness. This should have felt forbidden; instead it felt right. It felt lovely. It felt . . . amazing. Parts of her stirred, parts she had never before realized were alive.

He glowed with life, and it was that glow that attracted her, pulled her in. Her arms glided around his neck, and she slid close—or he did—close enough that her breasts almost touched his chest. Barely touched his chest. The contact caused her nipples to pucker into buds so tight they ached.

At the age of fourteen, when her father had sent her to visit the Lake District with an eye to giving her a sophisticated polish, she had stood on top of a peak, felt the wind on her face, viewed the sweep, the power of the mountains and the horizon.

Sitting here, against him, she again sipped that grandeur, breathed that fresh and glorious air that lifted her on the wings of . . . of life.

His fingers traced the cords of her neck, the thrust of her jaw, the height of her cheekbones. They slipped between their lips, breaking the kiss, yet extending it as he investigated the contours of her mouth, pressing and caressing like a man enamored. With her eyes closed, she let him caress the curves of her ears, the arch of her brows. To a woman who missed her mother's touch, whose father had been distant and critical, who had only a younger sister's love and had been denied that for four years, this exploration was a bounty of rapture, a feast of pleasure. It was sensation and glory. He burnished her lips with his touch.

Then he kissed her again.

She kissed him back. She welcomed the warm blade of his tongue into the cavern of her mouth and tasted him with a kind of amazement. Every part of her, her skin, her breast, her belly, her heart—expanded with pleasure.

He pulled her close. So close. Hard against him. His arms enclosed her at shoulder and waist. His palms moved along her spine and at the base of her neck.

They matched from hip to shoulder. The heat of him seared her with desire and burned away pretense.

She wanted, just once, to be the *femme fatale* who drove a man wild. Who drove Huntington mad.

She twisted her fingers in his hair and kissed him again, one last, deep and glorious mating of mouth to mouth.

When she was finished, he unhurriedly drew away from her. Her eyes opened, dazed with the bliss of giving a man such lavish pleasure. She looked into his eyes, into the glorious pure color of temptation, and wondered if she should kiss him again and halt the words that trembled to be spoken.

But she didn't. She couldn't. That would be beyond a single moment of indulgence. That would be stupidity.

His hands fell away. He cleared his throat, and with husky emphasis, he said, "We should not do that again."

"Of course not." Her voice squeaked. She moderated her tone. "I don't exactly know what got into us."

"Nothing more than the spirit of competition, I believe." His words denied his passion, but his hot gaze told a different story.

"Whatever it was we wanted to prove, we have proved." From somewhere in the shaken depths of her soul, she dredged up a smile.

"Absolutely." He eased away with a grimace of discomfort. "You should not think this is any indication of disrespect on my part. I hold you in the highest esteem, and admire you for every reason."

"I thank you for your assurance." With vague surprise, she realized that she never for a moment doubted his respect. "When one sits with a man on a sofa, one works very hard at attraction, and the whole lesson seemed to have developed into a competition between us, and we were egging each other on until we ended up . . . doing . . . things which . . ." She ran out of words.

He took up the thought. "It was almost a dare. An unspoken dare to see which of us was best. And I would say . . . what would you say?"

"Oh." A blush burned its way from her chest to her forehead. "I would say it was a draw."

"Exactly what I would say."

"Now our curiosity is out of the way, and we can go on and—" And what? Her mind went blank.

"And flirt," he said firmly. "These are, after all, flirting lessons, and it was the success of the lesson that carried us away."

"Exactly."

"You teach marvelously well."

She inclined her head, realized strands of her hair had once more slipped free of their pins. "And you learn very quickly."

"I'm naturally a quick study." He straightened the crumpled linen of his cravat.

"At this rate, you'll be ready for the party your father intends to give." She managed not to reach up and assist him. "A tea."

"You'll attend, of course." He sounded as autocratic as his father.

"I'll discreetly slip in and observe, but as I explained to your father, I can't pretend to be a guest. I'm not respectable." That aggravated her, too. She had been respectable once, until Lord Freshfield had destroyed her life.

And why did that suddenly bother her? Before she'd come to Nevett's town house, she'd considered the matter a bitter lesson learned by a foolish girl, one that Caroline had resigned herself to paying the price. Now, all of a sudden, it seemed so unfair!

The memory of Nicolette's words came back to her. *You were young. . . . You were inexperienced. What happened was not your fault—but you and you alone have suffered. . . . If it were me, I would be angry.*

It was as if Nicolette had given Caroline permission to be angry. Which didn't make sense. Caroline wasn't angry. She wasn't.

Things were looking up. Why should she brood about a past she couldn't change? She didn't understand the change in herself. She didn't understand it at all.

"We'll see about that," he said crisply.

Recalled to the conversation, Caroline asked, "About what? Oh, the tea. No, I won't be attending." While she pinned up her hair, she wondered at her annoyance at the thought of sharing him.

To her relief, he didn't argue. "What is the next lesson?"

"If the weather is good, we shall walk in the garden, pretend it is the zoological gardens, and flirt among the animals. If it's dreary, we'll practice playing cards and the many ways of flirtation at the card table. Or we can play instruments and sing. Or we'll practice indoor games like charades. As your governess"—she experienced the need to remind him of their roles—"I have a full schedule planned for you."

"So we'll do this again tomorrow."

"Most assuredly—although not the kissing."

"No." He sighed as if regretting the stipulation. "Not the kissing."

* * *

In her room, Caroline took her lesson journal, opened it, and stared at the words she'd written with such hope and care.

Week 1: Test Lord Huntington to see if his command of basic social skills are tolerable. Improve if necessary.

Taking up her pen, she dipped it into the ink and added below:

Lord Huntington is competent in dance and conducts himself well in the drawing room.

Then she nibbled on the tip of the pen, and added:

Although I know little about the matter, he seems also to be quite competent in romantic and physical matters, and his wife will be a happy woman.

Chapter 13

"Caroline, you have to come at once." Nicolette wrung her hands. "It's a disaster."

Caroline put aside her needlework and rose. "But the guests arrived not ten minutes ago. What's happened?" Her eyes narrowed. "What has *he* done?"

"The young ladies immediately started skirting wide circles around Jude." Catching Caroline's hand, Nicolette dragged her out of the library. "Come and see. He's boring everyone to death, and Nevett will have a fit!"

Caroline hurried behind Nicolette toward the great drawing room. She had planned to allow thirty minutes before she slipped in to listen and observe. Thirty minutes, she reasoned, would give the participants time to settle into their roles and Huntington time to work his magic on some poor, unsuspecting young lady. Using the skills he had exhibited in the past week, Huntington would be well on his way to at least one flirtation, and perhaps two or three. Caroline had been mentally counting her money—and ignoring any regrets. A single kiss between her and Huntington exchanged almost a week ago was no reason to imagine anything more could happen between them. After all, they had thus far resisted the temptation to taste the forbidden fruits again, although at night when the lights were out and all was quiet, Caroline worried that he would try to kiss her again . . . and she would yield.

"Listen to him," Nicolette commanded.

If Caroline and Huntington had been alone, Caroline wasn't sure she would have been able to resist Huntington. As he said, their kiss had been a natural outgrowth of their flirting, and every day since, he'd improved his techniques. It didn't help that they had the same sense of humor. When they argued, and they *did* argue, they did so with wit and logic. They made Nicolette laugh and Nevett occasionally poked his head in the door to observe, so he said, but mostly he stayed and laughed, too.

Caroline experienced a deep satisfaction in her pupil's progress—a progress that had apparently been temporary.

Standing outside the open door, Caroline heard the murmurs of a dozen conversations and the music of piano and harp, yet she picked out Huntington's voice at once. She thought—she feared—she would recognize his voice anywhere.

He was saying, "*I* predict that the newest French fashions will sweep London, and *I* shall be at the forefront of the revolution. A second French revolution, and in England! It will be named after *moi*. Ha ha!"

Peeking around the corner, she saw a party like so many others she'd attended: ladies and gentlemen of all ages sat or stood in the great drawing room, conversed, flirted, or gossiped.

By virtue of his costume and his mannerisms, Huntington made himself conspicuous. He spoke to a debutante seated beside him on a sofa. She must be in her second Season, or even her third, for she wore the arch expression that lifted the eyebrows and gave the illusion nothing worried her, when in fact she must perpetually fear she would be left on the shelf to become someone's maiden aunt.

And Huntington, oh dear, Huntington did the annoying handkerchief flip in her face—and his white handkerchief had a large JD embroidered in black thread on every corner.

Unfortunately for Caroline's peace of mind, she no longer winced at the sight of his clothing, for first and foremost she saw the man who wore them—and that troubled her.

More worrisome was her reaction to the kiss. She wanted to taste Huntington again, and for more reasons than inconvenient desire. An emotion she didn't recognize bubbled within her, a sort of savage satisfaction that she'd done exactly what she'd been accused of. She'd kissed a man in improper circumstances. She had lusted. She had tasted. She had enjoyed.

And she felt no regret. None at all.

"You must admit," Huntington was saying, "my ensemble is extraordinarily handsome and goes marvelously well with my teeth."

"His teeth!" Nicolette hissed at Caroline.

"I heard him." Caroline wished she hadn't.

"My teeth are extraordinarily straight and white, don't you agree, Lady Amanda?"

"Extraordinarily." The poor girl smiled gamely at him and stared as if she were fascinated.

"I find a liberal amount of toothpowder applied with

my finger is the secret." He inspected her own bright white teeth. "You should consider trying it."

Caroline's eyes widened in horror.

Lady Amanda's smile vanished. Standing, she flounced away.

"He's awful," Nicolette moaned. "I tell you, he was raised better than that!"

Everything Caroline had heard about him concurred. She'd made a point of inquiring of the servants what he'd been like as a child. She asked Harry to see if he could ferret out any gossip about the middle son of the Durant family. Everything pointed to a normal, even austere gentleman of sober tastes. "I wonder what happened?" Caroline mused.

"France happened," Nicolette declared heatedly. "France and Italy and Moricadia and Morocco and all those dreadful countries have given him airs."

"Has he been behaving like this at every gathering he attends?" Caroline, fascinated and appalled, watched him. Indeed, it looked as though almost everyone in the room observed him, unable to tear their gazes away from the spectacle of Lord Huntington making a jackass of himself.

"I don't know. We've been in mourning. I haven't attended any events. But this explains Jude's inability to attract a mate." Nicolette faced her. "You have to come in. You can make him behave. You *have* to make him behave."

Huntington's behavior might be a ploy to make Caroline attend the tea—she well remembered his intention to get her here—but that didn't explain his reputation as a crashing bore, nor did it explain those clothes.

As if she followed Caroline's thoughts, Nicolette said, "His clothing! What possessed him to wear that costume? The debutantes could overlook his prosing on and on, they're used to that from the gentlemen, but combined with that . . ."

"I'm at a loss." Caroline wondered if he'd gone to special lengths to be outrageous at this tea, or if that was his idea of appropriate afternoon dress.

He wore a white shirt, a black cravat, a quilted aqua waistcoat, and a short black cape. The outfit would be acceptable, if eccentric, but he had also donned striped trousers—aqua-and-white-striped trousers in a pattern that seemed to move when one stared at it. And to finish off his ensemble, one white boot had an aqua tassel swinging from the front; the other was plain. He was a symphony of bad taste, and in his behavior and his clothing, Caroline saw her chance of success slipping away.

"Very well. I'll go in." Caroline brushed at imaginary wrinkles on her new gown and steeled herself for this, her debut into society after years of retreat. When she thought about entering that room filled with gentlemen who, four years ago, had courted her, ladies who had been shocked by her downfall, and debutantes to whom her story had been a cautionary tale, she cringed inside. But she didn't complain; if humiliation was the price she paid to win her freedom, then she would suffer humiliation.

The agony of that emotion wouldn't last. The cash would.

As she walked into the gathering arm in arm with the duchess of Nevett, she reflected this humiliation was undoubtedly ameliorated by the sheer weight of Nicolette's noble title.

The murmur of conversation and the notes of the piano and harp died away. The gentlemen got to their feet. The young ladies glanced between the two arrivals as if uncertain. The older ladies looked alternately affronted or amazed.

Fixing a smile on her lips, Caroline took care to breathe slowly. She looked over the group without meeting anyone's eye.

Then one face stood out from the crowd. A grin broke across Turgoose's amiable face, and he left his place by the piano to come forward and bow. "Your Grace, what a marvelous surprise. You've brought us Miss Ritter!" He spoke clearly and calmly, as if about a pleasant but unsurprising event. "Miss Ritter, I've so looked forward to seeing you again."

"And I you, Mr. Turgoose." She was aware what an incongruous couple they made. Even with heels on his boots, he wasn't quite her height, and in his own way he was as much of a dandy as Huntington. Yet she would never forget his kindness four years ago. Nor did she underestimate his courage in greeting her now, for although she had taken care not to actually look at anyone, she had seen the birdlike black eyes of his mother fixed on her. Goose would be taken to task for his championship of Caroline.

The buzz of conversation started again, a little lower this time as the guests tried to discern why Caroline was there and what their proper reaction should be.

Huntington swooped in, his short cape fluttering behind him. "Goose always has the eye for the handsomest lady in the room."

The piano and the harp started playing again, sharply and quickly. Huntington had just made sure every female there eyed Caroline with disfavor, and her cool smile contained an edge she hoped he recognized. "A sincere compliment is a lady's finest friend, my lord, and while I doubt not your sincerity, I must ask—is your opinion of beauty to be trusted?" She heard a small gasp from a plain young woman seated stiffly between two young men.

Both young men, Caroline noted, wore cravats of brilliant hues.

Nicolette moved to rescue the conversation. "Or perhaps it is his sincerity that's at fault. For often he's told me *I'm* the handsomest lady in London."

Goose chuckled. "Right enough. Huntington's a ramshackle sort of fraud."

"Exactly." The accented voice came from behind Caroline. "Lord Huntington cannot be trusted with his compliments. Miss Ritter, depend upon me for the truth."

She turned to see an older gentleman. His shock of white-blond hair sprang in abundance around his thin, aristocratic face and in the middle of his forehead his hairline formed a point. His bow was courtly, European in flavor, and with a shock, she recognized him. "Comte de Guignard, my rescuer in the park." She lavished a smile on him. After all, it wasn't his fault she hadn't really needed rescuing. He had been as gallant as a dream. "Or one of my rescuers. Where is Monsieur Bouchard?"

"I am here." Monsieur Bouchard stepped forward, a man so overburdened by his mustache that it looked as though the weight of it had dragged the hair off his head. When she'd met him in the park, he'd been smoking a fat brown cigar, and he had smelled of the smoke. Although the cigar was gone, he reeked. He made an abrupt bow, and she thought he must come from a common background, more common even than her own, for his social graces seemed tacked on, learned late in life and not at all a part of his personality. "You are recovered."

"I am. Thank you both for being so chivalrous to a lady you didn't know." She spoke to them, but she directed the message at the hovering Lord Huntington. "Your kindness lit a warmth in my heart."

Comte de Guignard was in the prime of life; in other words, at that delicate age where men realized they were no longer the youngest and strongest males in the pack, and they always made fools of themselves over younger women. Caroline had seen it occur time and again; she smiled, she spoke, she teased, and the gentlemen became infatuated. She never intended for it to happen; she simply pandered to their vanity and their disappearing youth, and suddenly they fell in love with her.

Now she saw it occur again. At her words, Comte de Guignard straightened his already straight spine, pulled back his muscled shoulders, and jutted his chin. "It was a pleasure I've dwelled on, hoping to renew our social contact, but alas, although I looked, I saw you nowhere."

"Yes. Speaking of contact, Miss Ritter, I see you've furthered your friendship with Lord Huntington." Monsieur Bouchard's eyes flicked between her and Huntington. It sounded like a statement, but it was a question, and rather an authoritative one.

Obviously, Monsieur Bouchard didn't fall in love as easily as Comte de Guignard, and his query brought all the assembly straining to hear her answer.

But Caroline didn't have to—didn't want to— explain her connection with Huntington, so she used her smile with a hint of reserve. "I have." She glanced around the small gathering, and with humor in her tone, said, "He improves on acquaintance."

"Miss Ritter is a friend of mine," Nicolette said easily. "We had lost track of each other, and I was delighted to find her again. I'm sure you'll frequently see us together. In fact, she's staying with us."

Caroline saw the news travel from one ear to another until it had reached the far edges of the drawing room. She wouldn't have been surprised to discover that it hopped out the window and flew through the streets of London like some kind of gossip bird that squawked like a town crier. *Miss Ritter is the guest of the duke of Nevett and his wife, and their son visits frequently.*

As she'd feared, this arrangement held all the hallmarks of disaster. She had to move quickly to establish her presence was not of a romantic nature. Unless one could call one extremely glorious kiss romantic—which she did not.

"Like all English ladies, Miss Ritter appreciates my social graces and the advice I can give her about the ways of the Continent." Huntington preened like a peacock.

Ah. Her chance came at once. "I beg you, my lord, don't put words in my mouth. I can speak for myself, and while Comte de Guignard and Monsieur Bouchard bring a Continental flare to our gathering"—Caroline extended a gracious hand to Comte de Guignard—"it's the English ladies who make the gathering bloom."

"You are wise. It is indeed the captivating ladies who brought us to England." Comte de Guignard took her hand and bowed over it, then bowed again, a flawless, elegant bow that included all the company. "And their kindness to visitors that keeps us on your shores."

A spattering of applause proved they had the attention of the nearby company, and provided unexpected approval to Caroline.

"Well said, Comte de Guignard," Nicolette said.

"We're enchanted to have you and Monsieur Bouchard with us today."

"Ecstatic!" Huntington flapped his handkerchief like an overenthusiastic spaniel.

The ladies in the room turned away as if embarrassed by his gusto, and Caroline wanted to groan. He had to marry, and if he couldn't cajole a lady in this charitable gathering to sit with him, it would be impossible to find him a mate in society. Driven to distraction and despair, she caught his hand, halting the flip of the handkerchief, and hissed, "What are you doing? *Stop* that at once!"

She must have said it a little too loud, for conversation faded, then picked up again. She glanced from side to side, met gazes that sidled away, and blushed hotly.

"Of course." Huntington put his handkerchief into his waistcoat pocket. "I obey you implicitly."

"Pish-tosh!" she retorted sharply. "Ladies hear such promises, and none of us expect them to be fulfilled."

"Miss Ritter. You have wounded me deeply!" But Huntington's mouth lifted in an abashed grin.

The ladies tittered, the gentlemen guffawed, and the company relaxed.

At last Caroline dared to look around—and at once caught the cold, beady gaze of Lady Reederman. Lady Reederman didn't pretend to converse, nor did she make welcome the female she had once publicly and deliberately cut. Instead she observed, withholding her judgment for one reason and one reason only— because the duchess of Nevett sponsored Caroline. Lady Reederman might not like to keep quiet, but she prided herself on her exceptional propriety, and as Nicolette's guest she would do nothing that could be interpreted as a criticism of her hostess. But her basilisk gaze gave Caroline to understand that she would never approve of a young lady whose past was decidedly shady.

Turgoose must have seen the direction of Caroline's gaze, or noticed his mother's imitation of a lemon ice, for he said, "You're so amusing, Miss Ritter. The fellows all agree society has been a wasteland without your most excellent company."

Nicolette stepped between Lady Reederman and Caroline. "Miss Ritter, might I introduce those who are unknown to you?"

Caroline hesitated, and Jude thought she was tempted to beg off. Her conflict was real, he knew. She faced the prospect of chilly greetings, and those were kind compared to the reaction she would have confronted without his stepmother's patronage. Yet when he was done with her, she'd thank him for introducing her into society once more. And he would thank her for confusing and distracting the Moricadians.

"I would consider it a privilege to meet your guests, Your Grace," Caroline said with dignity.

No one read the look she shot him, but he followed on her unspoken command.

Turgoose hurried after them.

De Guignard and Bouchard put their heads together and spoke softly, no doubt wondering at Huntington's fascination with the woman he had had no time for before. Even now they considered him a fool, easily led, and he thought, with a little more prodding, they might try to use him in their plan. He couldn't imagine either one of them wanted to dirty their hands with the details, and he would willingly be their pawn.

With every evidence of keenness, he walked back to them, and said, "I have left off fighting my enthrallment, and surrender to her magic. She is almost French in her magnificence, is she not?"

"She is lovely," de Guignard agreed.

"As she was only a week ago," Bouchard added.

"Your admiration for her made me realize her quality," Jude said. "I find myself guided by your superior sophistication. Fancy that!"

"Yes." Bouchard considered him closely. "Fancy that."

"You must someday allow me to share your activities. For a single day, I would love to do as you do!"

"Perhaps it can be arranged," de Guignard said.

"Truly?" Jude laid a hand on his cheek. "Oh, venerable day! I await your notice." Then he left to rejoin the little group making a tour of the room, for although he wanted to look anxious to please, he didn't want to be too anxious; Bouchard was sharp and suspicious, and if he smelled the slightest whiff of conspiracy, all Jude's work would be undone.

"This is Miss Foley and her sister, Miss Lydia," he heard Mum say as she introduced Caroline to the pianist and the harpist. "They are the belles of the Season."

"For more reasons than their beauty! Miss Foley, Miss Lydia, your music is enchanting. I wish I had an ounce of your talent." Caroline displayed a remarkable ability to inject the right admiration into her tone, for the Foley sisters blushed, murmured disclaimers, and looked delighted.

"Miss Ritter, I believe you know my sister, Lady James," Miss Foley said shyly. "She says you are friends."

"She speaks of you often," Miss Lydia added.

Miss Ritter smiled a slow, incredulous smile.

Because he couldn't help himself, Jude smiled, too.

Then he noticed everyone in their circle was smiling, bemused smiles, unwilling smiles, amazed smiles. Her pleasure was contagious, a blessing they all shared. He felt the pride of ownership—foolish when she so obviously needed no man. He felt the tug of lust—madness when they'd shared only one kiss. A kiss that had seared itself into his mind and loins and made him want what he couldn't have. A kiss that had sent him all over town, stalking the Moricadians night and day rather than face hours in his bed alone.

"I do know Lady James!" Miss Ritter put her hand over her heart. "As you are, she was the belle of my Season, beautiful and gracious. When next you see her, extend her my greeting."

Stepping to Nicolette's side, Jude murmured, "I see you larded the guest list with people likely to be compatible with Miss Ritter."

"You cannot fault me for inviting guests whom I knew would be congenial," Nicolette murmured back.

"No hostess wants to be known for an acrimonious gathering." He glanced toward the circle of chairs where the matrons sat. "But I don't think it's all going to be smooth sailing."

Mum flicked a glance in that direction. "Ah, Lady Reederman. As always, the maggot in the punch bowl."

Jude coughed to disguise his laughter.

"Don't worry. I'll take care of *her*," Mum said in a steely tone. "I've grown fond of Miss Ritter. I have no intention of allowing anyone to cause her awkwardness."

"Lord Huntington, have you met these lovely young ladies?" Caroline asked. She drew him into the musical circle.

Under her tutelage, he became a likely suitor to the Misses Foley.

But he didn't linger when Mum moved Miss Ritter to the next group. Even without his plan to distract society with his courtship of Miss Ritter, he wouldn't have remained behind. The Misses Foley were sweet and attractive, young and insipid, and of no interest to him.

A tense moment occurred when Mum presented Miss Ritter to Lady Reederman, but Miss Ritter curtsied, and Lady Reederman inclined her head, and nothing untoward happened.

Finally, Miss Ritter and her ever-growing entourage arrived at the sofa where a vaguely familiar young lady sat with Lord Merrill-Sanersone and Lord Hollis. Both young men wore bright cravats, and they were trying to please the lady. Odd, for she was no beauty.

"Lady Pheodora Osgood of the Rochdale Osgoods, this is Miss Ritter," Mum said.

Lady Pheodora, Lady Pheodora . . . oh, Lady Pheodora. Ahh, Lady Pheodora from the park. Lady Pheodora whom he'd mistaken for his governess. She looked better than she had last week, not quite as plain. She sported a new hairstyle or had done something with her garments. Or perhaps it was simply an increased belief in her own charms. "Lady Pheodora, we meet again."

Looking disconcerted, she pushed her spectacles up her nose. "Yes. Yes, we do. Did you have more lessons in the park?"

Obviously, she didn't have any idea what she was asking, and everyone in the vicinity looked between Jude and Lady Pheodora with a puzzled interest.

She had probably thought him crazy, and thinking

back on their conversation, he didn't blame her. "I've restricted my lessons to the schoolroom," he said gravely. "But thank you for asking. You're most kind."

The suitors stood until the introductions were completed, then bowed almost reverently to Jude. "Lord Huntington," Lord Hollis said, "I think I speak for us both when I say how very much we admire your bold style."

"Really?" Jude's gaze lingered on those cravats. "Some say I've done a terrible thing by introducing such excesses into society."

"But you don't listen, do you, Huntington?" Lord Merrill-Sanersone said enthusiastically. "You go your own way without a care for anyone's opinion."

"Apparently," Jude said with a dry wit that no one noticed—except that Caroline cocked her head and examined him a little too closely. With a jolt, he realized he'd have to be careful around her. She was coming to know him too well, and pulling his handkerchief from his pocket, he waved it like a flag before a bull. He knew very well how that irritated her.

And as a distraction, it worked marvelously well. Her eyes narrowed on him, and as if her unspoken reprimand made him remember his manners, he tucked the handkerchief away once more.

Turning her attention to Lady Pheodora once more, Caroline said, "I know this is incredibly impertinent, but who made your indoor cap? I would love to imitate you."

Lady Pheodora touched the lacy bit of froth in her hair with astonishment. As if a dam had burst, she said, "*Do* you like it? Dear Mama said it wouldn't do, but I designed it myself and sewed it from Belgian lace. Mama said I had better listen to my cousin Letty about fashion, but I don't always agree with her, especially about this. I thought my cap was pretty."

"Not to disagree with your dear mama, but you have exceptional taste." Miss Ritter's voice was warm and persuasive.

Jude noted that the other ladies leaned closer and listened as the two discussed the style, and he realized that between him and Miss Ritter they would be responsible for some of the worst fashion quirks since his grandmother's dampened gown.

If he *were* in need of social instruction, she would be the ideal teacher, for she demonstrated a gift for saying the right thing to set everyone at ease.

And if he were Michael, he'd enjoy this brush with passion. He would kiss her because pretty girls were meant to be kissed. If she offered herself, he would take her. And when the time came for Miss Ritter to sail off to France, Michael would escort her to the docks. With great affection he would wave her off, and before the ship was out of sight he would have forgotten about her. Jude wasn't Michael, for he had begun to suspect he would never forget Caroline Ritter.

With a glance out the door at the hovering servants, Mum said, "The tea is ready. We shall serve."

At once Phillips appeared, leading a parade of liveried footmen bearing cups and saucers, pitchers of cream, and bowls of sugar. Without making a sound, they set up on the immense sideboard.

Goose took Miss Ritter's hand and started toward a sofa.

"Move aside, man." Jude jostled him. "Let the rest of us have a chance."

"I say!" Turgoose sputtered. "You shan't take my place."

"What about m . . . me?" Lord Vickers was not yet twenty and had fallen instantly in love with Miss Ritter, and he stammered with youthful indignation. "I should have a ch . . . chance with her."

"What about *you?*" The twenty-five-year-old marquess of Routledge smiled with all the confidence of a man with wealth, title, and comeliness. "What about *me?* I'm *desolated* by Miss Ritter's reserve."

Turning his gaze on Caroline, Jude got a shock.

As she gazed on the assemblage determined to admire her, she looked different. Like a temptress, like an accomplished flirt, like a woman who knew how to hold men in thrall with a glance of her slumberous eyes. He saw the woman she might have become if catastrophe hadn't overtaken her, and that woman was irresistible to him.

A swift look around confirmed his suspicions. Every man here watched her with hungry desire, their eyes alight.

Then she changed. She stood upright, looked stern, and spoke briskly. "Gentlemen, I value your flattery as it deserves. Now go"—she glared meaningfully at Jude—"away."

He did, spent the rest of the tea splitting his time between Lady Pheodora and the Misses Foley, and afterward remembered not a damned word they said.

But the memory of Miss Ritter's seductive moment haunted him all through the night.

Chapter 14

"*Dear*, you should have seen it." Nicolette swept into the library, talking as she came. "She made him behave."

"Miss Ritter made Jude behave?" Nevett put down his newspaper and looked over his glasses at his wife. Her eyes were snapping, her cheeks stained with color. She looked alive for the first time in months, and something inside him, something that had been tense for far too long, relaxed. "How did she do that?"

"He was acting like a fool, flapping his handkerchief and insulting the ladies by suggesting how they could improve their costumes and their teeth—"

"Their teeth?" Nevett showed his own teeth in annoyance.

"Yes, their teeth." Nicolette's exasperation couldn't be more clear. "I couldn't do anything with him. He ignored my glares, and he's a little old for me to take him by the ear and drag him away to sit in a corner, so I ran to get Caroline. She put up with his silliness for a few minutes, then she snapped at him—and from that moment on, he was the perfect gentleman. He charmed all the ladies. They're still gossiping about the change in him, I vow, and Lady Pheodora could scarcely take her eyes off him." Nicolette subsided in the chair opposite Nevett. "Although I thought her examination seemed more wary than infatuated."

Nevett cast the paper aside. Was this news of a potential daughter-in-law? "Who's Lady Pheodora?"

"Lady Pheodora Osgood of the Rochdale Osgoods."

Nevett searched his mind until he remembered the connection. "A family of singularly plain people. Is *she* a beauty?"

"Not at all." Nicolette giggled softly. "Do we care? She's female, she's English, and she's breathing."

"Are we in such desperate straits?"

"*I'm* not. You're the one who's so worried about grandchildren you hired a governess for your adult son." Swinging her foot, Nicolette flipped off her slipper. "Other females could easily be lured into his net if he used the proper bait."

"It irks me that he has to fish at all. In my time, I was chased by all the—" Nevett abruptly recalled his listener and shut his mouth.

"You were chased by all the debutantes." Nicolette dimpled at him. "*I* don't remember it like that."

"Not with you," he said gruffly. With one look he'd been smitten and felt a right old fool for imagining himself in love with warm eyes and a gentle smile. He had told himself he was the duke of Nevett, that he was doing Nicolette a favor by making her a duchess, and he had settled a substantial sum of pin money on her. He'd made sure his sons would treat her well in the event of his death, and the arrival of another son had puffed his conceit and given him yet more hope for the future.

Then Michael's death had broken both their hearts and set him on a new mission—to get Jude married and the future of the family secured.

It was only in the last few days, with that governess underfoot all the time—did she never return to her home?—that he'd realized he'd accomplished two goals. Nicolette no longer sat alone and read, or stared into space, and not once had he come upon her when she had tears on her cheeks. She was lively and amused, and for that he was grateful to his damned foolish-looking son and the spirited Miss Ritter.

As if she read his mind, Nicolette said, "I had to speak quite firmly to Lady Reederman about Miss Ritter."

"What did the old cat do now?"

"She *suggested* that I not invite such guests who would besmirch the other guests with a soiled reputation."

"Let me take care of the matter." He spoke coolly, but he was furious. Lady Reederman was, after all, only a countess, and one who frequently got above herself. This time she had gone too far. When he was done with her, she would never again admonish his duchess, nor would she ever dare criticize his company.

"I handled it." Nicolette's smile showed a hint of teeth. "I told her that if she wished to approve my guest list, she could take a position with the Distinguished Academy of Governesses as a social counselor and I would perhaps hire her. Until that day, I suggested she bully debutantes and green young men and others who are easily intimidated." She nodded firmly. "She didn't stay long after that."

"Brava!" Rising, he extended his hand to her. She

took it; he pulled her to her feet and into his arms. "You're magnificent."

"As magnificent as Miss Ritter?"

He wasn't blind. Miss Ritter was very attractive. But he wasn't stupid, either, and he blinked at his wife as if astonished. "I hadn't noticed. Is she supposed to be magnificent, too?"

Nicolette laughed and linked her arms around his neck. "That was exactly the right thing to say." And she kissed him.

He was the luckiest man in the world.

"I've never enjoyed the zoo as much as I have today." Jude lifted his mouth from Caroline's and watched as her head fell back against his shoulder.

Her eyes were closed. She gave a shuddering sigh, and the smile on her lips made him want to kiss her again.

As they walked through Nevett's gardens, they had pretended to be at the Royal Zoological Gardens. They had giggled at the monkeys' antics (which the unimaginative might say was nothing more than the waving of branches in the wind) and watched the elephants stomp in their cages (homing pigeons in their crates). It had been a carefree day filled with enticing banter. Even when he professed to be affected by French mannerisms and overwhelmed with concern for his style, she hadn't cared. She'd teased him, gently dragging him back to his real self, and he'd found her insight to be irresistible.

Finally, it had ended like this, with passionate kisses he knew should never take place.

"Now we must behave." She brushed her glorious, flyaway hair back from her delicate face. The sunshine turned her tan complexion to gold, and the color in her pink cheeks matched the early roses that bloomed in the arbor around them. "For we swore we wouldn't kiss again."

She was a splendid creature, with a husky voice and skin the texture of a baby's, and Jude couldn't keep his hands off her. "How can we help it?" He lowered his voice to a rasping whisper, and with exaggerated alarm said, "We're trapped behind the lion's cage. He's roaring at us, furious that I have taken his lioness for my own."

Caroline laughed a protest, her teeth gleaming, her exotic eyes sparkling with pleasure.

"He wants to rip my throat out, but I'll face any danger to possess the graceful strength and the glorious mane of the most graceful and dangerous cat of all— the Caroline-cat."

Lowering her head, she looked at him through her lashes. "You're ridiculous."

She was right about everything. He was ridiculous, and they shouldn't be hiding in the garden and kissing. But although he knew better, he couldn't resist the innocent taste of her mouth.

Leaning into her, he brushed her lips, again and again, until like a flower to the sun, she lifted her face to his. The scent of the roses was thick around them, but not so rich and sweet as the scent of her hair. He pressed his body against hers, trying to meld them into one, and he wanted to do so much more than that. He wanted to carry her off to his bedroom and ravish her like a lion triumphant.

Only two things stopped him. He couldn't take this woman who had been subjected to so much indignity and agony and strip her of the one thing she still possessed—her innocence. His actions were even more nefarious when he considered his intention to use her like a cape waved before the bull of society. The ton now knew that Lord Huntington paid court to the infamous Miss Caroline Ritter, and the resulting fuss would keep the two Moricadians distracted and entertained while Jude discovered, and put a stop to, their plans.

But he didn't want to think of the Moricadians just then. For the first time since Michael had been murdered, Jude felt alive. In fact . . . he'd never felt so alive in his life. "Teacher, will you give a good report of me to my father?" he teased.

Caroline caught her breath. "I always give him a good report."

"What does he say about that?"

"He wants to know why you're still wearing those ridiculous clothes."

Jude looked down at himself in feigned indignation. "Some men have no sense of style no matter how carefully they're shown the way."

"Hm. Yes."

He loved watching her prevaricate. "Don't you love my style?"

"I've come to accept it, which is not quite the same." She started to withdraw her hands from around his neck. "We should stop."

"We should." But he caught her to him, turned her until she was pressed against the warm rough stone wall, and kissed her again. Her breasts rested against his chest, and her lips opened beneath his.

Yet she did more than passively accept his attentions. She sought them; she answered him in a way that fired his blood. That was her secret; she was a maiden, yes, but she was no shrinking violet. She was brave, she was strong . . .

He murmured, "You're a lioness."

"I know." She used her teeth to nibble his lip. "Sometimes I think . . . I mean I wonder . . ."

"What?" he asked, intrigued by the diffidence with which his usually straightforward governess spoke.

"The duchess said something to me the first day I came here, and I've thought about it ever since. She said I must be angry about the way my father and society treated me." Caroline smiled as if inviting him to laugh at her.

Yet why had she brought it up? "Are you?"

"Don't be ridiculous! Why would I be? You know the story of my disgrace, of course."

"I do." He allowed her to push him away. "I agree with Mum. You were shamefully used and cruelly punished, while Freshie was lauded for his virility, and you were so much less able to care for yourself. If someone had played such a trick on me, *I'd* be furious."

"Well, I'm not," she said quickly.

Thinking of his reaction to Michael's death, he said, "I'd want revenge."

"No! Revenge. Indeed not." She fussed with the ribbons on her bonnet. "I take total responsibility for my foolishness."

"Yet you're still thinking about what Mum said to you."

"I am not still thinking about it."

"Of course you are, or you wouldn't have said—"

Her lips curled back, baring her teeth, like a lioness on the attack.

He recognized that expression. He'd seen his step-

mother wear it when one of her sons—or Nevett—
pushed her too far. Jude knew he had two choices.
Conciliate—or run.

He didn't want to run. He wanted to be there with
Caroline, so he set himself to soothing her. "I think the
tea yesterday was a marvelous success, don't you?"

Her tautness eased. Her eyes, which had been fierce,
became thoughtful, interested . . . focused on him. "No,
I don't. What were you thinking? Your performance at
the tea yesterday was a disgrace. Flipping your handkerchief! Prosing on about me when you should have
been praising the debutantes!"

"I didn't mean to displease you." Jude liked knowing
he had brought her attention back to him. To them. "I
got confused."

"Confused?" She rested against the garden wall.

He put one hand on either side of her head and leaned
toward her, close enough that his lips touched hers with
each movement. "I flirt with you during my lessons,
and it seemed natural to flirt with you at the tea."

"That's prattle." She strove to sound normal, but he
caught the faint breathlessness in her voice.

"Truly! It's easy to flirt with you. I know what to say,
how to act. Those other girls are young and silly. They
don't appreciate me or my advice."

"So few of us do."

He laughed. "Once I mastered the art of attending to
the ladies, I thought I did well."

"Yes," she admitted, "once you mastered it you did
do well."

She didn't realize how much attention had been paid
to her instruction and the meekness with which he followed it. She didn't realize that when she dispatched
him to visit with other young ladies, she sent a message

of absolute confidence in his attachment to her. Today society buzzed about Miss Ritter and Lord Huntington, and nothing the duke of Nevett said would make any difference to the rumors—that was supposing his father ever bothered to go into society, which he seldom did.

Did Mum know? Jude wouldn't venture a guess. She was an acute observer of human nature, but since Michael's death she hadn't bothered to look past the bounds of her own home. Perhaps she hadn't noticed the tension between Jude and Caroline, or perhaps she thought they had it under control.

He wished that was true. He couldn't resist Caroline. She was truly the finest flirt he'd ever met, but more than that, she tugged at his senses. For the first time since he'd returned from Moricadia, passion threatened to sweep him away. But while this seemed likely to become obsession, he held the reins in their relationship. She might tempt him unbearably, but ultimately, he was in control. He directed her movements. She would unwittingly help him, and be none the wiser and not hurt at all.

With that in mind, he incited trouble. "Comte de Guignard fell in love with you yesterday. I saw it happen."

"I know." Her eyes were serene.

"What will you do?" he asked curiously.

"Do?" She frowned, puzzled by the question. "Why, nothing, or nothing any different for him than for any other man who . . ."

"Who falls in love with you?"

She inclined her head. "It used to happen with great regularity. Now I'm more circumspect, and thus I avoid attention."

He wanted to laugh aloud at her artlessness. Goose was as in love with her as ever, young Vickers wallowed in love for her, even Routledge fancied himself a suitor. Still, he probed to see how greedy she might be. "But Comte de Guignard is wealthy, has a title, and he could take you away to a country where no one has ever heard of you."

"I've learned a few things since my debut. Just because a man loves me doesn't mean he wants to marry me—and I'm not going anywhere with anybody anyway." She made her statement with great satisfaction. "I'll never again expect a man to take care of me."

This situation required careful handling. "But Comte de Guignard is from the Continent, and surely older than your former suitors—"

"Most of them." She shrugged.

"You'll be considerate of his character, will you not?"

She looked startled. "Of course. I understand that men of his age are . . ."

While she hesitated, trying to be kind, he started laughing. "You're a dear, dear girl." He leaned down and with his mouth stirred the soft downy skin behind her ears. When she bent her head to accommodate him, his lips caressed her hairline. He took advantage of every movement, using each sweet yielding to make way for another wave of glory. He touched her face, her neck. A silver button rested in the base of her throat, and he found his fingers toying with it, opening it. Another button lay below that, and he opened that one, too. The baby-soft skin of her cheeks was softly tan; here the skin was paler, creamier, untouched by sun. He stroked her, exploring that tiny vee of flesh, and that one little liberty caused passion to rampage through him.

Swiftly he unbuttoned the rest of the buttons, opening them almost to her waist. Reverently he slid his hands beneath the material and parted the edges. Her undergarments were plain white and utilitarian, but he didn't care. It was the body beneath them that made his blood race. Her corset pressed up on her breasts, her chemise covered them, but in the sunshine, the material was almost transparent. He could see the glow of her skin and the darker shape of her aureoles and nipples. Cupping the sweet flesh, he moved his hands in slow circles and watched as her nipples tightened. He couldn't tear his gaze away from the sight, but he knew she watched him, lids heavy, and she made no move to stop him. The silence was profound; he couldn't hear birds or insects, he could hear only the panting as they breathed.

And he couldn't resist any longer. He wasn't going to hurt her. He wasn't going to take her. But he wanted, needed to taste her. Putting his mouth to her breast, he sucked on the nipple through the cloth. He drew it into his mouth, savoring the moment, the woman, the pleasure. Somehow he knew he'd never forget this moment in the sunlight and the fresh air with the scent of roses and of Caroline rich in his nostrils.

As he used his tongue on her, soft moans sounded from her delicately parted lips. Her head fell back against the wall. Her eyes closed. Her palms pressed tightly against the stone as if to restrain herself from touching him, and she trembled with need.

And he had to stop. It wasn't fair to use this girl, who had struggled so desperately to make a living, just because he couldn't maintain control of his own impulses.

Gathering her into his arms, he rested his cheek on her head and spoke into her hair. "I can't wait until the Lawrences' ball."

"Good. You want to go meet the ladies."

"Mum consulted me on your gown. I can't wait to see you in it." It was true. For the first time in his life, he was in the position of knowing just what a lady was going to wear—and anticipating her appearance. It was an odd feeling, almost proprietary, as if he were a husband.

"I'm not going," she answered coolly, but she allowed him to hold her.

"Of course you are. You have to supervise me." *You have to be there to charm de Guignard and Bouchard.*

"The gossip my presence would inspire would be disastrous for you and your cause."

"My cause." He was deadpan.

"Your father wishes you to be married, and you've said you wished it also." She disentangled herself from his embrace. Today, in this light, her eyes were the color of the green sea on a sunny day, and they ruthlessly considered him. "Is that not true?"

Of course it wasn't true. Jude had other plans on which to concentrate. The discovery of the Moricadians' plot. The instruction of his father as to the correct way to handle an adult son. But he knew that no matter whether he told Caroline that he wished to marry or not, she would still do her best to find him a mate, because she'd told him what she wanted—she wanted to take her sister to France to live with their mother's family in peace and happiness. And she would do everything to succeed.

He wouldn't marry simply to help her fulfill her dream; but after all this was over, he would reward her adequately. "I need my teacher at my side to tell me why the ladies resist my charms."

"They can't resist your charms." Her smile softened her refusal. "Not when you flirt with such marvelous subtlety. I predict you'll be a resounding success."

That night in her room, Caroline opened her lesson journal and read her entries. Week 1, Week 2 . . . and that was divided into days, and after each day she had listed the lesson and afterward divulged her thoughts on Huntington's progress. At last she got to

Week 1, Day 7: Teach Lord Huntington how to converse with a lady in a public place.

Beneath that, she wrote:

Lord Huntington comports himself well out of doors and will find himself much in demand as an escort.

Then, with an honesty that eased her troubled conscience, she added:

He obviously has much experience in pleasing a woman to the full extent of propriety and beyond, and is capable of making any lady forget his odd habit of dress and his equally odd idiosyncrasies. I fear that to successfully lure a young lady into the wedded state, she may have to visit the garden with Lord Huntington, where she can concentrate on his embrace. That is a sure cure to make a woman forget what he says and how he acts, and to ardently esteem the man inside the silly costume. I know this to be true.

With a sigh, she shut the journal and blew out the candle.

Chapter 15

*J*ude dawdled in the foyer, listening as Nevett's voice rose and fell behind the closed door of his study—mostly rose—and Jude grinned. He'd played an awful trick on Caroline, but he needed her at his side again.

Unfortunately, Jude's amusement led Phillips, on guard by the door, to let loose a nasty smile. "I knew she would get above herself, sir," the butler said smugly. "She's that sort of female."

"Did you?" Jude's grin cooled. "I would have said she was the sort of female whom I'll be escorting to parties."

"Only because she's your governess," Phillips said, with stiff daring.

"I would take it ill, very ill indeed, should gossip be spread beyond the bounds of this house about my governess." Jude stepped close to Phillips. The butler was shorter, older, set in his ways, but in his faded eyes Jude saw a hint of meanness. "Any kind of gossip, but especially gossip detrimental to Miss Ritter."

"Of course not." Phillips pokered up. "I don't gossip."

"Nor should your minions."

"Not a breath shall escape the household." All trace of Phillips's satisfaction was gone now.

"Good." A silence fell in Nevett's study.

Jude lost interest in the butler, for the door snapped open, and Caroline stalked out.

With a single glance, Jude knew he was in trouble now. "Miss Ritter, you look glorious this morning."

Caroline's morning dress of dark blue merino covered her from neck to wrists to toes. The skirt was wide, but not too wide, as befitting a woman of modest means, and she wore a white lace pelerine over her shoulders tied in a dark blue necktie.

She paid no heed to him or his courtesy, but stalked up to Phillips. With an indignation that made Phillips back away, she said, "I believe this would be a good time for you to go to His Grace and confess your sins."

"Such effrontery!" Phillips snapped. Then, "What sins?"

"The sin of eavesdropping." Still without acknowledging Jude, she strode into the library. He followed, and found her standing with her arms stiff at her side and her eyes hot and resentful. "You did it on purpose," she accused. "Don't tell me you didn't."

"Did what?" As if he didn't know.

"Behaved like a fool at the Lawrences' ball and alienated every lady there."

"Why would I do that?" Jude pretended a bland ignorance.

"So that I would be forced to go with you to Baron Atherton's ball tomorrow night."

Jude placed his fingers on his chest and sighed miserably. "I'm crushed that you can accuse me of such manipulative behavior."

She caught her breath as if she wanted to blast him, then slowly let it out. She was too aware of her position as governess to give him the upbraiding he deserved.

He glanced out the open door into the foyer, where he knew Phillips stood, ears straining to hear their quarrel. If they'd been alone, would Caroline have felt free to shout at Jude? Perhaps. He hoped so. He rather enjoyed seeing his governess pushed beyond the bounds of propriety. Wonderful things happened there. Marvelous things, seductive things. Recalling them, he took a step toward her, to gather her into his arms and kiss her as she was meant to be kissed.

But she made a sound, a rough sound deep in her throat like of the type one uses to discipline a dog.

And, like a well-trained dog, he stopped. He adjusted his cravat. He asked, "What is our lesson for the day?"

"You'll write letters of admiration to all of the ladies you met last night."

"But I must have met a hundred."

"Yes." Caroline pointed to the desk. "Compose them there. When I return, I'll read them, and I expect them to be in your best handwriting, and I expect them to be right."

Meekly he seated himself at the desk and dipped his pen in ink. "As you wish, Miss Ritter." He supposed this was a small enough punishment to get his own way.

Tomorrow night, Caroline would go to the ball.

"I'm apprehensive about facing the company." As the luxurious ducal carriage jostled along in the line waiting to disgorge its passengers at Baron Atherton's town house, Nicolette fussed with her ball gown.

You're apprehensive? Caroline thought incredulously.

"You're my duchess," Nevett said. "Why would you be fidgety about anything?" In the feeble lamplight, he looked amazed as only a man totally secure in his status could look.

In his position beside Caroline in the backward-facing seat, Huntington moved closer, close enough that his arm rested along the length of hers.

"I haven't been out for so long. People will stare and wonder how we're dealing with our loss." Nicolette glared at her insensitive husband. "I hate being the center of attention."

Huntington's touch warmed Caroline; he seemed aware that *she* would be the center of attention, not the duchess, and that she stood in peril of being treated with the rapt cruelty allotted to a disgraced female.

"You hosted a tea only a few days ago," Nevett reminded his wife.

"A small gathering of friends. It was almost completely appropriate for a family coming out of mourning. But this!" She gestured toward the brightly lit house, where carriages disgorged their fashionable passengers. "This is an ordeal."

"Blame Jude if you must." Taking her hand, Nevett patted it. "It's his fault we can't stay at home of an evening."

Caroline found two pairs of eyes focused on her and Huntington, and feared the duke and duchess would observe that they sat too close. So she looked at Huntington, also, and wished she hadn't.

He had arranged his hair in a perfect, understated

style. His profile was strong, his chin determined. He gazed at his father and stepmother through eyes that seemed both wise and wary—and he was a nightmare in purple and black.

Apparently Nevett had the same thought, for he said, "Son, you look like a bruise."

Caroline fought a desire to burst into hysterical laughter. Clenching her gloved hands, she told herself sternly that her disquiet meant nothing. What happened to her that night, what was said to her, was of no importance. What was vital was keeping Huntington on a tight leash, introducing him to the proper ladies, getting him married . . . doing her job.

"I wondered about that, but my valet assured me I would be the most stylish man at the ball," Huntington said in a fretful voice. "We should go back so I can don the sunrise neck scarf."

"No!" The other three spoke in unison.

"Not the sunrise scarf. It's preposterous," Nevett said.

"Wh . . . what do you mean, sir?" Huntington sounded hurt.

Caroline smoothly interceded. "He means it would look like part of your bruise is fading."

"We're almost there," Nicolette said. "I couldn't get up the nerve to leave and return. Please, Jude, I think you look very nice."

Nevett gave her an incredulous glance, then craned his head out the window. "By George, this baron fellow enjoys spending his money a little too much. His common roots are showing." He pulled his head back in. "Sorry, Miss Ritter. I wasn't referring to you."

For the first time that night she moved from anxiety to amusement. "I didn't take offense, Your Grace."

"Good. You're a sensible girl. No megrims for you."

As the carriage stopped, Nevett turned to his wife. "Nicolette, you should be more like Miss Ritter."

"Oh, Nevett," she said in despair.

"What? What did I say?" The door opened, and Nevett climbed out. He offered his hand to his wife. "That was perfectly reasonable."

Alone with Huntington, Caroline assayed a smile. "Shall we?"

"Don't worry." Taking her hand, he kissed it. "I'll be with you every moment, I promise."

She ignored the strong desire to agree. "I don't want you with me. I want you to flirt with the ladies."

"I'll do whatever you tell me to."

"You're being too agreeable."

"I can't make you happy." He descended.

"Yes, you can." Taking his hand, she stepped out of the carriage. "Find a bride. Marry before the end of the Season. That's all I ask."

Baron Atherton was from an old family with a minor title. He proved to have an aptitude for making money, and since he wasn't adverse to spending lavishly, the ton readily forgave him. Tonight, along with his much younger, very pretty, and vapid wife, he stood in his foyer and welcomed all of London society to his spacious town house.

He cast a sharp glance at Caroline when Nevett introduced her, but said nothing. He was damned lucky to get Nevett there at all, and he knew it. The duke's guest was acceptable . . . unless she caused another scene.

Nevett and Nicolette, Huntington and Caroline moved from the receiving line to the wide door overlooking the ballroom, and Nicolette took a long breath. "Here we go."

Caroline took a long breath, too, and prayed to be

unnoticed. She prayed that the evening would go well. She prayed they would indeed find Huntington a bride.

She frowned. But she wanted to find him the right bride. Before she knew him, she had thought any lady would do. Now she wanted a woman who would treat his costumes with humor, who respected his opinions, and who enjoyed his lovemaking. Of course, she wouldn't accept a girl who giggled at him behind his back. And she thought it wouldn't be appropriate if the girl was beautiful, or even too pretty . . . because Huntington wouldn't like the competition for attention. Yes, he needed the right bride. Then she remembered her sister, and amended that to—he needed the right bride almost as badly as she needed the money.

As the duke and duchess strolled forward, Huntington gave Caroline a lingering glance. "You look lovely."

She touched her modest neckline. "Thank you. It's a lovely dress." Made of nutmeg crepe, which matched her hair, it was decorated with rows of ruffles on the full skirt, and was far more luxurious than anything she had ever hoped to wear again.

"The dress doesn't do justice to the wearer." Huntington extended his arm for her to hold. "Shall we, my lioness?"

Caroline savored the glow his words brought her. Placing her hand on his, she said, "Indeed we shall."

Walking down the steps, they entered into the fray.

Chapter 16

*N*one of the guests circulating in the huge ballroom turned to look at Caroline or her companions. They were too busy gossiping and gaping at the decorations. Cool blue silks draped the walls. Long, feathered fans dyed in shades of the rainbow were plied by footmen dressed in exotic garb from India and the Far East, creating an atmosphere both decadent and opulent. An orchestra played behind a screen, and on the dance floor, couples swirled in great circles as they waltzed, and the scene was so colorful, so beautiful, it brought a lump to Caroline's throat. She had missed this.

"Look." Nicolette clutched Nevett's arm and broke into a smile. "There's Lisa and Mary and Constance and Elizabeth. And Teresa! They're all here. I haven't seen them since—"

The ladies saw Nicolette at the same time and emitted small shrieks. They rushed at her, surrounding her in laughter and friendship. They expressed their pleasure in her return with hugs and an exchange of gossip so intense it sounded like another language.

"I think Mum has nothing to worry about," Huntington murmured in Caroline's ear.

"I think you're right." Nor, apparently, did Caroline. With conceit and presumption, she had assumed her return to the ton would bring a storm of gossip. But the scandal attached to her name was old. The newest members of society didn't even recognize her. No one cared that she'd returned, and her relief was heartfelt and genuine. Caroline relaxed.

Nevett watched his wife until her friends bore her away to a corner where they could catch up on conversation. To Huntington, he said, "I'll be in the card room if you need me to, say, announce your betrothal."

"Not dressed in these garments!" Huntington looked shocked. "What woman would be interested? You yourself said I looked like a bruise."

"For God's sake, lad, you're wealthy and you're an earl. You could look like a toad with warts, and still the ladies would chase you! Just stand still"—Nevett waved a hand—"and don't talk!" Incensed, he stomped off.

"Your father's right, you know," Caroline murmured to Huntington. "That I should take his money for finding you a bride is almost theft, but you're making matters more difficult than they need to be." She gestured across the ballroom, where young ladies in shimmering silks and huge full skirts dipped and danced like a thousand colorful blossoms tossed on the breeze. Their light voices mingled with the deeper sounds of gentlemen's appreciation. The light of the candles turned their cheerful faces all aglow. "All of these youthful, pliant debutantes long for your attentions. Out of that number, we can easily weed it down to the half dozen who would suit you and make you a good wife."

"A half dozen? I don't need a half dozen. One will do, if she's the right one."

"You only get to marry one," Caroline said, amused. She didn't see his grave expression.

"But you mentioned a half dozen. Surely you believe that in every life, there's only one true love."

"Do *you*?" She pulled a long face.

"Yes."

His simple *yes* made their lighthearted kisses into something more. Something momentous. Something never to be forgotten. He looked into her eyes, and the expression there made her rush into speech. "How do you know your one true love isn't among this Season's aspirants?" *Don't look at me like that. As if I'm your true love.* Deliberately, she looked away, swept the crowd with her gaze. "Look, there are the Misses Foley. You liked them."

He paused before answering. Paused long enough to give Caroline that panicky feeling that presaged a scene. Then in a considering voice, he said, "Charming young ladies, although the youngest seems to be obsessed with handkerchiefs."

"What do you mean?" Caroline asked cautiously. She had thought she'd come to know this man. Now her confidence had been shaken.

"She couldn't tear her gaze away from my handkerchief." That sounded more like the Huntington she knew. The crisis seemed to be past.

"Then keep it in your pocket and don't flip it." Caroline located another debutante. "There's Lady Amanda. Her teeth look quite white."

"Unnaturally white," Huntington said in a fretful voice. "Freakishly white."

"All right." Caroline pounced on another face she recognized. "Lady Pheodora. She's looking . . . very nice." She couldn't keep the surprise from her voice.

"She is." Huntington seemed equally surprised. "Amazing what a smile can do. I wonder what created such a transformation?"

"I don't know, but her suitors like her." A respectable bevy of gentlemen surrounded her. She wasn't the belle of the ball, but neither was she the wallflower.

Caroline glanced around the ballroom again, and this time she caught a lady's eye . . . She looked familiar, although Caroline remembered a thinner face . . . "Edith," she breathed.

"What?" He followed her gaze. "Ah, Lady James. No, I don't think I can wed her. Lord James would complain."

"Don't be ridiculous. We were friends. Best of friends."

"That's right. I recall hearing you say that at Mum's tea."

Caroline smiled to see the dear face, but she didn't rush across the room. She knew better than to force her scandalous self on a former comrade, no matter how fond.

She needn't have worried. Edith's eyes widened, and she gave a squeal reminiscent of the squeal that had greeted Nicolette's arrival. As if that sound signaled a reunion, from around the ballroom five squeals sounded, and Caroline saw her old allies bearing down on her. They surrounded her in a rush, hugging, babbling about a hundred things, asking questions and telling her the news. Her eyes filled with awkward tears, but she brushed them away and returned each hug. "Alice. How good to see you. You're blooming!

Louisa, dear, I love your gown. Martha, when is your baby due? Volumnia, you're as beautiful as ever." She wondered if they'd heard she was coming and planned this, and thought how lovely it was to have such genuine friends.

Over the tops of their heads, she saw Huntington. He stood flipping his handkerchief and watching, an expression of amused indulgence on his face. And silly as the thought was, she wondered if *he'd* had something to do with this ostentatious display of support.

"How have you been?" Volumnia asked. "I think of you often."

"Especially when I see that cad Freshie," Martha said in a low voice. "Hateful man. He should be banned from society."

Caroline's smile twisted painfully. "There's little chance of that. Is he here tonight?" That was what she feared. He was what she feared.

The ladies exchanged glances. "I haven't seen him, but he and that dreadful wife of his are always late and fighting. He doesn't even pretend interest in her anymore, and she rips at him in public. A more miserable couple—"

"Tsk," Caroline said, with patent insincerity.

The ladies grinned.

"You always had a way of saying so little, yet so much." Louisa threw her arms around Caroline. "I have missed you."

"I felt so awful about abandoning you, but Mama wouldn't hear of me standing by you. Now I'm a matron, and Mama has nothing to say about what I do." Edith smirked.

"I wager she'll still have plenty to *say*." Caroline remembered how easily Edith's mama had been swayed by her dear friend Lady Reederman, and bitterly she knew that had she been of noble background, the older matrons wouldn't have been so unyielding.

"Probably, but I don't have to listen." Putting her head closer to Caroline's, Edith mischievously glanced at Huntington from the corners of her eyes. "Is it true Huntington is madly in love with you?"

"Not at all!" She had guessed the rumors might start, and she was glad for the chance to quash them.

The little circle of friends tittered as they turned to Huntington.

"Perhaps we should ask him if he's madly in love with *you*," Martha said.

He bowed to them all. "I harbor a deep and abiding admiration for Miss Ritter. Any other emotion in my heart is my secret to keep."

The tittering grew louder.

"Stop teasing." Caroline frowned at him and enlisted her friends in a manner that she knew they couldn't resist. "In truth, Her Grace asked that I accompany Huntington on his hunt for a wife. Ladies, who would you suggest as a bride for Lord Huntington?"

As her friends closed in on him, Huntington shot her a glance that promised retribution.

Caroline grinned as each debutante in the ballroom was pointed out, her merits weighed and her faults discussed. Regardless of his costume, none of her friends seemed to recognize any shortcoming in Huntington, proving that Nevett's presumption was right. A wealthy, titled nobleman need do nothing but stand still and keep quiet, and his bride would find him.

The gathering of young matrons around Caroline had attracted a kind of whispering attention, and as Caroline looked around she encountered glances that slid away before they touched hers. People were remembering. They were deciding. It wouldn't be long before she discovered whether the majority of society would vote with their black stones—then lift those stones and cast them at her.

She lifted her chin and straightened her shoulders. Last time, she'd cowered and cried. This time, she would stand firm, be poised, give no hint of weakness. As she cast her confident gaze across the assemblage, one man stepped forth. She'd feared Lord Freshfield, but this . . . she'd never expected this.

Her father. For the love of heaven, her father was there.

As always, he looked and dressed like a prosperous merchant, plump and conservative, and he looked out of place among the glamorous and the fashionable.

As he approached, the volume of voices around her grew lower.

He bowed without a hint of interest and affection. "I trust you're enjoying the ball, daughter."

Rattled, she answered, "Indeed sir, I am."

"Good. Good." He stood beside her another few moments, gazing out at the crowd. "You'll tell His Grace I spoke to you?"

"Ah." Now Caroline understood. This was the public display of paternal acceptance Nevett had promised. Her father had made the gesture on Nevett's command. "Yes, sir, of course."

He bowed again and disappeared into the crowd.

Why? After so many years, why had she seen him not once, but twice in such a small space of time? What was he after?

The volume of voices rose again, and it seemed the preponderance of approval from the duke and duchess, from her friends and from her father had swayed many of the guests. She answered greetings from people she barely remembered, and the single gentlemen drifted closer.

Comte de Guignard arrived at her side first, the ubiquitous Monsieur Bouchard trailing behind. "Miss Ritter, my greatest pleasure is to see you here." His bow was courtly, his kiss on her glove reverent. "Among a garden of beautiful English roses, you are the champion. Your beauty does not fade, but in fact grows greater with each passing day."

"Oh, it'll fade soon enough," she said prosaically. She didn't want to be wooed. Not by him, not by anyone. She wouldn't have Nevett accuse her of failing in her duty.

Goose hurried up with the eagerness he'd always displayed. Young Lord Vickers followed him and stammered a greeting.

Casting superior glances over his shoulder at the other men, Lord Routledge approached and bowed. "Miss Ritter, we met at Her Grace's tea."

"Of course, I remember you." *You supercilious little twit.* Her own savagery surprised her. He was the kind of man she'd considered eminently marriageable four years ago. Now his overweening confidence grated on her nerves, and her courtesy held an edge of irritation.

Not that he noticed. "May I have a dance?" He bowed again, obviously expecting her eager acceptance.

"I don't dance." She smiled to take the sting out of her refusal. "I'm here as a friend of Lord Huntington's family, and it would be inappropriate for me to indulge myself."

"Surely the family wouldn't have brought you to a ball and imposed such restrictions on you."

Monsieur Bouchard moved closer, and the stench of cigars was so strong she took a step back. She felt badly; he seemed a pleasant enough man, if rough about the edges, but he did smell of tobacco, and his teeth were the color of tea. "They did not," she said. "I imposed them on myself."

In varying stages of indignation, the gentlemen all turned to glare at Huntington.

And he, who had been discussing the merits of each debutante with Caroline's friends, had no idea of his crime. Yet right before her eyes, she watched him slip into the role of fool. He pulled out his overly large handkerchief and waved it like a signal flag. "What? My dear Comte de Guignard! My dear Monsieur Bouchard! Why do you frown at me so critically?" He glanced down at his purple waistcoat. "It's the clothes, isn't it? You've detected my charade."

"What charade?" Monsieur Bouchard bristled like a dog on the scent.

"I dressed badly tonight because . . . because . . ." As Huntington's lie collapsed, his handkerchief fell limply by his side. "You're too astute. You see the truth."

"Which is?" Comte de Guignard's hostile gaze studied Huntington.

"I listened to my valet instead of my own good taste, and now I'm dressed like this." The handkerchief flapped up and down his form.

Caroline closed her eyes in dismay.

"We were not speaking of . . . that," Comte de Guignard said, from between clenched teeth.

"Then what, my dear comte?" Huntington's brow knit. "I want nothing more than to please you."

"You could please the rest of us, too," Goose said.

"Yes, I adore Miss R . . . Ritter," Lord Vickers added.

"Do you know what Miss Ritter does in your name?" Comte de Guignard asked. "She refuses to dance. It is an outrage!"

This was the kind of scene Caroline wanted to avoid. "I beg you gentlemen, remember that I won't dance regardless of Lord Huntington's opinion. As much as I value that commodity, it's my decision."

"Ah, you have no man to make your decisions for you." Comte de Guignard kissed her hand again. "Pardon, but the gentlemen in your England must all be without sense to leave you so alone."

"I am not without sense!" Huntington said. "I'm perfectly sensible."

Caroline didn't understand him. When she was alone with him, he behaved like a reasonable man. But as soon as they joined a greater company, he became the same absurd gentleman she'd first met. If he was playing a game, she didn't understand the objective. And what other reason did he have for his behavior? She could think of no explanation.

"Yes, we see your sense now." Monsieur Bouchard viewed Huntington with a half smile. "At your convenience, my lord, we'd like to meet with you. Talk with you."

"Delighted!" Huntington lit up like Atherton's chandelier. "Shall we say tomorrow at noon?"

"Very good." Monsieur Bouchard clicked his heels when he bowed.

"And, Comte de Guignard, let me be clear. I live my life as I like," Caroline said. "I do not need supervision."

Comte de Guignard's eyebrows rose almost to the widow's peak in his hairline, but obviously he didn't believe her. He was an old-world gentleman, and for him, women had no thought beyond frivolity.

Caroline could almost see his mind working, seeking to rescue her one more time. Resting her hand on her arm, she looked into his eyes. "Truly. I have no desire to dance."

"A beautiful young lady must always dance," Comte de Guignard said.

"On command, my dear comte?"

"Non." He acceded to her gentle irony. *"Non."*

"But I asked you." Lord Routledge obviously couldn't believe he could fail in any endeavor.

"And I thanked you." He truly deserved a harder set-down, but she needed no more enemies than she already had. "Gentlemen, if you'll pardon me, I wish to introduce Lord Huntington to the young ladies." With alacrity, Caroline stepped away from their admiration. "My lord, shall we make a circuit of the ballroom?"

"Delightful!" Huntington said again and offered his arm. "That's exactly what I wish to do."

They strolled through the ballroom, speaking to Huntington's acquaintances. Caroline was well aware how they looked together. A handsome couple, well matched, complementing each other in looks. Despite Nevett's conviction, few believed she was only a friend of the family. So she steered them toward Lady Pheodora.

Lady Pheodora watched their advance with wary eyes, and Caroline wanted to snap that her notoriety wouldn't rub off. Then she noticed the direction of Lady Pheodora's gaze. She seemed to be apprehensive of . . . Huntington.

Huntington, who waved his handkerchief in huge circles to indicate Lady Pheodora's form. "Lady Pheodora, you look ravishing tonight!"

That was good, and so true. The fashion for low

necklines displayed Lady Pheodora's fine shoulders and bosom to an advantage, and her ring of suitors was growing.

"I must protest you giving attention to these other fellows." Huntington dismissed his competition with a white cotton flutter. "After all, I discovered you."

Everything he said was exceptional, but his voice rang with a false French accent he had unexpectedly acquired. Heads turned. People stared, then tried not to stare.

"My lord, you're too benevolent." Lady Pheodora shrank back when Huntington stepped closer. "I do remember you kindly."

Before she could react, he leaned very close and whispered in her ear. Then with a chuckle, he took Caroline's elbow and steered her away.

"What did you say to her?" she asked.

"I told her to take Lord Cunningham. He's the best of the lot around her, and he's ready for domestication."

Unwillingly Caroline laughed, then sobered. "My lord, you should be one of her suitors."

"No. Lady Pheodora is definitely not my one true love."

"True love, indeed." Caroline sighed in frustration. "How will we know this paragon?"

"I'll hear music." He slanted a glance at her.

"There is music playing right now."

"Then my true love is here."

"Let's find her," Caroline said lightly. Yet he unsettled her in his words and manner.

He steered his way toward Miss Edwina Richardson, where he flirted lightly before taking Caroline to yet another young lady. He declared none of them were his own true love, but on her command he put away his handkerchief and spoke like a normal English gentleman.

While they were conversing with Lady Rutherford and Miss Jordan (who showed a regrettable tendency to giggle nervously) Nicolette stopped by. In a low voice, she said to Caroline, "From a distance, it looks as if my disgraceful son is behaving."

"He is, and the mamas are allowing themselves to be convinced that he can be nabbed for their darlings."

"Good." Nicolette patted Caroline's shoulder. "Good. So they're starting to hope you're not his affianced wife?"

"No!" People looked at her curiously, and she lowered her voice. "No. I mean . . . no."

"I did hear the rumors that abounded." Nicolette's kind gray eyes sharpened on Caroline. "Yet I think the mamas have more to worry about than they might wish."

Caroline felt the color leave her face. "Your Grace, I would never take advantage of my position to press my suit with Lord Huntington." Yet that wasn't strictly the truth. She had kissed him. Guilt twisted in the base of her stomach and left a bitter taste in her mouth.

"I didn't suggest you had. But you're not the only one involved, and Jude behaves for you. When a fully grown man does what a woman tells him, he has a reason." As Nicolette walked away, she nodded as if imparting great wisdom. "Think about it."

Caroline didn't want to think about it. She wanted, she really wanted, to get Huntington married. She watched him with Miss Jordan, and he managed to put her enough at ease that she stopped giggling and started talking. When young Lady Claudia Leonard joined them, he teased her, and when she teased back, he laughed aloud. That made the heads turn. Caroline waved them over, and Huntington swiftly had his own group of admirers surrounding him.

Caroline relaxed. No, he hadn't formed an attachment to her. Soon he would be married and . . . and she would be on her way to France with Genevieve. Everything was perfect.

Occasionally someone spoke to her; for the most part, they contented themselves with distant smiles and nods. The debutantes and their mamas didn't want to endanger any marriages that might occur by appearing fast and consorting with a known fallen woman. She didn't mind. She stood off to the side and watched Huntington handle the ladies, flirting with the mamas as well as the daughters. He signed dance cards, and she thought she detected a special gleam in his eye for at least three of the debutantes.

Just at the time she had grown weary of standing, when the sound of the music and other people's conversations gave her a headache, Huntington said, "Excuse me, ladies, but I must find refreshments or perish."

The girls giggled.

"I hope to see you later," Lady Claudia said daringly.

"Bless you, child." He kissed her forehead. "I hope to see you and everyone again soon. For a while, I lost myself in your company." He offered Caroline his arm.

As he led her away, Caroline said, "I thought you liked Lady Claudia."

"I do," he said with some surprise. "She's charming. Why? Did I give the appearance of disliking her?"

"No, but that kiss was positively paternal."

"I'm old enough to be her father," he said, a tart note of exasperation in his voice.

"Not likely."

"No, but acquit me of lusting after little girls. She's not yet eighteen."

"So she's not your one true love?" Caroline couldn't believe she was asking that.

"No, but I think I have met the one. And do you know what I wish?" He looked down at her.

"What do you wish?" she asked indulgently.

"I wish I could kiss you right now."

"Sh!" Startled, she looked up at him. She observed no trace of the fop, nor any sign of the swain who obediently followed her from girl to girl. Instead, she saw a tall man with a strong chin and blunt features who smiled at her as if *she* were his one true love.

"No one can hear me," he assured her. "People are talking too much. The music is too loud."

He spoke of their kisses. She tried never to think about those kisses, and now, there in the middle of a ballroom, he used his voice and his gaze to make her remember . . . remember how much she relished those stolen moments in his arms. Remember the sensuality of his touch. She understood his kisses, and she supposed that was the greatest thing about it—and him. When they kissed, she slipped into his mind, reading thought and intention, gaining joy at knowing another being so well.

And while Huntington was right and no one heard him, one man was watching from behind a pillar, and that man saw her blush.

Lord Freshfield was not pleased.

Chapter 17

$\mathscr{B}$efore Caroline could subdue her blushes and remind herself she held the position of Jude's governess, a footman found them. He presented Jude with a sealed note on a silver tray, and when Jude broke it open and scanned it, his eyes narrowed. He looked intent, mature, serious: not at all like the trivial Lord Huntington she knew.

"Is something wrong?" she asked.

"Something wrong?" His expression became anguished. "Indeed there is. My valet writes that he dropped black polish on my white boots."

"Your valet interrupted your attendance at a ball to send you word of that?" Caroline was incredulous.

"It's an outrage! Do you know how difficult it is to find a boot maker who has the imagination and creativity to make white boots? I had to pay twice as much as normal, and the boot maker was almost crying with joy as he created them, and now . . . they are ruined unless

I can get them to the boot maker at once." Placing his palm to his forehead, he moaned, "I must go."

"No!" Caroline looked back at the clutch of debutantes he'd already met, then out at the young ladies scattered throughout the ballroom, all potential brides. "Not now. This is absurd. There are no boot makers open at this hour."

"For me there are."

She supposed that was true. When a man spent as much on fashion as Jude, the boot makers and tailors were always open. "But you've promised dances to those ladies—"

"And I will dance with each one at my wedding. In the meantime, they would comprehend the severity of my situation."

"You're making a fool of yourself."

"I promise"—he took her hand—"I'll dance with you at my wedding, too."

"You're abominable." She yanked her hand away. "I'll be lucky if Nevett doesn't throw me out tomorrow. Stay!"

"I *must* go."

Right then, she hated Jude. She hated that he'd reverted to his old self. She hated that she'd built hopes on his charming behavior that night and made plans for the money she would make from his wedding. Most of all, she hated that his defection relieved her, for that meant she had him to herself for a little while longer. With a spite increased by shame, she said, "Then go. I don't care. Just . . . go."

"I'll escort you to my stepmother's side." Taking her arm, he tried to move her toward the corner where Nicolette sat with her friends.

"I don't need you to take me anywhere." With chilly precision, Caroline removed her arm from his grasp.

He hesitated, glanced around, then nodded. "All right. If there's trouble here, it's hiding its face well. Go to Mum's side and remain there for the rest of the evening."

"Do you think I'll meekly do as you command?" For all that Caroline kept her voice modulated, she was in a rage.

A rage. She was angry. Ladies were never angry. *She* was never angry. Yet she wanted to shout at him, to strike him, for thwarting her so. And . . . for being as big a fool as he looked.

His eyes turned cool and sharp as steel. "I think you'd be a fool not to do as I command, and you're no fool." With a bow, off he went.

The swine was right, she reflected morosely. She would do as she was told. She'd go to the duchess's side and stick close. The night had been remarkable by its lack of drama. She intended to keep it that way. And on that thought, she realized she stood alone in the ballroom. Her friends were matrons, dancing with their husbands or visiting with the other wives about children, schools, servants, and household accounts. The debutantes had drifted away on whispers and giggles. Her suitors had gone on to more receptive maidens.

A chill slid up her spine. She was only too aware how precarious was her acceptance in society. It depended more on the company she kept than on her behavior, and at once she started toward the corner where she'd last seen Nicolette.

Of course people got in her way. They were talking, laughing, drinking. It was a ball, the kind of celebration that four years ago she'd loved so much to attend. Suddenly it seemed fraught with peril. Four years ago, someone was always with her—men who loved her, friends who enjoyed her, a chaperon . . . who betrayed her. Her uneasiness increased at the remembrance, and more than that, it seemed as if people were now aware of her disquiet and moving away. But her imagination was acting up . . . wasn't it?

No. For Lady Freshfield stepped into her path.

For one moment, Caroline was back in Lord Freshfield's study, a terrified, drugged young lady helpless under the onslaught of condemnation.

Now beads of sweat sprang out on Caroline's forehead. This woman had slapped her and marked her as a wanton.

Yet the past four years had changed Lady Freshfield. She was thinner, more worn, and the skin beneath her chin had assumed the shape of swagged drapes. Her huge skirt should have looked like the height of fashion; instead it overwhelmed her, shrank her to the dimensions of a decorated stick. Unhappily her eyes were exactly the same: brilliant blue, lit with flames of loathing directed at Caroline. Only at Caroline. "Miss Ritter, I couldn't believe it when my husband told me you were here tonight."

Caroline's gaze flicked behind Lady Freshfield.

And there he was, golden hair gleaming in the light of the candles, white teeth glistening with his derisive smile. Lord Freshfield. He had done this, waited for the moment when Caroline was alone and set his wife on her.

"How do you dare show your face in polite society?" Lady Freshfield's shrill voice sent a chill up Caroline's spine. "Do you imagine that anyone has forgotten what you did, luring my husband into his study and—"

"Being drugged by him?" Caroline didn't fidget. She looked Lady Freshfield in the face. "You know it's true. He attacked me."

"Even now you lie about that night—and to me, his wife."

So many people were staring. All those eyes, shocked and accusatory, just like last time.

"You went into his study on purpose. You knew what he wanted."

Caroline swallowed. That was the crux of the matter, the thing she could never explain away. She *had* willingly gone into his study. "I didn't understand what he wanted. I was a foolish girl. But you know—doesn't it repulse you that your husband seduces innocents?"

Caroline's courage seemed to take Lady Freshfield aback, and she chose her words carefully. "He's a man with a man's appetites, and when a pretty girl entices him he gives into temptation." Then fiercely, she returned to the attack. "But he's mine, *mine* by law and by vow, and you tried to take him."

The people around them were muttering.

Caroline stepped back from Lady Freshfield's barrage. This was so much like last time. So much like her nightmares.

Lady Freshfield followed, breathing hard, and her breath felt like fire and smelled like brimstone. "Get out of here. Go back to the streets or wherever you've been living."

"I haven't been living on the streets." But it had been close, so close, and Caroline backed up another step.

"We're decent women here, and we don't associate with the likes of you."

This was hell. Caroline had fallen into hell. She looked around at the encircling guests.

Eyes were wide. They stared in shock. They accused. They remembered. And everywhere she looked, she saw agreement.

And lingering in the background, the shining white teeth and glorious blond hair of Lord Freshfield. He was waiting for her. Waiting to catch her on her last fall from grace.

Turning on her heel, Caroline walked toward the door of the ballroom. A path cleared before her. She heard someone call her name, but she didn't care. She wanted out. Out, away from the stuffy atmosphere where cruelty to innocents was acceptable as long as it was entertaining. Out where the villains carried visible weapons and could be disarmed. She strode through the foyer where earlier she'd stood in the receiving line with the duke and duchess. She walked toward the outer door.

The footmen ran when they saw her, and somehow before she reached the door, she had her cloak in her hand. She didn't don it; she was overheated. Hell had a way of causing that. "Open the door," she said.

One liveried young man sprang to attention and obeyed her.

She walked out.

She heard the footman calling, "Miss, let me get your carriage."

But the air was fresh and cool against her hot cheeks. She took long breaths as she walked steadily down the drive. The coachmen all turned to look at her. They tipped their hats. One asked, "Can I 'elp ye, Miss?"

"No. Thank you." Unlike every other lady in the ballroom, Caroline wasn't afraid of the streets and the night. She knew how to hail her own cab, and when she got to the thoroughfare, she did exactly that.

As she climbed in, the driver asked, "Where ye going, Miss?"

Where was she going?

She wanted to wash away the memory of her encounter with Lady Freshfield. She wanted to forget the mortification at having her sins recounted for the debutantes and the gentlemen. More than anything, she wanted to forget her own ignominious retreat.

And she wanted to make Jude pay for abandoning her.

With a smart nod to the driver, she said, "Take me to Lord Huntington's town house on Fitzroy Square."

By morning, she would know what led a perfectly intelligent lady to abandon morals and prudence and take a lover to her bed. Caroline would be what everyone already thought she was—a woman of experience. And after she had settled her sister in France . . . perhaps she would become a courtesan. Not a mistress with no power, but a woman of experience with her own salon, where learned men and women would discuss politics, science and discovery, and after the lights went out, the gentlemen would beg to stay. After all, she had learned to flirt so skillfully, all the men in London had declared her to be a diamond of the first water. Under the proper tutelage, and Jude would provide the proper tutelage, she could learn to drive men mad with desire. It was— it had to be—a matter of skill coupled with the opportunity to learn. Being with Jude would provide the opportunity.

Despite the advanced hour, Huntington's butler was still in uniform when he answered the door.

Caroline tugged her hood close about her face. "I want to see Lord Huntington."

Not a muscle stirred in the man's face. "Is he expecting you, Miss?"

"Yes, of course he is. Why else would I be here?" She took care to keep her tone reasonable, but firm.

She would not be turned away. Not tonight. Not for any reason.

Apparently other ladies with dalliance on their mind visited Jude at all hours, for the butler bowed her inside. Without inquiring her name or business, he took her to a comfortable sitting room. "He isn't in right now—"

Of course. The boot maker's.

"—But you can wait here. Is there something I can get you, Miss?"

"No, thank you," she said. Then, "Yes! I'd like a glass of wine." Almost immediately, she held a glass of wine, ruby red and fragrant. She sipped it and smiled.

She couldn't believe she was here. She couldn't believe she was going to do this. She loved the idea of being in control of her destiny.

Not as she had been tonight in that ballroom, driven out by the shrill spite of a bitter woman. Caroline clutched the glass as she remembered, and the surface of the wine shivered with her distress.

Jude made her feel as if she were strong and brave. She, who had spent the last years living in fear. Fear of poverty, fear of starvation, fear of the dark, fear of losing her sister, fear of Lord Freshfield. But when Jude held her in his arms, she became a new woman, one who feared nothing. Everything in him challenged her, and she found herself rising to the challenge.

That was why she'd come here. Not because he'd abandoned her, and she wanted revenge. She needed to learn his indifference to criticism. She wanted an infusion of his unwavering spirit.

The wine slipped over her tongue, and she cast her mind forward. She loved the thought of being a hostess everyone clamored to meet, and she loved that she had taken the initiative and come to Jude to learn the necessary skills . . . to experience love one time. Just once, before intercourse became a matter of bargain and trade.

Odd, but standing here looking at Jude's possessions didn't cause her second thoughts. His belongings were masculine, dark, warm, and chosen with sophistication. So his taste in clothing didn't envelop his furnishings . . . she was doing the right thing.

She and Jude had kissed repeatedly. Each time she'd found herself more aroused by the passion that bloomed between them, and she had taken him by storm every time. She would bend him to her will this time, too.

The butler didn't return. Clearly, he thought she was one of Huntington's light o' loves, and he saw no reason to treat her with undue respect. All right. Then she saw no reason to stay where he put her.

She walked out into the foyer and with a regal nod at the startled footman, she climbed the stairs. Without difficulty, she located Jude's bedchamber and entered with all the brazen confidence of the courtesan she intended to be.

And she met Jude's valet.

The two of them stared, each astonished to see the other. But tonight, Caroline had changed. Or perhaps it hadn't been tonight; perhaps her life of the past years had been working its changes on her. Perhaps tonight all the changes had all caught up with her.

"I'm waiting for Lord Huntington, and I wish to do so here," she said with composure. "Is he out with his boots?"

"Miss?" The valet cocked his head as if he didn't understand the question.

"His boots," she repeated. "You dropped black polish on his white boots. Has he taken them to the boot maker?"

"Miss, I have no idea what you're talking about." His features chilled, and ice dripped from his voice.

So he didn't want to admit what he'd done. "Very well. May I suggest you seek your bed, and I'll care for Lord Huntington's toilette?"

The small, dapper man backed out of the room and shut the door. If his unflappable demeanor meant anything, it was that women regularly strolled into Jude's bedchamber and made such requests.

Well. Why not? Huntington was handsome, wealthy, and very much the man. He'd proved that in Nevett's lesser drawing room and the zoo that was really the garden. When she remembered his kisses, his mouth on her breast, her body softened, and any doubts—not that she had any—melted away.

Taking off her cloak, she laid it across the chair and looked around. Jude's town house did not have the grandeur of Nevett's, but handsome furniture filled the room, a fire crackled on the hearth, and, most important, the bed was large and imposing, with bed-curtains that would keep out the chill of a late spring evening.

She smiled at that bed. She curtsied toward it, and said, "Why, yes, thank you, I would love to." Lifting her arms, she pretended to dance and waltzed toward it.

Jude's valet had laid his nightwear across the bed: a brown flannel gown and a black velvet robe that would reach to his knees, and a plain white nightcap. How very dull for a man so enamored with color in his clothing.

Without art, without shame, she dropped her clothes, which had been, that evening, chosen with such care.

She donned the robe and it covered her from head to toe. The sleeves hung over her hands, and she rolled them up. She tied the sash loosely and climbed between the sheets.

They were heated. Apparently the valet had passed the warming pan between the covers before she came in. The mattress was soft, the pillows thick, the ceiling was plain white with cove molding and curlicues painted at each corner. She lay there, her arms outstretched, and smiled at those curlicues until she drifted into sleep.

Chapter 18

*M*urder.

Jude nodded curtly to his butler as he entered his house, and Wyatt read his mood exactly and refrained from chitchat. He took Jude's wool coat and tall hat, and when Jude dropped his gloves on the side table, Wyatt picked them up and stowed them.

Miss Gloriana Dollydear had an opera singer's ability to memorize and repeat words in a foreign language without understanding what they were. It was, after all, what an opera singer did. That evening at dinner, she'd given Comte de Guignard and Monsieur Bouchard information she'd "overheard" from Throckmorton; they'd sat before her and spoken in Moricadian of how that would affect their plans.

Before she could forget the confusion of sounds she didn't comprehend, Throckmorton had sent for Jude to translate. Although she didn't get all the words right, one thing was clear.

Murder. They planned to kill . . . someone.

Despite Gloriana Dollydear's best efforts, she hadn't heard, or couldn't remember, anything about who or where.

As Jude mounted the stairs toward his bedchamber, he loosened his cravat and unbuttoned his waistcoat.

The meeting, the secrecy, the revelation of one mystery that created yet more mysteries . . . all that reminded him too vividly how Michael had died at the hands of these men. Jude was no closer to justice for his brother, and now unless he was both lucky and smart, de Guignard and Bouchard would kill some poor sod here in London, all to keep control of a tiny country and its considerable assets.

Fury and frustration pounded away at Jude's good sense. He wanted to ride the streets, catch the villains as they left the ball, and eliminate them. That would be justice; those men killed without a thought to the pain and anguish they caused. They'd killed Michael.

Yet if *he* killed *them* without waiting for English intelligence to trap them and English law to sentence them, other Moricadians would arrive with plans to wreak havoc in the name of their freedom, and next time Jude wouldn't know whom to suspect and whom to follow.

Tonight, while the Moricadians were at the ball, Throckmorton's man would enter their apartment and steal back the presents that Jude had given them. He would take the other valuables, too, of course—he *was* a professional thief, and they *were* his wages. And he would search for any notes they'd made, any maps, any indication of who their target might be.

It would have to be someone important enough to make an international incident and ruin French relations. But who? The queen? Prince Albert? The prime minister? Until the Home Office discovered that, they couldn't make a move to thwart the Moricadians' scheme.

Entering his bedchamber, he tossed off his jacket, his waistcoat, and loosened his cuffs and his collar. Where was his valet? No matter. His valet loved Jude's clothing. Jude loathed it all. It fit his mood to rip off his purple shirt and kick off his black boots and . . .

He stood with one foot lifted above the floor, staring at the form slumbering in his bed.

Caroline. *What was she doing here?*

Here. And . . . naked.

Or at least it looked as if she were naked. As good as naked. One soft hand was tucked beneath her cheek. Her chestnut hair waved across the white of his pillow. His black velvet robe sliced across her pale skin and gave him a glimpse, just a glimpse of the plump circle of her breast topped by a warm, peach aureole and nipple. Everything about her was soft and relaxed, waiting . . . beckoning.

The brandy he'd imbibed with Throckmorton hit Jude hard. That must be the reason his head was swimming. It couldn't be because all his blood left his head for other regions.

He searched for his principles. No matter that she was here, and *naked*, he couldn't take her innocence. He'd be no better than Freshie if he did so.

But she'd come to him of her own free will, and she was *naked*.

His hands moved to the buttons of his trousers.

He wanted to be more like Michael, yes, but he understood what Michael didn't—that love carried responsibility, and sometimes love could hurt. He didn't want to hurt Caroline.

But she was *naked*.

He stripped off his drawers.

Something must have happened at the ball to send her fleeing to him. His stepmother would kill him for dishonoring Caroline. It would be unfair to take advantage of Caroline's turmoil.

But she was *naked*.

And now, so was he.

She was everything he needed. Arousing, female, so alive and vital, and Caroline, purely Caroline. Lifting the covers, he slid into bed and slid his arm under her shoulders. Her eyes fluttered open, and she smiled at him as if he were the man she'd been waiting for all her life.

"What took you so long?" she whispered. Putting her hands on either side of his face, she pulled him into her kiss.

The warmth of touch.

The taste of passion.

The scent of anticipation.

When he lifted his head, she was startled to see stark need and bitter desperation in his eyes. "Huntington," she whispered. "Jude." With a brush of her fingers, she pushed his hair off his forehead.

His expression cleared, became heat and pleasure in one. "Caroline," he echoed, and slid the robe off her shoulder. In a deep, silky voice, he asked, "What brought you here tonight?"

Then, for a moment, she lost her easy pleasure in his company. "I realized that I can do what I want to do because I'm"—*angry*—"in control of my life." Wrapping her hands around his shoulders, she pushed him over.

"In control of every single facet of my life." Lifting herself above him, she grinned savagely down into his face.

This was good. This was right. With this man, she could love and fight and win, and there would be no repercussions, no gossip afterward, for she implicitly trusted him to never, ever betray the secret of her visit.

His fingers rode down the slope of her neck, over her collarbone, and under the robe toward her breast. "Let me . . ."

"No." Taking his hands, she wrapped them around the bars on the headboard.

"You really don't think I'll be able to resist touching you, do you?" he chuckled. "You underestimate your allure and my restraint."

She sat up, pulled the robe up over her shoulders, and scrutinized all the long length of him. The blankets covered him from the waist down, but from the waist up, he looked completely different than a dilettante should look. Muscles corded his arms, and a fine, black hair, darker than the hair on his head, covered his armpits. His broad shoulders owed nothing to padding. His bones were better suited to a stevedore than an earl. Coarse black hair covered his chest, then on his belly it thinned and descended like an arrow under the covers. Every inch of his chest and arms showed the results of hard work, or hard loving, or hard fighting . . . her gaze shifted to the two red, round holes not far above his right nipple.

Hard fighting, indeed. God knew how, but he'd lived through two horrible wounds. Gunshot wounds. And all along his right arm was a long, thin, red line that ended in a divot in the muscle and a nasty looking scar.

"How did you get these?" She traced the scars on his chest.

"A silly duel. It was nothing."

No one knew about his wounds. She'd heard not a hint of gossip, but somehow she knew he hadn't won them in a silly duel. These were the marks of a warrior.

No. This was no man to toy with. Anything he wanted to do to her, he could do. Anything.

Not that he would ever do anything to hurt her, but in the heat of passion, he might—would—inflict his will on her.

She'd had enough of men's wills for one night. At least until the dawn, she would do what *she* wanted, take the pleasure *she* desired, dispense bliss as *she* decided.

"I'm your governess." Taking the velvet belt of his robe from around her waist, she used it to truss his hands together. "You'll do as I say."

His eyes grew wide, and he grinned. "Yes, ma'am."

"You think I'm jesting." She tied the whole contraption to the bed. She knew nothing of knots, nothing except what she'd learned in embroidery, but she knew these would last. "I'm not. Try to free yourself."

He twisted his hands against the velvet, but his hands, like his feet, were oversized, with broad palms and large fingers. His grin became a grimace. He jerked against the headboard, rattling the frame, but the solid wood didn't budge. "This is absurd," he said. "I have to be unbound to touch you."

"No, I have to be free to touch *you*. This way, I know you'll do as I say. This way, I'm in command. Now, my lion." She petted his hair, his mane. "Let me make you happy."

He growled, a low rumble of sound in his chest.

But she didn't experience any doubt, any fear. This was the right thing to do. The thing that would heal her anger and give her . . . she didn't know exactly what it would give her, but it was time she found out. She'd been so afraid, all this time, of ending up in a man's bed, a victim of his lust, that it never occurred to her she could hold the upper hand. She could take him, shape him, torment him.

"I wish you didn't have that smirk on your face," he murmured.

"Why?" She clenched her hands in his thick hair. God, he was handsome. He had a jaw that declared his strength. His neck, usually covered by a cravat, was huge, strong. Not like an earl's. Like a bull's. Like a man who worked on the docks or in the fields, or rode into battle swinging a battle-ax. Her fingertips skated over his ears, nicely curled and set close against his head. Over his jaw, rough with the growth of his beard. Down that neck.

And all the while, she stared into his blue eyes, which watched and weighed . . . and threatened, and promised.

"You're going to make me suffer, aren't you?" His gazed caressed the bare skin revealed by the opening of her robe. "You're going to make me pay for all the men who have hurt you, all the men who have judged you."

She kissed his lips, a long, slow, open kiss. She took his breath and gave him hers. Against his mouth, she asked, "Are you afraid?"

"No. No. . . ." His scowl betrayed his doubt.

"Good. Because I like being your governess." She scraped her fingernails across his collarbones and down his chest. "I like doing things to you. I like having you helpless and subject to my whims. Although I do wish I knew exactly what to do." Before her eyes, gooseflesh rose on his skin and in their nest of hair, his males nipples tightened. She was fascinated—and surprised, for exactly the same thing happened to her at exactly the same moment. "Oh." The word was a mere breath of air.

"You can do nothing wrong," he assured her in a deep, strangled voice. "Anything you want to try will be torture."

"Exactly what I want." She pulled the robe close at her waist, but as soon as she moved it slipped off her shoulder again.

His gaze followed her motions and eagerly sought out each glimpse of her bare skin. "I don't know how long I can bear it."

"You'll bear it until I let you go." She stroked the hair on his chest, taking pleasure in the rough texture and the way it curled around her fingers.

This was mesmerizing. Enchanting. She had never touched a man's skin, never imagined a man's reactions . . . had never cared. Now curiosity drove her on and on . . . her fingers danced over his ribs. She liked the smoothness of the skin on his belly, and gave in to the impulse to touch it with her lips.

He made a noise, not pleasure, not anguish.

She nuzzled him with a smile, laid her cheek against him, savored the warmth and the decadence of his prime body.

Something about her enthralled expression must have alarmed him, for he said, "You will let me go when I tell you to."

"If I allowed such insubordination, what kind of governess would I be?" she mocked.

She knew what tented the blankets below his waist. She'd lived in dreadful conditions where whores worked their trades. She knew what men were made of and how they rutted. But knowing in her mind and being there with him were different. With Jude, she didn't feel horror or dread. She wanted to see every inch of him, kiss him until he writhed with need, take him . . . lifting the blankets, she tossed them down at his feet.

His body was a sculpture, shaped by forces she couldn't imagine. His muscled belly, his long, muscled legs, his erection . . . knowing what a man had in his trousers was nothing like seeing it for the first time. His penis thrust out of the nest of dark hair at his groin, long, pale, and massive, with blue veins and a broad head. Revealing him made her want to . . . she didn't know what she wanted. To laugh with pleasure. To cry with awe. Instead, she whispered, "Oh, my."

He laughed, a short burst of strained amusement. "I think I'm flattered."

"You're magnificent. That's no flattery."

"I'd like to see you, too."

"No." Absently she pushed the robe up on her shoulder again. "Not yet."

She climbed between his legs and stroked his thighs, liking the way each heavy muscle was contoured. She traced the bones of his knees. She cupped his calves in her hands and allowed her hands to descend to his feet . . . "Huge feet," she whispered.

He smiled at her, but his eyes were dark with strain, and the skin on his face looked tight, as if it were stretched over his bones. His cheeks flamed with color, and his lips were bloodless. "For pity's sake, Caroline, untie me."

"No."

"Then put me out of my misery."

"You speak so forcefully. You should have more respect for your governess." Sitting up on her knees, she leaned forward and hovered over the top of him. "I shall have to teach you."

"Retribution will arrive when you least expect it." He no longer smiled, and his eyes watched her . . .

They watched her, and for the first time, he did remind her of a lion. A lion sighting its prey. Yet tonight she feared nothing. No man, no beast, could prevail over her. "I'm not afraid of you."

"And that's where you've made your mistake," he said ominously.

She caressed him with long strokes of her palms, down his chest, down his belly, over his hips. Each time, she got a little closer to his erection.

Each time, he writhed in silence.

It was a competition, like their kisses, to see who would break first.

At last, her hands drifted in the air inches above his erection.

Jude sat with his head propped on the pillows, watching her through slitted blue eyes. He looked furious and frustrated . . . and he broke. His lips barely moved as he begged, "Please."

"Please . . . what? Please . . . this?" She stroked, not directly on his skin, but just above it.

"Tease." His penis twitched.

She laughed. "Or please . . . this?" With one palm, she cupped his balls. With the other, she lightly caressed the length of him.

"God." His eyes closed. His body arched. An expression of ferocious bliss gripped his face, transforming him into a warrior of unquestionable savagery.

If he weren't tied, she had no doubt she'd be on her back by then, and he would be thrusting into her, taking her . . . her own eyes closed as the picture formed in her mind. She grew damp and swollen between her legs, and desire, never far away when she was with Jude, grew into fierce need.

But she wasn't done yet. She wanted to do everything tonight, everything she had ever heard of, everything she could imagine, everything that would brand her into Jude's mind so that he never forgot her. "What about this?" she asked. "Would you like this?" Leaning over, she kissed the thrusting head of his erection.

Jude groaned, a deep, anguished noise that she recognized . . . that any woman would recognize. It rose from the depths of his frustration, primitive and basic, and it called to her to finish this, to take him, to satisfy him and herself, to solve the mystery of their mating.

But that was too easy. Too fast. She had only this night, and she would make it last. She had only this man to conquer, and she would reduce him to desperation. Cautiously, she licked him, one slow, tentative taste of his skin.

"You've tied me to the rack. Caroline, you're torturing me." The bed shook as he dragged at his arms, rattling the headboard. "Free me."

She looked up and smiled. As he watched, she opened her mouth and took him inside.

He tasted salty. His skin smelled warm. He was in every way at her mercy. Beneath her palm, his scrotum tightened. She slid her mouth along the length of him, imitating the motion of loving without knowing the particulars.

She must have gotten it right, for he roared like a wounded lion.

She thought he would break the headboard. She sucked at him, then twirled her tongue around the head.

He rocked the bed in the throes of need. "Someday, somewhere, I'll make you suffer as you've made me suffer."

Sitting up, she viewed him sternly, as sternly as any governess with her student. "You're not a very docile pupil. If you don't improve your attitude, I'll be forced to take action."

He stopped fighting the knots, and he observed her. "Caroline, I am very good at seeking revenge."

For a second, she wondered if he would somehow free himself, and at the look in his eyes, the tenseness in his muscles, the length and width of his manhood, she experienced a frisson of alarm—and such a thrill she wanted to fling caution to the wind and release him.

Then she took a breath. She reassured herself. He was tied, and tied well. He couldn't touch her. She was in control. With a shrug of her shoulders, she allowed the robe to slither onto the mattress.

He took a gratifying breath. "Beautiful," he whispered. "You're every bit as beautiful as I imagined."

"So are you." She glided over the top of him, laid her chin on his chest and as he looked down at her, she smiled into his face. Stretching forward, she kissed him as she'd wanted to kiss him all evening long. And the magic seized her as it always seized her. His lips moved on hers, and she wanted to bite him, to enjoy this tiny bit of titillation all night, to let him wrap her in the intimacy of his tongue, his taste, until all the hours had slid away and the candles had burned down to nubs.

But there was no going back. Beneath the gentle desire of kissing, a greater need clawed at her. Below her, his body made demands, and her body responded. She came up for air. She wrapped her legs around him. She skimmed her palms up his ribs, over his armpits, up his arms, and clasped her fingers around his wrists. Stretched across him, she looked into his tortured eyes. "I want you so much. There's no other man with whom I wish to do this."

A slow smile stretched his lips. "Just as it should be."

It was less than the declaration for which she might have wished but, she reminded herself, she and Jude were about passion unfettered. She made no promises, nor would she ask for any.

She walked her hands down his chest, sat up, and positioned herself to rest directly on his hardness. She pressed herself down on him, experienced a surge of exhilaration, and slowly rolled her hips, wringing pleasure from every motion.

He watched her feverishly. "It's time to end the torment."

"You're right." She slid her hand between her legs and grasped him, positioned him. "It's time."

She looked into his eyes. She pressed herself down on the long, firm, smooth length of his member.

Beneath her, he trembled, holding himself still and letting her do as she would.

He stretched her. She had known he would, known there would be discomfort, but to her surprise her passage grew damper, easing the way. She wanted him. She pressed again, eased up, pressed again. The pain grew, but so did her exhilaration. She loved this. She loved having this strong man trapped between her legs. She loved the earthy scents of their bodies as they mixed and mingled. Her fingers curled in the coarse hair on his chest. She heard someone panting, realized it was her. Heard a deep groan, realized it was him. Her eyes widened as the pain reached its peak.

Then, suddenly, it was easier. She took him all the

way inside her, ending her virginity in a glorious flourish.

And his restraint ended. He couldn't pull her into his arms, but he could move. He surged beneath her, pushing her to find the primal rhythm of sex . . . and she did. The bed shook as she rose and fell, taking him inside herself, feeling the pull and stretch as he possessed her and she possessed him.

This was what the women whispered about. This was why men acted like fools. For this primitive grandness, the sensation of racing toward a togetherness that lasted forever. She was with Jude in a way she had never dreamed possible, joined body . . . and soul.

Over and over again, he lifted his body against hers. He strained at the knots, and his sleek muscles bulged and battled beneath his skin, visible testimony to the forces that strove within him. He watched, his blue eyes feverish, as passion pinched at her nerves, wringing moans of rapture from her throat. In the center of her body, delight ebbed and flowed, growing greater every time he pushed inside her. Their skin slapped together as their ride grew wilder, quicker, freer. Her hands clenched into fists. Her nipples puckered into tiny, painful beads. Everything in her tensed, waiting, wanting . . .

When climax took her, it took her with the strength of a great storm. Lightning streaked along her skin, turning it to fire. Her blood thundered in her ears. Her eyes were blinded by tears, and her lungs ached as she tried to get breath. But nothing mattered, not seeing, not breathing. Nothing mattered except chasing sensation with every thrust. She cried aloud and dug her nails into his shoulders. Beneath her, he drove into her as if he would fill her, fuse them, make for himself a permanent place between her legs, in her womb . . . in her heart. Inside her, her tissues clenched at him, trying to keep him there where it felt so good. Trying to wring promises of forever from him.

For one long, astonishing moment, she found total bliss.

But it was too much, too good, too magnificent.

The feeling began to slip away. Caroline began to subside, to sink atop him and rest.

But Jude wasn't finished. He thrust beneath her, seeking the same bliss that had consumed her, and when the storm took him, he gave a shout. His eyes closed, and he moved with such fury as if everything that went before was as nothing.

She didn't want to. She didn't think it was possible. But his climax forced her to another, and another. Her body was no longer her own. Her pleasure united with his and this time . . . this time it was more. It was bigger. This time as she took him inside her, he came with a magnificence that shook the bed. Shook the earth. In his seed, he gave her his promise of forever and she gave him . . . everything. She gave him all of herself.

Jude woke at the first light of dawn to find his arms free and Caroline gone from his bed. He sat up and looked around, but he knew without being told she had left the house. "Damned woman!" He cast his pillow across the room, but it bounced and settled on the floor, which didn't relieve his frustration at all. Nothing would do that except to have Caroline here, his arms free, and all the time in the world to exact his vengeance for her cruel and wonderful use of his body.

Springing out of bed, he looked down the length of his body. He had an erection. Of course he did. He always had an erection when he looked at Caroline, thought of Caroline, touched Caroline . . . now he'd possessed her. A smear of virginal blood that decorated it, proof positive last night had been real, but his cock didn't seem to realize it. It still strutted and strained, trying to find its way back between her legs to rut again.

Jude's fists clenched at his side and he stared, sightless, out the window, where London was slowly coming to life. How very odd that knowing Caroline carnally made him want her more . . . and not so odd that the manner in which she used him made him resolve to make her suffer as he had.

Yes, he missed Michael. Yes, he burned with the need to make those villains pay for that charred body buried in a land far away. But it was time to finish and move on, and he had not a doubt that the future somehow included *her*.

In a frenzy of activity, he rang for his valet and when the man stumbled in, half-dressed, Jude ordered a bath and his most absurd new outfit.

He had to get the matter of the Moricadians concluded so he could concentrate on dealing with Caroline—whatever that took.

Chapter 19

$\mathcal{T}$he streets were silent, waiting the first calls of the vendors and the creak of the street carts. Caroline walked toward her father's house and smiled up at the sky. The sun had just risen, promising one of those rare days in London, clear and bright and warm. Of course. How could it not be? Last night, Caroline had taken control of her life. She was brave. She would never be afraid again. She . . . she smelled the stench of an unwashed body.

Belated caution grabbed her by the throat. At all times and everywhere, London was dangerous. No one knew that better than she did.

Whirling around, she found herself facing a hulking fellow, as tall as Jude, but he was swaying, dirty, and drunk. She backed up, terrified, but her ball gown wasn't made for fleeing. "Back away!" she said in her best command voice.

The attacker laughed and reached for her with crusty hands.

She opened her mouth to scream—and caught a glimpse of something racing toward them low on the ground. She heard the clatter of wheels.

Harry.

The drunk looked down, aimed a kick—and yelled.

Harry went tumbling, but Caroline saw the bloody knife in his hand. He'd stabbed the drunk in the foot.

But gin made the brute immune to the pain, for he shook his head to clear it and started toward Caroline again.

Caroline kept moving. She stumbled. At her feet she saw an iron ring that had peeled off its wheel—and an opportunity. Grabbing it, she swung it as hard as she could into his chest.

He grunted and kept coming.

She swung again.

He yanked it out of her grasp and cast it across the cobblestones, clattering obscenely. His breath hissed through the gaps in his blackened teeth, and his red eyes flamed with rage. He lumbered toward her, his huge hands outstretched—

And Harry attacked from behind, his knife steady, and sliced him behind the knee.

The drunk's leg went out from underneath him. He went down screaming.

"That'll keep 'im down." Harry wiped his knife on his sleeve and tucked it in its sheath beneath his arm. He offered his hand. "Let's get out o' 'ere before someone comes t' see why 'e's bawling."

Caroline pulled him along as she hurried around the corner. Her head whirled. "I didn't know you could fight like that."

"Devil a bit. If ye want t' survive on the ships, 'tis best t' learn a thing or two. 'Aven't ever been sorry, Oi 'aven't."

"Will that man walk again?" The screams were fading as they hurried away.

"Do ye think Oi care?" Harry asked.

No, she supposed he didn't. Not when he wheeled his way through the mud and the refuse every day of his life, and took a kick because it was easy. "I thank you so much."

"'Ave Oi taught ye nothing? Ye 'ave t' pay attention." He sounded exasperated and angry. "There're always villains out 'ere, worse 'en me."

"Not worse than you," she teased, but her smile faded at once. She didn't want to think about caution, but neither did she wish to lose her life on the very day she'd begun to live it. "I'm sorry, I'll be more careful. Are you hurt?"

"A few bruises, that's all. Oi've 'ad worse." He cocked a knowing eye at her ball gown. "Nice duds. One would almost think ye 'adn't gone 'ome last night."

Caroline knew that Harry kept track of everything that occurred in London. He had eyes everywhere. She'd no doubt been seen leaving the ball last night, and just as likely been seen entering Jude's house. "Do you blame me for what I did?" she asked in a low voice.

"Do ye care what Oi think?"

"Yes," she said sincerely. "I value your good opinion."

"And well ye should." But a smile crossed his lips. "'E's got a good reputation, does yer fellow. Good thing t' see ye think o' yerself at last. But will 'e marry ye?"

"Heavens, no! That was never my intention." Last night hadn't changed her purpose. She was steadfast in her intent. Jude had to be married. She might as well collect the fee for accomplishing that feat. "But right now I have three choices—to be a spinster my whole life, to live with my family in France, or to become a courtesan. Just once I wanted to do as I wished without thinking of my reputation or my plans or my family."

"Hm." Harry's lips puckered.

The memory of his expertise with the knife rose in her mind. She knew he was fond of her, and alarm skittered along her nerves. "You . . . you won't say anything to him, will you?"

"'Oo? Lord 'Untington? Nary a word, dearie. 'Tis yer business and none o' me own."

She didn't know if she quite believed Harry, but they had reached her father's house. She gestured. "Won't you come in?"

Harry eyed the flight of stairs down to the kitchen. "No, Oi think Oi'll give it a pass this time."

Of course. "Can I get you some food or drink?"

"Now that ye can do. Something warm t' eat, and a bottle o' medicinal rum, if ye please."

She opened her mouth to remonstrate, then decided that if the man wanted to dose himself with rum, she wasn't one to dissuade him. Descending the stairs, she knocked, and when Cook answered, she hurried into the warm kitchen redolent with the smell of bread baking. "There's a man out there. He has no legs, but he just saved my life. Dear Cook, could you give him a hot breakfast and a bottle of rum?"

Cook stood with her flour-covered hands on her ample hips. "Saved yer life, heh?" She eyed Caroline's ball gown. "I can see why 'twas necessary."

Caroline ignored that. "I have to talk to Genevieve. Father out of the way?"

"Already left fer the office," Cook said.

"Good." Caroline collected two warm scones and devoured one as she flitted out the door.

The other she held under Genevieve's nose until the sleeping child stirred and asked fretfully, "What do you want?"

"To see my sister."

"Caroline?" Genevieve's eyes popped open. "What are you doing here? Now?"

"I had to ask you a question. I've seen Father twice in a week, and he asked me to come home."

"Really?" Genevieve sat straight up. "Are you going to do it?"

"Not if I can get Lord Huntington married instead." A pang went through Caroline at the words. Sitting on the bed, she put her arm around Genevieve. "Do you know what purpose Father had in asking me home?"

"No, but he's up to something." Genevieve rubbed the sleep from her eyes. "He paced around here for a couple of days, and once he actually spoke to me."

"And said what?"

"Told me I would never be as pretty as you, so if he gave me a Season, he still wouldn't have a chance at a title."

"He's wrong." Caroline pushed the hair back from Genevieve's face and smiled into the piquant features. "You're going to be much more than pretty. You're going to be beautiful."

"I hope so," Genevieve said resentfully. "I didn't used to care—"

A blatant lie, Caroline knew.

"—But now I want to be beautiful so I can catch a title and never, ever let Father visit me ever."

"That's a reasonable goal," Caroline acknowledged.

She hugged Genevieve. "I have to go back, but if you discover what he's up to, send me a message."

"I'll look around," Genevieve promised. "I'll find out what he's doing."

Jude walked into Throckmorton's office in the anonymous town house in London. "How did the operation go last night?"

Throckmorton looked up from his desk and shaded his eyes. "My God, man, do you have to dress like that to come here?"

Jude looked down at his fiery red waistcoat trimmed with jiggling gold fobs. "I'm on my way to see the Moricadians. I think this will distract them from any hint of intelligence I might display, don't you?"

"God, yes." Standing, Throckmorton walked toward the door. "Your valuables were retrieved, but Maltin found nothing in the way of information to give us a clue about the Moricadians' plans. Yet he brought us something that could prove of great usefulness."

Jude followed him. "What's that?"

"Their valet. He walked in on Maltin. Maltin grabbed him and brought him back here. He's being interrogated now."

"That *is* good," Jude said with satisfaction. "They'll think he took everything and fled. What's the interrogation brought out?"

"He won't say a word."

"Maybe he only speaks Moricadian."

Throckmorton cast a significant glance at Jude. "That's why we're going to see him."

They met one of Throckmorton's hulking guards hurrying down the corridor toward them, and without ceremony, he said, "Sir, you'll want to come and see this."

Throckmorton and Jude exchanged glances. The guard, as tough a man as ever they'd met, looked disgusted and more than a little ill.

In a small room in the interior of the house lit by a few candles, they found the single chair occupied by a man so thin he was a stone away from a cadaver—the Moricadians' valet.

Two men leaned against the wall; they straightened as Throckmorton and Jude entered. One of them said, "Sir, we've found out why he won't talk. Take a look."

Without being told, the prisoner opened his mouth— and where his tongue should be was an empty cavern. His tongue had been ripped out.

"God Almighty!" Throckmorton leaped backward.

"We didn't kidnap the poor sod," Throckmorton's man said. "We rescued him."

"Who the hell did this?" Throckmorton demanded.

In answer, the prisoner rolled up his sleeve and showed them a round red mark in his skin. Then another, then another. Some of them were scabs, some scars, a few were oozing.

"Bouchard and his damned cigar." Jude lifted his appalled gaze to Throckmorton. "I did warn you about Bouchard."

"So you did." Throckmorton headed for the door. "Call a doctor. Fix this poor fellow up. See if he knows how to write—"

"Not likely." Jude followed him back down the corridor.

"No, not likely. This puts a whole new complexion on the matter. The Moricadians must know he was too intimidated to leave on his own. They'll suspect he had help. They'll be nervous, ready to get the job done as quickly as possible." In his office, Throckmorton went to his brandy decanter, filled a glass, and swallowed it without a breath. "I never get used to that kind of cruelty."

"No." Once again Jude wondered at the tortures Michael had endured before he died.

With a glance at Jude, Throckmorton filled another glass and handed it over. "Are you having luck using your governess as a cover?"

"De Guignard has fallen in love with her." Jude swallowed his brandy, too, and hoped it would heat the chill in his blood.

"That's good, because we'd hoped he would fall in love with Gloriana Dollydear. Apparently she's too coarse to appeal to him." Throckmorton filled Jude's glass again, and the two men sipped their second glasses. "He's definitely the weak link in those two. Can you use your governess?"

"Why?"

"As the crisis comes to a head, she might actively have to assist us. Can she do it?"

"Yes." Jude put down his glass. Yes, Caroline was steady and courageous. But it was one thing to use her as camouflage. It was another to put her in peril, for he had tasted her innocence . . . taken her innocence. "Bouchard is dangerous. Deadly. Their valet has the scars to prove it. *I* have the scars to prove it."

"I'm not putting a woman on the front line. You know that." Throckmorton took a sip and added the corollary Jude knew was coming. "Not unless it's absolutely necessary. Desperate times require desperate measures. If you get queasy about using a woman, take a look at your signet ring."

Michael's ring. Jude stroked the warped surface, stared at the glinting ruby. Everything in him rebelled at the thought of Caroline in the hands of Moricadians. Yet . . . yet these men deserved to hang for what they'd done and what they were going to do.

"Go visit them. See what you can find out. Tonight I'll be at the opera putting on my play with Miss Dollydear for them to see"—Throckmorton looked disgusted—"and I'd like to get this wrapped up before the Moricadians can complete their plan to murder . . . whoever."

"As do we all."

"At least you don't have to spend your time pretending to be infatuated with an opera singer. Let's finish this matter before my reputation is blasted all to hell."

"It's far too late for that, too, my dear Throckmorton." Jude took a chilly pleasure in pointing that out as he walked to the door, fobs jingling. "Far too late for that."

Chapter 20

"We're going to walk into this tea, smile graciously, and if someone asks about your ignoble retreat last night, we'll say your sister needed you." Nicolette snapped out Caroline's instructions like Napoleon making an imperial declaration.

"Yes, Your Grace." The carriage pulled to a halt before Lady Emma's small town house.

"I'll be at your side for the first few minutes. Then if all goes well, I'll drift away, but I'll never be out of the room. If someone dares to make an inappropriate comment, I'll be back at your side at once. No matter what happens, you're not to run away again." The spark in Nicolette's eyes did not invite discussion.

"No, Your Grace." For Caroline's flight had been seen as an admission of guilt and was already the scandal of London.

"Lady Emma is a dear friend and immensely respectable, and she has agreed to completely support us, but you must promise not to panic again."

"No, Your Grace." Nicolette had been furious when Caroline got home this morning. She'd been pale with worry and sure Caroline had been killed on the streets, and she'd shouted at Caroline in a way Caroline had never been shouted at. She shouted like . . . like a mother whose daughter had scared her to death. Caroline had never been so touched in her life, and when she broke down and wept, Nicolette had wept, too. The bond of affection between them was becoming something more, something different. Something stronger, although Caroline didn't dare put a name on it.

Then Nicolette had made plans to rehabilitate Caroline's reputation—again—and a few hours later here they were at a ladies' tea to do just that.

"All right then." Nicolette's gaze swept Caroline's pale green gown. "You look completely handsome and appropriate. You're a friend of the duke and duchess of Nevett. You have no reason to fear, and you must not flee. One more time, and I can't rescue you from your folly."

"No, Your Grace." Caroline climbed the stairs beside the duchess.

"Are you afraid?" Nicolette asked as they stood before the gleaming door.

"No, Your Grace." She wasn't. Last night, Caroline had allowed an awful woman to rout her, and she'd done as Nicolette accused—she'd run away. Then she'd seized control of her destiny—and of Jude—and now she wasn't afraid of anything. Run? No. She had held a strong man in her hands and made him tremble. She was powerful. No one could change that. Not ever.

The door opened. Nicolette and Caroline stepped inside. Other ladies stood there, discarding their outerwear, chatting lightly, looking like pictures of kindness and gentility. They froze when they saw the new arrivals, then hurried to the drawing room, pretending they hadn't seen them.

"I'm sorry I put you in such an awkward position, Your Grace," Caroline said contritely. "I promise it won't happen again."

"I know it won't." Nicolette placed one of her hands on each of Caroline's arms and squeezed like a trainer encouraging a boxer. "Chin up!"

"And smile," Caroline added.

Nicolette did smile, a rather toothy grin that boded ill for anyone who got in her way. "Let us conquer London today."

When they stepped into the doorway, it was obvious by whispers and the shocked expressions the word had already spread—the infamous Miss Ritter was here.

Lady Emma, a small, slender, hunched spinster of seventy, hustled forward. "My darling Nicolette, how good of you to come. And Miss Ritter!" She offered her hand. "Is your sister better?"

Gracefully, Caroline picked up her cue. "She is, thank you. She has a weakness of the lungs and caused us much concern."

"So you were up all night caring for your ill sister? No wonder you look tired. You will allow an old woman the liberty of speaking so bluntly, won't you?" Lady Emma patted Caroline's hand. "Come and sit close to me and have a refreshing cup of tea. My cook is reputed to make the best crumpets in London."

Caroline murmured her thanks and joined Lady Emma while she poured, making small talk about the little nothings that occupied society's attention. Nicolette moved among the guests, greeting her friends, who behaved normally, and others, who flinched as if she carried the plague. But as newcomers trickled in and everything appeared to be normal, the level of conversation gradually rose. Lady James arrived and, with a cry of pleasure touched her cheek to Caroline's, and soon Lady Morrison, one of Nicolette's special friends, briefly joined them for a tête-à-tête about the opera they would attend that night. A tense moment occurred when Lady Reederman arrived, but although her sharp gaze focused on Caroline, her unerring manners allowed her to do nothing but politely join in the gathering.

When Lady Emma gave Caroline a discreet shove, Caroline rose and circulated through the room. And the ladies spoke to her. No one cut Caroline. Everyone solicitously asked after her sister.

So when the silence fell, it fell with a thud that shook the room. Caroline felt the small hairs on her body rise. Slowly, she turned toward the door, and there, framed like a bony goddess of vengeance, stood Lady Freshfield.

Her eyes flamed as she looked at Caroline. Hatred blotched her cheeks. She sneered with such vicious intent her lips looked as if they were drawn on with a shaky hand. Her overdressed figure vibrated with indignation, and she looked liked a caricature of a lady drawn by an underworld artist.

Absently, Caroline wondered how Lady Freshfield had learned she was here. Gossip must have flown across London; Caroline Ritter was at a tea party and would seize her good reputation unless you take action. Who would tell her?

Ah. Of course. Lord Freshfield. He had set his wife

on her last night. Probably he had done so again today, for he had hunted Caroline all these years, and he would not accept defeat now.

Yet last night, he had been routed from her nightmares. Jude made her feel immortal, as if she could conquer her troubles because she could handle him. She knew it was an illusion, but right now it seemed the truth.

Poor Lady Freshfield. Caroline realized she'd said it aloud. "Poor Lady Freshfield."

Nicolette walked to Caroline's side. "Lady Freshfield—"

Caroline waved her to silence. She didn't need Nicolette's help. Her body ached from holding Jude within it, a constant reminder of what love should be, and she was not going to cower before this pathetic reminder of love gone wrong.

"How dare you show your face in London society again?" Like a thin, venomous snake, Lady Freshfield glided forward, her unblinking gaze fixed on Caroline. "Did I teach you nothing last night?"

"You tried to teach me bad manners, but I am resistant," Caroline said without flinching.

A few of the onlookers gasped. A few giggled. And Nicolette whispered, "That's it, knock her out."

"You can't be here among good women. They'll never accept you," Lady Freshfield said. "You're notorious."

"Yes. Even after four years, people remember *my* name." Caroline watched Lady Freshfield as she absorbed the insult, as her hand lifted. Caroline caught Lady Freshfield's wrist.

Lady Freshfield struggled to free herself. Her claw of a hand held talons ready to rip out Caroline's eyes.

For the first time in her life, Caroline was truly glad

she was a tall woman. She was glad she was young and strong, and glad for the difficult years that had taught her to defend herself, for she wouldn't allow Lady Freshfield to hurt her. In a cold, clear voice that reached to the edges of the room, she said, "I beg of you, Lady Freshfield, remember—brawling is so vulgar. If we indulge, these ladies might think that we're common."

Amusement rippled through the room. Caroline heard the faintest call of, "Brava!" but what mattered now was staring into Lady Freshfield's eyes and enforcing her own will. This time, her voice reached only Lady Freshfield's ears. "You will not attack me. I will triumph."

"You're a whore." Lady Freshfield's voice was shrill and hysterical.

"That is quite enough." Lady Emma stepped forward, very much the aristocrat and the lady. "We don't use that kind of language in my house. It *is* common. Furthermore, I didn't invite you today, Lady Freshfield, and I know I didn't ask you to vet my guests. I suggest you'll be happier at home until you've recovered your softer sensibilities and are fit to be in gentle company."

Lady Freshfield looked around at the women who stared at her as if she were some unknown beast. She scuffled with Caroline for one more moment. Then, abruptly, she gave up. Her struggles died.

Caroline cautiously released her and stepped back in fear of a stealthy, slashing attack.

Lady Freshfield breathed heavily as if she'd run miles in her heeled shoes, and she spoke to the gathering at large. "I can't believe you would let *her* be here. You, all of you—you're not truly noble. You don't know proper behavior. All you care about is money and influence, and you let her join you because of the fortune,

and because a *duchess*"—the word rang with scorn—
"sponsors her. But when Miss Ritter steals *your* husband, and he never returns to your bed again, you'll be
sorry." Whirling, she stomped away, leaving an obnoxious aftertaste behind her.

"Well." In a parody of astonishment, Lady Reederman sat with her teacup held partway to her mouth.
"We've been properly put in our places."

Nervous laughter rippled through the room.

"Miss Ritter, I believe you were telling us about your
sister," Lady Reederman said. "Pray continue." When
Caroline stared at her in confusion, she added, "It was
time someone put that harridan in her place. Miss Ritter, I'm not surprised it was you."

*Week 2: See that Lord Huntington has comprehensive
exposure to ladies at teas and dances.*

Caroline stared at her entry, written with such hope
weeks ago, and laughed aloud. Exposure? Oh, yes, he'd
had exposure. She had exposed herself to him for their
mutual enjoyment.

Dipping her pen into her inkwell, with a flourish she
wrote:

*Lord Huntington does well in all matters of romance,
but like any high-spirited stallion, he requires a firm
hand on the reins.*

She laughed again. Yes, she had ridden him as if he
were a stallion, and like any good rider, she had kept
control of her mount. She patted her hot cheeks as she
remembered all that they'd done during the night.

With his encouragement, Lord Huntington imbues a woman with the audacity to discover the kind of female she was born to be before neglect and cruelty sapped her strength.

Caroline couldn't lie to herself. She wouldn't have had the courage to face Lady Freshfield as she had that day if Jude hadn't allowed her such liberties the night before. Knowing that a strong man had submitted himself to her rule made her appreciate her own power, and resolve that she would allow no man—no one—to ever use her again.

When Lord Huntington marries, I expect to hear his wife is the most blissful of women, for he is the most virile of men.

Chapter 21

"If you see me nodding off, dear, please give me a discreet jab with your elbow. It's considered bad form for the duchess of Nevett to go to sleep in the middle of an aria." Nicolette subsided into her chair at the front of Nevett's private box. "Although how anyone manages to stay awake is more than I can comprehend."

Caroline grinned at such cavalier indifference. "I don't understand how anyone can sleep during the opera."

"You mean because the singers are so unearthly loud, and we're so miserably close?" The ducal box sat to the left of the stage where, when one sat near the rail, as did Nicolette and Caroline, they could see everyone and everyone could see them.

"No, because the music is so grand and the singing so inspiring."

Nicolette snorted. "That's what they tell me."

"If nothing else, opera is fashionable." With a wave

of her gloved hand, Caroline's indicated the interior of the Royal Italian Opera House. The opera house had reopened two years ago, and every seat on the floor was taken, every box on all three layers was filled. The brilliant paint glowed gold in the houselights, and the dome rose far above the floor in celestial splendor. "Everyone in the ton is here."

"Ah, but one of the advantages of being a duchess, and I admit there are quite a few, is that it doesn't matter what everyone else is doing." Nicolette settled back with a smug grin. "I'm still a leader of the ton whether I attend the opera or not."

"In that case, you might as well nod off. Boredom can't hurt your social standing."

Nicolette admonishingly pointed her finger at Caroline. "*Don't* tempt me." But she laughed. "In truth, when the lights go down, I'll move to the back of the box. No one can see me there. Then all I have to worry about is snoring so loudly I can be heard."

Caroline chuckled, irrepressibly pleased with the night, her circumstances, and her companion. How could she not be? Although she knew it had never been Nevett's plan, his patronage had elevated her status from that of a soiled dove to the heady heights of companion to the duchess. She ate well, she dressed well, she once again dwelled among the society she had been groomed to join, and if some people looked at her askance, she had no fear of them, for the duke's status protected her . . . and after that day's tea, so did her own bravado.

Best of all, she had no reason to feel guilty. Her elevation came because she was diligently doing the work for which she'd been hired. She was helping Jude once again become an accepted member of society, and she was proud of her advances. By the end of the Season, she would have him married . . .

All right, she did have one reason to feel guilty.

A responsible governess did not sleep with her student. She most certainly didn't tie him to the bed first, even though he had allowed her the liberty. Her eyes half closed as she remembered the pleasure she had dispensed and the pleasure she had reaped.

No, a respectable governess didn't kiss a man until he writhed or ride him until both were exhausted; but it had been one time only, a moment of madness to prove to herself, once and for all, that she was in control of her life, herself, and her passions.

And Jude's, of course. She had conquered Jude in a fabulous and triumphant campaign. She was a woman filled with a sense of her own power.

Nicolette held her opera glasses to her face and examined the boxes on the other side of the theater. She looked down at the floor where the hoi polloi sat and talked and wandered. "Where is Jude?" Nicolette asked. "He's supposed to be here by now."

Caroline smoothed her silk skirt with careful hands. "I don't know." Was he avoiding her? Did he regret the previous night? Had she read him wrong, and his pleasure hadn't been as great as hers?

Or was he, perhaps, angry that she'd sneaked away? Angry that she'd refused to untie him and had forced him to do as she wished? At the memory, she could scarcely contain her breathing. How dreadful—or wonderful—that the mere thought of him sent her into palpitations.

"That's his voice in the corridor," Nicolette said. "See what he's doing, dear."

Caroline went to the doorway and looked out.

Jude stood there, speaking to Comte de Guignard and Monsieur Bouchard, and he looked . . . marvelous. He was heart-stoppingly handsome with a profile that defined masculinity. The brow, broad and sure, the nose, once broken and now battered, the purposeful jaw, those lips . . . Jude's lips made kissing an art, one whose memory alone made Caroline rest her hand over her heart to still its pounding.

"I'm still so shocked to hear about the burglary in your home last night." Jude's voice quivered with horror. "It's obviously the work of someone who hates the French."

"I am not French." Comte de Guignard was terse enough to be rude. "I'm from Moricadia."

Jude's costume in shades of mauve didn't offend her eye, but she suspected the clothing no longer mattered for she now knew what lay beneath. To her, all that mattered was Jude's sleek, muscled body, scarred by violence, the rough hair and smooth skin, the masculine organ that promised and gave so much rapture.

Tears sprang to her eyes as she recalled the pleasure, and more tears as she realized that once was not enough. She would allow herself no more of those sweet visitations; she'd done as she wished and discovered why women so readily gave themselves up to a man's embrace. She'd taken joy from him and given joy in return, and now she would be as she'd been before: celibate and solitary.

Pulling herself back into the box, she leaned against the wall, whisked the tears off her cheeks, and pretended not to care.

"But you're not Moricadian, eh? True Moricadians are not much more than peasants. If France hadn't taken over the country, they'd still be eating quail without a single sauce." Jude sounded like an actor declaiming, and a bad actor at that. "You and your fellow Frenchmen who rule the country are the real aristocrats."

"That's true," Comte de Guignard said softly.

To Caroline's surprise, he sounded like a hissing snake.

"The sooner Moricadia unites with France, the happier you'll be," Jude said.

Comte de Guignard said something in a language Caroline neither understood nor recognized, but the tone made her turn her head and frown.

"What?" Huntington asked, sounding bewildered.

"The comte said you have a superior understanding of his mind." Monsieur Bouchard's voice clearly told Caroline he was lying.

For the first time she wondered why Huntington seemed so enamored of the two men. They neither liked nor respected him. They didn't bother to hide their scorn. Jude said he worshipped all that was French, but as Comte de Guignard had taken care to remind Jude, they weren't truly French.

"I must thank you for including me in your shooting today," Jude said happily. "I'll wager you didn't realize I was an expert shot."

"You are an expert, indeed." Monsieur Bouchard sounded delighted. "And when I told a few of the kind friends we've made in your ton, they assured me everyone knows about your gift."

"Oh, please." Caroline could almost hear Jude blush. "I am abashed."

The orchestra struck up the overture.

"Ah. We should return to our box," Comte de Guignard said.

"Visit us during the interlude," Jude invited.

Caroline, afraid to be caught eavesdropping, started back for her chair, but when she heard her name, she stopped.

"Miss Ritter is with us, and she adores you both." Jude whispered loudly. "Especially you, my dear comte."

Caroline didn't know what to think. Why would Jude say such a thing? She'd told him what she thought of Comte de Guignard—did Jude think *only* of pleasing the Moricadians? Despite his frivolity and seeming insensibility, Jude was not a stupid man. In fact, Caroline realized she had great regard for his intellect. She couldn't quite put her finger on it, but something reeked of deception.

Hurrying back to her chair, Caroline told Nicolette, "He's still in the corridor holding forth with Comte de Guignard and Monsieur Bouchard."

He stepped into the box, and Nicolette instructed, "Shut the door and sit down, Jude. The opera is beginning."

"Yes, Mum." He pulled his chair directly behind Caroline's, and sat close enough that she could smell the clean scent of his masculinity, was aware of his every movement, felt crowded against the rail.

And her indignation melted. She knew what Jude was; he'd never pretended to be anything but a habitué of the Moricadians and the French. For the moment Caroline would be happy to have him close behind her and untouchable.

The lights dimmed in the house and brightened on the stage. The music swelled, and the soprano danced out on the stage. She was buxom, handsome, and had eyes so lively they reached across the distance to enchant everyone in audience.

Everyone, that was, except Nicolette. Nicolette slouched into her chair, and when the soprano opened her mouth to sing, Nicolette groaned without delicacy or a care to the company in the other boxes.

"Sh," Caroline whispered. "Those around us will think it's me."

Nicolette glanced from side to side. The walls between the boxes were thin, but solid. "The lights are down. No one can see me. Jude can take my place." And standing, she moved to the back of the box. She sat on one chair, pulled another under her feet, folded her arms across her chest, and let her chin sink to her chest. Her low voice wafted across the box. "Enjoy the opera, children."

Caroline expected Jude to move forward and join her, but he remained seated behind her, out of sight yet an ever-present being at her back.

"Did I tell you how very lovely you look tonight?" His voice stirred the tendrils of hair looped over her neck.

"Thank you." She smoothed the skirt again, loving the feel of her silk gloves over the velvet opera dress. The skirt was constructed of tiers of color, starting with a light blue on her bodice and the top tier and descending in color increments to a midnight blue at the hem. Caroline had been in doubt about wearing something so unusual, but she'd recognized the genius when she donned the gown. It was glorious.

Daisy had curled her hair into ringlets and placed a single red rose above her ear. The duchess had insisted on loaning her an intricate sapphire necklace set in gold and sprinkled with diamonds and matching earrings. The buzz that had followed Caroline as she walked with the duchess confirmed it—worn with a ruffled mantle of the same light blue as the bodice, this costume would set the trend for months to come. "The gown is beautiful."

"I would say it was the wearer who makes the gown beautiful."

She took a deep breath of air heated by Jude's passion. Or was it her passion? She didn't know. She didn't dare guess.

His arm reached around her. His hand took hers, and he held it. Just held it. She stared blindly at the stage where the soprano held forth and let the warmth of his clasp seep into her soul. Why did she care? If he'd intimately stroked her, she would have responded. Of course she would, because she couldn't *not*. But when he held her hand, just held it, she felt . . . safe. Protected. Cherished.

And no amount of common sense could convince her otherwise. Why did he affect her like this? She refused to look deeply into the reasons. Whatever they were, she didn't want to know.

As they watched the first act, her fingers tingled where he touched her—and the fingers on her other hand tingled, too. It was as if a single touch from him ignited her whole body.

On the stage, the baritone sang of love unfulfilled. The soprano flirted and danced. The music soared and reached, while Caroline's heart soared with it.

It had been so long since she'd felt like this, she couldn't diagnose her own mood. Finally, she realized—she was happy.

It wouldn't last. Experience had taught her that. But for this moment, she basked in perfect happiness.

"I think only of last night." Jude's lips touched her ear, moved with delicate precision as he quietly spoke. "I can't forget it for a moment. I want to have you touch me again." He freed his hand from hers. "No, more than that—I want to touch you."

The sound of his voice made her eyes close. She tilted her head down, enamored of his scent, his sound, his words. "We can't. What I did—"

"We did."

"What we did was a momentary wildness."

"You . . . you are wildness itself." His voice was buttery soft, gentle . . . inciting. "You're brave and courageous. You dare to bind a man and take what you want of him. Only you could do that, Caroline. Only you."

She thrilled at the sound of her name on his lips. She thrilled at his praise. She knew he was back there, out of her sight, lurking in the darkness, and the heat of his body transferred to hers. She needed air; she breathed deeply and took in more of his scent, his heat. He was infecting her with desire.

His lips slid to the tender place behind her ear, a whispery caress, a hint of a shiver.

Her breath caught, held, the shard of memory sharp and piercing. Of holding him within her, of pain and ecstasy.

His hand slid up her arm, massaged her shoulder, then slid down to cup her breast. He hadn't touched her last night. She hadn't loosened his hands to allow it. Now she realized her mistake. Her breast swelled, aching with a passion she remembered only too well. His fingers brushed softly across her nipple; it beaded.

Yet this was different. *He* touched *her*. Her toes curled inside her soft slippers. The blood rushed in her veins. The dark surrounding them loosened all inhibitions. She was wild, carnal, an element of nature, alone with the man who brought her to life.

On the stage, men and women sang.

In the other boxes and on the floor, people watched. Behind her, the duchess slept.

No one knew what Jude was doing to her, and Caroline loved the secrecy of it. The illicit thrill of knowing they should not touch here at the opera. They shouldn't touch at all, ever, anywhere, and they defied convention and propriety and everything she had worshipped and obeyed.

"Jude . . ." His name exited her lips on the merest exhale, an injunction, a plea.

"Yes, my darling girl."

She felt his smile against her cheek. He turned her head to his and kissed her. A single, close-lipped press of the lips. Yet she had sampled his flavor of passion before, and now she recognized his declaration of intent. She relished it. Blindly, she lifted her hand and laid it against his jaw.

Lifting his mouth, he whispered, "I've dreamed about you. About doing to you what you did to me."

His voice rasped along her nerves, deep and restive, compelling memory when she would prefer to be guiltless, without a past, without reliving the sensation of his skin against hers. Opening her eyes, she saw half of his face, dimly lit by the stage lights. The other half was in darkness, inscrutable, unknowable. His eyes glinted like dark jewels, all his purpose bent on her.

She had a sense about Jude . . . he seemed more alone than any man she'd ever met. She thought he was a man who carried a burden.

That was ridiculous, for he dressed like, acted like, a fool. Her imaginings were just that, imaginings.

His arm hugged her waist, then grasped her skirt and bunched it in his fist. He lifted and bunched, lifted and bunched.

"No," she whispered, but she didn't stop him.

"No one can see. It's dark. We're behind the rail. Mum is asleep," he whispered urgently. "No one knows what we're doing here."

But she shouldn't let him. This was disgraceful behavior at the opera. Disgraceful behavior anywhere. They could be caught. They could be humiliated. Yet she grew damp at the mere idea that he would touch her here in the magnificence of the Royal Italian Opera House while the sound of violins swelled around them and magnificent voices exalted love.

He pulled her skirt up to her waist. Her petticoats rustled. His palm stroked her knee above her garter, and the thin material of her drawers allowed her to feel each tender touch as if it were on her skin. His hand ascended her thigh. He opened the slit in her drawers, and when his fingertips brushed the curled hair over her most feminine parts, he goaded her toward anguish and pleasure.

She reached for his wrist, wrapped her fingers around it, tugged him away.

And he placed her hand on the arm of her chair. Again his voice brushed her ear. "No, Caroline. It's your turn to hold fast and suffer while I take my pleasure of you."

"Why should I do that?" she whispered, her voice tentative.

"Because that's fair."

"Fair? I don't care about fair. I like being in charge." She spoke with betraying honesty.

"You'll like this, too." Lifting the curls of her hair, he kissed the nape of her neck. He had made her a promise.

As he urged her thighs apart, she stared straight forward, her unseeing gaze fixed on the gilt and paint above the stage. His thumb slid into her folds and he opened her to his touch. Her lunge of desire took her by surprise. His fingers danced across her, gentle as a mist, yet she soared as high as the soprano's notes. She gripped the chair. She bit her lower lip hard enough to bring tears to her eyes, yet she dared not make a sound. If she did, someone might hear, and although they sang onstage, she felt certain that everyone would recognize the cry of a woman whose body ripened with yearning.

His fingertips taunted her. He fondled her, skimming her womanly nub in slow circles, then moving down and sliding around the entrance to her body. Her desire increased. The moisture increased. She wanted him to put his finger inside her. She wanted . . . she wanted *him* inside her. She was insensible with need, desperate for satisfaction. In the cradle of darkness, her hips swayed, moved in a seated dance that beckoned with primitive grace. She was woman. He was man. The trappings of civilization around them meant nothing compared to the demands of her body.

As if the whole opera house moved toward the same climax, the music rose to a crescendo. The singers gathered on the stage and warbled their approval—and abruptly, they were through.

The music stopped. The curtain fell.

Conversations broke out everywhere. The attendants moved rapidly through the crowd to light the lights.

Jude lowered her skirt. He kissed her cheek, a tender nuzzle that seemed to make promises—but he said nothing.

From the back of the box, Nicolette's voice asked, "Is it finally over?"

"It's the interlude. We have the third act to go." His

voice sounded reasonable, not gripped by unfulfilled desire.

Caroline was gripped. Caroline had been teased to the edge of climax . . . and abandoned. Abandoned, her body tense, swollen, ready. She remained in her seat, her gaze watching the box opposite as if interested by the footman who lit the lamp and the people who stretched and spoke.

Silently she cursed the opera with its dreadful timing and the lights and the noise. She disliked the audience and everyone in it. She hated the whole lot, because she needed release. Never had she been so aware of being a woman, of her body's urgent requirements. She needed to be alone with Jude, and she needed it *now*.

"We'll have visitors." Nicolette's chair scraped back, and her voice moved close. "My friends will be here, as well as Caroline's, and we'll have the people who want to view the woman who routed Lady Freshfield. In addition, we'll have the young ladies you're attracting, Jude."

Caroline didn't want to stand, but Jude put his hand under her elbow and urged her to her feet.

Of course she had to behave normally. She could scarcely howl her frustration to the crowd. But her legs wobbled and her smile stretched her lips in a parody of sweetness. She felt uncoordinated, her movements as jerky as a marionette's.

Something of her distress must have shown in her face, for Nicolette frowned. She took Caroline's hand. "Dear girl, are you all right? You're trembling!"

Caroline could scarcely tell her the truth. It would be too humiliating. It would result in her dismissal. And it wouldn't help. Nothing could help. "It's the music," she said. "It moves me."

Jude slid a sideways look at her, a smiling glance that mocked her story.

And in shock, she realized—he had done this on purpose. For some nefarious reason of his own, he had teased her, brought her almost to climax—then left her unfulfilled.

Chapter 22

$\mathcal{J}$ude saw the moment Caroline realized what he'd done.

Her eyes widened, her nostrils pinched. She fought with disbelief—so he smiled at her, sending her a message she couldn't misconstrue.

He had played her like the finest violin, taunted her with thwarted desire, and he relished her frustration. Let *her* know what it was to be at the mercy of a ruthless lover.

Yet he'd created one insoluble problem . . . he was as frustrated as she was. The footmen were even then lighting the lamps on their sconces. Guests would soon be wending their way to visit the duchess, her stepson, and the infamous Miss Ritter. If anyone glanced at his trousers, they'd see the evidence of his desire.

This would not do. This wouldn't do at all.

Turning away, he stood at the rail and looked down at the floor as if the antics there fascinated him.

Mum joined him. "What do you see?"

It was what he didn't want her to see that mattered, so he shrugged and muttered, "Just watching."

"You're so evasive," she said in exasperation. "You were always a private young man, very contained, not given to confidences or to wild acts of exuberance, and since you've come back from the Continent, you've been the exact opposite. I don't understand you and your clothes and your silly mannerisms. I swear that you show every emotion—and I wouldn't give you a ha'pence for any of them. I can't believe that you've changed so much."

And he couldn't believe she had chosen *now* to express her complaints. He didn't need word of Mum's doubts to come to the ears of Bouchard and de Guignard. That would be disaster indeed.

Even worse, Caroline walked up on the other side of Mum, and he did not want *her* to question his behavior. Not when she knew him better than any other person in this world. Not when he felt as if she'd been so close to him that she lived in his skin.

"I haven't changed," he assured Mum with equal parts bravado and deceit. "France opened my mind to a new life of fashion and pleasure. I always wanted to give myself over to those things, but until France I didn't know how."

"Is he really so different, Your Grace?" Caroline asked with taut civility. "To me he seems to be so perfectly without thought."

"Actually, I'm not without thought at all." He bowed mockingly at Caroline. "I am quite deliberate in my . . . pleasures."

Caroline tossed her head in disdain, and with her chin tilted at that angle and her mouth curled with scorn, she looked untouchable, distant . . . a challenge.

The memory of the night before, the sight and the feel of her today, drove him to a madness of need. Jude had always thought of himself as sensible, but a suspicion niggled at him; this recklessness, the madness of desire seemed to arise from some hitherto hidden part of himself. It was as if Caroline mined the depths of his soul and brought forth a new metal, unknown, shiny . . . and unpredictable.

"Jude is pretending to be someone else," Mum declared.

He took a sharp breath of dismay.

"Who is he pretending to be?" Caroline's voice was as warm as the North Sea in February.

"His brother." Mum placed her hand on his arm. "But he isn't Michael, and I feel as if I've lost both of my older sons. I want my Jude back."

"Oh, Mum . . ." Jude recognized a plea when he heard one. He needed to become himself again for, as he was, he was hurting his father, his stepmother, his younger brother . . . and Caroline. Once again it was borne in on Jude that he had to get this Moricadian business finished as soon as possible and at last go on to live his life as he wished to live.

In a tone that urged confession, Mum said, "If you have something to tell me, Jude, I wish you'd just . . ." She trailed off. She stiffened.

He looked where she looked. He saw what she saw. He wanted to groan. Walking down the stairs off the stage was Miss Gloriana Dollydear, and Garrick Throckmorton stood offering her his hand to help her down.

Throckmorton couldn't have been more ill suited to

the role of *bon vivant*. Jude grinned to see him look so uncomfortable and impatient.

Luckily, Throckmorton had such a reputation as a humorless stick that Mum didn't notice his lack of enthusiasm, and she hissed, "That jackass. His wife is increasing, and he's here romancing a lightskirt!"

"Now, Mum, we don't know that for sure." Jude could think of no one with whom he wanted to talk less about mistresses than his stepmother—unless it was Caroline. Caroline, whose eyes glittered with the brittle fury of a woman tormented and forsaken.

"He's kissing her wrist." Mum's petite figure radiated fiery indignation. "What would you call it?"

"Admiration for her singing?" Jude suggested.

"Feeble!" Mum said. "Jude Edward George Durant, you're not making an excuse for Mr. Throckmorton's activities, are you?"

Jude surrendered to the inevitable. "No. No, of course not. It's disgusting. The old lecher should be shot."

"Lord Huntington finds that it's not wise for him to make excuses for bad behavior." Caroline's voice was pure vitriol. "He's so splendid at wickedness himself."

"Comte de Guignard is in the box across the way, Miss Ritter, and he has bowed to you." Jude felt no compunction about changing the subject, and even less about what he'd done to Caroline in the dark.

She solemnly curtsied to de Guignard.

In the light of a thousand golden flames, Caroline's skin glowed like muted sunlight. Oddly, the blue-green of her eyes caught a gold tint, also, and shone so brightly Jude understood why men had attempted to kill themselves for love of her. He hoped de Guignard was ready to cast himself off a cliff for her.

Guilt niggled at Jude. He'd promised himself that she wouldn't be exposed to danger, and now he encouraged her kindness, knowing Comte de Guignard would construe it as interest—and knowing, also, that Bouchard watched his compatriot with a narrowed gaze. Jude saw his impatience with de Guignard's unrequited love, for Bouchard's intent never wavered. He had no weakness except for his impatience. He felt no kindness except for himself. He needed de Guignard for his entry into society, nothing more, and Jude sensed in him a keenness to finish the job for which they'd come, and an anticipation about its execution.

Bouchard loved to kill.

"Look, Caroline, there, down on the level below. Young Turgoose is trying to get your attention," Mum said.

"Yes, by making an idiot of himself." Jude grinned unrepentantly at his friend as Goose waved and pantomimed adoration for Caroline.

With a smile and a wave, Caroline curtsied to Turgoose. "It's good to know that no one is using me to attract dear *Goose* to our company."

Did she know . . . ? Did she suspect . . . ? As Jude stared at her, trying to comprehend her mind, he saw her rather than heard her draw a breath. A startled, terrified breath.

A glance showed him her nightmare. Freshie loitered in the box down and across from them. He stared directly at Caroline. He didn't smile; he projected menace, so much menace that he made the air toxic and the temperature plunge.

Caroline's hands crushed the rich velvet of her gown.

Jude met Mum's comprehensive gaze.

"Our friends have arrived," Mum said brightly.

Jude turned Caroline with a hand on her arm and gave her a gentle push toward the small, boisterous crowd that squeezed their way into the box. Then he turned back toward the spot where Lord Freshfield had stood—and Freshie was gone.

Of course. He was the kind of man who preyed only on those weaker, because those stronger would beat him to jelly.

Grimly, Jude decided that as soon as the Moricadian matter had been dealt with, he would do something about Freshie, perhaps speak to him in a manner Freshie understood, with his bare knuckles and a lot of ruthless purpose. When Jude got done with him, Freshie would never bother Caroline again.

Nevett's footmen brought in champagne and refreshments, and before long the level of dialogue rose to ear-splitting levels. Conversation died when Miss Dollydear arrived, dressed in her lavish costume and painted with rouge and kohl, but rose again to greater strength as young men swarmed her to express their admiration for her singing—and more.

With many a modest disclaimer, Caroline accepted exuberant congratulations for her rout of Lady Freshfield; clearly Lady Freshfield had few friends among the ton. Caroline hugged her female friends. She observed as Jude lavished careless praise on Lady Pheodora for her gown and her entourage of young men. She teased Goose until he flushed and grinned, and all the while she was aware of her body. As she stood talking, she pressed her thighs together, trying to relieve the desire Jude had aroused in her. She wondered if her skin glowed from the heat of her longing.

She conjectured that she was different than she had been a day earlier, a week ago, a year ago, and marveled that no one noticed.

She wished she'd never seen Jude, wished she had him tied to a bed where she could take her pleasure and leave him without redress.

"Mademoiselle, you seem distressed." Comte de Guignard spoke softly into her ear.

She jumped. "My lord! Sir! Comte! I . . . no, I'm not upset at all." She hadn't meant to show it, anyway.

De Guignard moved around to stand before her, a tall, handsome man with influence and money. If she were smart, she'd forget Lord Huntington and use her power to make de Guignard her slave. Instead she stood there miserably speculating which one of the debutantes Jude would wed.

Monsieur Bouchard joined them, reeking of the cigar he'd gone to the lounge to smoke. He curtly answered her greeting and watched Comte de Guignard with impatient eyes.

"I witnessed the scene last night at the baron's ball, and I swear to you, no such attack would have occurred in my country. A lady such as you would be treated with fairness, and a *canard* such as Lord Freshfield would be reviled for his cruel disregard for the flower of your womanhood. And as for your father"—de Guignard folded his lips tightly and took a long breath—"but I will not cast asperions on the man to whom you owe your very life. The man who should be protecting you with *his* life!"

"That is good of you." Actually, she thought Comte de Guignard's entire speech was presumptuous to the extreme. She knew very well he spoke out of softness for women and a foreigner's misunderstanding of what should and should not be said in conversation, but right now, she wasn't inclined to give de Guignard or any man the benefit of the doubt. They could all burn in hell . . . as she was burning.

She cast a glance of loathing at Jude. He looked absolutely genial and calm as he spoke to that lush and gorgeous opera singer.

Caroline wanted to push him over the rail.

"Have I displeased you, Miss Ritter?" Comte de Guignard bowed. "I meant no impertinence."

She yanked her attention back to him. "Not at all. I'm sorry I gave you that impression. I appreciate your kindness." How to say it? "But this is a struggle I have to win on my own."

Comte de Guignard bowed his head in acceptance— or homage. "May I at least offer you a place of sanctuary?"

Monsieur Bouchard made a noise of distress.

Comte de Guignard ignored him. "We've found, quite by accident, that the Moricadian embassy is no longer safe."

"I'm sorry," Caroline said. "Are you in danger?"

In the corridor, the attendant walked past, playing the notes to recall the spectators to their seats.

"That we do not know." Comte de Guignard struck a pose appropriate for a hero posing for a statue. "But not only have we been robbed, we also suspect we are under surveillance."

"I beg you, comte, do not," Monsieur Bouchard said.

De Guignard ignored him. "So we have moved all matters of import to a different location and taken great care that it remain secret."

Again the attendant walked past, playing the notes that announced the opera was about to begin its last act. In Nevett's box, the guests began to leave.

"Yet for you, most beautiful Miss Ritter," Comte de Guignard continued, "I will compromise my own safety and the safety of my compatriot and tell you the location."

"No, don't!" Caroline could see the trouble with this situation. If anything happened at their new embassy, she would be a suspect—and she'd had enough adversity in her life without wishing for more.

But Comte de Guignard waved away her objection. "Please. Set my mind at ease. Accept this information and keep it close to your heart." He pressed a slip of paper into her hand.

Accepting defeat, she took the paper and slipped it into her reticule. "Thank you. I'm honored by your confidence." And promptly forgot it as, through the thinning crowd, she saw Miss Gloriana Dollydear slipping a similar note to Jude.

"That is uncalled for," Caroline whispered.

"Miss Ritter?" Comte de Guignard followed her gaze.

So did Monsieur Bouchard. His little eyes narrowed. He stroked his flourishing mustache. "Most interesting," he said in his cold voice. "Most interesting indeed."

Jude caught them staring at him and the stunning woman before him, and he taunted Caroline with a smile.

"Really!" Caroline took a step toward him, ready to attack.

"What do you suppose she wants of him?" Comte de Guignard speculated.

"Fashion advice," Caroline snapped.

Comte de Guignard looked shocked at her temper.

"Yes, I'm sure that is it." Monsieur Bouchard chortled. "Look—Monsieur Throckmorton has arrived searching for his *jeune fille*."

Looking as suspicious as any cuckold, Throckmorton thrust his way through the last of the guests to come to her side. "Miss Dollydear, I lost track of you."

"I am here, my darling." Placing her hand on his arm, Miss Dollydear looked up at him adoringly. "Take me back to the stage where I must die for love . . . of you." As he led her from the box, she glanced back and rolled her eyes at Jude.

"Uncalled for," Caroline muttered again.

Jude wanted to laugh at Caroline's expression. His governess was frustrated and jealous, and the two emotions played havoc with her good nature. She refused to look at him. She nodded curtly at de Guignard and Bouchard as they took their leave of her. And when the last guest had left she seated herself with a flounce.

As the footmen dimmed the lights, Jude sat behind her again. He watched her profile against the light from the stage, and by her rigid posture, the way she held her head, and the way she ignored him, it was clear that she was livid.

Mum suspected nothing, but chatted in a whisper for the first few minutes of the opera.

Caroline answered without enthusiasm.

Mum slumped in her seat. Within ten minutes, her head bobbed. She caught herself, focused on the stage once more, then nodded again.

It was exactly the opportunity which he'd anticipated. Lightly he touched her on the shoulder. "Mum, do you want to sit in back?"

"Hm?" Blinking, she looked around. Standing, she

shook out her skirt. "No, I'm going to the retiring room."

He was the luckiest man in the world.

"There'll be other women there who are bored and want to gossip. Be good, children." Mum quit the box . . .

. . . Leaving an ever-deepening pool of silence. In the chair in front of him, Caroline sat stiffly. Placing his hands on her bare shoulders, he whispered, "Why are you angry?"

"I'm not angry." Her voice was too loud and very firm.

"I think you are," he purred in her ear. "I think you want me to finish what I started."

"Your *affairs* are of total indifference to me—as long as you keep your hands off me." She shrugged her shoulders trying to dislodge him.

He leaned close to her ear. "Really?" Gently he bit the lobe.

She swung around to face him. "Don't . . . do that!"

He couldn't distinguish her features, but he heard aggravation and something else in her voice—arousal. And her arousal brought his body back to full attention. His heart thumped in his chest; his cock strained against his buttons. "If we were where we could be assured of privacy," he declared with brutal candor, "I would take you here on the floor."

"Nonsense," she said crisply, "you're in total control of yourself."

A challenge.

He didn't pause to think. With his hands on both her elbows, he lifted her from her chair and propelled her ahead of him into the darkest corner. She tried to jerk herself free, but her words burned along his nerves.

He'd show her control. He'd take her where she'd never been before.

Catching a chair with his toe, he pulled it toward them and pressed her into the seat.

She tried to get up.

With his hand on her waist, he pushed her back.

She whispered heatedly, "I don't know what you're doing, but—"

"I agree. You have no idea what I'm doing." Snatching up another chair, he stuck it under the doorknob and wedged it tightly. No one would come through that door.

He didn't wait. He showed no finesse, bothered with no foreplay. Lifting her skirt, he slid underneath and between her legs. He heard her gasp muffled by petticoats and silks. He smelled the warm, sweet scent of woman. Of Caroline. She tried to shove at him, but he paid no heed. He was done teasing. She wanted satisfaction. He would give it to her.

If he'd thought about it, he would have realized how uncharacteristically he was behaving. He didn't think about being caught, didn't care whether his stepmother rattled the doorknob and demanded entrance. A part of himself he'd never before met now directed him, and he would do as he wished with the woman of his dreams.

He was already familiar with the lace and the make of her drawers, and unerringly he found the gap that covered her feminine parts.

She tried to kick him away.

He laughed, loving the danger and the excitement, knowing that she wouldn't fight him. Or not very much, anyway, for her antagonism was based on need, desperate, fiery need. With his fingers he opened lips still swollen with desire. When he put his mouth against her, he experienced the same jolt that went through her. She froze as if she didn't dare move again, as if a single motion would take her over the cliff.

She didn't yet know . . . he intended to push her over the cliff.

She tasted like desire, sweet and glorious, and his passion rose as she trembled. He hadn't much time. Soon someone would notice the blocked door. So he pushed her toward her climax, licking her in small, tantalizing motions.

Her trembling grew greater.

He probed her with his tongue, savoring her passion. He pushed into her, withdrew, pushed into her, withdrew.

Her body arched in the chair. Her thighs flexed as she struggled to control her reactions.

As if he would allow that. Taking her most intimate bud between his lips, he delicately sucked while at the same time he slid his finger in her.

Her inner muscles clamped down. Her body convulsed in a long rush of need. Climax swept her, and at last he heard it, the sound she could no longer contain—a sweet, reckless groan of completion.

He loved taking her to orgasm there, with the crowd all around and the music soaring. He loved knowing he forced her to explore a sensuality she had never imagined. So he drew out her pleasure, plunging his finger inside the warm, tight sheath, using his tongue in every wonderful way he'd ever learned. But at last she slumped, exhausted, her passion depleted . . . for the moment.

And he knew they had to return to their chairs. Swiftly he arranged her drawers to propriety, withdrew from under her skirt, and removed the chair from under the doorknob.

Helping her to her feet, he smiled at the dazed expression on her shadowed face. He seated her facing the stage, and seated himself beside her. Taking her hand, he kissed it, and when she turned her stunned gaze on him, he murmured, "Revenge has never tasted so sweet."

Chapter 23

"*M*iss Ritter, ye're home!" Daisy rose from her chair before the fire where she dozed and bustled through Caroline's bedroom to light the candles. "How was the opera?"

"It was inspiring," Caroline said. More than that, it was embarrassing, revealing—and arousing.

"I've heard the Italian Opera House is all painted pretty." Daisy helped Caroline off with her mantle.

"It's beautiful." Caroline discarded her outer garments into Daisy's hands and stood, dazed, in the middle of her bedroom while the maid put them away. Caroline had never felt like this before, as if her skin stretched across bones and veins and nerves all clamoring for possession. Jude's possession.

"Ye must have had a good time. Yer cheeks are all flushed pink and rosy. Ah, I'll wager the gentlemen fought to sit next to ye."

"Behind me." *And under my skirt.* Caroline stumbled on the fringe of the rug in her bedroom.

"Careful, Miss," Daisy warned. "Are ye tired?"

"I suppose I must be." But that wasn't the problem. Caroline's muscles didn't work. She could scarcely walk, had to think how to unclench her fingers to set her reticule on the dressing table.

"Then we'll get ye right to bed." Moving behind her, Daisy opened the long line of buttons down Caroline's back.

"Thank you." But bed wouldn't help. It would probably make things worse, to rest there, staring up at the canopy and thinking of *him.*

"There ye go, Miss. And yer jewelry."

As Daisy unfastened the intricate necklace and earrings, Caroline instructed, "Those must go back to Her Grace tonight." Nothing would ease this need . . . except Jude inside her, on top of her, beneath her.

"Aye, Miss. I'll see to it myself."

During intermission, Caroline had imagined that if she could simply experience one of those marvelous sensations of . . . of completion such as she'd experienced that night at Jude's apartment, she would feel fulfilled. But Jude *had* brought her to completion, and still she wanted. She ached. If she had Jude there, she would once again tie him to the bed and use him to her own satisfaction.

"Ye have such an odd expression on yer face." Daisy studied Caroline. "Do ye have the headache, Miss?"

"No, not a headache." Most definitely it was not her head that ached.

Obviously Daisy didn't believe her, for she asked, "When ye've donned yer nightgown, do ye want me to brush yer hair?"

"No, thank you." Caroline's voice held an unusual bite, and she softened it with, "Really, I am quite fine." She walked around the dressing screen in the corner, holding her dress around her shoulders.

It was dim back there. A row of hooks hung on the wall, with her nightgown on one and her nightcap on another. There was a small table with a bowl where she could set her pins and whatever other small objects she discarded, and a straight-backed chair—

She leaped back, stifling a scream.

Jude sat there, his shirt a blot of white against the dark wood, his teeth gleaming as he keenly smiled, his eyes observing every disheveled inch of her. He was as immobile as a statue . . . except for the long, sharp, thin-bladed knife he flipped over and over.

"Miss, are ye all right?" Daisy called anxiously.

Caroline clutched her gown in suddenly damp palms.

While he nodded, he continued to flip the knife, twirling it, spinning it with the expertise of a magician. His command was clear. *Answer her. Say yes.*

"I . . . I'm fine." Caroline's heart beat in her chest, her wrists, her neck. "I saw a rat," she murmured so quietly she knew Daisy couldn't hear her. She watched, rapt, as the spinning blade came to an abrupt halt.

His free hand reached toward her.

Her heartbeat accelerated.

He caught the loose neckline and tugged at it.

She swallowed. She knew this was a game, a sensuous game, but a thrill akin to fear slithered up her spine.

How ridiculous. Caroline could hear the sounds as Daisy busied herself in the open space just beyond the screen. Caroline had only to tell her that Jude was there, and he would be removed.

But she didn't want anyone to know that he dared enter her room, didn't want anyone involved in the affair between them. In the dark recesses of her soul she relished the secrecy and was flattered by his daring. To sneak into his father's house, into her bedchamber, and wait for her there . . . it was the act of a buccaneer and a lover.

So she said nothing to Daisy. But this was dangerous; she couldn't play without calamitous consequences, so she shook her head *no* to Jude.

His lips grew taut. A look developed in his shadowed eyes, a dangerous glint that promised retribution, peril and pleasure.

Without a word, he made his demand again.

And she realized she was frightened. Not that he would hurt her, but that he would change her from the woman she had been to the woman he would force her to become.

Yet irresistibly, she rose to his challenge and lowered the gown.

It caught on her wide petticoats, and he gestured. *Remove them.*

She stared at him—indeed, she didn't dare glance away. Jude looked as dangerous and as sharp as the knife he held. Reaching behind her, she untied the bows, one after the other, that held up her petticoats. Then she hesitated.

Without them, she would be clad in her corset and chemise, her drawers, her garters, her stockings, and her shoes. She would be covered, yet . . . she would feel nude. Why that bothered her, she didn't know. Only a day ago she'd been naked atop him, riding him as if he were a stallion, using his body in every way she could imagine. Doing what *she* wanted. But to disrobe there, now, stripping deliberately for him under his command, knowing what he ultimately would demand . . . somehow that was different.

He had no patience with her qualms. With brusque impatience, he reached for the gown and the petticoats.

With a rustle of starch and cambric, she dropped them into a rich pool of blue velvet and white lace.

He stared at her body, stared with a hunger so stark and fierce she felt like Aphrodite rising from a pool. There were only the two of them united in silence and precarious intimacy. Caroline didn't hear Daisy humming as she thrust the bed warmer between the sheets, didn't know anything beyond the world of Jude and Caroline. With audacious boldness, she slid her hands down the sides of her corset to her hips, outlining her curves for Jude.

She heard the hard pull of his breath. With the toe of his boot, he hooked the gown and the petticoats and dragged them toward him.

She stepped free.

He examined the swell of her breasts over the top of her corset, the lace trim on her chemise, her cambric unmentionables. The silence between them pulsed like a living being while she waited, trembling, for his next command—

When across the screen, Daisy's cheerful voice said, "So, Miss Ritter, I'll come and take yer clothes, then."

Caroline jumped. She looked between Jude and the gap that opened into the bedchamber. *Escape!* Without volition, her muscles bunched to run.

"Send her away." His voice barely reached Caroline's ears.

She shook her head.

He smiled, but he wasn't in any way amused. His eyes were cold, fixed on her, determined to bend her to his will, and the knife made a lazy arc in the air before he caught it again. "Send her away." His voice was a rasp and a threat.

"Miss?" Daisy called.

This was not the fop. Not the tender kisser. Not the amusing companion. This man commanded his world—and Caroline had tied his hands and used him. If she didn't do as he bid now, he would come for her another time, and she would never know when or how he would take his revenge. Her courage failed her . . . or perhaps her passion overcame prudence. "D . . . daisy?" Caroline kept her gazed fixed on that wicked blade. "You may go. I can finish by myself."

"Oh, Miss, you don't want to do that. You're tired." Daisy bustled toward the screen. "Let me assist you."

"No!" Caroline snapped. Gathering her composure, in a determinedly normal tone, she said, "No. Truly. I want to be alone. I'll see you in the morning."

"Aye, Miss, in the morning," Daisy said, her tone puzzled.

Caroline stared stiffly at Jude until the door closed behind her maid. "What are you doing here?" she asked in a whisper. "How did you get in?"

"Take off your clothes." It was not a request; nor was it an answer. "Take them off until I tell you to stop."

"Why would I do that?" She toyed with the lace at her bosom.

"Because you don't have a choice. If you don't, I won't give you what you want."

"And what, good sir, is that?" The heat of his gaze made a sheen of perspiration break out all over her body.

"Me." The knife started its casual arcs in the air again. "You came tonight. When I was under your skirt, licking you, you came against my tongue. I tasted it, felt it, heard the noises you made."

She couldn't believe he would speak aloud of an event that caused her such mortification . . . and such satisfaction. Every nerve leaped to arousal. "Shut up."

He paid no heed to her words, but watched her expression like a lion on the prowl. "But that wasn't enough. You want me to take you, to make you come again and again. You want the stroke of my cock inside you, probing deep, touching your womb, sliding out—"

"Stop." Her nipples were so hard they chafed against her corset. Her legs trembled. Deep inside, she ached with need.

"Take off your clothes."

"What? No." She put her hands on her hips, but thought that pose looked provocative. She put them on her stomach, then let them dangle . . . when had her own hands become objects that could so easily provoke a man? "Do you think you can sit there and demand whatever you want?"

"Strip slowly," he whispered, his voice rasping along her nerves. "Seduce me."

"I don't want to." She wiped her palms down the cambric legs of her drawers.

"Tonight isn't about what you want. Tonight is about what I want." He chuckled with moody amusement. "Strip . . . slowly."

She stood there in the dim little corner of the room. She was too warm. She was nervous. She breathed in short pants. She wanted to run away almost as much as she wanted to stay. And in some primal corner of her mind, she knew if she did run, he would spring after her, chase her, catch her . . . and that aroused her past bearing. This should have been her worst nightmare.

Instead it was an opulent dream that existed in a secret corner of her mind—and Jude had discovered it. Jude was making it come true.

She didn't know where to start. Her corset was pink, laced at the back, and very useful in keeping her upright. Her drawers covered her legs and, more important, the feminine mound between them. She could take off her shoes . . .

"Start with"—he used the tip of the knife to point—"those."

Her drawers. "But then I'll be . . ."

"Revealed. Yes. I want to see your legs. I've been thinking about them, how I want to cup your thighs in my hands and spread them, step between them and glide inside you . . ."

For a single heartbeat, she envisioned that—and capitulated. One by one, she stepped out of her heeled shoes. With clumsy fingers, she untied her drawers and slid them slowly down her legs. Her legs, bare and so long. Too long, she'd always thought. Her stockings were tied with a garter at the knee, a pretty garter in shades of blue. Caroline remembered asking Daisy what difference it made if her garters matched her dress, for no one was going to see them. And Daisy said, "Now Miss Ritter, when ye're pretty all over, you're cheerier, that's all."

Cheery, Caroline decided, was the wrong word entirely. She was not cheery, especially as she slowly straightened, sliding her hands up her own legs and cupping them over her exposed mound.

She didn't dare look up, but she could feel the strength and the power of Jude's gaze on her.

"Take down your hair."

To take down her hair would require that she lift her

arms and display herself, all her long length, to him. She didn't think she could do it.

"Take it down," he said, before she could shake her head. "I want to hold the silkiness in my hands when I'm inside you."

She wanted that, too. He painted pictures in her mind, each one more graphic and glorious than the last. Yearning weighed on her like a lover until she was desperate and embarrassed and aching with desire.

But it took all her nerve to lift her hands away from her body and up to her head.

Jude flinched as she did, as if the sight lashed at him.

While he sprawled in the chair watching like a sultan entertained by his dancing girl, Caroline removed each pin from her hair and one by one dropped them on the floor. As she did, her gaze lowered to his lap.

His manhood strained at the buttons of his trousers.

She thought she was discreet, but he chuckled, a noise so rough it almost sounded like anguish. "Yes," he said, "I'm so damned desperate I could take you here and now right on the floor."

"And why don't you?" she dared.

He half rose in his chair, the knife clutched in his grip.

Her eyes widened, her heart thumped.

Then he subsided. "No, you shan't taunt me into taking you. This time, you're performing on my command. Finish taking down your hair."

So he balanced on the edge of passion. One move on her part could move him to action.

As she pulled the last pin, the strands slipped into her cupped hands and she brought the shining mass over her shoulder. Releasing it, she let it tumble over her bosom in perfumed profusion. She tossed her head. The chestnut curls danced across the pale skin of her bare chest. She leaned down to put on her shoes, and as she did her breasts slid free from the support of her corset. Her chemise scarcely covered her nipples, and she heard the rough intake of his breath. She straightened, taller in her heels and feeling oddly victorious. With her foot, she pushed her gown aside and stepped between his knees. Grasping his shirt near his waist, she pulled the tails free of his trousers. "Let me . . ." she whispered.

He lifted his arms, and she pulled the fine linen off over his head, leaving his chest bare. The bullet scars were round and red, breaking the symmetry of the muscles. Yet the scars lent him a toughness that put her on notice; this man could rescue her when she faced peril . . . then place her in peril with a single triumphant smile.

She held her hands an inch above his arms, not yet daring to contact his skin, yet she felt his warmth. She rubbed her palms up and down above his skin, and it was as if sparks arced between them. She didn't have to touch him. The connection was there. His flesh drew her like a magnet. In a bold rush, she pressed her hand to his chest and felt the desperate rhythm of his heart. She flirted with her eyes—ah, the old skills returned so easily—and said, "How much longer do you think you can hold out?" She smiled a languorous smile that derided his self-discipline.

"You don't understand the forces with which you're playing." He slowly came to his feet. "But it's too late. You're going to find out."

She stepped back once, twice, half-laughing, half-frightened.

He thrust the point of the knife deeply into the wood of the table, and the haft quivered there. He stalked after her. Each footstep sounded heavily. He stared at her. His gaze scorched her. She felt like . . . like a lioness teasing her mate, knowing full well what the result would be. He would take her like the animal he was, and her desires would be satisfied at last. And in the end, that was all that mattered now. To be joined, to be filled, no matter what the consequences, pleasure . . . or pain.

Briefly reason surfaced in her mind. She wanted him too much. She felt too much for him. When they parted, there *would* be pain.

Then he reached for her.

Excitement vanished in a surge of good sense. She whirled to run. He sprang after her. Her shoes clattered on the floor. She stretched out her hand to touch the door . . . but before she could, he caught her around the waist. He held her against him, her back to his front, and she could feel the prod of his member against her bottom, the heat of his bare chest against her back. She stood docilely within his embrace, breathing as hard as if she'd run a mile, and she waited.

"What do you want?" he murmured in her ear.

"You," she whispered. "Now."

"That's the right answer." Going to the door, he turned the key and locked the door.

When he looked back at her, she trembled. He'd lost all the appearance of a dilettante; instead, he was steely, serious, frightening in his intensity. Coming back to her, he walked her toward her dressing table. A lace runner draped it. Her brushes were carefully arranged. Her reticule remained where she'd tossed it.

With a sweep of his arm, he pushed everything off

onto the floor. "Bend over," he said. "Brace your arms on the table."

"But—"

"What?"

But there was a terrible vulnerability to such a position. Except for her stockings, she was naked from the waist down. To bend over in such a manner would leave her so exposed . . .

"Do you want me to love you?" Jude's voice was deeply stern and inexplicably tender.

"God, yes." She looked into the mirror at the man behind her.

The flickering of the fire burnished his brown hair with gold. His eyes were shadowed with darkness. His face was strong and austere. Never had she been so aware of his height. He towered above her, a mountain of a man, unyielding and eternal. His chest was carved marble, a sculptor's dream, and his hands . . . he placed his hands on her bare shoulders, and they were big and capable. He slid his palms down her arms, wove their fingers together, and wrapped her in an embrace. He looked into the mirror at them, and with a smile he leaned down to bestow a kiss on her shoulder.

It was only a kiss, and only on her shoulder, but the touch of his lips was exactly what she wanted. How had he known?

Then he lifted his head. He took his hands away. "Lean down."

In the mirror, she saw danger and passion.

She feared his danger, but she wanted his passion.

She rested her palms on the dressing table.

"All the way over." He would not yield.

She kept her gaze fixed to his as she glided her hands

across the polished surface. Lower and lower she bent, but she must not have obeyed quickly enough, for he placed his hand in the middle of her back and urged her the rest of the way down.

Now it was as she feared. She was exposed to him. He could touch her, gaze at her, in any way he wished. It was a yielding of self such as she'd never imagined.

"Look at you," he commanded.

She stared into the mirror. Her hair tumbled around her shoulders in wanton disarray. Her skin shone smooth and golden on her shoulders and her chest. As she shifted, her chemise teased at her breasts, displaying the swell of one, then the nipple of the other. Her lips were full and red; her cheeks were flushed peach. And her eyes . . . her eyes were shadowed with mystery and slumberous with pleasure. For the first time she saw herself as Jude saw her: beautiful, wanton, and passionate.

"Look at *us*," he said.

He stood behind her, looking into the mirror, into her eyes. He was handsome in the sunlight, but he came alive in the light of flame. Each flicker of the fire bathed him in a sinister warmth that beckoned until all she craved was to do his bidding. He stood right behind her, his trousers brushing the backs of her legs, and when she stood on her toes, when she moved just right, she felt his engorged organ press exactly where she wanted it.

And she realized—they could make love like this, standing up, looking into the mirror, moving together in an odd, backward dance . . . and she wanted it. "Please," she whispered. "I'll die if you don't make love to me soon."

"You'll die when I do." He caressed her bottom, lingering as if the touch of her skin gave him pleasure.

"Wh . . . what do you mean?"

"Doesn't your heart stop when you come? Doesn't your breath cease? Is there thought in your mind, can you see, can you hear? It's the little death, and we're going to find it in each other tonight." He explored her, brushing the hair, stroking up and down her slit, then gently opening her. "Many, many times."

She whimpered from the pleasure of his touch, and whimpered more at the thought of the long hours of ecstasy. She stretched like a cat, arching her back as she tried to get close to his manhood.

It didn't work.

"Open your legs just a little," he whispered roughly, and when she did, he stood looking down at her most private parts.

She didn't want to be embarrassed, but she was, and a flush spread over her chest, her shoulders, and flooded her face with heat.

"You're beautiful, a goddess I must worship. You leave me no choice." His finger sank into her. "I could get lost inside you and never return."

She groaned with the bliss. Connection at last. As long as he did this for her, she could forgive him for teasing her at the opera during the first act. She could forget her shock when he slid under her skirt, put his mouth on her, and forced her to unforgettable ecstasy. She could embrace his despotism now.

He drew out his finger, damp from her desire, and used it to intimately circle her. He used his thumb to capture her feminine bud, then moving up and down, stroking it with leisure confidence that made her breath catch. She quivered on the edge of orgasm, almost there, so close . . .

His hands left her.

On the table, her hands clenched into fists. Her muscles tensed so desperately tight her shoulders trembled. "Please . . ."

"Yes." In a flurry of activity, he loosened his trousers and rid himself of them. Again he stepped up behind her, his bare legs against her bare legs, his cock brushing her bottom. "Now."

To line up their bodies, he bent his knees, and when he placed the head at the opening of her body, she jumped. It was an illusion, of course, but his heat was so intense she felt as if she'd been branded.

He worked his cock into her so . . . slowly. It was as if he were testing her, relishing every inch, taking the time to experience the friction. He wore a slight, anticipatory smile. That would have made her nervous, except that the feeling of having *him* inside her was an overindulgence past bearing. She could think of nothing else. He filled her. Inside her, the muscles clenched, trying to keep him inside, trying to hold him out. She found herself suspending her breath in anticipation as he slid closer, farther, grew larger. My God, so much larger. The sensation of satiation hovered just on the edge of pain . . . or was it pleasure? She couldn't tell. Again she sensed it in her mind and in her body; he branded her with his fire, and she would never be the same.

At last he touched the center of her, a firm contact that sent heat streaking along her nerves. She groaned, a heavy, desperate sound and pressed her bottom against him, seeking that magic stroke that would give her relief.

Instead he slid back, a slow withdrawal.

Her fingernails scraped on the wood.

He eased out so far he almost left her body.

She nipped her thighs together, trying to keep him inside.

"God. Caroline." He thrust back inside, all the way inside.

She groaned with relief, with growing desire.

He withdrew, thrust again, withdrew, thrust again, and suddenly they were moving together, the elemental rhythm driving them toward madness, toward glory, toward completion.

She watched in the mirror, her eyes so wide and unblinking they ached. No wonder he'd wanted this. He'd meant for her to see what before she'd only experienced. She loved the way they looked together. Loved his absorbed expression as he drove into her body. She wanted to watch it all, but as her delight intensified, she found her eyes drifted shut. She forced them open, but they closed again.

Completion approached. She tried to hold it off, wanting to hold him in her body, savor his possession. She wanted this pleasure to go on forever.

But there was no holding back. Spasms seized her, radiating out from the place where the two of them were joined, taking over her body. She couldn't hear, she couldn't see, she couldn't breathe. To the exclusion of all else, she was forced to concentrate on the sensations rampaging through her body. Jude owned her; he overwhelmed thought and will.

Or perhaps it wasn't Jude, but the power of them locked together, motion and fury, sweetness and madness.

The joining was complete.

                          * * *

In the early-morning hours, Jude once again woke
Caroline.

She groaned. In the dark, they'd made love so many
times she couldn't remember a moment when she
hadn't been either kissing or being kissed, full or being
filled, aroused or fulfilled.

Could she make love again? Her body ached, yet she
knew he had only to lie on top of her and she would
yield. More than yield. She would want.

He threaded his hand through her hair and held her
still for a long, wet, intimate kiss. "I have to go now."

"No." She stroked his waist, trapped him in her embrace. "Stay a little longer." She couldn't bear this . . .
this leaving.

"My father would kill you if he found me here, and
my mother would kill me." It was darker in the room,
the candles guttered out, the fire mere embers, but she
heard the humor in Jude's tone. "I want to die in your
arms, but not like that."

"Just a little longer." She caressed his cheek with a
kiss, a kiss he found with his lips and which quickly
turned to more. To passion.

He withdrew with obvious reluctance. Sliding off the
mattress, he paced across the floor, gathering his
clothes. "I have to go. Last night I received a message,
and promised I would visit this morning . . ."

"You're going to that opera singer's?" Only that
could have brought Caroline out of her passion-induced
torpor and into a sitting position.

"To Miss Gloriana Dollydear's. Yes." He returned to
Caroline, stroked her cheek, and although she couldn't
quite see him, she knew he smiled. "Not for the reason
you're imagining, my darling, although I value your

opinion of my virility. After this night with you, I couldn't go to another woman's bed without embarrassing myself. In fact"—his voice turned reflective—"after last night, I don't know if I could ever again go to another woman's bed."

"Then go on and do whatever it is you're doing. I trust you." With a smug smile, Caroline slid back under the covers. "And I've never said that to another man."

As the door shut behind him with a quiet click, she admitted, *Because I've never before trusted a man.* But she trusted Jude. She would trust him with her life. More important, she would trust him with her heart.

Chapter 24

*J*ude nodded a greeting to the two burly men who stood stoically outside the door of Gloriana's flat and hurried inside. Wild sobbing drew him to the door of the tiny drawing room, and with a glance he absorbed the scene.

Blood spattered the carpet, the desk, a chair. Gloriana's body sprawled on the floor, her breastbone shattered by a bullet. A young female, a girl he recognized from the opera's chorus, held Gloriana in her arms and wept.

"Dear God." Jude had seen Gloriana only last night. She had sung the lead in the opera. She'd passed him a note telling him to attend her in the morning. She'd been smiling, flirtatious, in good voice. Now . . . this. He had never imagined *this*. This carnage. This grief.

Throckmorton leaned against the wall, morosely watching the scene. "I don't know what happened yet. As soon as the girl stops crying, I'll get the details."

"Is it her sister?" Jude thought of Caroline's sister, and foreboding shivered through him.

"I don't think so." Throckmorton's mouth was white and pinched.

So the scene had sickened him. It sickened Jude, too, but they had to know the facts. "Throckmorton, have you tried talking to her?"

"I don't know what to say to crying women." Throckmorton shuffled his feet. "I would have brought Celeste, she can talk to anyone, but not here. Not to this."

"No." Jude didn't know how to talk to crying women, either, but he wouldn't stand there amid the carnage waiting for silence. As he walked across the carpet, he heard glass crunch beneath his heels. Something had shattered: a vase, a glass.

Kneeling beside the girl, he rested his hand on her shoulder. "Miss, I'm Huntington. Over there is Throckmorton. We'd like to help."

"Help?" She turned red-rimmed eyes on him. "What are you going to do, bring her back to life?"

"No. I wish we could." He handed her his handkerchief. "What's your name?"

"Mary." She wiped her face and her nose. "Mary Channing."

"Well, Miss Channing, what we can do is bring her murderer to justice."

"Aren't you the murderer?" She tilted her chin at Throckmorton. "You and him. I didn't want her to get involved with this spying, but she loved the thrill of it. She never saw she could be hurt. Be killed. Now she's gone, and it's your fault."

"My fault," Jude repeated calmly, but he exchanged a glance with Throckmorton. Miss Dollydear wasn't supposed to tell anyone what she'd been doing. Now they had proof she'd told this female. Who knew how many other people in whom she'd confided?

"You talked her into it," Mary lashed.

"She wanted to do it." Throckmorton didn't budge from his place against the wall. "She was good at what she did."

"I know." Mary lowered her head, and tears seeped from between her lashes again. "But what am I going to do without her?"

"I'll settle a pension on you," Throckmorton said.

"That's not what I mean. I loved her." Bunching her fist, Mary held it above her heart. "I thought we'd be together always, and instead . . . I'm alone."

"Oh," both the men said together. They understood now. Mary's wild grief was that of a beloved spouse.

Jude was ashamed, but he felt relief. He had feared Gloriana Dollydear had been indiscreet. Instead she had told her lover the truth, and it was to be hoped, only her lover. And on that thought came another; would he trust Caroline with the truth?

He would, but he didn't want to. He didn't want her exposed to danger, and like a coward, he didn't want to explain that he had already exposed her to danger without her knowledge. It would be better if Caroline never learned that information.

"Then, Miss Channing, you do want us to catch the men who did this," Throckmorton said.

She nodded and worked hard to stop weeping.

"Did you see it happen?" Pulling a throw off the small sofa, Jude laid it over Mary's shoulders.

"Not all of it. I was upstairs." She took a quivering breath. "I heard the men shouting at each other."

"What men?" Jude knew, but he had to quiz her.

"Those two foreigners. The count and the monsieur." A sob broke through Mary's fragile discipline.

"Wouldn't you be more comfortable in a chair?" Jude suggested.

She shook her head hard and clutched the body tighter. "No. When I let her go, I'll never hold her again, and I can't . . . I can't . . ."

"All right." Jude interrupted before Mary started crying in earnest. "May I cover her? I don't feel . . . it doesn't feel right leaving her exposed."

Mary looked down at the beloved face frozen in death. Reluctantly, she nodded. "Yes. You can cover her."

Throckmorton tossed him a knitted blanket, and carefully Jude laid it over the poor, broken body. "That's better." It was. Covering Gloriana seemed respectful, the least he could do for the valiant woman.

The only thing he could do.

Throckmorton moved away from the wall. He dragged a chair close, sat, and leaned forward, hands clasped. "Miss Channing, I have to ask you questions."

"I know." She sniffed. "Go ahead."

"You were upstairs. You heard the two men fighting."

"I came downstairs." Mary seemed steadier. "It was the monsieur shouting at the count. He asked what he thought he was doing. He pointed at Gloriana and said she wasn't safe. He said the count let any woman lead him around by his balls, and now everyone would know what they planned to do."

"Did the count say anything in reply?" Jude asked.

"I peeked in the door. The count was so angry, his face was bright red. I thought he was going to have apoplexy right there. He shouted back, said the monsieur got above himself. He said she was harmless, and anyway, it didn't matter. And the monsieur said"—

Mary's eyes got big as if seeing the scene again—"the monsieur said, 'No, it doesn't.' And he pulled a pistol out of his coat and shot Gloriana. Shot her. Just . . ." Like a striking snake, she turned on Jude. "It was dangerous. You knew it was dangerous."

"*She* knew it was dangerous." Throckmorton smoothly intervened. "Believe me, if I had thought this would turn violent, I would have pulled her out. I liked Gloriana. She was the best. She was my friend. She was my wife's friend. Please believe me. I'm sorry, and I'm guilty, and I would do anything to turn back time."

Mary took long, quivering breaths. At last she nodded, accepting Throckmorton's apology.

Gently, Jude led her back to the interrogation. "Monsieur Bouchard shot Gloriana. What did you do?"

"I ran in. The count was yelling at him again, but the monsieur didn't care. He threw the pistol over there." Mary pointed toward the desk, where shattered glass covered its surface. "He broke the . . . vase . . . she . . . gave me." Her tears started again.

"Handkerchief," Jude demanded, holding out his hand to Throckmorton.

Throckmorton pulled the snowy white square out of his pocket and passed it to Jude. Jude removed his damp handkerchief from her hand and gave her the new one.

She struggled against the crying, anxious now to finish her story. "I lifted her up. She wasn't dead. She tried to speak, but she couldn't. So she . . . she wrote . . ." Mary extended her bare arm.

A smear of letters extended across her white skin. A word written in brown . . . in Gloriana's drying blood.

Victoria.

* * *

In a daze, Caroline entered the breakfast room. She was late, for she'd fallen back to sleep after Jude left. Fallen to sleep as if she were still a debutante with no one to please but herself. Now she found Nicolette and Nevett wrapped in silence, but today it appeared that Nevett was the one walking on eggs. He clutched his coffee cup, but he stared anxiously at Nicolette as if waiting for her to speak.

Which she did as Caroline seated herself. "Caroline, tell His Grace how fortunate he was to avoid the opera last night. Tell him how long it was, how dreadfully boring, how the only diversion occurred during the interlude when the company was lively and in high spirits."

"The interlude was lovely." Caroline had the sensation of having stepped into a marital dispute, and she didn't know quite what role she should play.

"Tell His Grace that he should compensate me for my suffering, which he did not have to endure because he was home in his study, basking in peace and quiet." Nicolette shot Caroline a humorous glance from beneath her lashes.

Then Caroline comprehended, and she fought a smile. "It's true, Your Grace, Her Grace deserves a knighthood for attending the opera unescorted and alone."

"Or at the least a diamond necklace," Nicolette said.

Caroline almost heard the snap as Nevett realized he was being teased. "Very well, ladies, you've had fun with me this morning."

"Yes, I have, but I deserve more than fun," Nicolette said. "I deserve that diamond necklace."

Nevett's eyes narrowed on her.

"Or at the least, the double stand of pearls I admired at the jeweler's."

He sighed heartily, then pulled a long, thin box out of his pocket. "I liked this one better." Opening it, he displayed four strands of pearls on a bed of black velvet with a platinum clasp set in diamonds.

Caroline stared at the gift and her own words rang in her head—*A woman wants presents for no reason. Not because it's a birthday or Christmas. Just because it's Thursday . . .*

Nicolette took a protracted breath. "That's beautiful."

"It's yours." He put in into her hands and watched her delight with obvious pleasure. "To wear next time you desire to go to the opera."

Nicolette laughed a little at his joke, but her eyes brimmed, her smile trembled. "I'll wear it on a more special occasion than that."

Caroline recognized the vow she was making to her husband. She saw him take Nicolette's hand and lift it to his lips, and hastily lowered her gaze. This was private. This was the kind of love Jude said he wanted, the kind of love she hadn't believed existed. Yet as she sat there, looking fixedly at her lap, she inhaled the genuine affection between Nevett and Nicolette. Against her better judgment, Caroline wished that she could have this with Jude. *True love.*

"Caroline, would you help me with the clasp?" Nicolette's voice sounded almost normal.

Happy to do *something*, Caroline leaped up and fastened the necklace for the duchess, then stepped around to admire it. "It's stunning," she said.

"It's the wearer who makes it stunning," Nevett said.

Startled, Caroline realized she'd heard that compliment before, from Jude to her, and she wondered if Jude would be as good a husband to his wife as Nevett was to Nicolette. And she hoped she was in France before that happened, because she didn't know if she could bear it otherwise.

"Now, Miss Ritter," Nevett's gruff voice said, "you'll give me a report on my son's progress."

"Progress?" For a horrifying second, all Caroline could contemplate was the night Jude had spent in her bed, and she had no desire to speak of that progress.

Gracefully Nicolette proffered her opinion. "The ladies swarmed him last night, I thought. Didn't you, Caroline?"

"They did." Much to Caroline's concern, which produced a distress she didn't want to feel. She was Jude's governess. She wanted him to marry. She should not want him to make declarations like *I don't know if I could ever again go to another woman's bed.*

"Who are his prospects?" Nevett asked.

"Lady Pheodora Osgood seems promising, although she does look on him as if he is not quite bright." *Which proved that Lady Pheodora was not the wife for Jude.* "Lady Amanda seems to have forgiven him his early *faux pas* and now hangs on his every word." *The hussy.* "The Misses Foley are charming"—*distressing*—"and they seem much taken with Lord Huntington."

"Which one likes him best?" Nevett demanded.

"Does it matter?" Caroline snapped.

"No. No, it doesn't." He leaned back in his chair, smug and pleased with himself. "All that matters is that he marry and produce an heir or two. May I remind you, Miss Ritter, of what's at stake here. Should my son marry or even become betrothed before the end of the Season, you'll receive one thousand pounds."

Nicolette gasped. "You've bribed her?"

"Of course I did, dear." Nevett cast her a fond and

exasperated glance. "I want results, and money produces results."

Once again, Caroline saw the man behind the title: ruthless and utterly convinced he would have his own way. "Your Grace, I've been hired for less than a fortnight. Already I've produced a change in Lord Huntington's behavior, and that change, small that it may be, has attracted the notice of this Season's debutantes. They're a little more strident than I remember"—last night some of them had actually elbowed her out of the way in their mad dash toward Jude—"but I do plan to collect that thousand pounds." For no matter how much Caroline treasured the connection between her and Jude, no matter how compelling the passion between them, she had a responsibility to her younger sister. She clenched her fists as she remembered Genevieve's sullen face, her palpable unhappiness. No amount of pleasure could remove Caroline's responsibility. Nothing could diminish the bond of blood.

"I have the greatest confidence in you," Nevett said. "I look forward to paying you one thousand pounds."

Phillips appeared in the door of the breakfast room. He bowed toward Nevett, but he spoke to Caroline. "Miss Ritter, your sister has arrived and requests a consultation."

Caroline had been thinking of Genevieve, so it took a few minutes before the words made sense. She came to her feet. "My sister? Genevieve? Here?" She didn't wait for an answer, but brushed past Phillips.

"In the lesser drawing room," he said.

What was wrong? Why was Genevieve there?

Caroline found her sister pacing the floor, and as soon as Caroline appeared, Genevieve launched herself at Caroline, crying, "I know what Father is up to. I know why he wants you to return home! I searched his study and I discovered the truth. Grandmamma has died and left you ten thousand pounds in her will, and Father wants it!"

Caroline hugged Genevieve and tried to assimilate the information at the same time. "Stop. Wait. Slow down. What do you mean, Grandmamma has died?"

"Father has a copy of the will and a letter from Mama's French relatives." Genevieve was obviously incensed with Caroline's incredulity, so she spoke slowly and enunciated her words. "Grandmamma left you ten thousand pounds to be used as you wish, but she hopes you'll come to visit France and stay with the family, and she asks that you bring me. She said she would have left half of the money to me, but she doesn't trust the *canard* whom Mama married—that would be Father—to keep it in trust for me. She knows you're old enough to spend wisely and take care of yourself and me."

Caroline freed herself from Genevieve's embrace. She groped for a chair and seated herself, for her knees were distinctly weak. "Ten thousand pounds." Her voice sounded odd even to herself, and she could scarcely breathe for the relief. "Ten thousand pounds. I don't ever have to do anything I don't want to again. I don't ever have to be afraid."

"The money is held at the Bank of England for you." Genevieve knelt beside her and smiled sunnily. "Only you can sign for the funds."

"I can care for you as you deserve." Still stunned, Caroline stroked her sister's face. "My God. For the first time in my life, I'm free."

"When can we go? Can we leave now?" Genevieve laughed and shook Caroline's shoulders. "We can leave now!"

This was a dream come true. They *could* leave then, that minute. Genevieve would never have to go back to that cold, dim, silent house. They could live in the south of France and be warm and loved by a whole new family. Thank God. *Thank God.* It was the answer to all her prayers.

Caroline would never see Jude again.

She stared into Genevieve's face. Never see him, never touch him, never worship his body, never adore the way he swept her off her feet and plot the next time when she would sweep him off his . . .

"You look funny," Genevieve said critically. "Is your breakfast going to make a reappearance?"

"No. No! Where did you learn such a phrase?" Caroline asked, horrified.

"Oh, I don't know. Cook, I suppose." Genevieve shrugged awkwardly.

"Pardon me for intruding." Nicolette stood in the doorway. "But I was concerned. Is everything all right?"

Caroline and Genevieve came to their feet, and when Caroline introduced her sister, Genevieve dropped a gawky curtsy and said, "Your Grace, it's wonderful. Caroline is an heiress!"

"An heiress?" Nicolette entered and sank into a comfortable chair. "Caroline, is this true?"

"So it would appear, Your Grace." Caroline held her hands before her in a prayerful manner. "We were just discussing what we should do."

"Oh, dear." Nicolette's expression a mixture of delight and dismay. "Caroline, I suppose this means you'll be leaving us at once."

"Yes!" Genevieve said far too loudly.

Caroline patted her lively sister's hand. "I haven't decided—"

"You haven't decided?" Incredulously, Genevieve turned on her. "What do you mean, you haven't decided? Of course we're leaving at once. Why would we stay?"

"Because I promised the duke of Nevett that I would see his son married," Caroline explained, "and it wouldn't be honorable to walk out before I've completed my task."

"Stuff and nonsense!" Genevieve had a child's way of recognizing twaddle and an adolescent's impatient way of speaking. "He's a duke. He'll hire somebody else."

"No one else is as qualified." Caroline was aware of Nicolette's concerned gaze resting on her and resisted the temptation to meet her eyes.

"That's just dumb," Genevieve declared. "I'm not going back to Father's. You can't make me!"

Out in the foyer, they heard males speaking. Caroline forgot Genevieve. She forgot the duchess. She forgot her inheritance.

Jude had returned. Caroline would recognize his voice anywhere, and the now-familiar guilt and excitement brought her to her feet.

"Caroline, did you hear me? I'm not going back to Father's house!" Genevieve said.

Nicolette put her hand on Genevieve's shoulder. "Don't worry, I'll take care of you. Let's just . . . watch for a moment, shall we?" They followed Caroline out into the foyer.

Jude looked not at all like the giddy coquet Caroline had escorted to the opera, nor like the demanding lover of the night before. He had gone home to change, and his somber suit was echoed by the stern and distant gaze he leveled on her. He handed his hat to Phillips and his tone was clipped and impatient. "Miss Ritter, what did Comte de Guignard give you last night?"

"What did he give me?" What did Jude mean? Was he angry with her? He spoke as if she were some kind of lowly creature to whom he owed nothing, not even a smidgen of civility. "He didn't give me anything."

"Yes, he did," Jude said. "He gave you a slip of paper. What was on it?"

Vaguely Caroline remembered Comte de Guignard expressing his regard for her and insisting that she have somewhere to go . . . "He offered me a place of sanctuary."

"Where?" Jude's eyes narrowed on her.

"I don't know. I don't need sanctuary." She walked up to him and looked directly at him, trying to plumb the difference in him and the reasons for it. "Do I?"

"No, but I need to know where they'll escape when . . ."

"When what?" Caroline noticed the duke stood in the door of the breakfast chamber, but all of her attention was on Jude.

"Show me the paper." It was not a request.

"I'll go get it." She started up the stairs.

"I'll go with you." He followed on her heels.

She started to object, but he alarmed her with his intensity and his air of menace. No matter what she said, he would follow her, and propriety be damned. And maybe when they were alone he would tell her what had happened to turn him into a steel-eyed avenger.

As they climbed the stairs, Nevett watched them, then went to his wife. In the tones of a man making a horrible discovery, he demanded, "What is going on around here?"

With a smirk, Phillips said, "Your Grace, I believe *I* can answer that."

Chapter 25

"What's happening?" As they climbed the stairs, Caroline glanced back at Jude. "Tell me, please. What has Comte de Guignard done that you're so angry at him?"

Jude waited until they were out of sight of their audience on the curved stairway before he softly answered, "He plans to assassinate the queen."

Caroline's breath stopped. She stopped. "What . . . what do you mean? He can't assassinate the queen." Caroline turned to face Jude. "He's a count. He's not some scruffy anarchist. He's a gentleman. Why would the rich and titled Comte de Guignard try to eliminate our monarch?"

"He's wants to start a war between France and Britain by killing Queen Victoria and blaming France for it." Jude spoke as if his theory was fact instead of some madness he had fabricated out of his love for drama.

Except he didn't look mad. He stood on the stair below her. Their eyes were on the same level, and his face was different. So different. Intent, intelligent, driven.

"Is Her Majesty safe?" she asked breathlessly.

"We've diverted the queen. Sent her on a different route and substituted a mannequin in her place in the carriage."

"Why would war start if the comte killed the queen? Comte de Guignard isn't French. He told me so."

"How many people can tell the difference? He's been careful to make himself appear very French to the people who'll be brought in as witnesses, and who can be counted on to raise the alarm. Besides, he doesn't plan on getting caught. Today, while Her Majesty rides to Parliament, he's going to shoot—or more likely, have Bouchard shoot—and yell, '*Vive la France.*' They have paid innocent people to join in and probably to carry guns and confuse the investigation."

"That's absurd!"

"Not at all. I was supposed to carry a pistol, also, but I wasn't home to receive the invitation they sent me last night." He pulled it out of his pocket and handed it to her. As she scanned it, he grimly said, "I was here with you. If I'd gotten that invitation, then I would have understood the details of their plot much earlier."

Caroline read Comte de Guignard's message with incredulity, but that incredulity suffered more and more as Jude gave her the facts, and the proof.

"Go on. What else will the Moricadians do?" She handed back the stiff cream paper.

Jude crushed it in his hand. "They'll have written a letter purportedly from a French extremist and sent it to the newspapers. During the riot caused by the shooting they'll escape to their sanctuary. From there they'll catch a ship and leave the country."

Jude's sharp, flat tone made Caroline feel stupid, as if she'd missed the obvious. "How do you know this? When did you find it out?"

"I've always known they were here to do something horrible. It was a matter of finding out what, and where, and to whom."

"But the comte . . . ?" Yet she remembered his attitude when he spoke to Jude at the opera. She remembered the way Monsieur Bouchard watched people, with contempt and derision.

"De Guignard is a killer. *Bouchard* is a killer. Early this morning he shot Miss Gloriana Dollydear."

"That's impossible. I heard her sing only last night." Yet Caroline knew Jude wouldn't lie, and she could almost taste her horror. That beautiful young woman, so talented, and now . . . dead? "Why would Monsieur Bouchard do such a thing? Why would they kill an opera singer?"

"Because de Guignard told her too much. Because Bouchard was afraid she was working for us." With a firm hand on Caroline's back, Jude started her back up the stairs. "Because she *was* working for us."

"Us?" A sick feeling formed in the pit of Caroline's stomach.

"I'm part of Throckmorton's team at the Home Office."

Caroline walked ahead of Jude, putting together the facts in slow, inescapable logic. "So all the time I've been teaching you to flirt and trying to find you a wife, you haven't really been learning anything, and you're not interested in marriage. Instead, you've been trying to discover what Comte de Guignard and Monsieur Bouchard were planning to do."

"That's right." Opening the door of her bedchamber, he ushered her inside.

The blood drained from Caroline's head. She felt faint. She felt ill. And inevitably their confrontation was going to get so much worse.

Daisy busied herself picking up Caroline's clothing, putting the brushes back on the dressing table. She frowned at Jude. "Ye shouldn't be in this young lady's bedroom, m'lord."

"Daisy," he said, "wait outside."

"Nay, m'lord, I can't." The maid put her hands on her hips. "'Tisn't proper. 'Tisn't right."

"Daisy, please." So many emotions whirled in Caroline, all of them violent and alien, that she didn't know if she were wretched or angry. "Give us a moment alone."

Daisy looked them over, and perhaps she saw something in their rigidity that told her a confrontation was unavoidable. "All right, Miss Ritter, but I'm not going farther than behind the dressing screen," Daisy said stoutly.

"That will do." Caroline waited until Daisy disappeared. Moving to the far side of the room, she stared at Jude like a boxer facing her opponent. In a low tone, she asked, "Did you never think to *ask* for my help?" She answered before he could. "No. You thought if I knew the facts, I'd refuse. I didn't have a choice in this little farce."

"There wasn't time to explain the situation." He, too, kept his voice low. "It was a matter of some secrecy— and now some urgency. Give me your reticule."

"You simply didn't trust me to keep your secret." The agony of her own words caused her to reel in shock. She had used this man for pleasure, and allowed him to use her, and fallen in love . . .

Nausea turned to something worse. Something painful and horrible. She felt as if she'd swallowed something poisonous, and she was very much afraid that what she'd swallowed was the truth.

She had fallen in love with the frivolous, ridiculous, marvelous earl of Huntington. Now she looked at him in his dark garb and his serious mien, and she didn't know him. She had thought she did, but he wasn't the man she thought he was. "You used me." She wanted him to deny it.

Instead he agreed. "I did use you. But I used you in a good cause."

A good cause. His own cause. Like Father. Like Lord Freshfield. Without a thought to how she would feel. "You pretended to be a fop because . . . ?"

"We have to talk about this later." Jude glanced around. "Where's your reticule?"

"No." Caroline had been taught that gentlewomen were not stubborn, that it wasn't a ladylike trait. But for this man, she'd discarded ladylike behavior and a great deal of other things like virginity and propriety. "No, now. You said Her Majesty was in no danger, so . . . now."

Something in her expression must have warned him, for he said, "There are a great many reasons why I didn't tell you what I was doing, a great deal of them because when I was with you, I thought of nothing but you. Kissing you. Having you."

"Sh!" She glanced furiously at the screen where Daisy lurked.

"Because we had unfinished business." He lowered his voice, but it was just as intense. "I wanted you so desperately I missed that invitation last night. Doesn't that tell you something?"

"Yes. That you're trying to blame me for an evening spent in lasciviousness."

"And mutual pleasure, and no. That's not what I meant at all. I meant that you're more to me than I wish." He shook his head. "That doesn't sound right, but you know what I mean."

"I used to think I knew what you meant, but I've come to realize I don't know you at all. Now I'm sure that once I kissed you, once I gave you my body, you decided I was yours to use as you wished."

"That's not true." He sounded soothing, calm and sensible.

Which made her voice rise. "Which part? That you feared I'd refuse, or that you thought I was yours to use as you wished?"

"I never thought that because you gave me your body, I could use you." He spoke even more quietly as if hoping to hush her by his example.

"But you did, so it was that you didn't want me to have a choice." She clenched her hands to keep them from shaking, and the truth spilled from her in a dreadful, earthshaking rush. "If you'd asked me, I would have done anything for you. I would have done it for England, too, because it was the right thing to do, but mostly I would have done it for you. Because I was so infatuated with you that I surrendered the chastity I'd cherished for four dreadful years when selling myself would have made my life so much easier."

"I treasure the gift you gave me," he said, and she

thought he look stunned. "But right now, I really need that reticule."

"Paltry!" She loved him, and he so obviously didn't love her. She took a quivering breath. "You were laughing at me."

"No." To his credit, he managed to look dismayed— and distracted by that stupid reticule.

"You used me. You're no better than my father." She was crying, wiping tears off her hot cheeks. "You're worse than Lord Freshfield. I don't know if there's a man in the world worth having, but I do know you're not the one."

"I never meant to hurt you. I didn't think you'd ever find out—"

"So that's what you thought? That as long as I didn't find out it was all right? What kind of warped integrity is that?"

He took her shoulders. "Listen to me. I'll come back. We'll talk, I promise. But the Moricadians are going to shoot at the queen, and yes, we've sent a message to Her Majesty's guard and she'll be safe, but de Guignard and Bouchard must be apprehended or they'll try again. And if they succeed, the queen, our queen, will be dead. At the least, they'll ruin the fragile relations between France and England. We'll have another war, a war that'll make the devastation of the last war appear trifling. Other people's agony meant nothing to the Moricadians. Murder means nothing to them." He gently shook her. "Caroline, isn't the bond between you and me less important than our country's safety?"

All of her fire and passion died. A deadly calm took its place. She stepped away from him. Away from the love she cherished. "Of course it is."

He stared at her as if he didn't know how to handle her. "You're thinking you're not going to earn the sum my father promised you."

"What?" Was he really that stupid?

"I always meant to pay you. If you'll help me now, I'll double whatever Father pledged."

Without her volition, her hand flew out. She slapped him with the full force of her arm.

Disbelief in his eyes, he cupped his reddening cheek.

She shook out her skirts like a woman removing the paw print of a troublesome dog. An uncouth, offensive, loathsome dog, and she was insulting dogs by comparing them to Jude. Leaning over, she pulled the reticule from underneath the dressing table. "It was right where you kicked it last night." She threw the purse at him and consumed by her wrathful fire, she said, "Now—*do* go save the queen, and *don't* ever come near me again."

He seemed remarkably unimpressed with her ultimatum, for he opened her reticule. He removed the slip of paper. He read the message, and in a distracted voice said, "Stay here. You'll be safe. Gloriana Dolly-dear was shot because de Guignard told her their secret location. I don't want you shot for the same reason."

"I'm not going to follow you." She hoped her scorn hid her anguish. "I may be stupid, but I know when I'm not wanted."

"That's where you're wrong." Dropping the note on the floor, he tugged her into his arms and held her prisoner against his body. His lips touched hers, as he said, "I will always want you."

He took her mouth in a fierce kiss that sabotaged her wrath and ignited her passions. She responded without thought, without resistance, showing the love she denied.

Why not? It was the last time. She embraced him, tasted him, while he savaged her mouth as if he wanted to impress himself on her.

He kissed her like a soldier going to his death . . . and she kissed him good-bye.

He let her go. He stepped back from her. He stared as if he wanted one last look. "Remember me, sweet Caro. No matter what, remember me."

Caroline watched him walk out the door, and she was glad to see him leave. Glad. The tears that dribbled down her cheeks meant nothing!

Follow him. He dared think she was going to follow him. That swine had thought her loyalty could be bought. Worse than that, that her loyalty *needed* to be bought.

Sweet Caro, he had called her. Well, it didn't matter that he remembered her pet name. She meant what she said. She never wanted to see him again. Never. Ever. Not if he crawled on his knees . . .

And she wasn't going to follow him.

Yet she found herself running down the corridor to the top of the stairs, and got to the landing in time to see the door shut behind him.

She was only glad he walked out of there with the reddened imprint of her hand on his cheek.

Nicolette stood in the foyer looking up at her. "You hit my son."

"As hard as I could." Caroline braced herself for the duchess's reaction.

"If I know him, he deserved it," Nicolette said tranquilly.

"Yes. Yes, he did." Caroline needed to drag her thoughts away from Jude and back to her responsibilities. "Where's my sister?"

"I sent her into the dining room for a cup of tea and some scones. She's very upset, but like all youngsters that age, food seems to cure her distress. Don't worry about her." Nicolette indicated the outer door. "Where did Jude go?"

"He's off to capture the Moricadians and charge them with the attempted murder of the queen."

"Ah." The duchess nodded. "I had wondered."

Nicolette's lack of shock brought Caroline down the stairs to the foyer. "What do you mean, you had wondered? You knew about this?"

"Of course I didn't know. Jude would never tell a woman anything to cause her distress. He's one of those men who is determined to shield all women from strife, no matter how much it irks us."

"He might shield *you* from strife, but he was willing enough to use *me* in his little plot."

"I am sorry, but this has got to be all about his brother." When Caroline shook her head in ignorance, Nicolette continued, "Michael was killed in Moricadia. Jude hasn't been the same since, and if de Guignard and Bouchard are responsible for Michael's death, then Jude would have been willing to go to any lengths to take revenge. He would even have gone so far as to play the fool to put them off-balance and discover their nefarious plans." Nicolette gave Caroline a moment to absorb that. "You understand, dear. You have so much in common with Jude."

"I do not!"

"You're willing to do anything—stay in England,

work at menial jobs, even give up your chance at true love—to provide and care for your sister."

"That's different!"

"Is it?" As she walked away, Nicolette smiled enigmatically. "Is it really?"

It *was* different. What Caroline had done didn't involve treachery . . . although she would have done almost anything to provide for Genevieve. And if Genevieve had been killed, Caroline would have gone mad.

Then . . . "What do you mean, *true love?*" She stared at the door where Nicolette had disappeared. Nicolette knew? She knew that Caroline loved Jude?

Caroline ran up the stairs and to her room.

Was she so obvious? Did everybody know?

Would the humiliation of this day never end?

"Miss Ritter, what's this?" Daisy asked as Caroline entered.

Daisy's shocked tone yanked Caroline out of her fury and her sorrow. "What? What did you find?"

She glanced around to see Daisy standing beside the dressing screen . . . and holding Jude's long, thin-bladed knife in her hand.

He was going to fight the battle of his life. Because of Caroline, he had forgotten the knife he handled so cleverly. And the men he faced were brutal murderers.

She was an heiress. She never again had to do anything she didn't desire.

But being an heiress didn't free her of her moral obligations, nor did it free her from the bonds of love. She didn't want to love Jude, but she did, and even if she never saw him again, she wanted to know that somewhere in this world Jude lived and breathed. If she was responsible for his death, she would never forgive herself.

"Give me the knife, Daisy. Get me my cloak." Grimly, Caroline picked up the piece of paper with Comte de Guignard's handwriting and read the information. "I'm going to follow Huntington."

Chapter 26

 Harry had watched as that fine young lord left his horse in the care of a stableboy by Nevett's front steps. Huntington had gone in to visit Miss Ritter, and when he came out he looked none too happy.

Good. That would teach him to trifle with Miss Ritter. She deserved better than a trick and a tickle, and Harry knew that was exactly what Huntington had been giving her. Harry knew everything that happened in London and beyond, for he worked for Throckmorton—a good man, and one willing to keep Harry informed. So Harry shared the network of beggars and thieves who reported to him, and he divided his salary from Throckmorton according to who brought him the best tidbits. But Miss Ritter he tended for free. She had become his special project, sort of his own charity case.

Swinging himself into the saddle, Huntington gathered the reins, and trotted his horse down to the corner. He stopped. He looked down at Harry, and asked, "What's happened so far?"

Harry knew that Huntington wanted an account on the day's events, and Harry tersely gave it to him. "The 'oresons shot at the queen—not that it was the queen, ye know, but rumors that she's dead and that the Frenchies did it spread over London. There're riots all up and down Piccadilly. The trouble's spreading. Before long, the rioters'll go fer any Frenchies they know. Yer Moricadians got away, no one knows where, and Throckmorton's suffering quite a turn over at the 'Ome Office."

"I'm sure he is." Huntington leaned his arm on his saddle. "I know where the Moricadians are hiding. Get a messenger. Send word to Throckmorton. I need men at Whitefriars Dock at the warehouse. It seems empty, but be careful. The Moricadians are brilliant shots, and they have no qualms about doing what they must to survive long enough to make it to their ship."

"Aye, m'lord, Oi'll spread the word."

Huntington glanced back at his father's house. "Miss Ritter is very angry at me."

"So Oi see." Harry grinned at the sight of her handprint on Huntington's face. "Landed ye a good one, did she?"

"She was . . . distressed." Huntington touched his cheek. "She must remain here. She knows where the Moricadians are hiding, and this is the only place she's safe."

"If she tries t' leave, what do ye want me t' do?" Harry asked with exasperation. "Bite 'er on the leg?"

"Whatever it takes." Jude spurred his horse into a

gallop and was out of sight at exactly the same time Miss Ritter stepped out onto the stairs and strode toward him.

Harry groaned. "That woman'll be the ruination o' me." Gathering his money cup, he stuck it under his rags and pushed himself toward Caroline. *"She must remain here,"* he mimicked Huntington's noble accent. *"This is the only place she's safe.* So what does the lady do? She tries t' leave. Women. No sense. No sense at all."

Caroline saw Harry approaching as fast as he could and heard him muttering.

"Where do ye think ye're going, Miss Ritter?" he called as they got close.

"I have to go after Lord Huntington." She walked briskly toward the main street. "He left something that he desperately needs."

"And what would that be?" Harry planted himself squarely in front of her.

"His dagger." Opening her cloak, she showed him the blade tucked into her belt.

"'Is lordship and Oi have made each other's acquaintance," Harry said, "and Oi feel sure if 'e left without it, 'e can do without it."

"Maybe." She didn't wonder that Harry claimed to know Jude. Jude wasn't what he appeared to be; maybe Harry wasn't, either. "But I can't wait here and wonder if he's going to die for needing it. I'm an heiress. I have a choice now, and I have to do the right thing." She walked around Harry and made her way to the corner. She looked up and down, trying to decide if she should keep walking or if a cab would be by soon.

Harry got in front of her again. "Look, Miss Ritter, 'e's a man and a fighter, and ye're a woman—"

She glared at him.

"—And a fighter," he added hastily. "But this kind o' combat is brutal and ugly, and ye shouldn't see it."

"I'm not going to *see* it. I'm going to help."

"Ye'd just get in the way."

"Look!" She crouched down so she could look in his eyes. "I've spent my whole life being a proper lady no matter what my circumstances, and I won't do it anymore. I have the right to hate Comte de Guignard and Monsieur Bouchard for what they've done to my country. I have the right to hate Huntington . . . and the right to fight at his side."

"Ye're saying it's not the same kind o' hate," Harry said shrewdly.

"That's right. I'm done being a lady. I'm angry, Harry. Angry at everything that has happened to me. I've taken control of my fate, and I'm not giving it up. If somebody's going to kill Huntington, it's going to be *me*, not some assassins who think they have the right to come to England and use us—use me! For their purposes."

"Right." He was beginning to see her point and even agree with it. "All right then. I'll come with ye and—"

"No, Harry." A cab rolled down the street, and she waved it down. "You've done enough for England. I won't put you in danger again so you can help me." He tried to grab her skirt, but she stepped nimbly inside. "Thank you for understanding. You're the only one who does." She shut the door in Harry's face.

"Bloody stinking 'ell!" In a fury of frustration, he watched the cab drive away. He had been going to say he would go with her and keep her out of trouble. He should have known keeping that lass out of trouble took more than an aging, legless old sailor.

In fact, he wished Huntington luck handling *her*.

With his fingers in his mouth, he gave a shrill whistle and settled down to wait. In less than five minutes, although it seemed more, a skinny girl, one of the city's pickpockets, dashed up.

"What do ye want, Harry?"

Harry gave her the message to go to Throckmorton. "It's got t' go fast and it's got t' go right, and if ye do that, there'll be an extra reward in yer cap tonight. Now repeat it back." When he was sure the lass had every word perfectly, he said, "Looks like rain, so step lively. Ye don't want to be caught in the downpour."

He waved her off. She grabbed the back of one of the passing cabs and made herself at home as it drove down the street.

And Harry, with a lot more effort, did the same on a cab going in the opposite direction. He just hoped he got to Whitefriars in time to help Huntington, because Miss Ritter was chomping at the bit, and that dagger was no toy.

Jude hoped he didn't die there. He had found the warehouse with its square courtyard stacked with old barrels and littered with debris. At once he understood why the Moricadians had chosen this spot. It was on the river, their escape route. It was situated so that they had a view of anyone who approached. And it definitely looked uninhabited. As Jude dismounted, he wondered how the elegant de Guignard enjoyed living in a dusty hovel with broken windows and a healthy infestation of river rats.

Were they still here? The tide was going out within two hours. Their ship would sail on it. But Huntington prayed they hadn't boarded yet. If they had, they took the chance of being cornered, and these men were too wily for that.

So he had to stall them long enough for Throckmorton's men to get there. Overhead, clouds had begun to blow in, covering the sun, then whisking away . . . if the rain would hold off, Throckmorton would make better time.

Jude planned to go in as the foppish Lord Huntington and see if he could engage them in talk. The approach was the tricky part; if they decided to shoot him right away, all of his planning was for naught.

"Go home, boy. Go find your oats." With a sharp slap on the rump, he started his horse out of harm's way. Pulling a bright scarf from his pocket, he waved it above his head as he walked into the warehouse's courtyard. "Comte de Guignard! Monsieur Bouchard!" He called, "I received your invitation too late, and I'm so sorry I missed you, but I talked to Miss Ritter, and she said you were here!"

Silence answered him.

Did they believe him? Were they intrigued?

Well . . . he wasn't dead yet, and he counted that as first-class news.

"Comte de Guignard! Monsieur Bouchard! Miss Ritter sends her regrets." Jude saw the flash of a rifle in a broken window. A fine sheen of sweat broke out on his forehead. They were there, and God, he was glad, but he'd been shot before, and the suffering had been unbelievable. He didn't want to go through that again, but for Michael he would bleed . . . and for Caroline, he would live. "Miss Ritter wishes she could have come here, too."

When he was still standing at the end of his speech, he wanted to relax. Another few minutes of life. He had another few cherished minutes of life, and he wanted those minutes. He wanted all the minutes because, yes, he lusted for revenge on Michael's killers, but he no longer faced life with indifference. He wanted to be with Caroline, to sleep with her, to marry her . . . he loved her. How could he not? She was everything that was brave and strong and delightful.

Where were Throckmorton's men?

"Are you alone?" De Guignard's voice echoed eerily across the abandoned yard.

"I am." Smiling, Jude spread his arms wide. "I've come for the opportunity to shoot with you."

"Why isn't Miss Ritter with you?" De Guignard asked.

"She doesn't like to shoot." Jude injected surprise into his voice.

From another part of the warehouse, Bouchard asked, "When you came through the city, were there problems?"

"Problems?" Jude had had to pick his route to avoid the rioting, but if he told the Moricadians their plan had failed, they'd have to consider whether they could go home as failures. Prince Sandre did not accept failure lightly. Perhaps they would want to stay and try again. "No, everything is as usual," Jude said.

More silence. Then: "Empty your pockets," Bouchard called.

"My pockets?" Jude began. "My good man, why—"

"Do it!" Bouchard's voice lashed at him.

"Yes, of course, as you wish!" Hidden by his coat, Jude had a pistol strapped to his leg. He had a knife up his sleeve, a small sharp blade he could throw with great accuracy. He wished he had his dagger, but that remained in Caroline's bedchamber stuck in the arm of a chair . . . he smiled as he remembered last night, and supposed to the Moricadians he looked like an idiot grinning now. But that was to the good.

Slowly he slid his hand into his waistcoat pocket. "A watch!" he called. "What do you want me to do with it?"

"Put it on the ground," Bouchard instructed.

Jude looked down at the rough cobblestones at his feet and in his most fretful voice, he said, "I can't put my watch down there. It's filthy!"

"Put it down!" Bouchard said.

With a huge display of reluctance, Jude obeyed.

"What else?" Bouchard demanded.

"A handkerchief!" Jude waved the white square embroidered with his initials. "Really, Monsieur Bouchard, you aren't going to ask me to put this fine linen on the ground, are you?" He really, really needed Throckmorton's men to back him up. Mentally he tried to work out how soon they could get there.

Not soon enough.

"*Mon dieu*, Bouchard, this is ridiculous." De Guignard sounded impatient, and his voice moved toward the door. "We know what Huntington is!"

"Comte, please, you're too trusting." Bouchard was on the move, too, and he sounded frustrated and angry.

"We need to know what's happening in the city. We need to know whether the populace is angry." De Guignard stepped into the courtyard, a rifle cradled in his arms. His hair was perfectly combed. Medals decorated his chest. A long sword hung from a sheath at his waist. He looked every inch the foreign nobleman, and Jude appreciated the irony, for de Guignard had done so much that was ignoble.

"Angry?" Jude stuffed his handkerchief back into his pocket. "Why would they be angry?"

Bouchard stepped out, holding a pistol pointed right at Jude.

"Monsieur Bouchard! What are you doing?" Jude

backed toward the row of barrels behind him, shock and fear etched on his face. It wasn't hard to do.

"You heard nothing about a Frenchman shooting your Queen Victoria?" Bouchard demanded. "No riots? No Englishmen are tearing the French limb from limb?"

"Please, Monsieur Bouchard, we're not so uncivilized!" Jude protested, and put his hand on the butt of his pistol. He would roll behind the barrels and come up behind them, shoot Comte de Guignard, then do his damnedest to hide from Bouchard until Throckmorton's men got here.

"He's worthless." Bouchard said with relish. "We get to kill him."

And as Jude prepared to jump away, a feminine voice trilled, "Comte de Guignard, I've come to accept your offer of sanctuary."

All three men looked toward the street.

Caroline strolled into the courtyard. She wore a dark cloak, her blue merino dress, and a charming smile— and Jude couldn't believe she was here.

He looked behind her for Harry. She was alone. Damn!

"Why have you come?" Jude asked.

At his horrified tone, Bouchard's gaze sharpened.

"*Mademoiselle.*" Comte de Guignard started forward. "You are so welcome!"

She tossed her head in a coquettish manner. "What a beautiful rifle." She batted her lashes. "Are you having a shooting contest?" Her gaze flicked toward Bouchard. "Please be careful, Monsieur, that could accidentally discharge in Lord Huntington's direction."

Monsieur Bouchard lowered his pistol, but he stared fixedly at her, his black eyes suspicious, his mustache bristling. "You said you came to accept Comte de Guignard's offer of sanctuary."

"Yes." She smiled meltingly at Comte de Guignard. "I think it would be so charming to join you . . . er . . . here?" Her gaze swept the warehouse, and she looked prettily confused.

And even in the depths of his horror, Jude appreciated her flirtatious skills.

"Yet I wonder"—Bouchard pointed his pistol at *her*—"if someone here is lying."

Blind instinct swept Jude. Drawing his own pistol, he shot, a good fast shot that struck Bouchard in the side.

Bouchard whirled around, but he stayed on his feet.

While de Guignard gaped at the disintegrating scene, Caroline grabbed the rifle. She pulled it out of his hands and danced backward toward the street. With a mighty sweep, she smashed the barrel into the ground.

Blood spurted from Bouchard's wound; but Jude's shot was too far away, too fast, and not accurate enough to kill. Bouchard's grimace of pain became a triumphant grin. "I told you, Comte de Guignard, that all was not as it seemed."

De Guignard looked between Caroline and Jude and derived the correct conclusion.

Drawing his sword in one hand and his dagger in the other, Comte de Guignard stalked Jude. "It seems Miss Ritter is yours, Huntington, for as long as you're on this earth."

"Get out of the way, de Guignard." Bouchard pointed his pistol at Jude.

Caroline screamed and ran toward Bouchard.

Jude, helpless and in despair, tried to race past de Guignard.

With his sword, de Guignard slashed at Jude's chest.

Jude leaped back, but the razor-sharp blade peeled his padded waistcoat open. "Caroline, no!" he shouted.

And from the corners of his eyes, Jude saw a flash of motion on the ground. Wheels rattled across the stones. As Bouchard fired, the creature—my God, it was Harry—smashed past Bouchard.

Bouchard went down screaming, holding his leg.

Harry had hamstrung him.

Caroline whirled.

Jude's heart raced. Was she shot?

But no. She launched herself at de Guignard.

He stumbled, bewildered by the attack. *"Mademoiselle, non!"* He tried to turn his sword away from her— and she caught the blade in her hand.

He dropped the hilt.

She let it fall, then kicked it away.

Harry grabbed it.

"Mademoiselle, non, non, you're crazy!"

"Just leveling the odds." Ignoring the blood that dripped from her hand, she threw Jude a taunting smile, one that spoke of intimacy and triumph.

De Guignard's face darkened. He lunged for her.

She, wise girl, ran.

Jude charged after de Guignard, and as he attacked, Caroline called, "Here! Jude!" Clumsily, she tossed him his beautiful long dagger.

It tumbled through the air, the blade catching glints of fading sunlight.

Jude snatched it by its hilt. "De Guignard, for once stop chasing the woman and fight."

De Guignard skidded to a halt. Turning, he smiled a menacing smile at the advancing Jude. "I don't know if you realize it, my putrid English lord, but knife fighting is an honored tradition in Moricadia. I am an expert. I think perhaps you're at a disadvantage here."

It was true. Jude had seen it; in Moricadia every man and woman carried a knife, and they all prided themselves on their skills.

"I prefer a sword," Jude admitted. "But I like these odds better than the ones that have you holding both a sword *and* a knife. For that maneuver, some might call you cowardly."

De Guignard's smile vanished, and the monster behind the elegant mask showed its face. "I will enjoy spitting you on my blade."

The two men circled each other, knives and teeth bared. Somewhere on the periphery of his senses, Jude was aware that Bouchard still screeched, that Caroline and Harry stood hard against the building and watched them, that beyond this small area London pulsed with the riot the Moricadians had created. Above them, clouds gathered for a spring storm. Yet Jude's focus narrowed on this man, this knife, this fight.

De Guignard attacked first, a swift lunge to Jude's gut. Jude sucked in his breath. The point of Comte de Guignard's knife caught the flapping edge of Jude's waistcoat. Before de Guignard could disengage, Jude cut his cuff and slashed his wrist.

De Guignard snatched his hand back and stared at the small injury in amazement.

While he stared, Jude slashed three times in rapid succession—at de Guignard's chin, his heart, and his groin. He sliced a two-inch gash on de Guignard's noble chin and cut the clothes at his chest.

But de Guignard recovered from his surprise before Jude could open his trousers. He danced nimbly back.

Far away, lightning flashed. Slow, long, and deep, the thunder growled.

Jude smiled, a savage, challenging smile, and looked into the older man's eyes. "I didn't say I didn't know how to knife fight. I only said I liked a sword better."

The fight began in earnest. De Guignard was the expert that he claimed. He fought with a mastery Jude couldn't match, dodging, lunging, and parrying with unparalleled power and grace.

Jude responded with a younger man's speed and a clever man's caution. Michael and de Guignard were alike in their daring, and Jude had dueled with Michael often enough to know defeating this opponent required careful analysis. But while Jude watched for patterns de Guignard took Jude's flesh.

He nicked Jude on the wrist. "A payback for this small cut you gave me." He kept his free hand forward, and it clenched when he reached out once more and nicked Jude on the cheek. "A lesson to you for imagining you could defeat me." The hand clenched again.

Jude's lungs burned as he gasped for air. He watched unceasingly for an opening.

Closer, brighter, lightning blazed, and, almost immediately, the thunder rumbled.

With the next clench of the fist, Jude allowed Comte de Guignard to take a nick out of his shoulder, but he had de Guignard's measure now. All he had to do was avoid that wicked blade long enough to—

The fist clenched. De Guignard drove for Jude's chest. Jude caught his wrist, the one without the knife, and turned him like a dancer . . . onto Jude's own blade.

At the last minute, de Guignard spiraled away. The point drove deep into his side. Not his heart, as Jude had wished, but between his ribs.

De Guignard swung wildly as he went down.

Jude vaulted out of the way. The knife whistled past him and clattered on the ground.

The battle was over.

Jude stood over de Guignard, panting, in pain from his wounds, yet satisfied.

The comte looked down at the dagger planted in his chest. He looked up at Jude in absolute astonishment. "I've never . . . been . . . defeated," he whispered.

"You never tried to kill my queen before," Jude said.

In the background, he heard Caroline gasping in relief. Heard Harry's rough cheer.

Heard Bouchard's infuriated monologue as he clawed his way along the ground toward de Guignard, leaving a bloody trail across the grimy cobblestones. "Damn you, de Guignard. You never could resist the ladies."

Jude moved out of the way of this slow, crawling, vengeful worm.

"I begged Prince Sandre to leave you behind, but he insisted that a representative of the royal family come to supervise me. Me! I'm not the one who took their bait." Bouchard reached de Guignard's side, raised himself above his lord. "I'm not the one who chases every *jeune fille* who flatters me."

"Bouchard." Comte de Guignard drew in a long painful breath. "Shut up."

"If you had kept your mind on the assassination and not on the ladies, we'd have killed the queen already and be gone. But no." Bouchard yanked the blade out of de Guignard's side.

Blood spurted from the open wound, and de Guignard's eyes rolled back in his head.

"So now I'm going to hang from an English gibbet." Lifting the knife, Bouchard plunged it into de Guignard's heart. "And you're going to die."

Chapter 27

*C*aroline covered her eyes. She'd never seen death before, never imagined this kind of violence. Her heart beat so hard she might have been the one fighting, and when she pulled her hand away from her face and saw the blood from her own wound, faintness overwhelmed her. With a quiet moan, she leaned against the wall.

"Lass, are ye all right?" Harry tugged at Caroline's skirt. "The blood's getting t' ye, isn't it?"

She nodded. Especially her own blood. Especially—she flicked a glance at Jude—his blood, and the threat of death that had hovered too close.

"Better take 'er 'ome, m'lord, or she'll fall 'ere on the ground." Harry nodded sagely and pointed to the place where de Guignard lay dead and Bouchard writhed and cursed. "Don't worry about these two. I'll wait fer Throckmorton and 'is men."

Jude nodded curtly. He walked to Caroline and looked at her, his gaze a mixture of triumph, rage, and possession. He pulled her into his arms in a savage embrace.

She rested on him for one wonderful moment, then extracted herself and straightened until she stood on her own, ramrod straight and proud. "I can see myself home, my lord, I don't need any help."

"Really?" Taking her hand, he showed her the thin, bloodied slice that ran across her palm.

Oh, of course. He would make something out of *this*. "It doesn't mean what you think."

"What do I think?" He used his handkerchief to bind her hand.

"You think I'm yours to use whenever you like." The old bitterness and the new anger rose in her. "I've been used enough."

"That's right, dearie, make 'im suffer!" Harry cheered her on with a grin and a thumbs-up.

Jude used his scarf to wipe the blood off her face. He slipped his arm around her waist, and he was smiling.

Neither of them were taking her seriously.

Freeing herself from Jude's grasp, Caroline walked ahead of him out of the warehouse courtyard and onto the street. The thunder rumbled again. A fat raindrop fell with a plop into the dusty stones.

"I'll get us a cab," Jude said.

"I can do it for myself."

"Caroline, I know you're angry with me, but there's no reason to be stubborn." He sounded exasperated and patient. "It's not easy to get a cab in London. They stop for men and seldom for ladies, and in the rain it's almost impossible to hail one at all."

As he spoke, an aged cab drove down the street, the equally aged coachman bent forward, his eyes fixed on the reins in his hands.

Caroline threw back her cloak, thrust out her bosom and shot him a smile.

He pulled up so quickly the cab groaned, and the horse nickered. "Can I 'elp ye, Miss?"

"You're such a gentleman to stop when it's going to storm." She looked deep into his faded, rheumy eyes, and cooed, "Would you be so kind as to take me and this fellow"—she waved vaguely in Jude's direction—"to Mayfair to the duke of Nevett's house? I don't need to tell you that there'll be an extra fee for your trouble."

The rain was starting in earnest. "I was about t' go home t' me missis—"

Caroline fluttered her lashes.

"—But fer ye, anything," the driver finished extravagantly.

"Thank you." She opened the door and before she stepped in, said emphatically, "An *extra* fee."

Dumbfounded, Jude stood on the street.

She seated herself, looked out at him, and in a flat tone said, "Well, get in if you're going to."

He did, and seated himself across from her. The cab took off with a lurch. "Getting the cab was an impressive demonstration of your independence—and I suppose a well-deserved one," he said.

"I know how to handle myself on the streets. I know how to care for myself." She took care to space her words separately so that there could be no misunderstanding. "I don't need you."

"Yet the fact remains—you came after me because you worried I needed my knife. You ran in front of Bouchard's pistol to save me. You cut your hand on

Comte de Guignard's knife to help me." He touched her wrapped fingers, and burst out, "But Caroline, never do anything like that again. I couldn't bear it."

"I won't," she promised readily. She looked away from him and out the grimy window.

The citizens of London had responded to the rain by believing the announcement that their queen was alive and unharmed. They went home to their own fires, leaving empty streets and quiet lanes. The rapidly increasing rain made the interior of the cab dim and, she was bitterly aware, too intimate.

In a low voice, she said, "Oh, I love you. There can be no doubt of that." She sensed pain beneath her anger, but she couldn't feel it yet. All she felt now was a vast humiliation and a very real desire to hurt Jude. "But I don't trust you."

His complacency slipped. "Caroline, I know you feel I used you—"

"I don't *feel* you used me. You *did* use me. You admitted it yourself, but if I recall correctly, you believed it was all right because you used me in a *good cause*." She put a special sting to the last two words.

"I can teach you to trust me again."

"Really?" Lightning illuminated Jude's face in a flash, etching the sight of his bold features on Caroline's brain, and she realized—Jude was as arrogant as his father. What was she thinking, loving a man like that?

She hadn't been thinking. That was the only answer.

"You need to trust me now. You've proved your courage. You love me. After so many years alone, you gave yourself to me." Despite her struggles, he gathered her hands in his. "Marry me."

It should have been the most wonderful moment of her life. Instead, somewhere in the vicinity of her heart, the pain started.

"Trust me, I'll make you happy, for I've learned from a top authority what women want." He smiled with all his phony, overblown, confident charm, and he said, "Sweet Caro."

"Let me understand you." She kept her voice steady when she wanted to shriek like a fishwife. "You're willing to take me as your wife because I have courage, so I'm worthy, and I was virgin, so I'm virtuous, and I love you, so I'm bound to trust you." If she didn't know that Genevieve waited for her at Nevett's, she would jump out of the moving cab right now.

"That's not what I meant." He frowned at her as if that doomed proposal was her fault.

"It sounds as if you'll be getting the perfect wife. Well . . . except for that scandal attached to my name. But the fact that the earl of Huntington has condescended to make me his wife should make me grateful, too." Sarcasm rasped in her voice.

"I have never thought that you were anything but innocent. I've never thought that you were anything but wronged." The flash of lightning confirmed that a blaze of fury lit his blue eyes. "And gratitude is the last thing I want from you." The thunder growled in agreement.

"I do know. I beg your pardon. My pique got the better of me." It had; whatever sins Jude had committed, he wasn't so petty as to need her gratitude.

"So will you marry me?" he snapped. Then he visibly collected himself. "I mean . . . I would consider it a great honor if you'd consent to be my wife."

Pain grew inside her. "What is it that I'm supposed to say now? It's been so long since I received a proposal—of marriage, anyway—that I scarcely remember." Her every word was a mockery. With her finger on her cheek, she pretended to think. "Lord Huntington, I'm honored by your regard, but I find I'm unable to accept your proposal. While you've pointed out the great number of advantages to you, I see no benefit in matrimony for me. Therefore, I regretfully decline."

"You're letting your rage decide your destiny." He was so sure of himself. So sure of her.

"At least I'm not bending like a reed in the wind who bows before the inconstant wind." She explained the obvious. "The wind would be you, my lord."

"I am not inconstant." Temper still sparked in his gaze.

"A fop one day, a warrior the next. I would say that you are."

"It was a disguise in a"—he stopped before he could say *good cause*. "If nothing else, I can at least offer you security in the marriage settlement."

As they drove up to Nevett's town house, she took great pleasure in saying, "You haven't heard, have you? I do have security. My French grandmother left me ten thousand pounds and an invitation to bring my sister and live with the family in Aquitaine." The footman opened the door. He held an umbrella to protect her from the increasing downpour. Leaping out, she turned to face Jude. "I intend to accept. Don't forget to give our driver an extra fee."

She stormed up the stairs ahead of the footman and welcomed the splash of rain on her hot face. Heavens, how she hated Jude's arrogance, despised his subterfuge . . . and loved him despite everything. Loved him like any simpering fool whose heart fluttered at the sight of her one true love.

What an irony. Jude had said he wanted to locate his true love, but he hadn't truly wanted to find the elusive maiden.

Caroline had not believed in true love, but she had found hers, he had proposed to her . . . and she discovered that without trust, true love was nothing more than the storm that raged overhead, all flashes and booms and quickly over.

At least, she hoped it would be quickly over. She didn't want to feel so stricken and forlorn forever.

The door opened. Phillips stood in the entry.

Of course. It had to be Phillips.

She swiped the tears off her face and pretended they were caused by the rain.

"The duke of Nevett wishes to see you, Miss Ritter," Phillips said, and the glint in his eyes, the small smile on his face told the tale. Phillips had done something wicked. "The duke wishes to see you *immediately.*"

Jude pounded up the stairs behind her, picked up her hand, and showed Phillips. "That's not possible. She's been wounded."

"Yes." Phillips sniffed. "So I see. She does look quite disreputable. But you, Lord Huntington, have some wounds, also." For Jude, Phillips played the concerned elderly retainer. "Shall I call a physician?"

"Yes," Jude said. "Miss Ritter is probably going to need stitches."

"I'll see Nevett now." Gently, Caroline disengaged her fingers from Jude's grip and went to Nevett's study.

Jude followed her.

Nicolette sat in a chair beside Nevett, talking

steadily, urgently, but when Jude and Caroline walked in, she shook her head at them and sat back. Her whole attitude was one of resignation.

For Nevett held a green leather journal in his hands.

Caroline's planning journal.

She sank into a chair, her knees weak. She remembered very well every word she'd written on those pages, and they were, all of them, incriminating, revealing . . . embarrassing.

Jude knew his father well, and clearly Nevett was in a royal rage. "Miss Ritter, I gave you a task to do. A simple task, really—that you get my son, the earl of Huntington, the heir to a dukedom, married by the end of the Season. With that goal in mind, I gave you clothing. I've been informed I gave you shelter. Most important, I gave you respectability and my full trust." His voice rose with each word. "Perhaps you will tell me how it's possible to accomplish this simple task by sleeping with my son!"

Jude looked at her journal as if he'd like to rip it out of Nevett's hands and read every passage. "Father—"

Caroline gave him a look that reduced him to silence. She would handle this. "That's my planning journal, and in it I recorded my private thoughts about Lord Huntington's progress." Thoughts which she sincerely hoped Jude never saw. "I keep it in my bedside drawer. Perhaps, Your Grace, *you'll* tell me how you have it now."

"It fell into Phillips's hands," Nevett said, "and he very properly gave it to me."

Every head in the room swiveled toward the doorway. Phillips stood there, a pretentious smile stretching his lips. He thought he had won, and probably he had.

"It *fell* into his hands? Out of my drawer?" Caroline pulled a disbelieving face. "I would discuss Phillips's character with you, Your Grace, but I don't use that kind of language—"

That wiped the smile from Phillips's face.

"—And it's not *his* character in which you're interested." Caroline bowed her head in sincere contrition. She supposed she deserved this whole, horrible day. She should never have tried to snatch at that happiness she thought she'd had with Jude. It was a lie, a chimera, and now she reaped the results. "You're right, Your Grace. I do beg your pardon. I've violated your trust in every way."

"You violated my son!" Nevett snapped.

"Don't be ridiculous, Father," Jude said.

At the same time as Nicolette said, "Don't be ridiculous, Nevett."

"I didn't abuse your hospitality by *deliberately* enticing your son." Caroline looked Nevett in the eyes. "Our actions seemed to be an offshoot of the flirting that we practiced endlessly. But I don't want you to think I'm making an excuse for myself. There's no excuse good enough."

"We don't think you're making an excuse." Nicolette's smile warmed the cold that had crept into Caroline's heart. "You're simply a very good teacher."

"Nicolette, have you lost your mind?" Nevett pointed to Jude, then to Caroline. "We were trying to get our son married and breeding."

"*We* were not doing that. *You* were, and if you'll recall, I told you it was a plan fraught with peril." Nicolette shook her head. "Perhaps in the future, you'll consult me before you put one of your harebrained ideas into practice."

"Are you on *her* side?" Nevett indicated Caroline.

"Absolutely," Nicolette said categorically. "Caroline's a dear girl, and if you couldn't see the two of them falling in love, you weren't looking."

"Nicolette!" Nevett came to his feet. "You mean you knew improprieties were occurring, and you didn't warn me?"

Jude had kept quiet long enough. It was time to intervene. "That's because what occurred between Miss Ritter and me is none of your business, sir, and I'd thank you to keep a civil tongue in your head when you speak to her or about her." Jude glowered at Phillips. "And perhaps you should tell your butler to keep his filthy nose away from my affairs and to mind his own manners."

Phillips quivered with offended dignity. The silly old sod, did he think Jude would thank him for bringing this disaster down on them?

It was time to tell his father the truth. "I never intended to marry on your command. I don't know what megrim made you imagine I would."

"Wha . . . what?" Nevett's eyes bulged. "Has Miss Ritter made you lose all sense, too?"

Caroline made a restless motion and tried to stand up.

Jude restrained her with his hand on her arm. "Miss Ritter's going to become the toast of London, Father. She saved my worthless life and helped me eliminate the two men who tried to assassinate Queen Victoria. She was wounded in the service of the crown." Jude lifted her red-stained hand. "And if she would damned well marry me, I'd be the luckiest man in the world—but she won't."

Nevett turned an apoplectic red. "She refused you?

You, the earl of Huntington?" To Caroline, he asked, "Who do you think you are? He's going to be the duke!"

"I don't want an earl. I don't want a duke." Caroline wrenched away from Jude, her cheeks red with chagrin. "I want to take my sister to France and live quietly for the rest of my days."

While he sputtered in indignation, Nicolette told Caroline, "Genevieve is in your bedchamber waiting for you."

"Then I'll go to see her." This time Jude couldn't restrain Caroline. She rose and fled.

Nevett eyed Jude across his desk. "You, son, have some explaining to do."

"But first," Mum said, "Phillips, come in here."

The butler strode in, looking so proud of himself Jude clenched his fist and stepped forward, ready to forget their age difference and punch the old man.

Mum grabbed the back of Jude's jacket and pulled him to a stop. "Come here, Phillips." She pointed to the place on the rug before her chair. "Right here."

If Phillips had been smart, he would have recognized the danger signs. That was exactly what Mum had always done when she prepared to rake her sons over the coals. But Phillips strutted forward as if he'd done something grand, and stood before her with such a smug expression Jude's fists clenched again.

"Phillips, you've been with the duke for many years. In fact, more years than I have," Mum said. "So it's with a heavy heart that I must let you go."

"Your Grace!" Phillips's astonishment was satisfying to see. When he saw no yielding in Mum's expression, he turned to the duke. "Your Grace!"

Nevett stared at his young wife as if he didn't quite believe what he was hearing. "Now, Nicolette . . ."

She turned on him in a fury. "Husband, am I not in charge of your household?"

"Yes. Yes, of course."

"Then I regret to tell you we must seek a new butler. This one has proved to have a regrettable tendency to undermine my efforts and the efforts of your staff." To Phillips, she said, "You may go now and pack."

Phillips started to speak.

"You may *go*," Mum repeated.

He was the portrait of the offended dignity as he stalked to the door.

"Do you think that's wise, Nicolette?" Nevett asked. "Good butlers are hard to find, and at least we know he doesn't steal the silver."

"There are more important things than the silver." Mum must have really been furious, for she turned on Nevett. "Like the impropriety of reading others' journals."

"Miss Ritter was in my employ!" Nevett said unwisely.

"Yes, which makes my congress with her all the more despicable." Jude placed his fists on his father's desk, leaned over, and spoke right into Nevett's face. "It was me you should have been shouting at, not Caroline! I've behaved abominably."

"Son, you'd better tell me the whole story from the beginning." Nevett rubbed his forehead as if it ached. "Don't leave anything out."

So Jude started with Michael's murder in Moricadia, his participation in the pursuit of Michael's killers, and his unethical use of Caroline as a distraction.

Halfway through, Nevett poured himself a brandy, one for Jude, and at a glare from his duchess, one for her.

Jude gave his father to understand that Caroline had been untouched when Jude seduced her—and he did tell them he seduced her, for to admit that she'd tied him to the bed would lead to much guffawing at his expense—and he explained her part, and his, in the capture and killing of the Moricadians.

"That explains the blood on your shoulder and the cut on your face," Nevett said gruffly. "You might want to have them tended."

"I did tell Phillips to summon a physician." Jude's various wounds were starting to ache and throb, and the blood was drying and sticking to his skin.

"I'll go see that it's done." Mum rose and walked to the door, then backed away. "Caroline and her sister are leaving."

Jude came to his feet and stared as Caroline swept past wearing a worn gown and gripping her ragged old bag. Of course. She took nothing but what she'd brought, and she didn't spare him a glance.

Jude sank back down. He'd made a hell of a mess of things.

"Where does she think she's going now?" Nevett demanded.

"To an inn I would guess." Jude needed to make sure she got to a decent place, and safely.

"She's going to take her inheritance and her sister and move to France," Mum answered.

"How the hell does she think she's going to do that? Her father's not going to let her sister go. That old man's mean as hell. If he can't have Miss Ritter's money, he's not going to let her go away and be happy." Nevett stated the facts as he saw them.

"He's going to let her go with her sister because you're going to tell him to." Jude rose.

"Why would I do that? She was supposed to teach my son and heir to flirt, and she vowed she would get you married by the end of the Season"—Nevett pointed at Jude—"and I don't see a chance of that happening. Not even to her."

Mum sighed and looked at Nevett.

"Well!" He glared at her. "Why should I do her a favor like telling her father to let his daughters go off to France where the damned heathens live?"

"Because I ask you to." Jude locked eyes with his father.

"Nevett will be glad to speak to Mr. Ritter about his daughters," Nicolette gently interposed. "Now, dear boy, you should hurry and follow Caroline, or I won't know if she's safe, and I'll worry."

"Yes, Mum." That was exactly what Jude planned to do.

It was one of the things that women want.

Less than a week later, Jude stood on the dock and watched as the ship to France weighed anchor.

Caroline was on the deck with her sister, but even from a distance Jude could see Caroline wore none of the gifts he'd sent her. Not the necklace, not the lace shawl, not the warm mantle to wrap around herself during the sea voyage. Not even a single flower from his bouquet decorated her fichu. He might know what *most* women wanted, but he did not know what *Caroline* wanted.

Time, his stepmother told him.

But he thought that was too simple. Caroline wanted something more. All Jude had to do was figure out what.

As the ship moved away from the dock, Genevieve

ran to the stern to look back at the city of London. Jude waved at her, and she wildly waved back. She had met Jude on his visits to the inn, and she had confided she liked him. *It's too bad Caroline doesn't like you, too, but maybe in France she'll find someone who's just as nice.*

And that haunted Jude. He wanted to give Caroline time to miss him . . . but what if she didn't? What if she fell in love with a heathen Frenchman and married him, leaving Jude to spend his days in misery and loneliness?

He got drunk one night and told his stepmother his woeful scenario and she had, without any sympathy at all, told him that he should have thought of that before he used Caroline so ruthlessly.

Obviously, Mum had been talking to Caroline.

The ship moved farther away, and Jude kept waving, hoping that Caroline would at least lift her hand.

She did not. Her gaze went past him. Grasping Genevieve's arm, she dragged her toward the prow of the ship as if she couldn't wait to see the last of London.

Looking around, he spotted the trouble.

Freshie watched her from the shore, his stance menacing.

With the first feeling of real happiness he'd experienced for a week, Jude took off his coat and threw it on the ground. He walked toward Freshie, rolling up his sleeves.

When Freshie saw Jude's scowl, he started backing away, then with many a backward glance, he broke into a run.

Jude didn't give a damn about dignity, clothing, or a gentleman's rules. He sprinted after Freshie. He downed him with a flying tackle. With his hand on Freshie's collar, Jude dragged him to his feet. Smiling into Freshie's face, Jude said, "I really feel I must cure you of your regrettable tendency of stalking Miss Ritter."

And with a few well-chosen punches, he did.

Chapter 28

Seldom in a woman's life did reality match her dreams. Only twice had Caroline had that experience. Once when she arrived in sunny Aquitaine and met her loving family . . . and in the dark of night in Jude's arms.

She sat on a sun-warmed boulder not far from her family's chateau and watched as Genevieve romped up and down hills and around trees with two fat golden-haired puppies. Her sister and the puppies were very much alike with their gamboling grace, and Caroline thanked God for the haven her family provided for her and her sister.

In the three months they'd lived there, Genevieve had blossomed. She'd shot up two inches; she was now taller than Caroline. She'd filled out and showed the promise of beauty. Already the neighbor lad showed interest in her and watched her with worshipping adolescent eyes. But as she told Caroline, "I'm not interested in a man. They just make you unhappy. Right?"

Caroline had been forced to agree, for here she was, living the dream she'd dreamed for more years than she could remember, and all she wanted was Jude. Jude, with his intense blue eyes, his rawboned hands, the wounds he had suffered for his brother, for justice, and for her. Jude with his talented kisses and the passion he shared so brilliantly. As time went on, she forgot about the way he used her—dreadful man!—and instead recalled the way he looked at her, as if she were his one true love.

She tried to remind herself that he'd used her, but honesty forced her to admit; he wasn't like her father or Lord Freshfield. Yes, Jude had used her, but it had been in a—she hated to acknowledge it—a good cause. And he couldn't have told her what he was doing, for that would have compromised the venture and perhaps destroyed his chance for revenge against his brother's killers. She'd heard his explanations, but she hadn't known it in her heart. Now she did, and she wondered what would have happened if she'd stayed in England and accepted his proposal.

Caroline laughed aloud when one of the puppies went romping up the hill, tripped on his feet and came tumbling down. Genevieve chased him, picked him up, and kissed his slobbery face. "Ohh, Genevieve." Caroline shook her head, but she didn't remonstrate. Genevieve would tell her that a dog kiss was better than a boy kiss any day, and Caroline would be forced to agree—for Genevieve.

Pushing back her bonnet, Caroline lifted her face to the sun and closed her eyes. For her, only a Jude kiss would do.

Yet he would forget about her. He was the earl of Huntington, with a hundred debutantes from whom to choose. Caroline had tortured herself imagining him in love with a simpering young lady who was like . . . like she'd been four years ago during *her* Season.

Childish little twit.

"Hey, Caroline!" At the top of the hill, Genevieve bounced back and forth while the dogs frolicked around her. She pointed down at the winding path. "Somebody's coming!"

"Who?" Caroline stood. Whoever it was hadn't yet rounded the curve.

"This man. He's really handsome! He's coming around the path! He's carrying flowers!"

Caroline had the feeling Genevieve was shouting at him rather than at her. Carefully, Caroline pulled up her bonnet and brushed the wrinkles out of her simple blue skirt.

"He's glaring at me! He's changed direction. He's walking toward me!" Genevieve started giggling so hard Caroline thought she would burst. "I'm running away . . . !" She leaped like a goat down the other side of the hill and out of sight.

Caroline found herself standing stiff and straight, breathless and staring down at the spot where the path emerged from behind the copse of leafy trees and wondering if by some chance . . . "Jude," she breathed.

He looked better than she remembered, which was almost impossible because she remembered a fabulous man stuffed with every perfection. He was tall. He was powerfully built. Each strand of his brown hair shone. Most amazing, he was impeccably dressed.

He stopped when he saw her, and he stared as if he needed to fill himself with the sight of her.

She liked that sensation very much. She didn't like the irresistible urge to move toward him, to wrap herself around him, to melt into him and be one with him. The air between them heated, grew rich and stormy, and it seemed that lightning sparked on this sunny day.

But she'd learned her lesson. She'd given her body and her heart and received nothing but a patronizing marriage proposal in return.

Some women might call a proposal from the earl of Huntington no small thing, but it wasn't marriage she wanted from him. It was . . . everything. With a composure that was absolutely false, she walked toward him and extended her hand. "My lord, how good to see you."

He dropped the flowers. He reached for her hand. And with a confidence that should have made her bristle, he pulled her into his embrace and kissed her.

And she realized it wasn't confidence, but need. An all-encompassing, desperate need to claim and taste and reaffirm.

She suffered the same compulsion and answered him with everything that was in her, her hands clutching him, exploring the outline of his shoulders and absorbing the warmth of his body . . . until they broke apart for lack of air.

"The flowers." His heated blue eyes explored her face, seeking everything she'd refused him before. "I dropped the flowers."

"I know." She admired the passion that inspired such impetuosity.

"But I'm here to give you everything a woman wants."

"Are you?" She smiled. She liked that, too.

"My governess says flowers are very important to women. Caroline." He cupped her face in his hands. "I can't stand it anymore. I'm dying without you. You have to come home and marry me."

"Do I?" She drew away a little. "I *have* to come home and marry you?"

"No. No, of course not." He backtracked, a big, arrogant man who was far too sure of himself. "You'll do as you like, as you have done for years because I know you can take care of yourself. But here's the trouble." He tried to look pathetic. "I can't take care of myself."

"Really?" She liked his bent.

Getting down on one knee, he picked up the scattered bouquet. "Yes. I can't sleep. I'm not eating. I'm wasting away."

"You look good to me."

"Do I?" He looked up at her with a half smile, and she knew he realized how the sunshine caressed his hard features and how irresistible she found him.

"Tell me more about how you can't take care of yourself."

Still on bended knee, he offered her the flowers. "All your good work in rehabilitating me to be acceptable in society is for naught."

"Why's that?" She took the collect of broken daisies and battered chrysanthemums.

"I've developed bad habits. I don't like to dance with any lady but you. I spend too much time at the zoo looking at the lioness." He pasted an expression of sorrow on his silly, enticing face. "Worst of all, I talk to myself, because without you by my side, there's no one who understands me."

She was charmed. "Get up, you fool."

He made an offering on the altar of her womanhood. "I beat up Freshie for you."

She waited for the familiar rush of terror associated with Lord Freshfield's name. But she felt nothing. Sometime during the last months, she'd grown to believe she could handle Lord Freshfield.

Well. It was clear why. If she could step into the middle of a battle and disarm a man of his sword, she could handle anything. "Did you hurt him?" she asked Jude.

"Both eyes were swollen shut and he lost a few teeth. His ear will never look the same . . ." Jude rose and dusted off his knees, and the expression in his eyes was deadly. "He should never have tried to fight back. That just made me mad. Or rather . . . madder."

"Good." Caroline offered no false charity to Lord Freshfield. "I hope his looks are ruined so he can never beguile another young lady."

"Since the duke and duchess of Nevett have taken to cutting both Freshie and his ghastly wife, I think I can safely assure you his influence on the ton is over." He glanced around. "Is there someone to whom I should apply for your hand in marriage?"

"My grandfather, and you're assuming I'll consent."

Jude dropped to his knees again. "Please, Caroline, marry me. I can offer you nothing more than my fortune, my title, and my unworthy self, but—"

She started strolling back up the path toward the chateau.

He scrambled to his feet and charged after her, pulling to a halt directly in front of her so she had to stop and look at him. "—But I promise to be a good husband to you, and massage your charming feet and care for you in every manner."

"What manner would that be?" His expression told her exactly in what manner he meant. She watched his hands open and slowly reach for her; she felt the slide of his arms across her back. He tilted her into the crook of his arm and kissed her. Once more the blossoms scattered at their feet.

This time the first frantic edge was gone from his need. He took his time, layering kiss after kiss on her lips and her cheeks, teasing her with his tongue, stroking her spine with his hand until she stretched onto her toes to push closer to him. She had missed him, dreamed of his warmth, his scent, his touch. Now she reveled in the pleasure of his proficiency and wondered at the slight tremor that shook him. He was like a starving man given the merest tidbit from the table; he wanted the whole feast.

His kiss deepened until she forgot the singing birds and the golden sunshine and knew nothing except the dark inner world swirling behind her closed eyes. All that existed was desire, his and hers, uniting them in one need. No matter how far apart they lived or how much she tried to deny it, they yearned to be one, and neither of them would be satisfied until they were joined.

Finally, he set her away from him and stood, chest heaving, eyes smoldering.

And she . . . she suspected she looked as maddened and as reckless. She looked down at the bright, beautiful flowers that had formed the carpet for their passion. She had to think. She had to be sensible *now*, or she would take his hand and lead him into the trees. "I will definitely take that into account when considering your suit," she said breathlessly. She walked around him and down the path. He joined her, and they walked side by side, not looking at each other, but with awareness stretched tightly between them. When she could speak, she said, "I must warn you, my grandfather harbors no love for the English, and if I don't insist on having you, he'll refuse."

"I beg your pardon. You've had your way with me. It would be unchivalrous of you to turn away from me now." He gave a huge, phony sniff.

"I suppose that's true." She slid a glance toward him. "Are you increasing?"

"Are you?" he shot back.

"No." She was delighted to see his face fall.

"I had hoped . . ." His teasing mien vanished.

"What had you hoped?" she asked curiously.

"I had hoped that, if I couldn't prevail any other way, you would have to marry me."

"I see." She stopped walking. She faced him, and his seriousness brought a like response in her. "I've been thinking about what happened between us."

"Good. I'm glad I'm not the only one in constant torment." He checked her expression. "You were in constant torment, weren't you?"

"Not quite constant. But I wondered what it was about you that seduced me when no other man could interest me."

"Did you discover the reason?" he asked with a very real curiosity.

"I decided I gave myself to you because I thought you were the most masculine man I'd ever met. You didn't give a damn about what anyone thought of you. You wore what you wanted. You adopted silly mannerisms and prattled on fashion and France. You ignored the people who laughed at you and behaved as you wished. I knew you weren't stupid. But I didn't realize you'd donned a mask. I thought you were simply your own man. So when I discovered the truth"—she squeezed her fingers together in remembered anguish—"I was the stupid one. All my life, I had been the pretty girl who was not too bright—then it seemed true."

"Not too bright?" He separated her hands, opened them and stared down at the thin, white scar where the sword had bitten into her palm. "We were together for a fortnight. My father, my stepmother, everyone in society had seen me for months and didn't realize the truth."

"When I'd been here for a while, when the hurt wasn't quite so new, I thought of that. And besides, who would guess? What a stupid plan! Dress like an idiot, act like an idiot so the Moricadians would confide in you."

"It was a stupid plan," he said meekly.

Something—time, or just having him there with her—must have restored her lost sense of humor, for she shoved at him. "I suppose you're going to point out it worked."

"No. No, that I'm not, for it didn't work. Not without a lot of help from a singer who paid with her life and another lady who damned near got herself killed." For one moment, she glimpsed the bared teeth of a highly annoyed man. He looked rather like the lion at the London Zoo—ready to rend and tear. But when she looked again, he was merely a man, standing there accepting her scolding. "It occurred to me that you had no reason to accept my proposal, for I didn't tell you the advantages of marriage for you. Stupidly, I thought you knew."

"What would those be?" She found herself unable to look him in the eyes; the sparkle of his affection was too strong.

"Nothing more than a man who worships you for your courage, your intelligence, and your kindness. After I came back from Moricadia, I thought I'd never really see the sunlight again, never hope again, but you healed me. You made me look to the future. Caroline, you must marry me, live with me, bear my children."

She couldn't tease him anymore. There was only one place she longed to be, and that was with him. She slid her arms around his shoulders. She knew the answer, but still she asked, "Why must I marry you?"

He smiled at her, kissed her again, a warm, passionate, gratifying kiss. "Because, my darling, you're my one true love."

As the ship cruised close to its London dock, Jude watched Caroline lean over the rail and crow in delight. "Your parents came to meet us!" She waved vigorously at the couple standing so still and staring so hard. "What do you suppose they'll say about us spending our honeymoon in *France?*" She pulled a long face as she said the word, knowing full well what Nevett's father thought of everything to do with the French.

"Not a word." Jude wrapped his arm around her waist and smiled into her eyes. "Especially when we tell him about the heir to his heir."

Caroline's cheeks blushed a lovely rose and her eyes shone. "We'll tell Nevett that in honor of the place of the babe's conception, we're going to name him *Pierre.*"

She was beautiful, so beautiful, and Jude counted himself as the luckiest man in the world. "If it's a girl, he'll blame her gender on French drinking water."

"So he will." Caroline gurgled with amusement.

"I'm surprised they're actually on the dock." As the ship prepared to dock, Jude looked again at his parents and noticed their serious faces. "I would have thought that Father would wait in the ducal carriage."

"Yes, I can see him doing that. It would be so much

more suitable to his station," Caroline said humorously. "But Nicolette probably insisted." Her eyes narrowed against the sun. "Look! Over to the side. Isn't that Mr. Throckmorton?"

Jude whipped his head around and stared. "Yes, it is." Almost to himself, he said, "I wonder what he wants."

And because Caroline was attuned to Jude's moods, she sensed his tension. Putting her hand over his, she squeezed it. "Perhaps he wishes to give you the details of Bouchard's hanging."

"He's a grim fellow, but not that grim." Jude watched as the sailors placed the gangplank. He would be the first person off the ship.

Something was going on.

When the captain gave them the nod, Jude led Caroline down to his parents.

Yes, there was definitely something wrong, for although Nevett shook his hand and Nicolette exclaimed about Caroline's glow, they weren't smiling, and their eyes were anxious.

Jude's gaze went to Throckmorton. "What is it?"

Throckmorton didn't play games. "Do you remember the Moricadians' valet?" With a glance at the ladies, he tactfully added, "The one who couldn't speak?"

"Yes, of course." Jude could scarcely forget the man whose tongue had been cut out.

Caroline moved close, and watched him with worried eyes.

"He located Comte de Guignard's journal for us," Throckmorton said.

Nevett and Mum clasped hands, and Mum had tears in her eyes.

Jude had imagined the details of Michael's death. Were they now about to be revealed? "Tell me."

"According to the journal," Throckmorton said, "your brother Michael . . . is alive and imprisoned in Moricadia."

New York Times bestselling author

Christina Dodd

The Barefoot Princess

0-06-056117-3/$7.99 US/$10.99 Can

Since the powerful and wickedly handsome marquess of
Northcliff has stolen the people's livelihood, Princess Amy
decides to kidnap him for ransom.

My Fair Temptress

0-06-056112-2/$6.99 US/$9.99 Can

Miss Caroline Ritter, accomplished flirt and ruined gentle-
woman, offers lessons to any rich, noble lord too inept to
attract a wife.

Some Enchanted Evening

0-06-056098-3/$6.99 US/$9.99 Can

Though Robert is wary of the exquisite stranger who rides
into the town he is sworn to defend, Clarice stirs emotions
within him that he buried deeply years before.

One Kiss From You

0-06-009266-1/$6.99 US/$9.99 Can

Eleanor de Lacy must have been mad to agree to exchange
identities with her stronger-willed cousin. Worse still, she
finds the man she's to deceive dazzlingly attractive.

Scandalous Again

0-06-009265-3/$6.99 US/$9.99 Can

Madeline de Lacy can't believe that her noble father has lost
his entire estate—*and her!*—in a card game.